2/21

DATE DUE

P9-CQR-397

YA
Cha
The
Mechanists
1

RISE OF THE
RED HAND

BOOKS BY OLIVIA CHADHA

The Mechanists
Rise of the Red Hand

RISE OF THE
RED HAND

THE MECHANISTS: BOOK ONE

OLIVIA CHADHA

EREWHON

RISE OF THE RED HAND
Copyright © 2020 by Olivia Chadha

Edited by Sarah T. Guan

Erewhon Books
2 W. 29th Street, Suite 3S
New York, NY 10001
www.erewhonbooks.com

Erewhon books are available at special discounts when purchased in bulk for premiums and sales promotions as well as for fund-raising or educational use. Special editions or book excerpts can also be created to specification. For details, send an email to specialmarkets@workman.com.

Epigraph from *You Will Hear Thunder*, Anna Akhmatova, translated by D. M. Thomas, Copyright © 1985. This material is used by permission of Ohio University Press, www.ohioswallow.com.

Library of Congress Control Number: 2020946660

ISBN 978-1-64566-010-1 (hardcover)
ISBN 978-1-64566-015-6 (ebook)

Cover art by Rashed AlAkroka
Cover text design by Dana Li
Author photograph by Natalie Pigliacampo

Printed in the United States of America

First US Edition: January 2021
10 9 8 7 6 5 4 3 2 1

For David Miller—Of all the planets in all the galaxies. I'm so glad to have found you on this rock.

You will hear thunder and remember me,
And think: she wanted storms. The rim
Of the sky will be the color of hard crimson,
And your heart, as it was then, will be on fire.

—Anna Akhmatova

 **1 // ASHIVA**

SOUTH ASIAN PROVINCE
CENTRAL DISTRICT
155 N.E.
2300 HR

I know three things: (1) I am a prisoner of Solace Corporation; (2) I'll be sent to containment without trial; (3) According to my Info-Run, the rate of survival in containment is 0.0001%.

0.0001%

The green number flashes in the corner of my vision. My wrists are bound with metal cuffs. Ignoring the ache, I lift my hands in forced prayer to my forehead, and hit the I-Scan to turn off my monitor. Some data even I don't want to know.

The Maglev transport rickshaw barrels up, up and up through Central City. I've dreamt of coming here to the high Stratas of the neocity, Central, my entire life, but not like this. A girl from the Narrows in the Unsanctioned Territory has no business in Central, unless she set off an explosive device in the city and, say, that girl already has infractions for smuggling…

My new pals, the other criminals picked up by the gray-collar guardians, look about as happy as me. Grays are terrorist hunters; they can do what they please with us. The white-collar guardians are ticket-writers that police the SA, but the grays mean blood. The tall boy must be from the Northern cities because of how perfectly he wraps his turban. The tearstained Uplander woman to my right is pregnant; the pitch of her sari curves around her belly like a sand dune. She was probably taken because of the child growing inside her. An unsanctioned birth, I bet. Or worse, she falsified records to get her and her child into Central even though they were both declared unfit by Solace to live in Central.

And then there's the boy with the long black hair in his face. It fell across his eyes when they put the restraints on him. He's clean, looks like he just walked out of a holo-advert for an Uplander fetish product, and definitely doesn't belong in a criminal transport. Through his hair, it's clear his jaw has a replacement, chrome. He nods in my direction. Too cocky. But this was his idea.

"Hey, girl, where'd you get your replacement?" The turbaned Northerner yells above the transport engines. He winks and nods to my right arm, which had been disguised by my stolen white-collar guardian's jacket and gloves. But the recent explosion blew apart my jacket and my chrome peeks through the silicone skin like an exposed secret.

"Why? You want a referral?" I don't look up, but flex my robotic fingers.

His laugh is as deep as the Arabian Sea. "Sharp tongue in your mouth must hurt."

"Not always."

"There's only one person I know who can still do work like that," he says.

"Yeah. She's gone."

"Wahe guru," the Northerner chants a small prayer. "What happened?"

I look at my black combat boots, then at the Northern boy, making sure the guardians are busy. "That's what I'm going to find out."

The Northerner nods with conviction. I only met him an hour ago, but I already trust him.

The transport speeds toward the upper Stratas of Central, the towering city that twists higher and higher in the center of the Ring that cleans the air for the Uplanders to breathe. And the coastline that edges right up against the girders that keeps everything from sinking into the sea. Metal bridges like silver webs connect the crumbling old structures with the new. Animated holo-adverts project, on every surface, all the things the Uplanders should desire. What they desire most is power and perfection.

AllianceCon is a time for the remaining eight provinces of the world to show off their planet-saving tech to the Planetary Alliance Commission. The PAC holds the keys to the world bank, and they use AllianceCon to decide which province deserves continued funding. The province that shows the best tech that will allow humans to survive on this, our dying planet, wins the funding to survive another year.

Yeah, the South Asian Province has failed to secure additional funding the past three years in a row, and this is their last chance. The SA is coasting on fumes and loans. They've promised their newest tech will win this year. They haven't said what the tech is. The massive holo-screen reads: "Happy Alliance Day! This is our year!" And I want to tear it down.

We pass a twenty-story crumbling Buddhist temple with a holo-advert promoting Solace Corps' new divination program, Sign. The skyscraper beside it dances with gaudy neon lights of animated, pampered girls wrapped in immaculate fabrics, drinking the newest youth genetic edit. Garbage, all of it. Uplanders have everything but souls. The whole neocity was built on the backs and blood of my people who aren't even allowed to live here.

The holo-screen at the next intersection flashes with a series of faces. The transport moves fast, but I know that face. How could I not?

The pregnant woman stops crying and looks at me. "Are you...?"

"Hush, Auntie." The boy with the long hair in his face whispers. I don't need his protection. Even he knows I'm the fighter, he's the brains.

"I'm no one," I say, and something in the woman changes. She smiles and subtly presses her hand to her chest and nods. The secret sign of the Red Hand, only for my eyes.

"Quiet," the guardian yells to us all. "Or we'll muzzle all of you animals."

The woman presses her hands together and prays silently. The city rushes past the windows. Millions of scenarios pour through my mind, wave after wave. We went over the maps. We know the steps back and front. Stick to the plan, I repeat over and over until the words are tattooed on my brain.

We'll reach the entryway into the general prison containment in a few minutes, but not before crossing the tallest bridge in Central that connects the upper Stratas to the lower. I've heard the Uplanders on the other side of the barrier glow from the inside out. If I didn't hate them so much, I'd envy them a little. A crowd gathers below. It pulses like a swarm of ants consuming fallen fruit. They are cleaning up for Alliance-Con. Central must be taking down another memorial for the fallen from the Last Vidroh, the uprising in Central at the end of WWIII. The memorials were their way of quelling the population's need for retribution after so much bloodshed. They'd hate for the important visitors arriving during AllianceCon to see the SA as anything but perfectly content in our completely divided world. My teeth slip from clenching too hard and I bite my lip; my blood tastes like metal.

A guardian comes through the transport to test us for various viral agents.

"Arm, Downlander scum," he says to me.

I stick out my replacement arm and smile. "Nice gray collar. Never seen one up close," I smirk.

He bristles. "Not that one, girl. The human arm, unless you'd like both arms to be replacements," the guardian says.

The test hurts every time. And every time I'm cleared from the Fever. I wonder if it even exists or if it's just a government plot to keep us in line and afraid. They're looking for symptoms of fever, blue rash, the beginning marks of paralysis, but mostly for a way to humiliate us. It's been a problem for a decade. They get it figured out, but then it returns. The guardian hits up the boy with long black hair and then the Northern boy. Clear. And then he approaches the woman. She sits before him with her face turned away. What's she looking at through the thin glass of the transport? Her reflection, or something in the city?

The view from the bridge we cross is terrifying. We are at least fifty stories in the sky. I see the deep brown electricity clouds flash in the distance beyond the dome like bellowing sky beasts. Hundreds of miles across, the Barrens wasteland is a scorched dark brown and red desert surrounding Central. And though no life is said to be able to thrive there aside from cockroaches, its volatility is as striking and hypnotizing as a tornado.

"It's beautiful," she says to no one in particular.

The guardian bends down to administer her test. "Arm," he says.

She doesn't respond. Her long braid hangs down her back gracefully. She stands and faces him. Her body is thin, frail, aside from her belly, like most of us from the Narrows. He raises his pulse baton. I hate those things. The weapon is allowed under the New Treaty laws because it's not considered lethal, but the guardians turn up the voltage high enough and know where to strike to cause heart attacks. I've seen it.

"Watch yourself woman. There's nowhere to go from here," he says.

The woman's eyes pass through the guardian. "You would have been perfect." Her hands rest on her belly. I notice a bluish bruise on her hand the shape of a cloud. The Fever. She recites a prayer in Gurmukhi, Masiji's language.

"Sit down, now!" the guardian commands.

The woman takes another few steps toward the guardian and then backs up as far as she can in the transport.

"For the Rani, the Lal Hath," she yells.

The Red Hand.

I try to stop her. "No!"

She runs and throws herself against the transport's cheap excuse for safety glass. It shatters into shards that flash across our faces like razor rain. She doesn't scream, but I do. Her body falls down and down and down, and there's no sound when she lands, not from here at least.

The guardians signal an alert and ready their weapons, but there's nothing to do about the woman. The transport stops. They yell and push us back against the unbroken side of the vehicle.

My stomach is a nest of vipers.

"Wahe guru," the Northerner prays. "She's better off. God knows what they'd do with the child of a criminal."

Bitter tears cover my face and sting my new wounds from the shattered glass.

I nod at the boy with the long black hair.

We cannot fail.

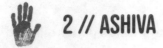 # 2 // ASHIVA

Look casual. Like you really belong here. Waiting. Alone. At night. No big deal.

The center of Strata One of Central is always dark as smoke. The light has trouble getting in through the towering buildings that sit inside the Ring. But I'm only awake at night anyway, when the heat breaks and it isn't dangerous to be outside without protective gear. The air smells sweeter in the Stratas, under the protection of the Ring's clime-controls and filtration system, than the air back home in the Narrows, in the Unsanctioned Territory, but still: Permanent midnight is all I know.

This place is wet and wired. Two things, saltwater and electricity, usually make a mighty conductor, but for the most part the old wires don't work. Otherwise we'd all be fried.

I stand outside the mediport. Its aluminum wall is cold, damp and slick, but I lean on it anyway. A hospital for the poor, the mediport is a pathetic excuse for medical assistance: always filthy, lacking resources, doctors. It's a place to die, or hide, or both.

As the thick clouds and smog part high above me, I see the Alliance Space Colony floating in the moon's orbit around the Earth. Only on a full moon can you truly appreciate its size, the extraordinary ring that spins around the banded cylinder. They say it's built for two million people to explore the universe for Goldilocks planets and mine the rare earths that our governments fight about on Earth. There are many living up there already, building, fixing. Who will be chosen to live up there and how is anyone's guess.

They think we are stupid. It's for the rich. We know it. Though the Space Colony was designed before WWIII, the construction went into hyper drive shortly after the New Treaty was established. We don't believe in coincidences.

I try to stretch my new right arm, but it only shrugs. Ugh, my lazy plexus isn't connecting with my replacement arm again. It will be the end of me. Masiji says I need a new one. You can't have a replacement if it doesn't properly connect to your brain through the plexus implant. Yeah, let me get right on buying that very expensive biomimetic part.

My shoulder and thoracic back ache every day. The thanks I give to The Mechanic for making my broken body whole is so loud sometimes that my pain becomes only a ghost, only a whisper in my mind. The nerve roots where the replacement begins in my shoulder joint are redirected into the replacement, but their phantom memories remain. The agony takes its turn on days when it's quiet, when I'm still. Silence and stagnancy are just for decay; they invite death. It's only when I'm still that I look at the arm she gave me, the metal bones and joints, the cables and ports, wires and circuits . . . and feel its weight pull on my body, unequal to the rest of me. It's heavy. It's me, but not me. But when I'm running, there's no time to think or feel. In motion, doubt becomes a whisper again. Then, I am unbroken, with purpose.

I hate waiting. And people who make me wait I hate even more.

Across the alley is a small bhelwalla stand, Mr. Belochi's.

The last human stand, all others have been sold and converted
to bot machines. I can smell the warm spices and my dry
mouth salivates. Well, might as well eat if my meet's going to
be late, again. Gotta keep moving.

I press my hands together and nod at the old man. "How's
business, Uncle? You still have a snack for your favorite customer?"

He is short, as though time and work has forced gravity to
pull harder against his body. "Achcha, Ashiva. If it weren't for
the AllianceCon spectators pouring into town."

I take in the area for UAVs and instead see the new holo-
screen projecting above his stand on the building wall behind
him: the PAC's emblem of fists hammering down and crushing the broken body of a massive war mecha. This is how they
see themselves. The heroes who ended WWIII. The ones who
united the world and stopped a complete nuclear holocaust.
When the American Province unleashed their war mecha in
the Middle East to claim their rare earth's mine, the world
shook. Then Asia launched its war mecha to counter the
American mecha. Soon American nuclear missiles fell in Central Asia and the Middle East. Asian mecha retaliated with
their bombs on the American Province. Damage was extensive. While the planet survived for the most part, it was
changed. Millions burned to ash. Their ghosts rightfully haunt
us. The Provinces almost ended it all.

"But isn't AllianceCon good for business?"

His glare is sharp, like the tip of a sword. "They've lost the
taste for our kind of food. The kind made by hand." He shakes
his head.

I take in the posters on the surrounding walls celebrating

the 25th Alliance Day—the birth of the PAC, end of WWIII, and what the PAC calls the reunification of the world after nuclear catastrophe. The New Treaty that ended WWIII makes sure the Provinces of the world play nice: no genocide, no weapons of mass destruction. PAC holds the marks. The posters are covered in graffiti calling for reparations for those lost in the Great Migration. Someone crossed out "celebration" and spray painted "murderers." We all celebrate the end of the war because we are still alive. But we also remember why we were fighting over resources, and how the sky turned orange from pollution then, and the seas swallowed thousands of miles of coastal cities. End of a war, beginning of the New Era.

But being alive is not always living.

"Never mind, beti, I have something special for you today." He claps his calloused hands and searches behind the stand, humming a strange song as he moves. When he rises again, he's giddy. "Here, I traded for this on the undermarket. Thought you'd enjoy it."

The fist-sized yellow fruit tumbles into my human hand. I breathe in its sugary sweet smell. "No, it can't be. A mango?" I turn it round and round, marveling at its ugly, wrinkled skin. It's soft and rough and a bit squishy and smells like burnt candy.

"You said you'd never tasted it. I want you to try my favorite fruit. Came from the Eastern District." Mr. Belochi hums as he turns the hot potatoes around on his small flat top, and sprinkles spices and chopped onions into the mix.

"It's unsightly. I adore it. Thank you."

He laughs. "Yes, and it tastes like it's from the gods."

"I'll share it with my family."

When he is done cooking, he pours the snack into a metal cone and hands it to me. And I lift my veil and swallow it in a few slow bites.

I slide him a few marks. More than I can spare, but I need to believe that a human can compete against the bots all over Central.

"Thank you, Uncle."

He smiles and continues to hum.

I can smell them before I see them: A giggling group of uppy girls with rose-scented hair and perfumes, and long flowing saris they let drag on the wet, dirty streets because they have more. One guard in front and one guard in the back, both Northerners with turbans, who look like they have very rough senses of humor. Probably on their way to a virtu-club. Girls like them come down to Strata One to party, take designer drugs, eat exotic food, and rebel against their strict upbringing without damaging their honor in their homes in the upper Stratas of Central.

Their shiny neural-synchs glitter with chrome and jewels, proof they passed the Solace test, live in Central, and now are permanently optimized through the Solace Corporation, a connection I don't envy. The tall girl has a gold butterfly at her temple, the other's is a crescent moon. Each piece goes for a quarter-million marks. Enough to feed the entire Narrows for a year. I know they don't remember the floods, the Great Migration, the Crimson Riots. They don't remember that twenty-five years ago their people locked the gates to Central and let climate migrants drown and die in the heat at the end of WWIII. They don't remember, but I do. I wasn't there, but it's in my DNA. My people never forget the choices the SA made when they responded to the guidelines of the New Treaty.

I lean against the wall with an AllianceCon poster. The one with President Ravindra standing tall and smiling in her blood-red suit. Always red. Always smiling. I hate that woman. I press a di-cut metal sticker onto her face with a red stenciled hand and the words "Red Hand Asleep Not Dead." General Shankar's profile is in the background of the sticker with a wild grimace as he wields a cannon over his shoulder during the Last Vidroh against Central. That could cost me one transgression, a ticket, and a slap on the wrist.

When the girls see me, they point and cover their mouths with the edges of their sleeves and distance themselves. It's my respirator mask dangling unclipped at my chest and the veil that covers half my face that makes them think of disease. They think anyone not perfect is contagious. My mask shows I live down here or in the Narrows. Like poverty is infectious. I kick the wall and choke down my pride.

Finally, a man exits the mediport carrying a large bag. He follows me into the alleyway. He's so nervous I'm sure he'll give us both away. When we reach the wall, I put my cyborg hand over his mouth and speak to his panicked eyes.

"You're late. And obvious. What'd I tell you last time?" I let my hand go.

"Sorry, Ashiva. Z Fever is moving through the city. I've been triaging for days."

"You're telling me it's here then? The Fever?"

Dr. Qasim nods. "The GHO is calling it Zephyrus Fever. Z Fever. It's viral and ugly. We don't know how it's spreading, but it is in the SA. The GHO is about to approve initial quarantine protocols here—same ones as in the Americas. Central wants to keep it quiet for now, but they want it dealt with quickly before AllianceCon and their 25th anniversary party. They know we all hear 'pandemic' and think about Ebola 4."

"Oh," I step back. "That bad?" Ebola 4 killed tens of millions of people globally, two decades ago. The PAC and GHO's responses were overreactive, but they missed the mark. They didn't realize it was spreading through contaminated food, so quarantines only kept the disease from spreading locally—but still it carried on the winds of trade across the globe anyway.

"I don't know, yet. But crowd mentality, you know. I wouldn't blame people for—"

"Taking to the streets, rioting, joining the Red Hand to resurrect them from the ashes?"

"Achcha . . . we're working on an inoculation and treatments. But the GHO is reporting new cases in the Americans and Asian Provinces. It's spreading fast." He presses the bag to my chest. "Here. Spared from the Arabian Sea," he says and tucks a scrap of paper in my hand. "Don't ask for the details and be careful with this one. It's not—"

"Okay, okay." I open the top of the bag and shuffle through the valuable vegetables and fruit. Good cover.

"Gentle, please." He turns to head back to the mediport. "This is the last time. The gray-collars are monitoring my flat, my family. They said they'd take my daughter and wife if I step out of line."

"Dr. Qasim, remember where you came from." But even I know. The gray-collar guardians are the ones you have to watch out for. They have a free pass to do anything they want to get what they want.

He puts up his hand, metal fingers glimmer in the dark. "I need no reminder. I am thankful for The Mechanic's mercy every day. I'll contact you. But it won't be for a while. And sorry about this. They said they'd take me to containment for questioning if I didn't prove useful."

I roll my eyes as the white-collar starts closing in. "Sorry about what?"

He signals to the guardians on the corner and they storm me.

And he scurries off like a scared mouse. The Internal faction of the Red Hand won't be able to rely on him much longer. I'll have to find another doctor on the inside, and it can take months for a smuggler to make a new contact. At least I have this package—every delivery is as important as the last. I take two steps forward and freeze.

"Oye, pickpocket! Identification." The guardian marches towards me with the confidence that his weaponry instills. A baton, electro-pulse gun and other intimidation devices bounce on the belt that cinches his long, white tunic.

Flit you, Doc. Here we go. I place the bag swiftly in the shadows and make a mental note to add his name to my throttle-list, right under Jai and Khan Zadabhai and the rest of the Lords of Shadow.

"Dhat," I whisper under my breath. I am no thief. Any jackal can steal a few marks from an Uplander because they always have their head in the clouds. If the Red Hand has a tricky transport, they tell me. What I do takes talent. And real talent gets you to tomorrow.

I bite my tongue and turn my wrist to his scanner to display my books. Essential for everyone in the Red Hand.

They're good. The best. But if he checks them in Central in So-lace's main, he'll see creases in the tampered data, and I'll be charged with curfew violation—one transgression that'll give me a one-way ticket to waste my time in questioning.

I straighten my tunic and feign Uplander boredom. This murkh halfwit is going to make me late.

"You are a long way from home in Strata 12. Let's see your face, girl."

"Sure, sahib. Just taking a walk." I hide my surprise in hear-ing my Strata. In my next life, maybe. Zami must've added that as a hidden message in my fake ID books, my lucky number. I unclip my veil from above my ears and grin. Fake books: two transgressions, one night in basic containment.

He flinches. "Accident?"

"A hungry, wild dog. Er, during a vacation in the East." I'm not sure what beast caused the scar on my cheek.

"Left you a permanent reminder." A note of disgust glim-mers on in his face. "You're going to have that edited soon, I suppose."

"Right away, sahib." I'll never have a genetic edit. My scar isn't terrible, but it makes Uplanders squirm. When I go to clip my veil again, my shoulder whizzes and whines under my black jacket. Stupid moody arm has impeccable timing.

The guardian cocks his head sideways. "Is your replace-ment registered?"

"Yes, of course, sahib," I say. My forced smile hurts my dry lips.

I don't know if he believes me, but he's just a white-collar, not here to take people in, just a scout, a writer of fines. A pain in my ass.

"Did the doctor give you something?"

My empty hands are clear. "A slim diagnosis, and smashed hope."

"Why don't you move along? President Ravindra's curfew is still in effect." He looks me up and down. Even with the books it's obvious I'm not a member of the elite class.

"I'm waiting for a friend. Last I checked that is still a right of the citizens, even in Strata One."

"If I see you outside in a half-hour, I'll have to take you to Central main," he says and moves on to hassle others.

"Okay, sahib. I'll be only a moment."

And I slip into the shadow's shadow. When he's gone, I lift the bag across my shoulder.

It twitches against my body.

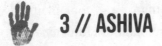 **3 // ASHIVA**

The bag is heavier than its size. I walk down the narrowing streets through the Liminal Area, the ten broken city blocks between Central's gates and the entry into the Narrows slum. With its forgotten buildings and anarchists, it's important to rush through. There's always a fight to be had here. I move quickly toward the edge of the platform to the Narrow's entry line. Returning home feels like sinking below the city, between dark, unfinished buildings, ancient structures in ruins, like faint memories still grasping onto life. Bygone buildings the SA keeps promising to fix, to finish. We're all still grasping. After WWIII, the sea levels rose hundreds of feet and caused the Great Floods which led to a panicked, bloody mass migration inland to the South Asian Province's center. Cities flooded. Millions drowned.

As I walk toward the line, I pass holo-screens projecting News One and the PAC's President Liu's weekly State of the Planetary Union that is more of his heartbreaking dung: "In these impossible circumstances, we will continue to allow each province to decide how to survive, and who will survive. It's not the PAC that will control the decision. We are giving the decision and power back to the people." Blah, blah, blah.

Power is never really with the people, is it?

The SA is desperate this year. I can feel it. They'll do anything to secure funding to build the three remaining neocities, East, West and North. And I mean anything. In our overpopulated SA, President Ravindra decided to use the algorithm Solace to determine who was genetically the best choice to continue in this new world and live in the first of four planned neocities, Central City One. But really, President Ravindra was just too cowardly to make the choice herself. Let a computer decide. Give the ones deemed "fit" a neural-synch to optimize their brains so the fewer can work harder, better. Distance yourself from the suffering and maybe it didn't happen. Maybe those deemed unfit by Solace will disappear or jump into the ocean themselves. Yeah, that'll work out.

After WWIII, when the SA crushed the Red Hand with their mechas during the Last Vidroh, they created the gray-collars and their extensive UAV system to track us. The Red Hand was forced deep underground and separated into Internal, External and Liberation cells. We switched our all-channels comms to closed internal comms. General Shankar's Liberation Hand detached completely, cut off all communication. They're the ones who do the hard work of arson, kidnapping, arms smuggling, and political assassinations. We've gone quiet, but we're still here, waiting for the right moment to join our hands. Asleep, but not dead.

I never knew the Red Hand when it was united. All I've ever known is Masiji's Internal Hand and our protection of civilians in the Narrows. I dream of the day when I can become a lieutenant in the Liberation Hand and walk alongside General Shankar. When we can raise our resistance from the ashes and demand equality for all Downlanders. For now, I'm just a trainee. Some day. One day. I hope.

It's not in human nature to recede and give up. We all fight. Life wants to continue even if Solace says you're unfit for the future.

I stand shoulder to shoulder with all types of poor slops who'd traded their jobs in maintenance and data centers to maintain the new automated systems. While we are in this together, when they push me, I push back harder, but not at my full strength. If I don't shove, I'd be trampled. None of us are allowed to live with the Uplanders in Central's Stratas inside the Ring, not without money and a proper neural-synch, and that's a Solace test we didn't pass. We can only visit to work, to be their lowly assistants.

Or work as agents of the Red Hand fighting to undo the system that kills us.

I walk to the booth and hand the gatekeeper the scrap of paper Dr. Qasim gave me. "How's the night shift, Romil? Catch any smugglers?" Romil is Red Hand, but we never talk about it in public. He lifts his gaze toward me, and it always knocks me off balance. His two bright blue, electrified eyes, backlit and cybernetically enhanced, fit squarely where his flesh-eyes should be. They make his scarred, round face look obsolete somehow. I've never asked him, but rumor is he lost them in a chemical fire. But his smile makes him seem kind, to me at least. As the leader of the clandestine spy network of the Internal Hand, he can literally see through walls, though most don't know about the added upgrades The Mechanic made to his standard ocular replacements.

Romil's belly shakes when he laughs. "Eh, not yet. Declaring . . . produce? That's a new one. What happened to metal scraps, cables, or batteries? That would be less . . . er . . . conspicuous."

Above Romil's head are holo-screens of the missing. Peeking out from beneath a poster announcing AllianceCon is a black and white image of some poor kid from the Narrows. "Lost," it reads. "Will pay for return." There are too many missing and lost to count. And where they are is anyone's guess. Most kids were abandoned on orphan trains during the Great Migration from coastal areas. When parents couldn't afford to move their whole family to higher ground, they'd send their children to the cities hoping someone would care for them. Decades later, people still hoped to be reunited. But lately, kids go missing all the time from the Narrows and no one knows why.

I open the top of the bag to show him the tops of wilted greens and vegetables. "For your sick mother." I wink and slide a vial of medicine under a pile of wilted greens. I know his mother. She trades the best sweets in the undermarket.

As he slides my papers back to me, he winks and says, "Tell your sister hello."

I nod and lift the paper and whatever he's put underneath it into my jacket pocket. Cameras all around, better safe than in containment. He turns up the volume on his holo-screen that's projecting the State of the Planetary Union. I stand back and watch as Romil checks another person's books. A small crowd gathers alongside me to watch the screen.

President Liu was recently elected by the Provinces to lead the PAC. The Province leaders all look angry even though they are sitting at a half-moon table side-by-side, like they're best friends. He sits between the leaders of the American Province and Asian Province. That's no mistake. They wouldn't enter the room if they had to sit next to one another. Snippets of quotes from the meeting run across the bottom ticker: "Liu says the Planetary Union is strong. Our provinces will work together to redistribute resources equitably across the union." Another reads "Alliance Conference to determine funding." Another quote reads: "Trade War Eminent: Rare Earths Declared Protected Commodity." And: "Stalemate on Neodymium Trade."

Neodymium. The element inside everything important. From robots to transports to computers, and the turbines that propel the Ring. Even in my replacement's plexus. The Asian Province has the largest mining operation in the world. But the processing of neodymium pollutes like crazy, so the PAC funds them, but only so they get what they want. It's all shady. Australian and American Provinces also have mines and are trying to build refineries, but with their limited pollution credits, they'll never compete. The African Province just announced their new mining operation and all the world leaders are now panicky. This was exactly how WWIII began. A fight for resources. We disarmed each other of war mechas and weapons of mass destruction, but they failed to fix the problem. We have no rare earths to share. It's only a matter of time before we fight again. And no, the Space Colony will not save us. I flip off the shadow of the Colony's toroidal rings as they careen across the moon.

The buzz tells me there's a UAV about ten feet above me. I clip my veil and pull my metal-threaded hood low over my head. Always move the same way, slowly, carefully. Don't draw attention to yourself. The drones see sudden changes as threats. The UAV flies closer.

"Better move along, Ashiva." Romil waves me through as he crunches the greens. "And be careful."

"Thanks." The crowd dissipates.

The scan clears me from a list of diseases, then I place my hand on a circular pad and tiny sharp needles perforate my skin like ten wasp stings. A pleasant new test for the Fever. I follow the masses to the edge of the encampments, a city outside a city. Clipping my respirator across my face, I look at the gift for my sister, Taru: a few vials of dust of different colors. Chemicals. Stuff only she understands.

As I move quickly through the Liminal Area into the Narrows, I pass familiar faces and tens more strangers. Over a million bodies down here. But I can count on my flesh hand those who know I'm Red Hand. Children play with a small rubber ball. It looks to be made of parts of tires, melted, cut, and stapled together in an awkward circle. They move fast and slow, some limp, some seem to fly. Each has a replacement body part. Either a replaced hand, foot, face, arm, leg or wires embedded in stents and replacement internal organs not visible to the human eye. But I see. I know. A girl steals the ball from a boy, pivots, then kicks it to another girl on her team. I cheer. The lucky ones get replacements. The lucky ones who survived the orphan trains, the floods, nuclear fallout, the Crimson Riots, the explosions from the Last Vidroh, disease, starvation . . . the lucky ones. Those who survived, they are now like potent stars crushed into a tiny speck of power, infinitely stronger. Not physical strength. Remade again with scraps of biotech smuggled by me and my team, the Red Hand runners. We bring the parts to the Commander and she completes their replacement surgery in her laboratory. We might be poor. But we are scientists, engineers, soldiers. The Uplanders closed the gates. But we survive. The boys laugh and cheer as the girl kicks the precious ball hard and far into a makeshift goal between two concrete blocks in the distance. For them. It's all for them.

The Narrows is a shanty city that blooms at the neocity's edge. Population: one million. The Narrows project was abandoned when Solace Corp decided that automation and construction of the neocity Central would be more efficient for the South Asian Province and so would investing in neural-synchs for Central's smaller, elite population. They built the Ring that filters the air and installed the neural-synchs linked to Solace to the minds of the genetically clean and wealthy. So out here in the forgotten landscape of the Narrows, some buildings have windows, others don't. They just left the area unfinished and the Downlanders took them apart, piece by piece, and rebuilt our houses, the undermarket and schools. Reused and remade, our shanty city stands, half-finished skeletons of concrete and metal. We built a latticed canopy that covers the entire length of the Narrows to block the sun, but more so to cover us from the UAV drones. We stay inside, they don't follow us. Many of us live two lives: one in Central, as their grunts, and one outside in the Narrows, as ourselves. They can take our jobs, our lives, our city, but we continue in spite. Though we don't have a Ring controlling the climate and cleaning our toxic air, Central installed a sea wall to protect us from the rising water. Another pathetic attempt to show their sympathy through empty, useless actions. All show, all the time. The civilians in the Narrows put their trust in the Red Hand. We are their secret, unofficial protectors— they guard our identities and don't ask questions. We make sure they're fed and have replacements. Make sure their children can just be kids sometimes.

And though we rest, the Red Hand never sleeps.

The Arabian Sea is to the right and Central City to the left, with the light dome the electricity makes covering it like a ter-rarium. The joyful sound of children laughing carries in the air, but I can't see a soul. Then it comes, a UAV buzzing, hover-ing like a massive metal insect. We call them machchar be-cause they make the annoying, high-pitched whizzing sound of a metal mosquito. One child appears suddenly from behind a dumpster. She's smiling, happy, just a girl waiting for the UAV to inspect her.

"Unfit," it says and buzzes around her, flashing a blue light.

Then another child appears, then another, and before long the UAV has at least ten faces to take in and survey. They're all trying not to laugh, but someone lets out a nervous giggle. Then I see. Standing atop the dumpster, a boy holds a sling-shot and aims it at the UAV as it is busy with their faces. The projectile tethers around the UAV just below the Solace Corp logo without disrupting it, a rock attached to a thin rope that's carrying a long sign. As it finishes with their faces, declaring them all "unfit" but "registered & cleared" and moves on, I see the sign reads, "kick me."

We all die laughing. Defacing a UAV is two transgres-sions, but not if they don't get caught. Kids even in dire straits need to be kids or else we lose. If we live only in fear, we lose. If we can't be human anymore, we lose. Small acts of rebellion are as important as large-scale ones. As soon as the sign's in place they all scatter like dust. I whistle to the gatekeeper and he signals to the girl on guard duty. We all take shifts, which is easy considering there are so many of us.

"Open the gate," he yells.

The massive metal wall shifts on wheels to the right and I walk through, waving to the crew as I pass. While I want to sit and watch the sunrise caught in the smoke-thick air, speed's important.

"Hey, behanji. Thought you finally slipped up," my little street brother, Zamir, stands from his seat on a metal barrel and walks alongside me. He's called me sister since the first day he saw me in the orphanage, the day we were selected by Red Hand.

"Still got it, hero. What'd I tell you?" I ask.

"'They can't catch the righteous.'" Zami looks tired. He must've waited for me for hours. "Sure, even with your replacement arm you're only human. And still only a runner, not a Red Hand Liberation lieutenant yet, if I remember correctly."

"That's more than I can say for them. And hey, any day now." I laugh and watch Zami's half remade face glimmer chrome in the fluorescent torch light. He doesn't laugh with me.

"If the Liberation Hand is still alive, you mean," he says.

"Oh, they're alive. General Shankar is still leading."

"How do you know? We haven't heard from him in years." When Zami grimaces, his replacement jaw and cheek glimmer in the light unevenly.

"I know. I just know." He has to be. If he's not alive, we have zero chance of reuniting the Red Hand cells in order to make a coordinated assault on the SA and Central one last time. If he's not alive . . . I can't even imagine that future. "What's really bothering you, bhai? No water at the chug-chug today? Your face looks worried."

"Shiv, Taru went missing."

I stop. "What happened?"

"We don't know. They gave level one Red Hand recruits their assignments today. And all we know is that after she got hers, she left the Narrows to go into the Liminal Area. Probably to take a walk. But..."

"Dhat, the goonda crew has been searching for a kid with her talents. She's been talking about them like they're better than us. I've gotta go."

"Sister, relax. You've done everything you can, and she knows how fragile she is. You've told her not to fall. She knows to be careful. But you've built a fence around her. People don't like being in cages."

"So, it's my fault?" It is my fault. Anything that happens to Taru is my fault. I should have done more to keep her safe. Her fake diagnosis of juvenile osteoporosis doesn't seem to keep her very still anymore. It used to when she was younger. But she's getting braver. Sometimes I wish I hadn't falsified her records. Sure, her bones aren't great. She had several fractures from a training skirmish when she was little. But I had to do something more. Right when she had her casts off after the accident, she wanted to leave, to go into the Liminal Area. She wouldn't sit still. It was dangerous being so young, stupid, and so mobile. So, I exaggerated her medical records and talked Masiji into supporting my lie. For Taru's sake. For her. It was supposed to be temporary, just until she learned the ways of this world. It wasn't supposed to go on this long. But the lies piled around me like landmines.

No one knows the weight of my lies and the regret that fills me like liquid hot metal.

"No, I didn't mean that. She's weak, I know. She can break

at any time. But the more you push, the further she will go. Just let her return when she's ready."

I swallow hard. "I know she went to find Ravni's crew." I put my arm out to stop Zami's pace. "Stupid kids." The goonda crew runs the Liminal Area outside the Narrows. They are anarchists, outlaws, daaku. All they care about is agitating all sides. Damn the chaos makers.

"Maybe. She did mention she wanted to make fireworks to sell for AllianceCon as a side hustle. But—" Zami pauses.

"But what?"

"What if the daaku used her to build an explosive for another plan to take down the Ring?"

Zami averts my gaze. "That'll blow all the good groundwork the Red Hand has been doing."

"It would hurt my chances of going up for lieutenant in Liberation Hand; any noise will derail the whole thing. More UAVs. They don't like messes. I'm going to kill Ravni." Everything goes white. Ravni, the leader of the goonda crew is a killer. She coaxes you in close with charming conversation, like a lovely little spider. Then, suddenly you realize she's built a web around you and you're done. Her crew of thieves strip you of everything. My heart thumps in my ears like a laser cannon and I want to throttle her. "I need to go. You take the package to Masiji."

"No. You can't just solve everything with fists. You'll never find Ravni anyway. They're laying low in the tunnels." Zami holds my shoulders. Even though he's younger than me, he's taller. "Shiv, you are a warrior. Fearless. But so, so stupid. The dumbest smart person I've ever known."

I throw my hands in the air. And they'd love to get ahold of my little sister's gift of alchemy and chemistry to make a thing of destruction.

He shakes his head. Zami lifts my chin so we are eye to eye. "Taru needs you. When she turns up, remember that she has probably already learned her lesson."

"Right, okay." I nod and gently pat the bag at my side. "Fine. Need to get this to Masiji, then I'll find Taru."

Zami nods and presses his forehead to mine.

We duck through a low doorway and enter a sea of tunnels. At the end of the maze is an entrance with a sign for a seamstress. The secret compound, our home, is the orphanage called The Children of Without. Rooms border the central courtyard, that house the children and caregivers. The latticed roofs connect all the makeshift structures to avoid the UAVs above, but they also cut us off from seeing the sky. I miss the sky, even with its yellow-orange haze and shocks of electrified clouds filled with acid raid.

"Hello, Ashiva. Zamir."

We both stop.

Mrs. Zinaat is the Red Hand's Internal Recruitment Commander. There was a rumor that she was a professor once, that she had a large family with three small children who all died in the Last Vidroh, collateral damage as people fled Central into the Narrows. She makes me nervous every time I see her. It's like she can see I'm full of lies and trouble. Next to her tall, peaceful, thin-nosed, and pious form, we all look shoddy. She's delicate and strong, like iron lace. Always wearing a dupatta to cover her long hair, but never sweating like the rest of us.

"Salaam, Mrs. Zinaat-ji. Have you seen Masiji? I have a package," I say and look down at the broken concrete to avoid her piercing gaze. She caught me stealing a ration pod at langar when I was six. Instead of turning me in, she made me put it back, and taught me the five lessons about respect and the way of the Red Hand. That if we steal we are taking from the most vulnerable and are as bad as the Uplanders. That every day our job is to undo the PAC's work, and free our people and those around the world who are also suffering at the hands of their governments. I never stole again. Not from the Narrows, at least.

She presses her well-worn hands together and smiles the best someone her age can. I think she is probably only forty, but breathing our polluted air for that long causes lung-rot and damages the joints. Most only live to fifty, middle age is thirty. My future is like a slowly closing door and those around me are illustrations of various endings. It probably wouldn't be so bad if this is all we knew. But humans were living well beyond one hundred and twenty only a quarter of a century ago. Central steals time from us, the most sinister punishment. She looks me and Zami up and down carefully, then points to the temple door. "She's been waiting for you. But she's in the middle of Open Speak."

"Shukran," I say, thanking her.

We walk back to the main area, enter another tunnel, then stop at the doors made of thick scrap metal, the strongest stuff.

Zami whispers to me, "Let's go inside."

I pull off my combat boots and rinse my feet with the filtered water in a small bowl before entering the temple room. Inside, time stands still. Images of gods and goddesses, gurus and teachers hang on the walls, an unbiased, multi-belief room of hope. Poverty is nondenominational.

Open Speak in the temple is the weekly civilian grievance session. When we enter, I inhale the rich smoke of incense, and hopes, dreams, and frustrations of the Narrows. Mostly, people voice their concerns about food and supplies, or the odd gripe with a neighbor or domestic problem. But it usually devolves to a complaint about food or the heat. The two ways we die.

Masiji's shadow is wide and dark in the center of the room. She's surrounded by a hundred people or more. People are sitting on the floor, standing, and those who need a chair have them. Zami and I keep to the shadows and listen. Civilians and Red Hand alike share the room. Though most civilians don't know and don't want to know who are part of Red Hand. We protect them, feed them, train those who want to be fighters, and they forget our names and faces when they are questioned by guardians. Safer for all, plausible deniability is key. Masiji is known as the Mayor of the Narrows here by most. But to me . . .

She is strength incarnate.

Our leader. Our Mechanic. Our Savior. Our Commander.

The metal on her body jostles as she paces. "There will be a time when we will face an impossible choice. We worry about our survival, the chug-chug bots that are constantly breaking down. We argue about how many ration pods they send us. We can fight all we want for more food and water, to eliminate the UAVs. But that's missing the point. We have to imagine a future outside the Narrows. This is an encampment. It was never supposed to last more than a year. But here we are, twenty-five years later."

People are agitated. These aren't the same complaints about the water machines going awry again, or fussy bots that find it harder and harder to de-sal and decontaminate and de-radiate our food and water. No, this is not the same problem of broken sewage systems and food supply that is late, again—forever. There's a desperate urgency in the air.

"We need to take Central for ourselves," chimes in a boy I know is a runner for the Red Hand. Chand, the big, old teddy bear of a smuggler. He knows better than to speak up now. Masiji sends him a dagger look and shuts him up fast.

A petite girl stands. "We need to see if we can gather our forces. We need to reach abroad to the world. We need unity now across all people suffering in the world. It's the only way." She makes me so proud. I know her from somewhere, but can't place it. From the orphanage, or maybe she's a new recruit.

I turn to Zami and whisper, "That one. Is she inside?"

"I'll look into it. She'd be good for us. She's got first-rate recruit vibes," he whispers back. The girl sits down again, respectfully cross-legged on the floor with everyone else.

Masiji's replacement leg is naked chrome uncovered by the silicone that many choose to hide their cyborg parts. The joints hiss and puff as she paces. Her tunic is dark brown and black with shocks of orange woven with metal, like a warrior. Her gaze is fierce.

Masiji continues amongst the moans and affirmations. "That's right, beti. Those of us who are old enough to remember have witnessed a paradigm shift of the human mind and body." She taps her forehead referencing the plexus we have that runs our replacements and the uplanders' neural-synchs.

A woman stands and says, "Mechanic, what about the rumors of the Fever? Is it true?"

"Is it a pandemic? We'd see the GHO at our doorsteps if it were. So far, there have been unconfirmed cases in the Upland, but not here. It's not to worry about," Masiji says.

"They don't care about the Unsanctioned Territory, or the districts in the East and West. The neocity is their focus. The North hasn't been in contact with us—not since the nuclear bombs triggered the avalanches. They herd us like cattle. Treat us like we're animals even though we don't have the diseases they're looking for," the woman continues.

"Once the GHO makes a recommendation, we'll know more."

Some nod, others shake their heads.

Masiji takes a step back and says, "We have bigger things to worry about than the Fever. Planetary President Liu will stand by Planet Watch's statement that our rights should be protected by the higher courts—even under the New Treaty."

"How do you know they will? Why would they care?" A woman's voice is tired, strained.

A young man chants, "The New Treaty should burn with the PAC!" Others join his call.

Masiji is unfazed. "The Treaty only states that resources should be redistributed within the population as seen fit by that particular Province's leadership. It only states that we can't use weapons of mass destruction or kill a population outright. So, our anger should be directed at our Province government, along with their solution: Solace. Once the world sees the fallout of Solace and Central, they'll be forced to change the treaty. We are not alone. Once we reconnect with our allies, we will undo their laws."

"Why don't we all just move to Greenland?" someone blurts out and the crowd laughs. "Or the African Province—their new forests are rooting well." Wishful thinking. We all know we aren't allowed to leave our home Provinces. No migration under the New Treaty.

"We can't trust the PAC again. Not since the Void." The girl trembles this time when she stands. The one who spoke up earlier about joining forces, the one we marked for recruitment.

A heavy silence falls on the room like a thick shadow. And all eyes turn to Masiji.

She faces the girl with a click of her heels. "The Void was just a story cooked up by Central to scare us into submission. There's no PAC-sanctioned prison." Masiji says with a finality that shuts the crowd up.

The Void. Whispers of a planetary prison set on the boundary between territories. Larger than just a regular containment prison, it was said that once someone was taken there, they would cease to exist. No funeral. No letters. No visitations. Erasure. Most say it's a lie, that no one group has this power. But sometimes I wonder if it's real. People have searched and failed to find it. A rumor buzzed about it being in orbit in space. But that would cost too much. If it is real, it has to keep moving somehow.

The girl stands with a bowed head. "Masiji, forgive me, but my father..."

Then I remember her. The girl. The family. The whole story. Her father went missing after working in Central as an assistant to a city official who was under investigation for corruption. Disappeared. Never seen again. She's been speaking up to anyone who will listen ever since. But we all have so many problems that our ears are full.

I hit Zami in the arm. "See? Real."

"I still think it's just a bad fairy tale," Zami says.

"Someone will find it. Hold them accountable," I whisper.

The rising voices hush when an elderly man tries to stand from his chair. Daadaji, Red Hand's Internal Colonel, but the civilians only know him as Old Grandfather. He was a soldier in the Last Vidroh with the Liberation Hand, but retired when he was unable to run field missions. He came to the Narrows to assist in the duties of managing the resistance messaging in the Narrows and grow our movement. Daadaji wears drawstring pants that are too big on his body, save for the frayed rope that holds them up on his slender hips. But his T-shirts he gets from the donation pile. Today he's wearing a ratty gray T-shirt that reads "Have a Nice Day" in pink cursive. He's a cheeky old bastard with eyes that are younger than the face they're set in. It takes him forever to rise, but we wait for him and for his comments out of respect.

The old man clears his throat. "We have been angry for a long time. I fought at Central's gates. We have died for this cause. Central's weapons are bigger. Their numbers are greater. Their resources and people are optimized. They spend all their time and money building the Space Colony, for what? We have nothing. Belief is not enough to change this. You can believe all you want, but that won't help us trade places with the Uplanders. When will we fight?"

Masiji walks toward him. "Daadaji, I have made our children stronger than theirs. They just don't know it yet. Sometimes those who can't hear us or see us need to remember. Solace has silenced the Narrows. They wait for the seas to rise so they can blame our erasure on natural disaster."

A woman says, "So, Mechanic, what are you saying?"

"We should make them remember us. We worry about food, shelter, thermal death when what we need is for the world to see us. We need to take the battle to their door with our allies."

The crowd pulses with energy.

"We need the world to see the reality of their Central city, their precious Solace!" Masiji presses her right hand to her chest and the crowd does the same. The Red Hand. Suddenly, she sees me and Zami. Her eyebrows rise. "We are all Red Hand."

This act of defiance shakes the crowd. All suspicions confirmed. Masiji just announced she's a member of the Red Hand. Though not everyone in the Narrows is a part of the Red Hand, we are their only government, their only hope.

"Calm down, brothers and sisters." Masiji's voice rises above the rest.

A girl says, "Death to the uppers."

A boy says, "No more war."

Masiji waves her hands and in her deepest voice speaks above the din. "Enough!"

All voices inside hush.

She continues, "Langar is served. Please exit the temple and move to the courtyard." People are hungry. Hunger outweighs anger every time. The crowd dissolves and when a path is clear, she comes towards us. We follow her into a quiet room and close the door behind us.

"There you are. I thought you were taken to contain-ment, or worse," Masiji says, whipping her long braid over her shoulder. She still wears her protective mechanic gear, metal apron, gloves, and goggles on her forehead. Masiji must've been in her workshop, as she smells of rust and soot.But her gear is polished and perfect. It's how she shows she is of the people.

"You'd miss me too much," I say. "I brought you some-thing. Dr. Qasim remembers you well." I set the bag down carefully on a thick mat.

Masiji removes her gear and piles it on the floor. Her gait shifts from left to right heavily because of her replacement leg.

"Tiger," she hugs me.

Under the wilted vegetables is a box the shape of a mas-sive egg. With a click, the box opens and inside we all see a sleeping infant. Dr. Qasim insulated her transport box with padding and an oxygen system around her small frame. She must be only a few months old.

"This is the youngest yet," I say.

Zami smiles at the baby and asks, "What should we name her?"

"Jiva, for her soul that's kept her alive. What a gift." Masiji presses her hands together in prayer. She picks up the pink brown baby and kisses her cheeks. "Beti," she says, and turns the baby around carefully in her hands.

I ask, "What's wrong with her? Why'd they throw her away?"

"Nothing's wrong with her, beti." Masiji says. She inspects the infant's body. "She didn't pass the tests. Solace somehow determined her unfit for the future." She runs her fingers over the stitches across the infant's tiny chest. "Probably asthma or lung deformation was her downfall. They must have tried to do a lung transplant, but failed."

"What some Uplanders will do to pass the test is disgusting," I say.

"What they do with their children who don't pass is even worse, throwing them away like garbage," Masiji replies. "All they care about is their population number. Keep it small or else they can't support their system. Overpopulation is the biggest security threat to the SA's neocity Central. If it weren't for Central's exorbitant Human Tax, many more would keep their children even if they didn't pass the test."

"But it's too expensive, so if they don't pass, the parents stay, but they have to let their children go," I comment.

"Central only offers impossible choices," she says.

"I wouldn't want to live there. Even if I had passed the test." I stroke Jiva's chubby cheek and she giggles, then drools. Masiji opens the door and calls to a woman deep in prayer.

"Poonam," Masiji whispers, "come here please."

"Haanji," she replies, without missing a beat, and enters our room. Poonam Auntie is the Red Hand's Internal Medic. She's stout, muscular and odd. Her eyes have ghosts behind them, like she's seen too much. And she probably has as she was a field medic and explosive specialist before the Red Hand went underground and separated into cells. Even though she's a bit kooky and odd, I adore her. The way she dresses, like she does so in the dark, to her thick, curly black hair that spills all over the place. Her cheeks are wide and childlike. But most of all, I adore her shiny replacement hand.

It's outfitted with extra devices that make her medical tasks easier.

"Please take all look at this baby. Let me know if she needs any assistance and get her settled in the nursery." She hands the baby to Poonam Auntie who coos a little too loudly and wakes the baby, who shrieks.

"Oh, oh sorry, beti. Sh sh, beti." She sings her an odd lullaby about the war.

"We will have the naming ceremony after langar tonight."

"Right-o." Auntie bows her head to Masiji and winks at me before exiting.

My stomach growls. It's been nearly a day since I'd tasted a ration. The snack from Mr. Belochi's stand only woke the massive pit growing in my stomach. The mention of our communal dinner is a sharp reminder. Every evening we gather for a meal of rice, daal, and bread. The ration tablets Central airdrops to the Narrows are pounded into a flour for blue flatbread. Taking a pill strips the humanity from meals, so we do our best. Since the Red Hand split into cells and separated from our Liberation Hand completely, we are alive but ineffective. The pods make Central look good. And a sharp reminder to us of the uselessness of charity. We're tolerated like a mosquito on a crocodile's back.

Masiji fidgets with her pile of things, like she is taking inventory. "Okay, Zami go on to langar. And you, Tiger, go find Taru."

Zami smirks and leaves me alone. Jerk.

"Can't I take a meal first? It was a hard day—"

Masiji takes my arm and we leave the temple room. "I know you would rather avoid her, daughter, but don't let the work you do for the Red Hand become more important than your duties as a sister. Don't get so laser-focused that you become blind."

"Blind to what?" I ask.

"Ach, Ashiva, do you remember when you found Lomri, our little Taru wandering the streets, hungry? Do you remember what you said to me when you brought her here against my wishes? Our broken little Lomri?" She looks at me and waits for me to let her words sink in.

"Of course, that I would give her my ration at least until she was stronger. So?"

Masiji looks lost in thought. "That's what's important."

"I'm a good smuggler. A good runner for the Red Hand. I'll be promoted to a lieutenant station with the Liberation Hand soon. Haven't I done everything you asked?"

Masiji stops walking and holds my hand a little too tight. "You are the best at what you do. But don't forget what we're fighting for. Each other. Don't lose sight of that. Taru needs you as a sister today, not as a warrior. Her day was harder than yours. Have some empathy, girl."

I take in my bare feet. All scratched and calloused and stubby toes.

"Ashiva." Her voice is not a question. "Today she was given her assignment. She was placed with the Internal Hand." She looks at me with raised eyebrows.

A stinging heat runs up from my stomach to my eyes. "Okay, good." I nod, but I'm not sure this is good. In fact, this is very bad. I am relieved she was assigned to stay put. But that's why she took off. She was ticked.

"She'll be safe in Internal Hand for now. She can work with

Poonam Auntie as a medic assistant and later maybe she can work on her weapons projects. Just as you wanted. But she won't be happy. And if she ever finds out what you've done ..."

"Achcha." Yes, I am afraid at what I did. Threatening my allegiance for Taru's safety inside the Internal Hand. All she's ever wanted was to be in the External Hand, to go far away from here, to work in science and be placed as a spy inside another government. To get out of the Narrows, to have a future beyond the slums. All she wants is to leave the Narrows, leave us. And I've just gone and built a concrete wall around her. If it keeps her from breaking, so be it.

"She'll hate you for it, but maybe in time she'll realize it's your way of showing your love."

"Promise me. Never tell her."

She salutes me.

I return the gesture.

Masiji says, "Just remember: Keeping someone from dying isn't the same as letting someone live."

"Copy, Mechanic. Loud and clear."

She shakes her head at me and I shrug. Agree or disagree, I'll never win with her.

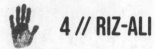

Being a data tech intern for Solace Corp has its perks and drawbacks. Perk 1: I work with the first-of-its-kind central neural network operating system to take on the management of a neocity. Perk 2: I live in the exclusive Solace Towers, Strata 95, in the center of the Ring. Perk 3: Once I launch neural code programs at work to train Solace, I play mecha robot fighting games for the rest of the day, secretly, on the underweb. Perfect life. If it was my own life, I'd be envious of myself.

But it isn't mine. I'm a prisoner of my mother's design. She moved me here, away from everyone I've ever known, because she thinks I've been on the underweb playing mecha fighting games again, and her career can't risk another upset. Real war mechas armed with WMDs are illegal, but some feel games that even hint at them should be banned also, which is rubbish. She's threatened to send me to Ahimsa, the luxury wellness center where the rich kids go to get "better," so many times that finally she said she was just going to move me to where she could know I was safe. She put me in this high-security, automated apartment building. It's all punishment even though it won't stop me from being myself. And it's not like she's wrong. I am playing Mecha Wars again to spite her.

I lean out the window and blow my ether smoke as far from my bedroom as I can. Ten pedestrians, fourteen transport rickshaws, twenty-five surveillance cameras and three UAVs hovering, reading faces, heartrates, intentions. Wait—

twenty-six. They just placed a new one on the corner of the building across from mine. The small blue lights are blinking. Always scanning, sorting, whispering. But I know who is on the other side of the lens: Solace, Central, my mother. No one is ever alone in Central.

Central wakes up through the misty sunrise. It's perfect. Just like everything here, on the inside. Designed for convenience, the walkways, Maglev roads, and bridges were built with the lightest-weight metals and glass. I marvel at the domed farms inside every community, growing food with cloud mist technology to feed each neighborhood. Even the people are optimized; the neural-synch sees to that. The city shimmers in the rising sun, on its girders, high above the Arabian Sea. My view from this corner flat is rare: the sea and the Narrows on one side, and from the other window, the vast uninhabitable inland. Central is set at the edge of two worlds. When I cock my head, I can make out the outline of the electromagnetic field that runs between the Ring's towers in a dome above Central. It is only visible at dawn and dusk, and it mirrors the city below, creating a doubling effect. The Ring that keeps the temperatures livable and filters the air to the nanoparticle. That keeps the chosen alive. I should appreciate all I have while so many others are fighting for breath in the Narrows and the Liminal Areas.

In the distance inland, through the electromagnetic dome, are the noxious clouds that hover in the beyond the city in the Barrens. Clouds hang like steel wool and flash with lightning as they hover, always searching to land a strike on a physical object below. Perma-lightning and acid rains scorch the earth. Central's electromagnetic field redirects the charge when lightning strikes the dome. The inland expanse beyond the neocity is not habitable, the nuclear fallout from WWIII made sure of it. Between the lightning clouds and the acid rain that falls from them, scalding the world below, the desperate animals that are still there have undergone strange and dangerous adaptations. The world outside Central is a wasteland.

And the dead war mecha half-buried in the sands of the Barrens sits and stares at Central like a broken god. The storms swirling around it make it look like a mystical creature, not a hunk of metal that it is. But as I peer inland, through the perma-lightning and storms, past the decommissioned war mecha the size of a skyscraper, I see my uncle's machines.

They move in the distance. A hundred agribots, tall and lanky, like giant crane people, lean over and lift pallets the size of trucks, pallets full—I assume—with some sort of lentil or grain sprouts being grown in the giant aeroponic dome . They move like stiff people, but always working, never sleeping. These mechas are New Treaty-approved. Built for—and only for—the purpose of sustaining life on Earth. My uncle's last project before he died. His project continues without him.

Exhaling the smoke again, I recount the people now on the street below: twenty-five. Always the same numbers, every day.

The few minutes before my house-bot, Taz, wakes are the few minutes I own. Sliding back into my console chair, I roll and unroll Kanwar Uncle's precious pieces of synth paper. The plans for his new mechas he was working on at the time of his death, ones that might have been used in agriculture, in peace missions, in protecting humanity and the planet. If he had survived. Kanwar Uncle was an engineer who worked for the SA on The Future of Agriculture team. His projects were focused on making agribots that could farmland that was un-inhabitable by humans in places like deserts, atop ocean barges, even on the Space Colony. His last project was high security and he promised to tell me about it when he could, but he never got the chance.

I've stared at these plans for four years in secret. They were his last gift to me. On the synth paper are his agribot projects that consumed all of his time, complete with details of power sources and networks. But I've only just realized that they're much more than plans. In the code, all these years, was a simple message to me. When I see it, I wonder why it took me so long to discover. In the code, through the data and equations, there's a pattern. But it's so rudimentary that I previously disregarded it. Or maybe I just wasn't looking. But it's there now, clear as day. A message to me: "It's not as it seems. Contact the Red Hand. The Commander will tell you everything." My heart soars. His message to me. To keep going. To believe in the world as we see it, as he saw it. But the Red Hand is labeled as a terrorist network by the SA. It's hard to know what to believe when the boundary between survival and hate, starvation and war are so thin and permeable. In the past, the Red Hand committed arson and armed civilians. Of course, it's rumored they also feed, house and educate the people of the Narrows, and there hasn't been an act of war since the Last Vidroh. Maybe they went underground. The PAC takes credit for defeating them, of course. But why does uncle's note say to connect with the Red Hand? I don't know. But I must follow through, to try to continue his good work. To trust in humanity and nature again. I press the synth paper to my chest. I always knew something was terribly wrong about his death. If the Commander has answers, I'll do what I must to connect.

The authorities said Uncle was performing illicit weapons work in Central, which was against the New Treaty. But non-nuclear armed robots are still legal and superfluous. They said that his work was highly flammable, and he died in an explosion. But I always knew that was a lie. Uncle was a brilliant engineer; there's no way his lab would have an accident like that, not with the precautions he took. He was only involved in robotics to save the world, not to weaponize it. Mother didn't even mourn Uncle at his funeral. Not a tear. She said it was important to move forward, past the tragedy, or else the SA might think we were co-conspirators in his work. I've hated her ever since.

I grew up with him at every birthday and most dinners. He went to university with my father. They were flatmates for years. He was a bachelor, never had a family, so he adopted us as family, and spent his days and nights building machines that would save our world from ending. When my father and mother worked late, Kanwar Uncle would come to eat dinner with me. He brought me presents. Not candy. Not toys. Puzzles. Real books of poetry and history and stories. Video games. We played chess. He taught me math and principles of engineering through games. When I was five, we built my first robot. When I was seven, I coded my first computer program. I owe everything to him.

But robotics is a precarious field. So easily can one make a battery system that can be used interchangeably between an agribot and a war mecha. The colossal shields he designed for the agribot farm to withstand the acid rain and electrical storms could be used as shields for a mecha suit. Damn, even my annoying little house-bot could be retrofitted with comms tech used to transmit info to a war mecha. Intentions are everything. The PAC and SA can make the case that even the use of nearly any tech is an act of war. I see that now. I borrow the tech that Uncle taught me to build the mechas on the underweb RPG in Mecha Wars.

He was my world until, one day, he stopped visiting. I waited to show him my plans for my newest robot, and he never came. I was alone for two days with a nanny-bot. Mother and father were working. Mother said he was a traitor. Father said nothing, like the death of his best friend took his voice. We all stood beside one another during his funeral and cremation, Uncle's only family. I cried for days. Father left a week later for Greenland to begin his new job reassignment at the Foundations Institute to work for the PAC on their new Alliance Space Colony. Mother kept her job and said Uncle was a villain. That was that. I was forbidden to talk about him from that day forward. But I never stopped looking for the truth.

I roll up the synth papers, place them back into their thin box, and slide it back into the hole in the wall I cover with a perfectly painted panel. Hidden like a true treasure for the past four years.

Today is the day I do something about it.

Shaking my head at myself, I tap a few buddies on the underweb: Generix and MechTech.

KID SYNCH: YOU THERE?

They both ping me back.

GENERIX: HEY LOSER.

MECHTECH: MORNING TO YA. SUCKS ABOUT MAGTAR, YAAR.

KID SYNCH: I'M SURE YOU'RE REAL SORRY FOR WINNING THE MECHA WARS™ 10.0.

MECHTECH: YOUR EXO-SUIT WAS PRETTY LAME, ANYWAY, SO I THOUGHT I'D GIVE YOU A CHANCE TO BUILD A NEW ONE. MAKE IT BLACK THIS TIME. HEAT RESISTANT.

KID SYNCH: HAHAHA. THE RED HAND CHALLENGE? ANYONE?

GENERIX: WORST IDEA EVER. NOT TO MENTION WE CAN'T FIGURE OUT IF IT'S A SET-UP FROM CENTRAL. IT'S A CLOAKED REQUEST.

MECHTECH: NAH, IT'S LEGIT. I CHECKED ITS ORIGINS LAST NIGHT. NOT FROM CEN-TRAL.

KID SYNCH: WHERE THEN?

GENERIX: YOU KNOW THEY'RE NOT THAT STUPID.

MECHTECH: YEAH, NOT DUMB LIKE YOU. HEH HEH.

GENERIX: HEY.

KID SYNCH: IT SEEMS LIKE AN EASY JOB.

GENERIX: TELL ME YOU'RE NOT GOING TO DO IT.

KID SYNCH: NO WAY. CAPITAL OFFENSE AND ALL.

MECHTECH: BUT THE GLORY! ALL OF THE GLORY!!! ONLY THE GREAT KID SYNCH COULD POSSIBLY PULL THIS OFF. AND YOU GET TO CLAIM A DIGI-PET OF YOUR CHOICE. YAAR, THEY'RE, LIKE, SO CUTE.

GENERIX: NOW WHO'S THE DUMB ONE?

I don't mention I've already hacked Solace twice and pranked Central by shutting down the Ring once for five whole seconds. The Ring's software is near un-hackable, and anyone who even attempts it gets slapped with twenty trans-gressions and possible eviction from Central. I'm growing tired of my anonymity. My buddies know I've done a few things, but the specifics I've never told a soul. While I've come close to telling MechTech and Generix, I've never met them in person. You never meet underweb pals. For all I know they could be anyone. Keeping my felonies to myself is the best for now. Everyone talks big on the underweb. Anyway, the Mecha Wars is an undermarket game.

I hear a voice in the gathering space calling, "Good morning, Riz-Ali Singh. I sense a contaminant. Perhaps we should close the window and run the eco-filter?" Taz, the most troublesome bot in the world, buzzes around the flat. Must be ten to five.

KID SYNCH: MY NANNY-BOT JUST WOKE UP. GOTTA GO.

I disengage from the underweb and burn my history, just as the bot wheels into my room with his round, white head permanently smiling and wide-eyed, the flat-screen on his chest flashing with touchscreen comms and instructions. The height of a small child, he has an unassuming quality about him, which is essential for all nanny-bots, so that humans lower their defenses and trust them. Taz seems basic, but I'm not fooled. He has extensions set for all sorts of emergencies, a fire extinguisher, medi-kit, even a talk therapy setting. I don't have access to his system to know for sure what he does with the information he collects on me, but I have a few ideas.

"No need, Taz." I cough and toss the ether smoke into my teacup, sliding the ignitor into my pocket, out of view.

"It seems your neural-synch is on deep-sleep mode still. Shall I turn it on for you before I perform the tests?"

"Um, I was just recalibrating," I press the button in my temple and reestablish the full connection. Not like I can ever fully disconnect. "I'm ready."

Taz rolls toward me and I stand still, my arms at my sides, head looking straight at my poster of Talvinder's newest film, *War*. It doesn't hurt, the crisscrossing beams of lasers he uses to X-ray my body for defects. When he's done, I sit on the edge of my bed and hand him my arm. His needle is thin and I can't even feel it anymore. One poke. He pulls the blood sample into his system and the screen on his chest flashes as it runs a report. Taz's face is smiling the entire time. Definitely a design defect. It should be more interactive. No person is that happy all the time, or ever, really. I never see the results or exactly what I'm being tested for, but I assume infectious diseases and viruses, and genetic defects that may not have appeared during the Solace test. Not everyone gets the five-minute, daily once-over. My numbers were barely passing at best. This was part of the deal my mother struck with the SA to allow me to stay in Central.

Info-Run data spills down the right edge of my vision. Comms from the Minister on behalf of President Ravindra about the unrest building in the Narrows and more funding promised for the Narrows to clean it up. Another red alert about the new Z Fever report and how to stay clear of those showing symptoms . . . blue rash, tremors, and other things that turn my stomach. The GHO reports that it has appeared in three Provinces thus far. There's more information about AllianceCon, and how the SA is so proud they won the chance to host it and show the world how *well* they're doing with Solace. How they have something special they're revealing during the conference. I bet—they're going all out since it's the SA's last shot for additional funds from the PAC. They'd better win the marks or else they'll just have to find another way to deal with the worst population problem in the world.

I shake my head. Well? We're doing well? They sure know how to put on a strong front to the world and the PAC. If Solace and Central even appears to fail, the PAC will pull funding and redistribute our money to other Provinces that are stronger, more viable. It's all a show. But one people actually believe.

As the data runs an update, I feel the skin on my scalp crawl. With each new comm, a nerve twitches, pinches on my scalp. I lean on my console and let my head fall heavy into my hands.

Don't think of it. It will just make things worse. Stop.

But it comes anyway. I imagine my neural-synch is alive, embedded around my brain. Its tentacles growing like arms twisting around my temples. My hands tremble, eyes twitch with involuntary movements. Stop. Just stop. This is not a normal side effect of the neural-synch. I no longer tell the medical team about these quirks I have. I stand and let the thoughts dissolve. "Sometimes, to find the right solution, you need to relax into it, Riza, puttar," I hear Kanwar Uncle's soothing voice and see his face like a shadow.

"Sir, are you ill? May I check your—" Taz's voice pulls me hurtling back to reality.

"No," I push the bot away. "I'm alright. Just a, a . . . memory. Something you don't know about."

"Memories, yes, I do know those. Memories: the unconscious mind's process of ordering and reordering..."

He always takes the romance out of things I find beautiful. I imagine what it would be like to toss the little nanny-bot from my window. There'd be a fine for littering probably, and it might actually hurt someone walking below. But it would be worth it.

"Taz, has my father responded yet?" Taz's eyes light up green and he pauses.

"No messages from Mr. Singh. He is . . . away at a scientific research trip currently at the Space Colony."

Mother has been on my case lately and I miss my father's jokes. He hasn't responded in a month. I know his work is important, but I hope he comes through, and soon.

My father purchased Taz before he went to Greenland. Like a bot would make it okay that my father chose a position in the PAC rather than staying with me. Mother says it was his way of leaving a piece of him with me. A nanny-bot for a teenager.

"Taz, play my last message from Anik Singh."

Taz's face goes blank and I hear my father's bellowing voice laughing. "Too busy for your old man, nah? Puttar, son, it's your father. It's been so long that I'm sure you've forgotten me by now." His laugh is a flurry of chuckles. "But do me a favor. Tell me how you are doing. The Colony is beautiful. I wish you could see what I see, looking down on Earth from such a distance. I'm looking down on you right now. Remember that. Don't let your mother boss you around too much. Love you, Riza."

"End of message, Riz-Ali." Taz's face returns to the ever-present smile.

"Make me breakfast, please," I say.

Taz wheels out of the room and into the main kitchen area.

I pull on my white tunic and twist my long black hair into a braid, and head to the dining room. Sidharth is already watching the Info-Run on the holo-screen in the common area at full volume. He's dressed like a Solace director rather than the intern he is. His hair is shiny and combed, smelling like the newest genetic scent that should be pleasing to others around him. Everyone but me, obviously. I've lived here for months, but my hate for my flatmate grows. The kid is nothing if not perfect. And a damn fool. I picked him out of a list of flat-mates my mother made because he was straight-up the oppo-site of me. I didn't want to be friends with whoever lived with me. I knew it wouldn't end well. People leave, disagreements turn to resentment. This way we'd never even pretend to like each other. And it was fun to verbally spar with him. Mother was pleased at my choice. It was clear she'd rather have him as a son than me. His neural-synch is chrome, the newest cover. Mine is a matte, faded copper because I'd rather have it disap-pear completely.

"Good morning," he says.

I nod, once.

"What's that smell?" Sid's nose scrunches.

I smile. "I don't smell anything aside from your cologne." I laugh.

"You know ether smokes are illegal, right?"

"Are they now?" I say and pick up the fresh cup of tea Taz holds out to me on the white tray.

"Yeah, but you already knew that, yaar."

"I'd rather be educated by your vast knowledge of the world, Sid. It's so astounding. First in your class. Youngest in the training center." I puff out a laugh.

"You wanna learn something? This summit is all for show." He stares intently at the holo-screen. "Liu has to get some courage if he's going to actually lead the planet. No Province should be forced to give away their rare earths to have them redistributed among the other Provinces."

"What's mad is that we're still trying to solve the problem that got us into the war in the first place. And to get enough materials we'll have to make it all the way to the Kuiper Belt. The few provinces that have pollution credits should process them for the rest of the world. We shouldn't compete against each other. If we don't work together, we'll be on the edge of war again."

"Now you sound like the opposition. Why don't you go a work for the Planet Watch Group? Or go plant some trees in the Eastern District on the border of Asian Province." He laughs, rolls his eyes.

"Planet Watch has a point. We need more than one neoc-ity to house the population in the SA. They need to begin building the others right away. It's madness. They promised four, one for each district."

Sid doesn't even hear me, but switches the Info-Run to Celebrity Insider instead, and pictures of models, actors and other wealthy faces populate the screen. He sits at the white dining table and Taz brings us breakfast: boiled eggs, fruit, bread—same every day. White linens, white table, white marble floors, the lack of color is enough to make me want to burn the whole place down just to give it a tint.

"Talvinder looks happier since he got back from Ahimsa wellness center. Check it," Sid speaks, with his mouth full. Tal's career in film blew up the past year. He's in everything these days. "Has that rebooted glow they talk about."

"Maybe you should go. Go drink brainwashing smoothies, get your soul-cleansing enemas, whatever you think will make living easier," I say.

"Nah, my friend went. It's not all brainwashing. He was a little shaken up when he came back, but then smooth sailing."

Sid chews loudly. I push my food around the plate.

"Shaken up?"

"He wouldn't talk about what happened. His parents put him there because he was sneaking to Strata One a lot. They didn't want him to get booted from Central."

"That place is messed up. No connection, sign your life away, come back chill. They have to do serious damage to your psyche there somehow. It can't be just a massage, beach, and juice."

"Yeah, I guess you're right." Sid scarfs the rest of his food into his mouth. "You coming?"

"Yeah, where else would I be going?" I say.

Taz buzzes. "Your mother, Shiraz Singh, is on the comm, Riz-Ali." My fork slips out of my hand onto the marble floor.

Sid smirks. "Better get that. Don't want to keep the Minister of Communications waiting."

I flip him off as he closes the door behind himself. "Taz, connect."

A screen projects from the center of the dining table and my mother appears like a goddess, with all these disembodied hands around her face. Her hair and makeup people are fussing with her as she speaks to me. "Oh, good morning, beta, are you eating? You look so thin," she says. "Or sick. I can't have my son starve. Maybe I should send a medic ..."

"No, I'm eating, see?" I show her the plate in front of me. "But you could program Taz to show a little more finesse in the kitchen." I want to scream at her. That I'd found a clue. That I was right all along. That Uncle wasn't a traitor like she said. And for a second, I forget she hated him at the end, and nearly tell her. But my mouth clamps down on my words like a trap.

"Look," she moves closer to the screen, pushes the hands

away and whispers. "You need to take the auto-inject today. It's the fifteenth."

That's what Mother needs, a kid who doesn't fully integrate with the neural-synch. Usually, Solace-approved parents give birth to Solace-passing children. I passed, but Solace's neural-synch has never been completely compatible. Or, perhaps, I am just not compliant or compatible with the technology—maybe I just don't want to be.

There is something off about Mother's appearance. Just in that one instant, she looks at me, really looks at me, and she seems afraid. I watch her face intently as a gen-bot the size and shape of a metal beetle crawls across her nose, tightening a wrinkle with the light of a laser under its belly. Though gen-bots are commonplace, they always turn my stomach. "And remember, it's the last day of your internship at Solace, so try to not mess it up. You're heading to work for the SA government next, in the Western District. It's the only position I could find for you." Her glare has the venom of a thousand vipers.

"Yes, Maa, I know, I know. We've talked about this for weeks."

She glares at me, through me. "Don't mess this one up."

Bile rises in my gut. "Got it, Maa." Last day, last chance to access Solace, and do something really risky to connect with the Red Hand and find out the truth about my uncle. See if they can tell me what their Commander knows about him.

"And don't take any additional edits. I know you've been busy in the underweb and it's not good to try to optimize further when you aren't calibrating properly yet. Be a good boy. No messing this up. Your father is settling in with his new position and I'm finally getting somewhere here."

"Anything else?" How does she know I was on the underweb? I know she monitors me, but how much she can see I can't determine.

Another voice says, "It's a big day here. How about some congratulations for your dear mother?"

"Congratulations? For what?"

Another face enters the screen from behind mother. Geena. She's been working with Mother for years, and has a son younger than me, so she's always been a go-between, a messenger of spite. "Her big announcement about the next campaign for Solace. It's called Shaanti. The rollout is soon, with President Ravindra herself. I think you'll be impressed." Geena raises her eyebrows as if to say *this is important, acknowledge your mother*. I hate her. She probably hates me too.

"Congratulations, Maa."

"I'd better go. And remember, give your father space. He's very busy."

It's been like this since Kanwar Uncle died. I bite the inside of my cheek and close my eyes, imagining a different world where I can sneeze without signaling an alert.

"Riza?" The hands of the makeup and hair techs return to the screen and continue to apply. Each stroke makes her look more and more beautiful. One wand adds elasticity to her skin, the other brightens. One transdermal laser delivers an edit that adds a flush to her cheeks and another deletes a new freckle. Mother loves her beauty fixes.

"Achcha, Maa. Thanks," I say.

Before I can say anything more, the comms disconnects. A whirl of giggles and chatter from her design team end the call.

The flat is nice, and somewhere deep inside me I don't want to really burn it all down. But still, today I can't have the idiot nanny-bot watching me. Not if I'm going to get the help I need to find my uncle. I've planned it out for weeks, how I'd do it. To hack Solace, grab the bit of data the Red Hand want and trade for information. It's my last chance to have full access to Solace because my internship is ending.

"Shall I bring you the immunosuppressant auto-injection device, sir?" Taz asks.

"Yes." The bright light in the penthouse buzzes. I click my ignitor in my pocket over and over again.

Taz brings a cold, metallic tube filled with medicine that will allow me to continue to use the neural-synch for another month at least. My body has rejected it since installation last year. My neural speed tests are barely passing. The device isn't meant for me, but Mother won't hear of it. She says it's for my benefit, but I know it's for hers. If the Minister of Communications had a child who didn't make the cut, it will be an all-out embarrassment, and I'd get shipped out of Central with a one-way ticket to anywhere but here, fast.

The silver medicine rolls back and forth in the tube-like liquid metal. No, not today. I shove the medicine deep into the back of my desk drawer and pull out a nano-optimization drug called THink instead, a small syringe with a tiny metal dot in the tube, suspended in a purple gel. I bought THink off the underweb weeks ago. If I were to take them at the same time, I'd probably die of a heart attack. Today, I need to be able to match Solace to meet the challenge. I'll come back for the auto-inject later, after THink wears off and exits my body. I take a breath and stick the needle into my thigh. I wonder when it'll take effect and hope I didn't buy a dud.

I flick on the ignitor and a bright white heat appears. The

curtains take to the flame like paper, definitely a construction shortcut. Eighteen steel beams on every floor, tinted windows, climate control—and thin-ass curtains.

Sizzle, a little smoke, nothing too extraordinary. Not a revolution.

Taz buzzes around and his alert flashes all sorts of lights and sirens. The flames catch, just enough, then Taz uses his extinguisher wand to spray out the fire in one burst.

"What a mess, Taz."

"Yes, I must mend this before it stains."

"Yes, clean this up, all day, okay?" For the rest of your life would be perfect. I don't care if he reports this to my parents. Why does a bot have such pull on me? I go to my computer set up, pull a few key parts I'd need, shove them in my work satchel and take off.

"Yes, sir."

I am free. Or at least somewhat.

My apartment door slides shut behind me. I calculated the contaminant effects of the small fire and knew it wouldn't trigger the building-wide alarms. At least I am glad my calculations are accurate even though I am not fully optimized with my neural-synch. Mother always wants me to be perfect, like her. Guess I'll just have to do better to show her what I am really good at.

I let my long hair out from the braid and pull on a black tunic, leaving the white one on the floor of the hallway. The lift takes me down and down and down from Strata 95 to the sky rail in Strata 25. It is so quiet without Taz buzzing behind me. The smile pressing into my cheeks feels foreign because I haven't felt it in forever. The strange laugh that escapes my throat feels silly, powerful, and everything I'll ever need, all at the same time.

As I cross the street, I grin up at the Solace UAV and see it register my face, then watch as it quickly moves onto another passerby.

 **5 // TARU**

She likes to say she found me, but I think I found her first. My memories are like clouds blowing across the hazy sky: Some settle into shapes, others don't figure into much and dissolve to nothing again. I don't trust them. But beyond the sounds of the rising sea, the echoes of transports screeching, the hands and bodies and memories that blend into black, I can see her face. Through my saltwater-crusted eyelashes, her face glows like the brightest, most beautiful star. And in my memory, I follow her.

Ashiva.

She picks me up in her arms from the docks and carries me to the orphanage in the Narrows. Poonam Auntie bathes me, dresses me like a doll. She returns my necklace to me afterward, and tells me it is important to keep it, to never let it go. The type of gem, purple surrounded by silver, is from the south. A place that's under the sea now. They mend my broken feet with casts, and after my feet heal, only a few thin, dark scars remain on my skin above the replacement joints and metal bones they gave me. When I run the first time, I am free again.

Gifts of The Mechanic, my savior.

When I got older, Masiji said my parents were probably displaced after the Great Migration to the SA's new capital: Central. But that they clearly loved me and wanted me to live. That's why my parents risked their lives to put me on the orphan transport that dumped children into the city. Most children died. Central wanted little to do with us, unless we cleared the Solace test. But some continued anyway, and that gave people hope. The survivors are taken in or they joined a street gang in the Liminal Area.

But the luckiest ones are adopted by the Red Hand.

I owe them my life. I owe them everything.

At first, in my memory, I am just a silly baby Ashiva plays with, that the helpers in the nursery tend to. But after a couple years, Masiji takes interest in me. I finish puzzles quickly, faster than any other child in the orphanage. So, she tutors me privately, teaches me to read. It's right around that time, when there are at least fifty of us of different ages and sizes, different capabilities and temperaments, that the training begins.

And with it come the nightmares.

Rao is my partner in sparring because we are the same size even though he is a year older. His hair is always messy because of the cowlick. He doesn't want to fight. He's such a soft boy with a tender heart. He wants to be a cook, but our world doesn't allow for hobbies and dreams. And the lieutenants of the Red Hand come at us with bamboo sticks and threaten to lash us, lash our friends, so we fight. We can't leave. Where would we go? Why would we want to go? The New Treaty laws make sure no one can officially emigrate and only the wealthy can travel because it is so expensive. Of course, we could go to the Eastern or Western Districts, but they have their own poverty problems and the SA is stalling on the development of their neocities. I dream of the Northern Fort, but they tell us stories about how after WWIII's nuclear winter, the radiation still pulses in the North, and how they live in snow caves, how millions turned to ash as they ran, suffocated in avalanches, or died from starvation. They tell us of the deformed beasts that lurk in the Himalayas around the impassable roads, waiting for people to eat. None of us have ever seen snow and, though we die of the heat, the opposite death also terrifies us.

"The Uplanders will kill you if they get a chance. Don't you want to live? Show me!" Masiji yells so loud our bodies tremble until they don't anymore. And behind her, Mrs. Zinaat watches us, always watching for weaknesses and strengths.

And we believe them.

After a few months, we are used to hitting each other with closed fists, wrestling, even winning. The rewards are worth it. Fruits we've never tasted. First pick from the scrappers' load. One time, it's a small piece of hard candy on a stick from one of the smugglers' cargo. I've never tasted anything so sweet. The other children are jealous. But that candy is stained in blood. I never forget that I broke a girl's wrist for it. She is fine. She isn't mad at me. I didn't set out to break it. It's just what the lieutenants tell me to do, to fight her and not lose. To not cry because tears are weak. I don't know. It's all confusing. My memories. They change and move like clouds. Some bleed like impossible scars, others dissolve and reform. It's hard to remember what is true and real aside from the scars.

This is how we became strong.

I am not so lucky in the next challenge: three against one. They come at me with sticks in the darkness, an ambush. At the end, I can't hear anymore, and am near unconscious and my friends are crying too. They are my friends. I am barely breathing. Ashiva comes to my side.

Ten broken bones and I may have died if Ashiva hadn't

gotten there before the teacher. We are taught to fight, but it is hard to sense when to stop. They turn us into animals.

Much later, I am in the infirmary when they tell me I have a brittle bone disease, juvenile osteoporosis. That I can't fight anymore, not like that, not again. Ashiva was there when Masiji told me the diagnosis. I thought I was just in a bad fight. The body cast they put me in is expensive. Ashiva makes sure that I never have combat training again. Warns everyone I can't be touched—or else. And they leave me alone. Anyway, I am afraid I'll break again, so I am thankful for her protection.

I am in bed for nearly three months and Mrs. Zinaat comes to me with daily assignments. I can't move my arms, my legs, but my hands and head are free. And my mind is sharp. I love learning, and she treats me like her special student, gives me tests, exams, lectures, books. She knows that thinking will heal my body and mind. This begins my fascination with science. When all you do is study day and night, you learn quickly. That's when my dreams of working toward being assigned to the External Hand began. I dreamt of being planted as a spy inside the PAC, another government, or company. I'm smart and can compete on their level. All I want is to be far from here, researching how to make the world better. I think somehow, Mrs. Zinaat thought I might die soon, and that I should feel special in my last days. We are all surprised I fully recover.

When I am discharged, I move into the orphanage with the other children. The others are scared of me, not because I am fierce, but because I lived.

"Taru, you're the glass girl!" Rao calls to me. Our cots are beside each other's, almost touching, on the thick rajaiyan on the floor. I was jealous of Rao. He collects all sorts of treasures in the folds of his comforter. Shiny things like beads, bits of thread. Things. I don't have anything aside from the clothes I'm wearing. I decide to start a collection that day.

"Glass is sharp when it breaks," I say, and we become friends again.

When we are older, we are organized and given jobs. The fast ones become runners, others become basic hands, assistants, organizers, grunts for the lieutenants. The best job is with the External Hand working as a spy because you get to leave this place. It's a competitive position, but I'm good enough. I study day and night to pass their tests, to prove my worth. I love Ashiva, but I am not like her. She is a chameleon; she loves smuggling, fighting, running. I only want to learn. We all study basic coding and hacking. It's necessary because our replacements need daily calibration and updates, and because of the surveillance in the Narrows, Central always watching us. But I want more. To never fight again. I don't care if it makes me look weak. Anyway, Ashiva says that if I fight, I might shatter.

But now, today, here on sorting day in the Narrows' central office, for the first time ever, I feel that all my hard work has been for nothing.

"There has to be a mistake." It is all I can say after the trainer ignores my request to rerun my results. "I'm the top student. I'm supposed to move into External Hand."

The grunt who works for Mrs. Zinaat doesn't even bother to take off his glasses or even look at me. He just says, "No mistake, behan. This one was triple-checked by even The Mechanic. You're on Internal duty for now. You'll continue to work in the nursery as seva and assist Poonam Auntie as your assignment. It's an official order from the top. That's a great position."

From the top echoes in my ears an impossible phrase. "But I don't want to work with Poonam Auntie. I'm . . ." I let the words dissolve in my mind because the grunt is already talking to another kid. The room is stifling.

There are three options for children after they move through training: Internal, External, or, the most difficult, Liberation. Nothing is guaranteed, and only the best end up in External and Liberation. The rest are usually kept here in the Narrows, running errands, working on projects to keep the Narrows going, recruiting new members. It's just treading water. External means we could get out and run missions in other governments to take the system down from the inside. The training room's walls get smaller, the floor and ceiling tip, and I'm trapped. I look at the blood stains on the wall that have been there forever, faded to a dirty brown and no one would ever know it was blood. But I know. Go. Go now. Or you'll lose your chance to ever leave this place. I think about the hours I've put into my studies. The life I've imagined beyond the walls of the orphanage. And they want to keep me. Working with a pagal lady who talks to herself and tells stories about explosives she used to make. It's so below my ability that the insult is sharp.

I push past Rao, who stops me.

"Hey, where're ya going?"

"I just need some air."

"It's pretty amazing you're with Internal. Look, I'm just an assistant. Not even ready for an assignment yet. Probably won't ever be." He laughs, but I'm tired. I'm not useless.

"I'll be back, Rao." I make my way through to the outer al-leys of the Narrows. Ashiva, she said I could be anything, do anything. I wish she was with me to receive my assignment like she said she would be. She'd fix this. She could. I'm not good at fixing things. Science problems, yes. Not people things.

The heat takes a toll on my body before long, and I head to the edge of the Narrows. Before me is the line into the Liminal Area and then Central. Behind me is my family and a world I belong to. People who saved me. Those I can't defy.

One step forward. Then another. I've been through the boundary before, but not often. It's easy for children to get picked up by guardians in Central for no good reason and then disappear. We don't come here. Especially not me with my health condition. If I fall and have no one to help me, I could shatter. That's what Ashiva told me. I'm not allowed to leave the Narrows without direct approval from Internal Red Hand leadership. Move with the fray, people moving into and back from Central or the Liminal Area for their daily jobs. I'm just another person. Just nobody. Nothing.

The burping chug-chug machines sit at the edge of the en-campment, making our lives possible. Our water is acidic; I've tasted it unfiltered. It was sour and gave me a stomachache. Probably from the filth though, since acid rain alone can't kill you. So, we built several chug-chug machines in the Narrows, each the size of a small transport. Bots gather rainwater in storm barrels and wheel them to the chug-chug machine, named for the belching sounds it makes. The machine injects sodium carbonate into the water and runs it through a calcium filter. Then the magic of what I like to call the demud-ding process begins. It takes the longest to remove the dis-eases and bacteria. I've helped work on the machines. We each take turns maintaining them and yet people continue to die from dysentery or algae. We keep trying.

The UAVs hover around us like buzzing insects. They pause, listen, look, and invade our bodies and space without ever touching us. Then as quickly as they arrive, they move onto the next person or group. My hands feel wet, but I don't show my fear. We all have the right to pass through the gates. We check in and out. They track us. I see people begging on the streets, like anyone has anything to give them. They're all dying, of heat, of starvation, of hopelessness.

My feet stop short of a small form on the damp, broken concrete. I kneel and pick up the dead bird and shake off the ants that are swarming it. When I hold it in my hand, I'm not convinced it's real. It's small, probably a sparrow of some kind. It weighs close to nothing, an impossibility. Its body feels hol-lowed out, lacking breath, deficient of blood. It's not dried—probably died recently, but there's something different about this one. It's like it was in flight just moments ago, wings spread, its beak open and ready for food. It appears as though it was surprised by death, and that takes me aback. What a pure feeling. I've never felt that. I want to wrap its broken wing with a bandage. Instead, I tuck its little body aside where it won't be trampled, and a rat can benefit from its demise.

Mammals and fish have suffered the most. But the insects thrive. Ants the size of beetles march at my feet, carrying bits and pieces of materials. Crickets, locusts, and other inverte-brates flourish. They weren't affected by the bombs twenty-five years ago. While forests, fish and animals died within a thousand miles of the bombs, the insects just shrugged and kept going. Sure, some died, sensitive creatures, like the butterflies. But most insects bounced back faster. It's funny to think how we could learn so much from the simplest beings.

When I'm through the gates, the stress and anger that consumes me feels a world away. I try to hide my limp. I need an adjustment on my feet, but haven't had time to check in with Masiji. Or, actually, I want to avoid her as much as possible. Sometimes, running is the only way to gain perspective. I don't have anywhere to be, so I keep moving. Through the Liminal Area. Finally, to the abandoned Trans-Ocean Bridge Project. Even though it's a skeleton, there's hope in the broken structures. As I take them in, I imagine fixing what's broken: In my mind I see cranes and air-transports to lift that girder, to support that pylon, to seal the walls. I can see what it'd be like finished: a beautiful feat of engineering.

"What're you smiling about, girl?" The voice behind me is soft, gentle.

"The building could be beautiful and useful if they just tried harder," I say.

"That sums up just about everything."

I turn and see a girl about my age and height, with very short hair, which makes her round face and enormous eyes even more extraordinary. "They'll never do the right thing, finish their good ideas, find a solution."

I ask, "Why? Why do you think?"

Her laugh echoes against the surroundings. I don't think she's laughing at me, but I take a step back, not able to fully smile with her.

"You really don't know, do you." Her face goes cold somewhere between shock, and complete and utter hopelessness.
She has to be older than me by a few years. I see it now. She
closes the distance between our bodies with two steps and I
lean closer, wanting the secret she knows so well. "It's not that
they can't fix this problem. This world. God, all the scientists
probably figured it out long ago. It's that they'd be out of a job.
They'd lose their power. And that's all that people in power
want: more power."

This hits me like a block of concrete on the chest. Words
escape me.

"Come on, you look thirsty," she pulls my arm.

"Don't touch me. Please." I shrug her off, wary of my brittle
bones that could break under the pressure of her grip.

"Sorry, I didn't mean to scare you."

"I'm fine. I'm just different." My legs follow her anyway.
She's like a magnet and I'm drawn to her.

The small structure she leads me into is cramped. There
are kids everywhere, smoking ether, eating, playing, laughing.
I don't see a single adult, but there are a few older teenagers
lingering, mostly reading on their hacked comms readers or
playing games on the underweb.

They are all having fun.

"Here," she says, handing me a bottle of water. "I'm Ravni.
What's your name?"

My tongue makes a "t" sound, but I quickly change my
mind, "T— Lomri."

"Fox, cool. You Red Hand or civilian? No, let me guess."
She sizes me up like food she's buying in the undermarket. "I'd
peg you for Red Hand, but you seem too pure."

"What do you mean?" I know about the Liminal daaku. They're a gang of thieves, robbers, scammers. They defy the Upland and the Downland, and instead run anarchy in the badlands between Central's gates and the Narrows. Even the mafia, like the Lords of Shadow, have rules. The Red Hand is a revolutionary group, a vast organization with different arms of structure. But these daaku are just criminals who live off of the scraps of both sides. Nihilists. I try to be as clueless as possible to learn as much as I can. Though I know they're killers. I'm not afraid. I've done some things.

"The Red Hand, you know, they're militant terrorists who bomb buildings, bridges, and transports. They make it harder to just live in the Liminal Area because Central assumes we're all Red Hand terrorists now. Gray-collars breathing down our necks. But," her arms spread wide, "we don't like fighting in government-sponsored wars."

"I see," I say. I'm not up for a political discussion. Not now. Not today. "I'm not Liberation, if that's what you're asking."

"Really? I see you with . . . computers or science? Yeah . . . I can see it. You're a smarty. Puzzling things out all the time."

She got me.

I like her. She sizes me up again and says, "You completed basic training?"

I nod. I don't mention I helped make the curriculum and completed all training for External Hand. Top of my class, but assigned to Internal like an ullu.

"Then maybe you could help us with a project. It'll be fun, I promise."

"Sure, but I only have an hour."

"It won't take long. Not for someone like you."

I decide to help her with her project, but I know I don't belong with them either.

She leads me into a room. On the table are containers,
duct tape, metal pipes cut short, plastic tubes, hollowed-out
balls, and thin cotton rope. I know what she's making and
move closer to the table after I take stock from afar to make
sure nothing's active.

I lean down and read the containers. "Potassium nitrate,
black powder, flash powder, ammonium nitrate, copper
plates? Wait, do you have nitro?"

She smiles. "Not here, too volatile. But we can get it. We
can get everything. Wanna make some crackers? Light up
Central? I figure with your know-how, you can teach us how to
make some fun things, so we don't blow ourselves up trying.
You can be our safety expert."

The sight of their arsenal makes my heart race. I've been
building explosives, working on a large project in the Narrows. It's my secret. I've spent months collecting materials,
and here I walk into the Liminal Area and this girl just opens
the door for me. It can't be a coincidence. But I can't resist. "I'll
show you one. After that I have to get back."

"Deal."

The artificial neural network, Solace, is everything to anyone in Central. The heart of the corporation, she is a fussy machine, and omniscient enough to control the entire South Asian Province's transmission of information, even in the districts outside the neocity. She was developed by scientists who were chosen by President Ravindra in secret to find a solution to our resource and population problems. They're heroes here. The quote that's sculpted in glass when you enter the Solace Corporation dome is: "Without Sacrifice There Will Be No Tomorrow." My internship specialty? Data. Organizing it, rearranging it, calibrating it. My neural-synch allows me to match Solace's lowest neural network speed, but barely. The neural-synch is a device that links us directly to Solace. It optimizes us in terms of brain activity speed, RAM, memory capability. Some say the next step in the neural-synch would be to take the leap to connect with a larger cloud beyond what the human brain can possibly ever allow. But I won't allow it. Ever. I'm defiant. Even though they say it's just theoretical, I am terrified that truly linking with Solace would then allow it to control me somehow. Or worse, that I would cease to be a human with a consciousness. Some say it could never happen, but anything is possible. The neural-synch is just a device necessary for the Central elite to be able to do the work of ten people each—they're the chosen. And with a smaller population, we need to be optimized.

But I don't belong here.

The techs are lined up in small office cubes made of glass

on the highest floors of Solace's dome. One after another, they spread out like glass beads on a very tight chain. I used to think they were like the hexagonal chemical compounds I'd read about in boarding school. But they are truly like cages that don't have the decency to show their bars.

"Heya, Sumi," I say to the girl sitting in her workspace as I pass. Suddenly, I feel a vibration across my entire body, like a strange wave of electricity. The THink is working, I hope.

"You're late again." She looks worried for me, which makes her even more, I don't know, pleasing to me. Sumi's long black hair is tied in a spiral of a braid today. It's so intricate and beautiful. But words dry up in my mouth.

"Yes, again. I guess. Hey, I like braids . . . never mind," I say. My face goes volcanic and all moisture in my mouth evaporates. Now or never, dummy. "You going to AllianceCon?" Good one, yaar. Way to sound slick.

"Of course, I'm going," she says, sort of laughing, loud enough for our co-workers in the surrounding offices to perk up. "Isn't everyone?"

The silence that stretches between us is as vast and deep as dark matter.

Retreat.

"Okay, maybe I'll see you there," I say, and I bump into the glass wall and dump out my work bag. I don't know why I said that. I'd rather stick an injector in my eyeball than go.

"I bet you have first-class passes, given your mother's position and all," Sumi stands up. I want to collapse into a black hole as I stuff my things back into the bag.

"Nah, I mean, I could use hers, but then I'd have to hang with her."

"She's brilliant. I love her newest campaign on Solace's program." Sumi watches me pack up.

"Yeah, I guess."

"You use her connections for everything else, don't you? I mean, that's how you got the tech internship right after you were expelled from boarding school, right?" She speaks so fast that I have a hard time keeping up. She isn't mean, just hyper-honest. Candor is a side effect of turning up the neural-synch to the highest speed for the workday.

I hear a few snickers. "No, um, well . . . I actually applied like everyone else. Never mind . . ." She's right. But in my secret defense, I wasn't really expelled, but moved because my parents were relocated. It was all part of a grand, fabricated narrative that was out of my control. My mother has been on my case ever since, and my father, the fun one, has been MIA. I yell this response in my mind. But my mind is buzzing. I'd better get to the system fast.

"Right, okay. See ya." And she goes back to her workstation. "What's up with your skin today? Are you sweating?"

"Oh, excuse me." I touch my face and I'm slick with sweat, so I hurry to my office. When I'm seated in the console chair, I take a deep breath in and connect a cable to the input in my neural-synch. First vertigo and then it feels like I am falling backwards through space. Just as soon as it begins it stops and I am inside Solace, ready to set up new sequences for her machine-learning training. The world of the computer surrounds my vision like a tunnel of code. I can't see where I end and it begins.

I type the code and press my hand against the glass reader. The test runs, and the results are normal. When I am sure all systems in Solace are active, I begin. Once I run the Solace maintenance program, she'll be busy for two minutes. That's how long I have to complete the task. Find the file in storage and copy it to my drive. If I go over the two minutes, the consequences will be swift: infractions, possible time in containment, maybe even booted from Central if I'm considered a security threat.

"Launch maintenance, Solace." The countdown begins on my info-screen.

2:00

When she is set to learn, Solace can't see me. It's the only time she is blind and I am free from her gaze. My chest tightens, my heart thumps uncontrollably and my vision expands to 365 degrees. My mind has never felt so clear. I know the drug is working. I'm not weighed down by thoughts. I'm free of doubt and processes. I follow circuits, leap over connections, duck through doorways, and enter Solace's back storage like I've trained my whole life for this. My brain and body buzzes with excitement. I could definitely get used to this.

I grab the coordinates to a small data packet from the Red Hand's underweb hack challenge. The collective said it was somewhere inside Solace's storage, hadn't been accessed in decades, and was just a dusty antique. Why do they want this packet? I don't care. All I care about is connecting with them for the reward when it's done so I can find out what they know about my uncle and his connection to their Commander. The last challenge they put out on the underweb asked for someone to shave Solace CEO Mr. Gupta's cat and post a holo-vid to prove it. To my knowledge, no one participated in that challenge. Or at least, no one succeeded. But this little dusty data?

No one will notice if I run a duplicate. I search for anything hinting at the name Himalaya.

1:00

The packet proves more difficult to find than I thought, even with THink. Come on, come on.

00:10

I find it in one minute, fifty seconds. Saved and cleaned up my tracks. Thank you, optimization nano-bots.

I descend the spiral layers of Solace Corp, and ride the mechanical bridges down, down and down the dome, until I reach the central entrance to sign out.

"Good day, sir," the security guard says as he runs the blue light over the chip in my wrist.

"Good day."

The guard looks at his screen and squints. He types a few notes, and then the glass doors open for me. I pause for a millisecond, but then walk out with the data packet in my neural-synch like nothing at all is the matter.

I did it. The air outside is clear and clean. Too clean. It smells of nonspecific fresh flowers that I can't place. I rush past the massive fountain park and through the thick forest of rare, floral trees that decorates it. The haze from the pollution past the Ring keeps the sun at bay. But I'm free. No bot, data packet in hand, I'm in control for once.

A wave of heat fills my stomach and my steps stagger, but my legs move in the right direction, away from Solace Corp. Each step brings me closer to a group that can actually help me.

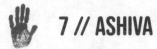

7 // ASHIVA

When I was ten, I used to sit on the metal sea wall and watch the fishing boats bring in their catch from the south, before the red tides, born from the extreme heat, killed the surface sea life. The fisherfolk were thin but strong, and their boats were incredible feats of engineering built from construction scraps and recycled materials. I'd wait on the edge of the port until the last few moments before curfew to try to catch the sun rising above the water. It was usually too hazy to see, but it happened sometimes. And when it did, it lifted my heart.

When I saw the girl wandering slow, like a sleepy fox in the dawn light, near the edge of the deep water three yards from me, I called to her.

"Oye, ladki, careful." She couldn't have been older than four, and her bare feet were worn and bloodied from the unkind streets. They had to be damaged, possibly fractured, the way she was limping. The orphan transports overflow with children sitting on the top, hanging on to the sides. There was never enough room for everyone. Many kids died or were injured from falls.

She seemed numb to the world around her, like she was caught in a dream. And for a moment I wondered if she was a ghost or spirit. I realized where that word came from that Uplanders called us: the forgotten. Fisherfolk scurried past, robot maintenance machines buzzed by, rickshaw transports blasted above on the Maglev tracks, but the little girl kept moving toward the water, the world around failing her in every way possible.

An old man who was mending his nets nearby said, "She's a shell. Empty. Soul has already left the body." His hands mimicked a butterfly flying in my direction. "It happens to the forgotten."

Her eyes were lined with charcoal—someone had cared enough to ward off the evil eye and pray for her, but not enough to feed her and give her shelter. Street children didn't need prayers, we needed rations and love—even if Solace labeled us "close to expiration" and "un-fit."

I shook my head at the old man. "She's not dead. Not yet, Uncle." I pushed myself up to stand. The sunrise was caught behind the haze. It wouldn't show itself this morning anyway.

The old man waved me off like he might a fly, like I knew nothing, but he was the one who told me the week prior that the world was coming to an end and that the Arabian Sea would swallow the world. Superstitions had no place in the SA anymore, but they still leaked in like viruses. Maybe that was all some had left. Even when all the coastal cities had succumbed to the seas, and the government had used all remaining PAC funds to build the neocity Central on the highest land inland, displacing millions and making everyone except the wealthy a refugee, an exile, people prayed, like it did any good. I never understood it. Gods wouldn't make this world.

"Girl, you hungry?" I asked. I knew my pockets were empty, but I searched my satchel anyway.

She didn't respond, but continued to walk toward the sea across a broken concrete jetty that angled down into the water and below its surface. When she reached the water's edge, she fell to her knees and collapsed hard on the damp, broken slabs. The water and ocean detritus lapped her bloody legs like an apology, like it was trying to wash away the city's failure. She made a small sigh when I picked her up in my arms, her eyes blinking with saltwater. She weighed so little, maybe ten kilos. She was so fragile. In her, I saw myself. I saw the world and what it thought of us. I saw a chance to protect one precious life.

"Come on, little fox," I said and carried her easily with my replacement arm. She was still breathing, but barely. I knew Masiji would want to reprimand me for not finishing my errand and bringing home a girl without approval, but she'd never beaten me, so it was worth the risk. Anyway, she put me back together, saved me from the same fate, so why wouldn't she take in this lost girl?

I look for Taru in the alleyways. She isn't in our room when I arrive. She isn't in the central courtyard, the general dormitories, or the play yard near the schoolroom. I check with the entry gate and they said she'd come through, but not where she went. The rooftop of the abandoned building is hotter than hot when I lift myself up and over the ladder, but there she stands with her back to me, watching the sea from the highest point in the Narrows. In front of her are a pile of her important things, things I don't understand. Bottles, jars, experiments in process, containers of all kinds with powders—elements she calls them. There are even small rockets she's fashioned from scraps of fabric and metal, connected to computers. Off-market drones she's programming. Beautiful pieces of artwork that have a dual purpose of entertainment and destruction. She has a gift for chemistry, computers, and science. None of which I understand. She was tutored by every specialist in the Narrows when Masiji saw her potential. Now, she's a master.

"There you are, sister," I say.

She shakes her head, back still turned. "You made a promise, Shiv. You said you'd be there with me today. I needed you. They assigned me Internal Hand. What the hell, Ashiva?"

"I'm sorry. Dr. Qasim was late and then I was interrogated by the guardians. Narrowly missed that one, if you ask me." It's one thing to lie. It's another thing to perform the lie. I would have given it all away if I was there when they gave her Internal.

"It's always something."

When did she get so grown up? "Taru, look at me," I say. "It'll be safer here."

She turns around and says, "I just want— never mind," she says.

I try to be what Masiji tells me I need to be. What Zami thinks I'm a failure at. What Taru needs. But it's so damn stupid that I can't help myself. I grip the wall and a bit of rock breaks off in my hand.

"What were you thinking?" I don't yell, but my words are heavy with anger. She looks defeated, but it was dumb. "To get back at me you run with the Liminal daaku? You're smarter than that."

She groans and makes to walk away. "Don't start with me!"

"You know their crew is dangerous. Why'd you go with them today? After all I've done to keep you safe."

Her eyes fill with tears. "I didn't mean to. I just went on a walk. And they're not so bad . . . and they told me they needed help with fireworks, just to have some fun. For AllianceCon.

That they'd sell them. They wanted my guidance. They said I was an expert. I didn't know ..."

"Thugs, all of them. They have no allegiances to anyone."

"I know, I know." Taru sits on the ground and crosses her arms.

"So, why'd you go? You know the risks."

Her mouth makes a funny, thin shape, like she's locking words behind her lips.

I sit down beside her. "Taru ..."

She doesn't look at me when she speaks. "You're a smuggler. You have a job to do. I need to help with the cause too. I thought that if I did this for them, I could build a connection. Use my skills for the Red Hand. Just like you." She's holding something in and I'm worried she knows what I've done. She can never find out I've sabotaged her path. She won't understand. She continues, "If the Red Hand doesn't give me the right assignment ... I just need to feel useful."

All I can do is hold her, gently, so I do. I wrap my human arm around her small body. She shuffles her replacement feet closer to mine and relaxes. I'm the only one in the world she lets touch her like this.

"Once we go through assignments, we have two jobs: seva and Red Hand. Your work in the nursery is service. We all have to do service here. We run the gates, take turns fixing and running the water machines, you know. And you'll be an asset in Internal. You'd be an asset anywhere. That's how you're helping. You're going to assist Poonam Auntie. Think of the lives you'll save here."

"I know, but I want to do more. I want to go on missions outside of the SA. I want to go to Greenland. Ashiva, I even want to travel to the Space Colony. Something went wrong. I'm the top student. It's a mistake. I know it."

"I don't know what to say." The words are lies, thick in my throat, and I wish I could make it right. But if she went to the External Hand, I wouldn't be able to take care of her. I know what she feels, even though I won't say it. If I had to stay inside the Narrows day and night, I'd lose my mind in twenty-four hours flat. But I can't take care of her if she's not here. When I leave to work for the Liberation Hand, I need to know she'll be safe here.

"Why do you get to go?" she asks.

Now it's my turn to hold it in. "I'm built for this, my replacement. To run the missions."

"Why didn't she build me for something? Why can't she fix my skeleton to be stronger, so it will never break again?"

I look at her and melt. Guilt fills me like poison and for a second I think about just telling her everything. But I'm in too deep. If she found out how I've orchestrated her safety, I'd risk losing her even more. "You're brilliant. Masiji only fixed your body to make walking easier for you. You are exactly as you should be. I'm the freak. You know I weigh ten pounds more with this arm?" I shake my head. "Toss me in the water and I'd sink."

She laughs a little. "Nah, you're still the best swimmer in the Narrows. I hate you, Ashiva."

"I know, Lomri, my little fox. I hate you too," I say.

I feel a small, cold thing slide into my hand, a necklace.

"Made this for you," Taru says.

"Now, I feel even worse. All I brought you was this wrinkled old mango." I pull it from my pocket.

"Wow, it's amazing ... I've only heard about them."

"What is this?" The charm on the necklace is all twisted metal, like a nest of stars.

"It's us. See, the gear is a star, and the edge is a smaller one. Me and you."

I bend down and she slides it over my head, around my neck. "Thank you. Not that I deserve it."

"You don't." She smiles.

"Just the same, I am sorry."

I consider hiding the powder vials from her, but I'd never forgive myself. "Here, the gatekeeper gave me these to give to you."

Her eyes widen and she rushes to take them from me. "Amazing!"

"What are they?"

"You wouldn't understand." She winks.

"Smart-ass. Probably true."

"I can finish my project. It's big. When it's done, it'll be very useful. I'm going to keep it just outside the Narrows at a safe distance to avoid any accidents. In that place we hid when I was little. You remember?"

I nod. I know she's making an explosive. I can't stop her from dabbling in the dangerous. The whole world is dying around us; how could I tell her not to?

"Just promise me—" I start.

"I won't run with Ravni's crew again. Okay? Can I go now?"

"Not that. Just take a weapon with you wherever you go. Use this big brain of yours to puzzle things out first. If you get in a tight spot, grab a weapon, find a ration, something. Do everything to keep yourself alive."

"Promise," Taru says.

We lean our foreheads gently on each other's and it's all I need, even though it's impossible to know if she takes me seriously. I've done my work to protect her, maybe too well. If only I could watch her all day and still do my job, I'd believe everything would be okay. But it won't be. It isn't. Which is why I fight. If I fail at saving Taru, I've failed at everything.

And this world isn't worth saving.

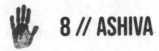

8 // ASHIVA

The meetings of the Red Hand Council are brief and virtual for a reason: We don't exist and, if we do, we don't exist in the same place at the same time for too long for security reasons. An in-person council means a representative from each cell of the Hand is in attendance and that's never happened before. Not since before the Red Hand split into cells after the Last Vidroh, when we were still connected to the same body. I know because I've run security for the meetings the last year alongside two other runners about my age: Chand and Maigh. Before the split, we ran coordinated missions together. But since the UAVs and the SA's anti-terrorist gray-collars have been around, we had to go underground. The communications have been sparse and coded. We've been waiting, like tigers sleeping in thick elephant grass, for just the right time to connect our cells back together to form a powerful, united group.

I can tell by the shifting feet and clearing throats that no one, not even Masiji, is comfortable here. She called us suddenly to come to exit drain 11 for an emergency meeting. A coded message went to those far across the entire SA Province, from our Central District to the Eastern District, to the Western District and up to our border with the Asian Province, in case the Northern District can still hear us. Those in the Narrows received a brisk shake on the shoulder by a child runner. Not all came; some can't risk the trip. Masiji said there was a security breach on the all-channel coded comms, which means the SA's gray-collars or the PAC was listening in now. The Red Hand had to stop even the coded comms until they could find a better mode of communication between the three cells. But for now, Masiji was clear there is an urgent matter they need to discuss. Everyone knows she wouldn't call a council meeting if it wasn't imperative.

The drain is massive, and there's a small room, just before the water falls to the ocean, where we stand. The rushing water is loud enough to cover speaking voices. And the thickness of the concrete and metal surrounding us keep our heat signatures from being picked up by a UAV. I peek out at the water pouring over the edge into the sea and my stomach is in my throat at the thought of going over.

"Don't like heights?" Chand asks, looking down at me. Tallest by far, Chand is intimidating, but I know he is just a big softie.

I shrug. "I like them fine. I don't like us all here together." I whisper that last part.

"Take a peek over the edge, Ashiva. It's not that far down." Maigh says and I laugh. She's always trying to get my spot as the top smuggler. But she'll never catch up.

"It'll be over soon," Chand says.

Maigh has a look on her face like she just ate the biggest sweet. "Spit it out, girl." I say.

"Okay, word is there's a shipment coming to Central of rare earths. It's on a tech transport from the PAC with batteries and other supplies. But this one has it all. And I've got a contact who can let me inside the cargo bay for five whole minutes."

"And how do you know this?" I ask. If we could get our

hands on some neodymium it could fund us for years.

"I have my ways. I hope this meeting ends early so I can catch it. My contact won't wait for me."

"Okay, Big Time." Chand laughs. Everyone knows Maigh revises the truth. But sometimes I wonder if she's real. We all run cargo for the Narrows, but it's usually tech, batteries, food, and med supplies. There are sanctioned donations from international charities, gifts from the Eastern and Western Districts of the SA, and some crap no one wants or needs. Sometimes we make a contact for the real stuff. Like my contact for the children. Chand is really good at getting high-level tech. Maigh has been bringing in some expensive metals lately. I hope she's not a double-player. After training our whole lives, the more daring among us have the Liberation Hand in our sights. There are only a few positions every year because the journey is extreme. They say they smuggle the new lieutenants to their secure and secret location. Rumor has it that it's a trip that takes being drugged and smuggled in a cargo box. I've heard they don't even tell the new lieutenants if or when it's happening to cut down on potential braggard kids. Even knowing how dangerous the journey is, I'd do it. I want to fight.

Anonymity is our best mode of survival. The Red Hand is everywhere, is nowhere, is everyone, is no one. It's necessary to maintain our power, our reach across the world. Sure, there are those who are known in Central, power figures like Masiji. And if President Ravindra and her government killed her, it would start a war they wouldn't be able to stop. Besides, she's a literal ghost. Never left a print or traceable picture. There are only poorly-rendered drawings of her being ten feet tall and having weaponized mecha armor. Propaganda inspired by WWIII when war mechas wiped out nations and millions of people. Masiji let those rumors fly because it builds fear, hope, the reasons for fighting certain death. With a leader like that... maybe we can overcome the impossible.

But the rest of us have dual identities for our sakes and for the betterment of the Red Hand's mission: to undo the Upland; to defend all lives, as all are worthy of saving; to redistribute wealth and tech across all classes; to lead the revolution to allow natural survival of the fittest; to find a better solution to the PAC's New Treaty. External Hand connected to different resistance efforts across the globe in the African Province, Asian Province, and even as far as the South American Province. Anywhere a government's response to the New Treaty was to pick and choose a few lucky to survive on this dying planet, we made allies fast. The rest of us move quickly, lightly, with cloaking tech, sleight of hand, and our wits. To get in and out of Central. To work as gatekeepers, as comms managers, and smugglers. To fight.

I've never seen the Liberation Hand leader. And I mean never. You don't meet him until you've survived the new lieutenant transport. General Shankar is a mythological person whom I heard about, but never knew was real. His group focuses on militant modes of resistance and doesn't report to anyone until after the fact. They are doing the hardest work, after all, risking their lives to blow up bridges and transports, all to save Downlanders. He looks sweeter than I imagined, though weathered by war. Both his arms are replacements, covered by silicone disguise, and he has an air of impermeability about him that is awe-inspiring.

To bring us all together with the Liberation Hand in one space is to build a target on our heads and send our location on an all-comms to the world.

"You all know it must be serious otherwise I wouldn't have called," Masiji starts the meeting. "I'll make it brief, so we can all get the hell out of here and back to work."

"Where's the fire, Mechanic?" Romil, the gatekeeper and Internal Hand's head of spies, looks around the room with his back-lit blue eyes. He winks at me from across the room.

Beside Romil stands kooky Poonam Auntie, our weapons specialist and medic. She's fiddling with a small piece of scrap metal. She folds and unfolds it, and it whines with each bend, sending a tiny shiver up my spine each time.

Leaning against the wall is Mrs. Zinaat, the educator and head of recruitment. She looks like she'd rather do a million other things than be here, like have her trainees do studies on the environmental impacts of radiation, or teach the children how to disarm each other in hand-to-hand combat. Her tall and thin form is even taller and thinner as she stands beside Daadaji, the head of our Internal Hand in the Narrows. The old grandfather, who spoke up in Open Speak, looks wide awake, even excited by the urgency. Even with the lack of resources, his face is shaved of stubble and his "Cheer-Up!" T-shirt is clean. His voice was always gentle during our training, which was always philosophical: how to communicate the plight of the people of the Narrows to the world. His task is to keep the message alive here and around the world, to somehow plant the seeds of unrest even in Central. He has trainees infiltrating Central in the lowest levels of society.

General Shankar stands in the shadows. I can't believe

how close I am to him. I must have a goofy grin on my face because Chand elbows me hard.

There are others I don't know, but I guess they are the leaders' lieutenants. Many more aren't here; some are imbedded in companies and governments around the world. Those who are in deep cover will never surface. They only help as they can, but if things go south, they'll do what they have to, to survive like the rest of us.

"As I mentioned, our all-channels comms was hacked. An Internal tech found a trace on the line. We've been very careful, and they didn't get any info. It was a ping that originated with the SA. They were trying to locate our comms line. It looks like they're using the satellites on the Space Colony to track us now."

"Arre, kya?" I whisper louder than I intended. That would give them range, that's for sure. But anyway, what the hell.

"It was vital we come together here. I would have sent a comms or we would have had a holo-meeting as usual, if circumstances were different."

General Shankar clears his throat with a growl. "Out with it, Commander."

Masiji paces. "We've all spent the better part of our lives dedicated to the Red Hand. We've gone dark, we've been patient." Masiji looks around the room at the different leaders. "I know that not all of us agreed with our separation in the first place." She stares at General Shankar, who grunts. "We even lost some members through the separation. But we continued because the mission is too critical to let go. We have sown the seeds of dissent. We have fed the civilians, trained the next generation of fighters. Some of you have smuggled arms, placed spies inside other governments and PAC research teams. There are now thousands of us around the globe." She stops pacing, squares her shoulders, and turns to face the leaders. "It's time to come together again." The words escape her mouth breathy and heavy—like she wished to say those words for so long they grew covered in dust in her lungs.

General Shankar speaks with a deep voice thick with skepticism. "What the bloody hell do you mean? Why now? What do you know?"

"AllianceCon presents a unique opportunity. To attack them here, where they stand, while the world watches on all networks," Masiji says.

Muffled cheers are exchanged, people pat each other on the backs. Everyone except General Shankar, whose shadow grows exponentially.

Masiji says, "We've done our best to reach out to the GHO, but they seem to be preoccupied with what's happening in the Americas. This will be our best chance to get our message to the world and connect with other groups, like the Planet Watch."

"Not to mention the SA has the GHO in their pocket," General Shankar says.

"Are you not pleased, General?" Masiji asks.

He shrugs and all heads turn to him, waiting for his response. "What do you know?"

"What I've told you."

"No, there's something that's triggered this in you, Commander. I've been waiting, begging to unite forces again for years. There have been other times when it was favorable. Like when the SA went through the reconstruction on the wall and

Ring supports. They left us an opening we could have marched an army right though. You're not telling us something. If we're risking our lives, you need to come clean."

Masiji doesn't flinch. "There might be an attack coming."

I gasp and hit the wall behind me accidentally with my replacement arm, sending an echo through the room.

She continues, "The details are unknown. But our Internal tech who got pinged was tracking the SA."

"They gave our location away?" Mrs. Zinaat speaks up. "Your tech revealed us?"

"It's happened before. We all spy on each other. But this time we seized an opportunity to follow the ping and managed to enter the SA's comms system. The tech intercepted an SA comms that showed the Narrows as the number one hot spot."

"We're marked." I whisper.

"The SA are going to tighten their grip somehow. Damn," General Shankar says.

Masiji continues, "Last time we were on the active list, the SA released the UAVs and gray-collars. We don't know what to expect. We need to reconnect before we lose our chance."

Quiet Poonam Auntie clears her throat. "Commander, may I?"

Masiji nods. "Of course, Poonam."

Poonam Auntie moves to the center of the room. "You know, I was there, many of us were there, when the SA closed the gates. I was young. I watched as they used mechas against unarmed civilians. They lied and said that we, the Red Hand, put explosives on our children to infiltrate their front line. They open fired on children and covered up their actions with lies. The SA did that. The things I've seen, I—" She shakes and squeezes her eyes shut as though she feels the heat and roar of an explosion in her mind. Then she takes a minute to steady herself. "I'm in." And she presses her right hand to her chest.

"Thank you, Poonam." Masiji presses her hand on her chest and looks around the room. "The Red Hand will rise again." One by one the leaders each show their solidarity by pressing their hands to their chests. All except for General Shankar. The Red Hand is nearly reunited. Chand and Maigh and I turn to each other, almost forgetting we are on duty. But then Masiji's voice brings us back to the planet.

"Shankar, let us continue our discussion. Perhaps we can address your concerns in private."

He nods once then he puts up his mask and hood.

Masiji says, "Good. We will have a lot of work to do. We will regroup in our underground headquarters. It's secure, for now. Let's leave separately and meet there."

Masiji signals us to step outside and close the doors behind us. So, we do.

"Tired of the kids' table," Chand says. "I still can't believe it."

"Shh, yaar, keep your cool."

"Right." Instead, we exchange hand signals.

"I'm taking off." Maigh starts walking down the massive pipe.

"You can't leave," I say. I watch a pile of trash bounce about in the water like a child's boat.

"Who's gonna stop me? Anyway, looks like you two got this." The girl gives me a thumbs-up and says, "I've got a big cargo to pick up right about now."

Dhat. "Wait, aren't you going to stick around?" I ask. She's going to beat me to the next assignment and walk out with a chance to be involved in an assault on Central?

"I'll be back before you know it. I wouldn't miss a thing, trust me."

"Eh, let her go." Chand holds me back from following. His replacement forearm is almost as strong as my full replacement arm. "We'll get on The Mechanic's good side, right?"

After a few minutes, the heavy metal door swings open and the Red Hand Council members leave, one at a time. Dispersing in different directions through different exits. General Shankar disappears through a hatch and another tunnel entirely.

Masiji is last. "Where's Maigh? Eh, no matter. You can go." She nods to Chand. "I need to have a word with Ashiva."

Chand raises his eyebrows at me, then leaves.

When only the rushing of water surrounds us, she leans in close. "Ashiva. I have your trust?"

"Of course, always." I put my hand on my chest signaling the Red Hand.

"Good. I need a favor."

"Anything."

"I want you to keep an eye on General Shankar's whereabouts. Make sure he stays in the Narrows. I fear he might do something drastic that could ruin our chances of having a successful mission."

"A basic trace? I ... I can have Saachi run it."

"Yes, a trace. But this one needs to be quiet. Thik hai?" she says.

"So, a quiet trace. You need me to have Saachi set it up, but keep quiet about it and you need me to clear her tracks?"

She nods. "Just set up a line to ping me his whereabouts every hour."

"No problem." Silence separates us. Her mind seems full, but words don't come. It's like she wants to tell me a story, but now's not the time. "Anything else?"

Her heavy hand rests on my shoulder. "You've learned the lineage, correct?"

"Of course. We all have. In order to keep the Red Hand going, we all need to be prepared for a cataclysm."

"It must continue regardless of who's at the helm. I know I can trust you."

"Masiji, what are you saying?"

"These are funny times, is all. I need to know I can trust General Shankar to work with us, to act together as a united front. I'd hate for him to launch an attack without coordination. My biggest concern is the care and well-being of the Children of Without."

"I know." I think about Taru, about protecting her above all else.

"Good, Ashiva. That's all," she leans against the wall and nods her head, asking me to leave.

But something doesn't sit right. As I walk back to the Narrows, I listen to the water rushing around me and wonder if it's rising. Rats run along the tunnel as I pass, awakened by my heavy steps. I watch a large rodent scurry away on its six legs with a small bird wing in its mouth.

9 // ASHIVA

When Solace came online and the Uplanders' neural-synchs linked, we anticipated menial labor would be eliminated in the city. They'd be optimized and would have no need for low-level workers, as bots would do the smaller jobs. We prepared for that. We weren't surprised when middle- and upper-management went too. Push people further towards the inevitable and they end up accepting crazy things. But then they lined up those who didn't pass the Solace test, and most went peacefully to the Narrows encampment. Okay, well, not peacefully, but we went. The algorithm split up families, friends, colleagues, governments.

But what we didn't expect was the sound.

It was deadly quiet. No riots, no fighting, no complaining. In a city that was rarely content even during festivals, this wasn't just unusual. It was unnatural. Like the neural-synch made them inhuman.

And after such a disastrous build up to the neural-synch, to the Ring, to Solace, any sane person in the Province would have expected bloodshed on both sides: anti- and pro-techs. In a place where discontent was commonplace, peace marked a different kind of terror. A terror the Red Hand has been trying to understand and undo since the rollout.

It wasn't just quiet, it was otherworldly.

Me and my crew were all young then, and most of us couldn't tell you what it was like before Solace, the UAVs, the Ring, and tests because this was the world we were born into, existing on the cusp of tomorrow, the future just out of our reach. We know what they did wasn't right, pushing us out of Central to die, and that's enough for us. That and Masiji's Narrows. We live by the Red Hand laws.

And the Commander just asked me to break one of the most vital laws that carries a punishment of the corporal kind.

It's illegal to track each other in the Red Hand, particularly the leaders. It shows distrust. At first, I had no doubt because when the Commander asks me to do something, I do it. Don't think. But each step away from her allows doubt to grow like a bacterium, making me feel sick and confused. Infected by the thought of betrayal. Back and forth my thoughts go, until finally there's no way to avoid it: I need to do what Masiji asks. If she's right, and General Shankar runs an op without coordination, it could tear apart all we've worked for up till now. Lives could be at stake.

But he's hopefully going to be my new leader, and the two have had bad blood between them. People could die even without us achieving our ultimate mission of disrupting AllianceCon, and making our situation known to the world and Planet Watch, in order to unhinge the PAC.

Decision made. I just hope I don't get caught.

Zami and I hurry along the New Ocean Road, past the submerged ruins of the city, to the undermarket. Old neon signs sway in the growing ocean breeze announcing their wares: jalebis, samosas, medicine, charging stations. Hawkers selling storage devices, cyborg parts, and offline hacked tech whisper in code as we pass. All illegal and essential.

To the left are Central's new structures, spiraling upwards; to the right the dark sea churns and rises, higher and higher.

Soon there'll be nowhere for us to go.

"Psst. Check out my newest ladders, cleaned them myself."
A small boy named Rao always sits at the same corner. His
fuzzy cowlick on the back of his head makes him seem young,
silly, and sweet. Something precious. He's in the Red Hand,
but just as an assistant. He's kind, not a bit of fight in him. So
Masiji allows those like him to work as errand boys to keep
them out of trouble.

"Nahi," Zami pushes the eager boy back. "We don't need an
uplink, chota bhai."

"What about my sweets? Ma makes them every morning.
Well, not every morning, but weekly. You know what I mean."
He lifts a scarf from a platter of square, blue sweets.

I toss him a mark and take the sweet snack he's selling.
"Your mother's a good cook."

"Shukriya, sister. And if you ever have an errand . . ."

I stop walking and lean closer to him. "Thanks, Rao. Not today. Leave the hard work to us." I tousle his hair and we keep
going.

Zami says, "Makes me not want to walk through the market. Maybe we should find a new space. He's chatty."

"It's alright. One mark can change his night from bad to
fine. It's better if we keep our location in the market. Everyone
feels safer because of it. Civilians protect our identities, and
we protect them."

"Yeah, I know, I know. And the Red Hand needs a location
in the market. Stay at the front of people's minds. But still, you
see one person and stop to help them."

"That's a problem?" I split the snack with Zami, who takes
it willingly.

"Yeah," he says as he chews. "All it takes is one rat, you know?"

"Have faith, Zamir. He's a good kid."

"You can't save everyone, behanji. Not everyone in the Narrows can be trusted."

I stomp past Zami.

"What?" he says to my shadow.

"You don't get it."

"Get what?"

"If Solace decides who is good enough to be optimized to live and work in Central, what's the difference if we decide who should live and die here? If we can't believe in our allies, we are lost," I say.

"Ahh, come on, behanji. I was just being real—wait for me!"

Zami reminds me of me when I was younger, before I understood the cost of it all.

I step over the hawker selling refurbished wires, batteries and various torches. A sentry for the Red Hand. Kneeling, I let the light from one of her lanterns illuminate my face without my veil. She flips a lever, unlocking a door behind her. As I push open the door to the abandoned office building, I switch on my flashlight and make my way through the darkness. Zami catches up, and when we reach the elevator, he jumps in too. In our office space, I unlock the door and lock it behind us again. The old locks are beautiful; the key turns with a satisfying click.

Screens flash with lines of code and I hear Saachi's voice before I see her. "I was beginning to think you weren't showing up tonight."

"Why would you think that?" Zami puts his arm around

her and gives her a half hug. "I'd never leave you."

Saachi punches him in the chest, and he feigns pain. "Sometimes I wish you would leave." They laugh. I'm about to burst with my orders. Even though I decided to go forward with it, it's cutting me up inside.

Saachi is older than us and has vast connections. She's one of the tech leads for the Red Hand—the tech we aren't supposed to have. And she runs a team of biohackers who trade materials on the underweb and refurbish them for replacements. She's tall and smart and boyish, a chameleon. And the best experimental scientist in the SA, maybe even in the Province, in my eyes at least. We run our programs on machines not connected to Solace. Our network is so old and slow, but it's usually undetectable and is our one connection to the underweb. If Solace looks for us, it'd be like a mecha robot looking for microbes underfoot—wishful, but impossible.

"It's been quiet tonight," Saachi says as she keys in code and watches the virtual screen like she watches ocean waves. She holds a snack in one hand and nibbles her fingernails. I don't know how she multitasks like she does.

"Were you the one who got pinged?" Zami blurts out. I hit him in the arm with my flesh fist.

"Nah, not my gig. I think that must have been someone closer to Masiji's inner network. I heard though. Damn crazy. You ready for the reunification of the Hand?"

I nod. "Been waiting for this my whole life." For the first time ever, I am excited about the possibility of putting my training into action. To use my knowledge of weapons, formations, and battle studies in the field. But then a cloud hits me. "But first, I've got a high priority project," I spit it out. "Orders from the Commander."

"Of course. What is it?" Saachi and Zami listen.

"To keep tabs on General Shankar." I watch their faces, waiting for the questions.

Saachi turns to me with surprise. "What? Isn't that against the Red Hand law? The Liberation Hand isn't governed by anyone. Not even the Commander can tell them what to do. Not even if the Red Hand is reunited. It's treason."

Zami shakes his head and lifts his hands like he's letting go of an invisible weight. "Yeah, no thanks. If he finds out, we're as good as dead. He scares me more than Masiji."

"Masiji says that she thinks he's planning something big. That they need to stay in the Narrows until the tensions clear. I ran security for the Council meeting. He was there."

"You saw him?" Saachi says. "What's he look like?"

I nod. "Tall and impossible, like a mountain. We have to run an hourly trace is all. He'll never even know. If he finds out, she'll defend us. I know it."

"Fine. But I— it wasn't me."

"Didn't do it, didn't see it, don't know. I know." I nod silently agreeing to take the fall if it goes south.

"Oh hey, I finished something for you." Saachi pulls up an image on one of her screens. It's a squarish, super pixilated image with two ear-like shapes on its head, and a wagging tail out its side. It could be an animal. "Tada!"

"What the heck is that?" Zami laughs.

"Come on! It took me hours to make it look so bad. It's the replica that you needed." We stare blankly. "That ancient artifact digi-pet? For your hacking challenge. You have to feed it every few hours or it will die. See?" She sends a square to the digi-pet's mouth and it wags its tail. "Originally they were inside these little plastic bits. But my underweb version is pretty cute, I think."

"Oh! Wow, it's so basic. I thought it'd be more . . . I dunno . . ." I say shocked. "Why were these ever a thing?"

"No one knows." We laugh together. "But they're gold on the underweb. I made a program to replicate the original. At least I think I did. Whatever. It's all about pride for the challenge anyway, right?"

"It's adorable." Zami sighs so loud it's more like a grunt. "Someone'll pick up the challenge, right?"

"We should plan for the worst, guys. Solace is tightening the pipeline and in a few short weeks, we might not be able to get onto the underweb. Then what?"

Zami talks with his hands. "Wait to die, I guess. That or pull some Rani of Jhansi style maneuver. All-out attack, swords drawn, you know. Right at the heart of Central. Solace's liquid memory system. Or take out the Ring."

"Suicide. They underestimate how many of us are down here, but they have bigger, better weapons. We'll get electrocuted before we make it into the Ring. Let's just hope that the bosses figure out a strong assault."

Zami jogs to his corner of the room and his massive home-made computer station. On the black screen of the comm panel is a window into the underweb, and a short message in white type flashes.

RED HAND: I ACCEPT THE CHALLENGE. THE TASK WILL BE COMPLETED TO YOUR SATISFACTION. —KID SYNCH.

I laugh aloud. "Whoa, Kid Synch's got this one? Then it's as good as done." I know Synch's work. They're a trickster with a nearly invisible signature. Small attacks here and there, nothing too big to draw too much attention. Brilliant stuff.

Zami spins toward me on his black chair. "Check and mate, Synch. This could be everything, Shiv. I mean, with this we would prove our theory of accessibility into Solace, and we could gain Synch's trust and bring him on as an insider. I need to know why that file is important to Masiji. We'll finally find out what this Himalaya file is all about."

"Shh, I know. Let's not get too excited. They're probably going to lose their nerve anyway. They always do. But at least this time we have a real coder at work."

"The Red Hand has made a name for ourselves on the underweb. What can I say? We are cool."

I tousle Zami's curly hair. "Don't let it go to your head. On the underweb you're a god, but here in our place, you still have to clean up this junk."

"I know, I know." He smiles and scans the room full of wires, broken computer parts and motherboards.

Zami looks up at his screen at a flashing red light. "Trouble."

"Shh." I signal to Saachi to go dark.

"Someone's coming. They bypassed my security."

"Stay here," I say and Zami doesn't disagree. "Lock it behind me."

The empty data center is dark with one light illuminating the entry, just barely.

I say, "Keep walking. This place is taken."

A voice I don't recognize speaks in the dark. "I've come for you, Ashiva."

"Me? Good luck with that." I dig in my heels and stand with my hands in front of me, ready to strike. "Come out of the shadows."

A figure the size and shape of a man stands in the center of the office ruins. Then I see the glimmer of gold on his teeth and know.

"Jai, flit you," I say and let my hands hang. "What in the gods' names are you doing here?"

"What? Aren't I dangerous enough to warrant a bit of fear? Come on, Ashiva. You always wanna fight." He shadowboxes like a fool.

I turn to head back inside.

"He wants his marks. Your family is late this quarter," Jai says.

"Khan Zada." I face Jai. "Tell him he'll get his marks when we have marks to give."

Jai steps so close to me that I can see the edges of his chin's scar; he smells of machine oil. "That's not how it works."

I shrug and my replacement shoulder moves weakly.

"He knows you have enough, Shiv."

"What does he know."

"He has ears, and eyes, and some other body parts working for him," Jai says.

"Gross." I turn to reenter the lab.

"Tithe is the only way he can protect the Unsanctioned Territory. Without it, there'd be chaos. You know that." He winks and I want to pull out his eyelashes one by one.

"What I know is that we pay and pay, and never see anything in return. Only to get hassled by his goons when he wants more in the beginning of our workday. Khan Zada doesn't help us. He's a disgrace."

"Careful, Ashiva."

"We all know he made deals with the Uplanders. He

should only work with us."

Jai moves toward me to strike, but when he is inches away, he goes in for a kiss instead.

And then I punch him hard in the arm. He'll have a lumpy bruise for a while. He's lucky I don't break it.

"Try that again and I'll rip off your lips, scoundrel. To match your chin."

"Okay, okay, Tiger. But remember whose place this is."

"Er, mine, clearly."

"No, his. This is his." Then he uses his chin to point at my arm, my replacement. "That's property of the Lords of Shadow, girl."

"You can't be serious," I say, but I know he is real as real. "No, it's not, haraami."

He leans back against a wall. "Call me a bastard all you want, Ashiva. Khan Zadabhai sees it like this: He gives the Red Hand a pass, the undermarket, your little smuggling operation, all of it. It only works if he faces the right politicians in the right direction, turns their eyes away, see?"

I swallow hard. Not a fan of threats. "He wants my arm?" My heart shakes, but I make sure he doesn't see me waver.

"No, he wants you and yours to keep their replacements."

"Look, I'll get him the tithe tomorrow, okay?"

"Fair enough." Jai turns to exit. "And, hey, Ashiva, you know, long ago, I was a recruit."

"What, too hard for you?"

He shakes his head. "I got caught up in a side hustle with the Lords of Shadow, and Khan made me a deal. I was too young and stupid to know what I was signing up for. No way out now, not until I work off my debt."

"Sad story, Jai."

"Look, Ashiva, I like you. I'm mostly just a messenger, so this one's for free. You might want to take a break from smuggling Uplanders. Noise is the Minister of Comms is dying for a reason to cut the Narrows off completely, rations and all. The AllianceCon is making them nervous."

"How'd you know about the smuggling—?"

He points his large finger to his eyes and his ears, and clips his mask on his face. "See you soon."

"Not likely," I say to the shadows.

A pit grows in my chest as I flex my arm. I know Khan will do it, just to spite me. Make an example and they all fall in line.

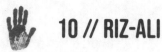# 10 // RIZ-ALI

Getting the data packet is only half the challenge or else any tech with access to Solace and a fully optimized brain might try it. Not that they would, but they could. There was some talk on the underweb about a team of techs ready to go, but they all went dark when the recent updates from Solace came. They say they're busy, but I know they're scared. All talk until it's time to act.

But to deliver the packet to the Red Hand on the underweb is the actual challenge. I'll have to cloak the data, send it through an unmonitored line, and delete all traces of my fingerprints on the data. It has to be perfect, or else I'll be pinged by the authorities before I disconnect. Hacking is a massive transgression. And I have to get back home to take the auto-inject in time, or else I might end up dead.

Can I do it?

Sure, it's risky, but I need to know what happened to my uncle. He was connected to the Red Hand Commander somehow. This is the best way to gain their trust.

There is only one place to upload a colossal data packet undetected. The Liminal Area, vastly unpatrolled and unprotected, the badlands that slipped out from under Central's control after the riots. Still under the edge of the Ring because they couldn't manage to kick out the population still squatting there. People in the Liminal Area don't want to associate with the Narrows or any leader. They only believe in one thing.

Anarchy.

Maybe this is the real reason I beat my underweb pals to it. An Uplander in the Liminal Area is easy pickings for all sorts of peripheral hacks, and it's dangerous. An Uplander was kidnapped twelve months ago and they found her body dissected, like the Downlanders tried to detach her neural-synch, but failed to realize how far it attached inside the brain and just made a mess of everything. Of course, detaching would take surgery and the device, over time, organically imbeds itself deeper within the body's nervous system. Anyway, it was messy. I don't know what to believe though. Mother taught me we shouldn't believe any of the Info-Runs. She would know; she creates half the Info-Runs with her team.

I walk past the transport stand where other Solace employees wait for their concierge lift home or ride on the skyrail that wraps around Central's Ring. They are so carefree. A woman and her son are feeding the geese in the central pond. The genetically modified geese were flown into Central from the North American Province, as most wildlife had died or escaped to the north after the floods and the acid rains had started. They sent gifts like this to all Provinces to help mend their relationship with the world. It's all guilt and show, though. The North American Province will never live down the launch of the nuclear missiles twenty-five years ago. The mother and her son look so peaceful, like we're not living inside a precarious bubble. My mind races. Twenty-two employees in line, same as every evening. This is it. Last chance to change my mind. It will take twenty minutes to cross the ten blocks to the old Bridge Project and into the Narrows.

Twilight fades to a yellow-orange haze that covers the city like a gauzy curtain. I never walk these streets because Solace

provides transport for all their tech employees, but I know
Central is a basic grid. Sixty roads crisscross, making larger
and larger blocks as it goes toward the Liminal Area and out
into the Unsanctioned Territories.

Transport rickshaws buzz past, honking at everything and
nothing, their sleek bubble-like frames coasting just inches
above the ground on the Maglev roads. Uplander workplaces,
Solace Corp and other tech companies made Central a forest
of glass and metal. Elegant, perfect buildings shoot to the sky
like temples of technology. There are some remnants of the
past, lingering like scars. The Downlanders made sure to
protest the removal of their old buildings. Most of the ancient
temples and statues were moved or encased in the same glass
as the buildings in an act of preservation. I wonder if they'll be
the ones to outlive us all.

The air changes from sweet and humid to a sharp, bitter
stench. The Ring's cooling system isn't as effective in reaching
the outskirts of Central, even with the electromagnetic field
that covers Central. Air is cooler inside and nearest the center.
My lungs hurt with every breath. And then there's the heat. It's
like being face-to-face with an open flame. My Info-Run alerts
me:

WARNING: TEMPERATURE RISING

Thanks for the insight. I set my neural-synch to silent and
see alerts in my vision rather than in my mind.

The buildings are less and less refined. Some buildings
are just beginning to take shape; others are still wrapped bun-
dles of construction materials waiting to be opened by the
builders who dreamed them up, but will never build them after funding was cut.

Portable fencing narrows the lane, forcing people to walk through and line up in the area. The guardians are wearing masks and clean suits even though the signs read, "Precautionary Check Point."

I turn to a man next to me. "What's this? This wasn't on the map."

He doesn't look at me, but seems tired, bored. "The Fever, yaar. Just be cool and they'll let you pass."

They take our temperatures with a wand and we move through. As I pass, I see an Uplander woman who has been pulled to the side. Her face is terrified, but calm. Everyone else ignores her, walks faster. But I can't help but take her in. Does she have Z Fever? I wonder.

I enter the first empty Information Portal Station, strip, and shove my work suit in the refuse bin. The metal room is small and narrow, but I manage to pull on my gear: a pair of cargo pants, a T-shirt with the sign of the revolutionary hand emblazoned on the chest. Over that I put on a nylon vest, and then tie my hair into a tight bun. The gear is all black and dirty, and acquired from the underweb over time so as to not draw attention. I added tech to the clothes, ladders and ports, and one very small, very temporary disruptor that would kick me off any searching network. Solace can only locate anyone with a neural-synch inside Central. My handheld electro-pulse device gives me a sense of security, though I'd have to be in close proximity to danger to use it.

My reflection on the screen is fragmented. It's difficult to see between the massive touch screen projecting news, transportation information, and adverts from nearby stores. Is it enough? I rub some dirt from the ground onto my face, and cringe while doing it. The damp wall feels sticky through my tunic, and I slide down to sit on the city street. The holo-advert spins across the side of the building across the way. A "Solace Shaanti: The Next Stage of Evolution" campaign advert bleeds across the metal face of the sky-rise building, in flashes of lights and colors. Images of bots, civilians, and Solace Corp's logo mesh into one, fast-paced, blurry video. Other adverts show beautiful people dancing. The parties my mother wants me to attend, but I never do because, well, she wants me to.

I press my neural-synch and turn it on to status. It runs a report.

TEMPERATURE: 98.60
FLUIDS: HYDRATED
LOCATION: CENTRAL BOUNDARIES

All set then. The temporary body disruptor I've made will keep my location looped inside Central even as I continue to the outskirts.

A small street-sweeper-bot bumps into my foot several times before I lift it out of the way and it continues on its path. Someone decorated it with a string of beads and dried chilies to ward off the evil eye. No matter how far we've come, our superstitions follow.

As it spins away, it mumbles in multiple languages, "Zara rastha dijiye. Excuse me. Chalega. Clean the road. Clear the road." There's a piece of paper stuck under its wheel, making a swishing sound as it spins. Little bot. I put my foot down in front of it and rip the scrap away.

A propaganda poster for Rani, the girl who died in the Crimson Riots. She became the face of the Downlanders, the symbol of their oppression. Her form is painted and outlined in black. In the background is a hand outlined in red. The poster reads: "You were lied to. The Rani is alive." The symbol every Uplander fears.

During the Great Migration, the rich were whisked away on high-speed transports to the neocity Central, while the rest were left at the gates. Riots broke out. Then the girl was murdered, butchered by the Uplanders. The video went to all the comms. Central was pressured to open the gates. And met with the Red Hand to make an agreement about a settlement community, the Narrows.

"Trash." I crumple it up and toss it in front of the sweeperbot to consume. The stuff people believe is crazy. It's propaganda. She died. It was terrible. We should feel guilty. It's crazy what people will believe.

I calculate I'll reach the edge of the network in about three minutes, which will be only about fifty paces toward the Unsanctioned Territory. Fifty paces closer to the truth. But suddenly my feet stop. I didn't stop, they did. It's like my body is freezing up. Like an invisible hand is holding my ankles back, making my steps heavy.

"What the . . . ?" I look around. My hands tremble and my vision goes out and all I see is the Solace Corp logo on a black background, similar to what I would see during updates, but there's none scheduled today. My vision returns as quickly as it went, and I take in my surroundings. I wiggle my feet. Bad place to lose control. Could Solace have just interrupted my movement? I don't have time for this. I take a couple steps forward and find I can move normally again.

"Oye, check out the svachchh," I hear a small voice echo from the walls of an unfinished building.

My clothes are dirty, so I don't know what they are thinking, calling me spotless.

I feel a small hand tug at my work bag. "Pretty things."

The younger-than-me girl child is scrawny, hollow-eyed and yet so sharp at the same time. I shrug her off.

"Take off, choti behan. Not interested." I hear my words, but I don't know where they came from. She hasn't offered anything.

"Sure, bhai. Whatever you say," she says and walks alongside me for a few paces before disappearing into the building's shadows.

I've got everything, the gear, the tech, but the darkness is shocking. It's all encompassing. Every inch of Central is lit by solar torches. But there hasn't been one in the two miles since leaving the middle of the city. Skeleton buildings surround me, climb and reach over me, and that's when I know I am getting close.

The Bridge Project was supposed to link the one coastal border of Central directly to the Last Island. They were going to turn it into an exclusive luxury resort island. But when the island fell into the Arabian Sea, they stopped construction, leaving behind the expensive materials. It is a sight to behold: the girders tip together like the legs of a fallen giant robot, four stories high. My connectivity through my neural-synch is limited here, at best. Ideal.

At the foot of one of the girders, I set up shop. I link my neural-synch to the uplink in my vest, then slip that into my work case's uplink. By connecting the information in a circular loop, I'm able to create an independent network. Solace could have detected this if I was in Central, but here I'm free to do as I please.

Uplink open.

The temporary memory card slips into the port and I wait for it to load. Meanwhile, the start screen pops up and I get to work, punching in the code and opening the main source list in the port.

The screen freezes on my last command and I wipe my forehead.

"Just like sending code to Solace," I say to no one and everyone.

My fingers flash across the keys. Finally, the system opens up a pathway and I set the screen to cloak. I pull the data packet from my card and send it on its way into the underweb, C/O the Lal Hath from Kid Synch. No one will dare steal from them, and it'll make its way to the hacker collective within an hour.

Click. And done.

My ether smoke feels cold in my hand as the ether fills my lungs. Three, four clicks on the keys and I exit my session, making sure my actions aren't traceable. Done and done. I pray it works. That I can set up a meet when I'm declared the winner.

The Unsanctioned Territories surround me. I've never been here before. All my hacking has been completed in various parts of Central. So precarious. Their buildings twist on the edge of the sea like unwelcome guests, slums proliferating as they will, as the city allows. It's dark now, and I need to return to Central before the population of the Liminal Area wakes up and finds me here out of place. More importantly, I need the auto-inject to avoid a serious illness from the neural-synch.

"Why the rush?"

It's the girl again. When I show her my electro-pulse device in my hand, she laughs.

"Scared? I'm a friend. I could show you around. This your first time in the Liminal?"

She's cheerful enough, but I shake my head. "No, I have to get back."

"Why? You're from Central. There's no curfew for you. You can do what you want, when you want it. The air might make you sick, though. Right, bhai?"

I pause for a millisecond. "Certainly, but if you'll excuse me . . ." I take a few steps up the hill and that's when I see their shadows in a line in front of me, like a chain of bodies walling me in. Twenty kids or more.

"You should really stay, we have so much to talk about," she says and takes my hand. The sun is setting just over the water, diving into a cloud of haze.

And just like that, I am a captive of a gang of child goondas.

"Ach, sit still, Tiger." Masiji's words are muffled by her welding mask. Her workshop in the Narrows is hot, always hot. Smelting metals, smoke and grease, incense and music. Little robot projects of hers zip around her feet like metal mice.

"I am sitting still," I wiggle on the table. My surroundings are blurry through the fogged-up glass goggles Masiji insists I wear. My right arm is held in traction above my head and it's split open at the shoulder joint, wires and all. The joint's unclipped, I'm flayed, and feel too vulnerable. Through a reflection in a metal panel above me, I see my shoulder stump and the joint base she installed years ago at my scapula, like a receiver for the replacement. The metal wires reach around to my clavicle. I wonder if I should have the reinforcement surgery she offered that would bring supports at my ribs and spine, so it feels more stable. But another surgery like that sounds like horror.

She lifts her respirator and shakes her head. "Beti, you're about as still as electricity. If you can't sit, I'm going to have to remove the whole replacement arm to work on it, and we're back to square one. You wouldn't get much work as a one-armed smuggler." She laughs.

She always says I am like electricity, always buzzing around for the nearest conductor. "What? That's the option? You make this so easy." The tension in the traction fights back as I struggle.

"Beti, just sit."

I'm dying to know if the Red Hand will unite, but I'm sure they're still in negotiations. So instead I say, "You've received my info on the General?" Saachi's words about our trace being treason echoes in my head every second, ever since we set it up.

"Thank you for doing that for me. There's no need to worry. It was necessary. He's stayed put, so I was overreacting. We are working on rebuilding now. I know you're anxious to know." She smiles.

My heart soars.

The lanterns hanging from the ceiling flicker and buzz. Everything runs on generators down here, which makes Masi-ji's work even more miraculous and insane. Unsanctioned work in the Narrows is not for the weakhearted. If you ask me, it's a technical craft, art, and miracle, all at the same time.

She laughs and gets back to work. "And you make everything difficult. It's in your stars, so I shouldn't be surprised. Beti, when people try to help you, for god sakes, just take the help."

"Okay. I'll try." I bite my bottom lip and focus on watching a little robot scurry about, picking up small scraps of metal and shards of wood from the floor, and putting them into a small fabric sack hanging on its chest like a marsupial pouch. "What's that for?"

"Chota is my clean-bot prototype," she says with admiration. Like he's a pet. He has two small, black wheels and a tiny, white, metal body with a head that's a soft, square display screen. His digital blue eyes blink at me sweetly.

"Well, I guess he is small. You've got your work cut out for you, Chota baby. You'll need a much bigger refuse pouch to clean this place," I say. The bot looks up at me and squeals his wheels, then speeds off to pick up a bit of wire with his tiny arms.

"No thanks to you," she grumbles and pulls her mask down. "Now sit."

As she solders, I hum to keep my mind off of the surgery.

"If I only had access to what the Uplanders have, I could . . ." Masiji sighs. "Ahh, just as I thought. The plexus is nearly dead; the motor is burned out. Good thing I got my hands on a new one. A better one."

"Wait, what? Where did you get one?" I sit up, restraints be damned. "Let me see."

She hands it to me carefully. It sits in the palm of my hand, all chrome and small and beautiful. "This must have cost a fortune." The rare earths inside the new plexus are the most contested resource in the world and what led us to the mecha wars. The elements are necessary in all forms of biotech, transportation, turbines, computers—everything we need to live, to thrive. After we burned all that we could, all the fossil fuels and trees and coal, we finally made renewable energy sources. But, now, we fight over the elements that keep them going. People would sell their loyalties for just one nano-magnet made of neodymium alloy—the permanent magnet that keeps the motor in the replacement moving forever.

"What I wouldn't kill to have Uplander tech. But a good mechanic doesn't share her secrets. I got a first-class deal. It's used, of course, but I've tested it. It's spotless. No trace of Solace code. It'll run with your tech offline."

"I don't know what to say." I throw my arms around her and

she steadies herself against the worktable. I'll never know how she has such vast knowledge and connections, but it's something we all accept, happily.

"Can't have you complaining about your replacement drawing attention to itself. What use would you be to any of us locked up in containment?" She smiles. "Now, can you sit still?"

I nod through my smile. Her workshop is small and filled with parts and pieces of experiments, things that make us whole. Masiji replaced her own foot before I met her. She said it was deformed by arthritis and hard living; she knows what it's like to live with a replacement, and constantly need to repair and mend it.

"Masiji?"

"Yes?"

"Do you ever think about just leaving to the North? It's been a quarter of a century since the bombs. It must be recovering. What if the fort is still there?" I fall into a daydream of flying over the Himalayas to Red Hand operatives in the North.

"It could be. Northern Fort could be there, buried in a mountain, in the valley with the river, and the village like mushrooms on the mountain. But we can't go now." The clank of metal on metal tells me she's put her tool down.

"Why not? What if we could unite the Hand and launch our assault from somewhere they don't expect?"

She smiles. "We can't leave the Narrows. We would still know that we walked away from fixing a problem that we created. We can't just leave this injustice the way it is. Problems would follow us."

"What do you mean, 'we created'?" Masiji's body language bristles at my question.

"It's just that we can't walk away knowing how people are suffering here. If we don't do everything to stop the SA and disable the PAC, they'll just as soon kill everyone outside their gates. Their biggest regret is the truce." She picks up her tool and says a prayer.

She's right, but she's sometimes hard to read. "Sometimes I wonder, you know, about all this and can't help but think that people made these choices. They did this. Why haven't they been held accountable? Shouldn't that be our number one agenda? As the Red Hand, that is ..."

She whispers, "They will be ... in time. Every wrong will be righted. But first we need to get through to the world about our plight. Our biggest priority is the children. They need to survive this at all costs. Even if ..."

"Even if what?" I ask. Masiji's face is half covered with shadows and half in the light.

"Even if that means we make difficult choices to get there."

"I understand," I say, but I don't. It seems clear to me. What's happening here is wrong. The New Treaty is wrong. Where is justice? Why isn't the world revolting?

Masiji stands upright and uses a clean rag to wipe her forehead and clean her goggles. "War is not easy to understand. The Red Hand has been fighting since before WWIII, but our mission changed as the world changed."

"How do you mean?"

"Before WWIII, we were recognized by the SA government as a legal community group. We were nationalistic and wanted to help usher the SA into the future along with its population. We were idealistic. We wanted to save everyone."

"Don't we still?"

She nods and her lips turn white from pressing them together. "Yes, but everything has a price. We had to fight.
Shankar's militia joined the Red Hand. We became bigger,
stronger. We will be strong again."

"I don't understand..."

She smiles as though she's caught up in a memory. "Does-
n't matter now." She leans over my body and I hear metal turning and a satisfying clicking sound. "And—just about done.
Ready to test. Okay, you can open your eyes now."

"They're not . . . oh." I realize my eyes were closed tighter
than tight.

"Well, child, synch, and let's see your best stretch. Gently
at first."

It's been so long since I've had a perfectly working limb
that I'm not ready for the disappointment. I sit up and look at
my reattached arm, a good model titanium alloy and steel. The
silicone skin was removed before the surgery and my cyborg
arm is in full view, every inch of it. It hisses as the motors react
to my suggestions. I push my plexus at my temple and let the
machine bridge both systems: human and machine.

My mind fills with images of stretching my replacement
to the sky. "Is it moving?" I don't want to look. But suddenly I
feel the fire of my ghost limb wanting to come to life.

"Open your eyes, girl. And see for yourself."

It is. At this moment, the world seems possible. Smiling
feels good, and only then do I realize it's been a long time
since I'd allowed myself to do so.

The workshop lights flicker again, and then go completely

out. "Ach, useless things," Masiji says as she turns on a few battery lanterns. "We still have work to do. I need to set the regulator and recalibrate the new plexus. It will take another hour or so. But you can relax. We are through the tough work," she says as she lifts little Chota and puts him safely in his box. He spins his wheels, blinks his big camera lens eyes, then shuts down.

Finally I have an arm that works without giving itself away on my undercover trips to Central.

"Could we reattach the silicone too?"

"Of course. And I've installed a new liquid disc reader as well."

"Nice upgrade! Thanks."

She sits at her station and attaches cables to my arm and the computer. I close my eyes and listen as Masiji prays. This is the miracle portion of her surgery. No one else knows how she calibrates our replacements. It's her secret. I've watched a hundred times, but never understood the final step. It has to be her prayers. She strokes beads on her wrist.

Just then, my wrist comms flashes with a message.

FROM LORD ZAMIR: THE PACKET WAS DELIVERED. WE GOT IT. KID SYNCH CAME THROUGH. NEXT STEP, THE WORLD!

"What's so funny, Ashiva?" Masiji asks.

"Zami just surprised me, that's all." I switch off the comms. "We sent a hack challenge on the underweb and some techie actually did it. They sent the data packet Himalaya to us. The hacker must be an insider at Solace—it's just impossible to break in from the outside. We might actually have found ourselves a techie at Solace Corp to . . ."

Masiji gasps. "Himalaya? Why—?"

"You mentioned it a long time ago." Caught in a trap, I realize I wasn't supposed to have heard the information when I ran security for a Red Hand Council meeting in the past. "I thought it would be old and dusty and no one would miss it."

"That's dangerous. Solace knows every bit of data, where it goes, how it moves. That's what she was made for. Trust me, I know." Something in her changes. She is actually scared. The Commander is never afraid.

"Sure, but it's just an old bit in off-site storage. The hacker is the one who would get caught, not us . . . they're taking the risk. Anyway, now we have someone inside Solace. I thought you'd be proud."

Her voice catches. "Why would someone agree to dig into Solace's storage?"

"I promised a digi-pet."

"Girl, what the hell is a digi-pet?"

"Ugh, it doesn't matter. And anyway, the Red Hand has built a sort of name for ourselves on the underweb. There's a lot of cache that comes with winning a challenge."

"I don't like you drawing attention to—" Masiji is about to start into one of her treatises on safety when the world shakes.

BOOM.

It's the kind of sonic burst that drops your stomach to your feet. A bin of metal tools falls off the shelf, scattering across the floor.

BOOM.

"What in the gods' name was . . . ?" Masiji asks as she picks her things up.

Still attached to the wires, all I can do is crane my neck out the window. A plexi-wall that wasn't there before stands about ten yards from us.

"What the—?"

BOOM.

Guardian aircraft land in each corner of the Narrows. Suddenly, my comms flashes in emergency mode. The flood lights pour in from outside, a brilliant 3D image illuminates the sky outside, spinning for all to see.

I'll never forget President Ravindra's careful, even-toned, better-than-you voice. Her penchant for red is out of control. Red lips, red cheeks and eyes. Even her center part is painted with red powder. She looks beautiful and dressed in blood.

"THIS IS AN UNSANCTIONED LIVING QUARTER. BY THE MINISTERS OF THE SOUTH ASIAN PROVINCE, YOU ARE ORDERED TO QUARANTINE."

"Why is this happening?" I scream to Masiji. Though she's a few feet away, she can't hear me over the comms.

"OUR PLANETARY HISTORY HAS TAKEN US ON A UNIQUE PATH. BEFORE THE WILLFUL SEPARATION OF OUR DISTRICTS, WE WERE EMBATTLED AND ON THE EDGE OF NUCLEAR ANNIHILATION. SINCE THE ESTABLISHMENT OF THE PAC, THE EARTH HAS A CHANCE. SOLACE AND CENTRAL ARE BURGEONING. NEW TECHNOLOGIES ARE LAUNCHED DAILY. AND OUR POSITION ON THE GLOBAL MARKET HAS BEEN SECURED ONCE MORE . . .

The sound of scraping, moving metal brings a bad taste to my mouth.

"HOWEVER, AGAIN, WE ARE FACED WITH A NEW ENEMY IN THE NARROWS. AN AREA BUILT WITHOUT LAW, WITHOUT MORALS, THE UNSANCTIONED TERRITORY MUST BE REMOVED. IT IS A HOTBED FOR TERRORISM AND HATE. AND NOW, SICKNESS. THE Z FEVER IS NOW A PANDEMIC, AND IT HAS BEEN DETECTED IN THE NARROWS, AS WAS SUSPECTED. BECAUSE OF THE DANGER OUR GUARDIANS FACE WITH THIS NEW CHALLENGE OF SECURING THE NARROWS, WE HAVE DECIDED TO EMPLOY THE MECHAS OF THE FUTURE. NAMED AFTER OUR GOAL, OUR FUTURE MUST BE DETERMINED BY OUR WILLINGNESS TO PROTECT THE PEACE: SHAANTI. WE PRESENT THE C.O.R.E - COMBAT OPERATIONS RESISTANCE ENVOY MECHA-SUIT. THEY WILL UPHOLD THE PEACE THROUGH THEIR ENVOY AND PROTECT US FROM THE IMMINENT THREAT OF DISEASE. UNDER THE NEW TREATY, THEY ARE ARMED ONLY WITH THE NEWEST NON-LETHAL WEAPONS."

President Ravindra's smile is wide, and behind her stand all the ministers of our Province.

I detach myself from the wire clips. "Mechas? Central has mechas?"

They finally come into view: four monstrous-sized, black robot shells with guardians at their helm. They are nearly twenty feet tall, solid black metal and emblazoned with Central's symbol on their shoulders, and Solace Corp's logo.

"The newest addition to Solace Corp. What they've been talking about. I never thought that war could be mistaken for peace," Masiji's voice is pain. "Shaanti. What have I done…"

Peace.

"But mechas?" I yell to Masiji. "What about the Treaty?"

"They must have found a loophole. Maybe they're saying it's a peace mission, with non-lethal weapons."

We watch the guardian ships hover and land in the area, dropping more C.O.R.E soldiers in place, making it impossible for us to exit. They place transparent temporary walls on the edges of the block, sealing our passage, our fate.

"You need to go," Masiji says as she hides her valuables and the Chota baby bot in a small hatch beneath the ground. "Now!"

"We need to go, come on. There's still a passage in the Narrows road through the undermarket," I say and drag her through the rear door into the alleyway. She is frozen by the sight of the C.O.R.E.

It's dark, at night, and we can hear the screams of children and adults as they are being pulled from their communal houses in the Narrows. As we run, guardians line people up and test them for disease. Diseases they don't have. An easy excuse to say the slums house the disease, the Z Fever. For once, I pray that Zami isn't home. I pray that Taru ran away to the Liminal Area. That the Red Hand Council members are safe. But they're not. I know. Because I tracked them all. They're in and around the temple area in the underground catacomb. Dhat.

An old man takes a little girl in his arms and tries to run, and a C.O.R.E soldier hits them. The sound is terrible. I know the result. They'll say they were resisting, to justify all of this, all the deaths.

"Run, Ashiva. Run and don't look back. You have to live, otherwise all my work was for nothing." Masiji pushes me with all her strength.

"I'm not going without you, Masiji." She's slower than me, so I jog a few yards ahead, scouting what's to come.

We keep to the shadows and hurry along the alleyway between the shanty structures as it snakes and finally turns into a single-file passage down, underground. A wave of relief washes over me. We'll get out and then we'll free Zami and Taru somehow. I can use my connections on the underweb. We'll find a way.

"Halt!" A guardian's voice from behind us slashes my heart.

"Run. Hide," she whispers. "When it's clear, get to the undermarket. Seek out the Lal Hath originators. They'll help continue the work."

The concrete holds my legs.

"Stay strong. Stay strong for all the children," she says and takes a few steps back.

Before I can protest, she pushes me forward and then runs

toward the line of guardians.

"No!" A thousand screams say no, but I know she's right. I have to run. If I am free, maybe I can help everyone, even her. Carry on the work. Thoughts spin in my mind like pulses of electricity.

And so I run.

My boots hit the ground as I run through the puddles in the tunnels. Masiji's screams echo as the guardians beat her with their electro-pulse batons.

The sounds of nightmares. I want to turn around. But a fire carries me through the tunnels, deeper and deeper under the city, until my legs burn and my breath is ash.

When I'm at a safe distance, the horrific sight is clear. The entire Narrows that houses a million people—children and adults, Red Hand members and civilians—is on fire. The C.O.R.E uses some kind of sonic cannon to blast the crowd. Some people fall to the ground, clutching their heads or their ears. Another C.O.R.E uses a sort of heat-ray at the crowds and to burn the structures as people flee. None of this can be legal. Screams fill the air. Lines of people are being sorted, put into transports. Finally, the smoke moves and I can see that the temple structure is leveled and what's left is a smoldering pile of rocks and rubble.

The Red Hand Commander is captured. Who knows how many were killed in the raze? Please, please, let them be safe.

I run. And all I have with me is regret.

# 12 // TARU

I'm on seva duty when the little ones' cries begin. They were sleeping. All of them. But suddenly they became uneasy, all the children in the nursery. Sunny, the good sleeper, starts fussing and crying. At only two and a half, she's already had a few surgeries to repair her left eye, and inner ear. She had injuries when her Uplander family tried to have her modified to pass Solace's tests.

It's like Sunny knew something was coming, like she felt the vibrations in the ground before the monsters even reached our village.

I go to her cot, to comfort her with a song, a lullaby, her favorite.

Sleep baby sleep,
Sugar, roti, milk,
Milk and roti are finished
Sleep baby sleep...

But a child never cries alone when others are near. Soon, everyone is waking up, crying, asking questions.

Nothing soothes Sunny. Her cries are different, too, deeper. Her thick black hair reminds me of an endlessly dark night, far away from any city's lights. A place I dream about going to with Masiji, Ashiva, and Zami. Somewhere far away from here. Where we can live on our own. Grow food. Surely a place like that exists in the Northern District; the Red Hand's fort has to exist. Or maybe beyond the mountain ranges in the hill stations. Somewhere where it's still cold. One day...

"Taruji, I hear a nightmare," Sunny says in her smallest voice.

The ground rolls like an ocean wave.

"Earthquake?" I ask. Mrs. Zinaat, who's on nursery duty with me, shakes her head.

She is solemn. "Can't be. All comms would have reported seismic activity. This is man-made. We must gather the children. Take them to the catacombs."

"What if it's nothing?" I ask, still rocking Sunny in my arms. The process of leading all of these half-awake children into the dark for a drill is the worst idea. "It's too dangerous. We could lose one in the dark. There are only so many we can carry. We're safer here."

Her gaze and voice are concrete. "Do what I say, Taru. Now." She lifts an electro-rifle over her shoulder, transforming immediately into a soldier.

"But—let's wait for Ashiva. She'll come and..."

"And what? Save us? Taru, we have to protect the children. Get going!"

The twelve children we have in the nursery are all under the age of six. The oldest children carry one infant each. Leaving four for her and myself. I carry two and she pulls the rest in a wagon made from metal siding scraps. I stash pieces of roti and ration pods in my pockets and the older children's pockets as well. Inshallah willing, we'll survive whatever is to come. Apocalypse or not, they'll need to eat sooner rather than later.

We go into the darkness without a solar lantern. That's why we can't see them clearly at first as we climb above the shanty town. When the first mecha soldier enters the Narrows

and smashes the gates, it's lit by the entry torches. Like a demon coming to life, the monster soldier storms through the
gatekeeper's tower, armor glinting in the night. At least two
people are inside. Sunny's adoptive father, Sunil, and her
mother, Gaura. They don't emerge from the rubble. She is now
a double orphan. Most of these children will be. We work so
hard to place them in homes in the Narrows once they are
ready. My screams are drowned by fear.

The sounds are sickening. I pull the children close to my
chest and pray to all the gods for mercy as I stumble down the
broken trail.

"Move faster, Taru," Mrs. Zinaat's voice is out of breath.

My foot isn't agreeing, so I stumble. Masiji has begged me
to come in for a tune up in her workshop.

The second mecha solider and an armored transport
crush over the broken gate. The voices of guardians giving
and receiving orders through their loudspeakers fill the air.
"LINE THEM UP. TEST THEM HERE. THE REPLACE-
MENTS ONLY."

"Where is the GHO? Planet Watch?" Someone screams.

Then we all see the holo-screen play above the Narrows.
The voice of a polite and calm President Ravindra blares over
the bloody chaos below. I can't help but stop to see it, if only
for a second. They call them C.O.R.E. To keep the peace. This
is not peace, it's hell.

But before long, the guardians are pulling people from
their shanties and lining them up in front of the burning buildings.

The catacombs are a natural cave-like structure built under the Narrows. It was a city once, from long before. It sunk

into the sea, and then they built another city above it. But then the water was redirected by the sea wall, and now it's safe from flooding. We drop the children down, one by one, onto the narrow rocky stairwell. We push them back and back and back inside. We prepped the catacombs with the basic survival materials: lanterns, tins of rations, tins of water. I am last to go inside. That's when I hear the metal monster crunch up the side of the trail towards us.

What would Ashiva do? I have to run. I can't just sit and be useless anymore. I have to lead it away. This is my chance to do something.

"Taru, no!" Mrs. Zinaat yells as I hand the babies to another child and step outside the catacombs. The camouflaged metal sheet is heavy as I drag it in front of the entryway into the catacombs. It's stuck. It doesn't close all the way. The large opening is big enough for them to be found under a search light. No, no, no. They can't find them. No. A search light picks up on me and there's a rush of wind in my face.

BOOM.

The ground shakes. A sonic boom vibrates the world around me and shakes my brain in my skull. My nose bleeds. But I move. Go.

My body carries me back down the hill. Back into the Narrows. Let them follow me. Follow me away from the children. Toward the burning buildings, and danger. The C.O.R.E soldier hunts me with its metal robotic steps crushing the rocks and earth below.

"Stop! Compliance is required." The guardian's voice projects from its speaker.

The dim light and sonic blasts are disorienting, and the

broken concrete in the path ahead is a surprise. I fall and a rusty spear of rebar slices my arm. The C.O.R.E lifts me by my injured limb and drops me in front of another guardian. Its grip is inhuman, and it feels like my bones are going to give way and shatter all over again. Every inch of my body cries. I'm screaming. I know only because my throat is on fire.

Something pushes me from behind. A guardian shoves me into a line. "Stay here, replacement scum."

All feeling leaves my body. I want to cry for the wound on my arm, for the fear in my heart, but I am still, frozen, like an animal waiting to die. And I can't do anything to wake up from the nightmare. All of our training and we are no match for the mecha. I want to find an electro-pulse rifle or an explosive, anything, to gather our forces together, to fight, but there's no way. They hit us with such surprise that no one had a chance to organize. Instead, my eyes scan the world around me, burning like a warzone, children screaming, our city crumbling. UAVs hovering everywhere with their stupid blinking lights and idiot words for us. I scream in my mind. I'm thankful the children will be safe with the Mistress, but I wish I could have taken more people to the catacombs.

The line is filled with children, from toddlers to teens. They're familiar to me from langar, from training, or just the line at the chug-chug. We cry in each other's arms. Some look for their family in other lines, others tremble uncontrollably. I gather the smallest ones together and say, "It'll be okay, we'll get through this together."

"Silence," says a guardian with a baton in his hand.

A boy says, "We don't have to take this. They have no right."

"Hush, bhai," I pull him close, but he tears away from my hand.

"No, it's not right," he says and takes off running. The guardians yell a warning, but he doesn't listen. Finally, a C.O.R.E follows him and stops him cold with a baton to the back. He lays flat and doesn't move again. Ever.

I cover the children's eyes and try to distract them as the line moves. Our turn comes to check in, and the guardians demand our arms. They extract serum, blood. Then they shove us into a dark transport vehicle where they tell us to strip our clothes. My clothes are everything I have. Masiji taught me how to sew them properly. I run my fingers over the shells that Ashiva showed me how to fashion into buttons. I fold my clothes carefully and put them in a pile at my feet. Ashiva's voice is in my head: Take something, anything, a pod, a weapon. The ration pods fit neatly under my armpits.

They burn our things and say it's for vermin infestation and Z Fever contamination.

A guardian gives us each a basic tunic and I carefully move the ration pods in the pockets. I'll keep them as long as I can. The other children need help changing.

We are organized by size and age, and replacement type. Then they force us into small air transports. We sit on one bench with a bar across our laps to keep us in place. A few minutes later, about twenty adults file in, all wearing similar tunics. They sit on the bench across from us with the same restraints. Some are familiar.

"Taru, thank god." Masiji's voice is hoarse. Her face is battle-scarred from what I assume is a recent beating. "This is not how it's supposed to happen."

I've never seen Masiji so afraid.

"What happened? What do we do?" Tears come quickly. Her presence gives me permission to be weak because she is always so strong.

"Sh, sh, bachcha. There's nothing we can do now. By international laws, they can't kill us. Relocate, yes, they can do that. Torment us, but not—"

"They said there's a disease here..."

"No, Taru dear," Masiji says. "I don't think it's here. They are liars."

Once the transport is full, the doors close, and we rise into the sky and fly. We don't know anything yet, so I try my best to listen to what Masiji says and not worry. But it is impossible. Instead, I try to find peace inside myself, in a place they cannot reach me.

I've never flown before.

I wish there were windows, so I can see Central.

I bet it's beautiful from above.

And our home is a burning scar at the edge of the sea.

13 // RIZ-ALI

The room they keep me in is windowless and damp. An old control room or off-grid storage facility. Which grid, I can't tell from where I am sitting. I count the cracks on the concrete floor instead: forty-seven. I press my neural-synch futilely, knowing there's nothing I can do externally. The one time I need Solace to see me, it can't. The buzzing in my mind grows louder and louder, and I cover my ears and try to snuff it out. When that doesn't work, I hit my temple. Anything to shut off the sound. They stripped me of my gear. Even though the thought kills me, I should have taken the injector of medicine like Mother said. A sickness is creeping across my brain, side effects from the THink nano-optimization drug, compounded with my lack of compatibility with the neural-synch. I've pushed it too far this time and I might not come back from possible neurological damage.

The vent at the bottom of the door lets in a centimeter-wide scar of light, allowing me a glimpse of the space. The room they tossed me in isn't bigger than a closet, with metal walls, and an ancient computer control panel of some kind that has large buttons and a strange screen. An early computer, perhaps? Once the government updated the city's sewer systems decades earlier, the old defunct machines and systems went by the wayside. The air is humid, thick. The smell is oceanic with a touch of metal, tinny, and sharp. I try to steady my breathing and heartbeat, so I can listen closely: Water is rushing through pipes. Pipes, damp, old machines...

Suddenly, it becomes clear. I might be sitting inside an abandoned sewage control center, at end of the line in no-man's land. No one would ever find me here even if they knew where to look.

The door opens with a crash, and three individuals clamor into my room. The girl who followed me in the Liminal Area, a young boy with wounds on his scalp, and an older boy who has a scar from his lip to his chin. All of them can use a day at the genetic edit spa. I'd pay for their treatments and put it on my mother's tab to trade for my freedom.

"I need water," I say, though they all ignore my words and look right through me.

The girl who followed me speaks to the older boy with the lip scar, "We found him crawling around the Liminal Area. We weren't sure about his intentions, but he's not street enough to be a member of the Lords of Shadow. So, we ran him against records, and he's listed as a missing person. There was his precious mug, a perfect, white-suited Solace techie. I couldn't get more info because it was only surface bits. But he's probably important, or wanted for something or else they wouldn't have reported him missing after only what, a day? Looking at him I wouldn't think he had crime in him, eh?"

The young boy says, "His return will pay big, yes? Buy us a favor with the boss, Jai?"

"You'll get his thanks, don't you worry," says the oldest boy.

"Just keep your gang off our backs for as long as you can. We don't have a leader for a reason," the girl says. "And I don't like you." My, she has bite.

The oldest laughs. "I'll take it from here, Ravni. Not that I won't miss your company."

"It's mutual." Then she turns to me and says, "Water?" In her hand is a small aluminum cup. There's small debris floating, like fish, in the water.

"Um that water is..."

"Not good enough for you? Oh, right, it could kill you since you don't have the antibodies. There's no quick fix for infected water other than not drinking it." She takes a swig and wipes her face with the back of her hand, smiling with full teeth. "Or growing up slowly, building your immunity to it."

"Killing me is that funny?" I ask.

"No, just, you're, well, so weak, and perfect." Her hair is cut short and her big eyes sit deep in her face, like the weight of it all is carried inside.

The boys around her laugh as they back out the room. "Check out behanji. She's into him."

"Chup, murkh. Never seen an Uplander up close," she says to the boys. When she turns to me, her eyes cut me like glass. "See you round." She winks.

"Wait! What's going on? You can't just hold me without reason." I almost say, You can't hold the Minister of Communications' son because she's a frightening person who'll as soon as disappear your lot than talk to you, but I stop myself. If they know, I'll only be worth more. Better to be an unnamed wanted loser than someone of consequence.

"Come along then, get up," is all the scarred-chin boy says. He sounds, well, strangely put-out.

I push back as far away from him as I can go, unsure that my legs can hold my weight after sitting so long in the dark. How long has it been? Hours? Days? It feels like forever. Without my ability to connect to Solace through these massive walls. I might as well not exist in space or time.

He takes a step closer. "What? Don't they make Uplanders with legs that work anymore? Or do you need an upgrade?" All three kids laugh like I am a toy, an anomaly, a joke.

"This is a violation of my rights," I say, shielding my eyes from the bright light that pours around his form, showing that he's a thug, a goonda.

"Oh, my apologies, sir, would you like some water with sliced mango and ice? This isn't a vacation colony, white suit. Get up." He kicks me with his boot.

My legs are weak, and he laughs when I slip.

"Yeah, don't care, techie boy. Walk," he says.

He holds me up by my shoulders to the one luminescent bulb dangling from the tunnel, peering at me like a curious scientist. With the close-up of his face, it's clear he is just a street thug: dirty, angry, possibly insane. But I envy his conviction. I assume he hates me for my money and the life I live. But he can sign up for the Solace Corp program scholarship. It chooses the fittest few to join the ranks in the Upland every year. He might make the cut, with a few edits. Maybe.

He pushes something sharp into the small of my back, so I move forward. "Where are we going?" I ask.

"You just don't worry about that, thik hai?" He tosses a heavy fabric hood over my face. It smells old, unwashed. And just like that, I am blind. "Walk."

I have no choice but to walk to wherever this goonda wants me to go.

"You sure you've got a neural-synch? Isn't that supposed to make you smarter, or, what do the holo-ads say, 'optimize your future'?"

"Yes, obviously."

"Well, then, if you're so smart, how did you end up here? I bet if you actually ran the stats, they'd come up flat in our favor of finding you."

"Yes, statically."

"Then, a girl. You got yourself a Downlander girlfriend? What a scandal!"

"No, not even close, Jai."

"On a first-name basis?"

"I was, well, doing some underweb work."

His laugh is real. He even holds the side of the tunnel to support himself. "That's the best one I've heard in ages. Working on the underweb. You've got stones, ya do."

"It's true. I'm a freelancer."

"Whatever makes you feel better about yourself, uppy scum." He pushes me down the tunnel ahead of him. "Now, get on. And one more lie and I'll have to take out that tongue of yours."

14 // ASHIVA

I was an animal fighting to survive when I woke from my first replacement surgery. I was five. I didn't know where I was. I struggled and scratched and hissed at the wires and tubes. Masiji had to sedate me. When I finally came to, she laughed and called me a chrome tiger. Disoriented, I couldn't feel my body, but she said I was filled with a raging fire to live. Not everyone makes it through the surgery. Many bodies reject the replacement or can't synch with the plexus. I'm lucky Masiji nearly finished installation of the plexus before the raid. My replacement is functional, but needs a final tuning.

I've made up stories about my replacement arm. One of my favorites is that I was a small child on the migrant train, one of the falling-kids sitting atop the train. That when I crashed to the ground, the train wheels took my arm off, clean. Another story I told nosy people was that a guardian tried to take me and my mother, and his electro-pulse baton melted my arm away. We all make up stories because none of us really know the truth. The Children of Without have been injured by this world, by disease and war, and terrible tests. They are not less for their injuries; they are beautiful just as they are. Some require lifesaving surgery, while others don't want replacements. No one is made to feel less. But I need to join the Liberation Hand and so I augment my body to fight. The truth is my replacement took care of the wounded arm I had at birth, Masiji said. She told me she found me on the streets, arm shattered, born of a mother who had Z Fever and died. Sick mothers once gave birth to sick children. And sickness wasn't allowed in the protection of Central's Ring. Back then, the Fever was contained. They stopped in-utero transmission with medication. Now, the disease doesn't transfer to the child, but it causes other systems to fail. Genetic mutations, injuries, brittle bones, poor weight, all the things Central doesn't want in their optimized population.

When I left the Narrows and ran into the tunnels, leaving Taru and everything I knew behind, it took everything inside me to keep running away. To know that Masiji was taken, beaten. To not know where Taru and Zami are. And the children . . . my blood turns to an impossible fire. But I can't do anything. Not yet. Not until I make my way to the outer region. I keep going.

Fighting tears, I run harder, faster. My home is gone; I imagine what the C.O.R.E soldiers will do to the area, to the children. I need to find the Red Hand leaders. There's a protocol that I don't know for dire circumstances like this. If they are alive, they'll know what to do, where to go, and how to reconnect with each other. The protocol is above my rank. Masiji's reminder plays in my head: "Red Hand needs to continue. Go find the Lal Hath originators." But how? So many inside the Narrows are gone. The image of the mechas standing guard, their jet-black armored bodies creaking dangerously, like they can crush us without even flinching, snuffs out any fight I have. For now.

The crazy thing about heat is how slowly it kills. First, you get dehydrated and dizzy. Then, thoughts become muddy, meaningless and thick in your mind. Soon you get a headache and a horrific stomachache. Then suddenly, some just die. Without my mask and the cover of the structures in the Nar-

rows, I'll be dead in a day. When I stop sweating, I'll be in trouble. I make it to the edge of the Narrows and up against the
Liminal Area. They'll have trouble finding anyone here; it's a
maze and full of goondas. I force open the first door with my
fist. The abandoned building is dark, quiet, and if I'm still, it's
cooler than outside.

But I'm not alone.

A few junkies and a couple Liminal goondas strung out on
designer drugs they can't afford take the first floor, so I go
down into the basement. They don't even seem threatened by
me, they're so glitched. Enviable carelessness.

For the first few hours, guardians patrol the area. As a
C.O.R.E walks the streets of the Liminal Area and shakes every
bit of the structures, my body quivers from teeth to toes. But I
hold my breath and pray to no one in particular that they can't
access my plexus. Masiji designed it to be offline, and I have to
trust only the Info-Run and comms can intercept my plexus.

I cry, but my tears evaporate before they fall.

When I'm hungry, the nearest glitched-out goonda's pack
is wide open and a quick look gets me a ration pod and a quar-
ter-full water bladder.

I have to find the elders of the Lal Hath, get help, free my
family. But first, rest.

Resting is never easy for a tiger.

Suddenly, an Info-Run shoots down my vision, leaving me
with no other choice but to read it.

ALERT
FROM: MINISTER OF COMMUNICATIONS
THANKS TO THE EXCELLENT POLICING, CENTRAL WAS ABLE TO STOP A TERRORIST
ATTACK BEFORE IT BEGAN IN THE NARROWS TODAY. ALL PARTIES INVOLVED HAVE
BEEN TAKEN TO AN OFF-SITE FACILITY, WHERE THEY WILL BE QUESTIONED.

ALLIANCECON AND CENTRAL'S 25TH ANNIVERSARY CELEBRATION WILL TAKE PLACE AS PROMISED. THANKS GO OUT TO THOSE WHO KEEP OUR NEOCITY SAFE. OUR NEWEST TECH, BUILT TO KEEP THE PEACE, ASSISTED IN THE MISSION. AS PER THE NEW TREATY, THE LIMITED CASUALTIES WERE FOR THE GREATER GOOD.

Frustration builds until tears come. A terrorist attack? Newest tech? Their mecha-suits?

Now it's clear. Central's lies can't hide the truth: The Minister is done with the Narrows and everyone inside. It all makes sense now. They wanted to test the C.O.R.E before the AllianceCon to gain the graces of the PAC. And their money. But most importantly, Central wanted to clear the Narrows to wash their hands of the guilt. I wish we could put out a comms to tell the truth to Planet Watch. Even when we do, though, Central will spin it as a lie.

But we won't be forgotten.

My internship training prepared me for every situation Solace Corp could foresee. From how to calculate issues of scalability with our energy sources, to managing the data capacity of the network, we studied everything. Everything Solace Corp deems vital information for the development, maintenance and survival of our chosen society in the South Asian Province, that is. I've never been allowed to deep-dive into Solace's algorithm to search for the primary guidelines that formed her code. Why one person is better than the next seems an impossible choice to make. Solace's original code is confidential. But it keeps changing anyway, every day, learning, growing from those initial few lines. Supposedly improving. But humans wrote the original code. What those few people valued, what they considered important to determine who would continue onto the next apocalypse remains a mystery.

Regardless, kidnapping isn't in her program and I've no idea what to do.

We aren't supposed to leave Central. We aren't supposed to want to leave it. Even as the last in my class, I am trained to use my neural-synch to calculate code, data, and solve large problems. And, yes, this is a very large problem. Uncle would say to keep puzzling out the pieces and not give up. But I keep coming up zero. This all began with my attempt to connect with the Red Hand. At this point, they might still be my only hope.

Tongue intact, thankfully. Jai is all threat and little bite. But he is filthy and smells unwashed.

"Jai, is it? My parents are looking for me. Doesn't that worry you?" He has seven scars on his face alone. One curls from his chin to his lip, like he got caught by a fisherman's hook. His thick curly hair is a mop.

He doesn't even look up. "Are they now?"

"Yes, of course they are."

"Huh," the goonda exhales spite.

I try to look him in the eyes, but he doesn't budge. "Why do you think they won't be? I'm an Uplander. There are a hundred ways to track me, to monitor me."

"Sure there are, yaar. But these walls are made of ancient concrete. It just happens to be so thick and airtight that not a single bit of data can get in or out. It's like a tomb. You're on your own, so let's get on with it."

"At least tell me where you're taking me."

"Now, where's the fun in that?"

The way he walks, I can tell he's had a few parts replaced in his legs, and that they desperately need tuning. I can hear the gears and electronics push and reset every few steps. It amazes me, the resilience of the Downlanders. Without a thing, they've figured out how to operate, adjust and calibrate. Imagine what they could do with access to our tech.

"What are you looking at?" Jai spits his words at me. "Don't get funny and think about trying something, eh?"

"I wasn't. It's just . . . I could help you with your limp. It's a flash easy fix edit—"

His fist is hard on my face as soon as the words come out my mouth. A rush of blood fills my mouth, leaving a strange metal taste. So much blood. My hands are covered in it. I'm not sure if it comes from my nose or mouth or where. I've never seen my own blood before, let alone tasted it.

He pushes me against the tunnel wall. "Do you think I want anything from you? Do you think for one second that your life is worth anything to me? It's not. I'd sooner toss you into the sea than have to babysit you. But I'm a good soldier. I do as I'm told. And right now, you're going to keep your mouth shut and make this journey a lot more pleasant for us both. Nod if you get me."

I nod my head.

"Don't cry, Uplander. This will all be over soon. I'm not going to kill ya. You're not worth much to us dead, eh?"

My shirt catches the blood. For a second, he almost looks like he feels sorry for me.

"You have no idea what's coming, do you?" Jai says before he pushes me to walk ahead of him. "What they've done to you, to us all?"

No way to answer that one. But maybe it's not even a real question, so I just stare.

"You think I'm pathetic. But it's worse for you. So sad." He flicks my neural-synch and says, "No control, kid."

"I'm not like them," I say.

"Everyone thinks they're on the right side. Scary thing is, even the villains think they're right. If everyone's a zealot, who can be right?"

When we reach the end of the tunnel, we climb a makeshift ladder that leads to the world above. The first breath of air is life-giving, but the second smells just as badly as the air below. I don't know how the Downlanders do it. A violent coughing fit chokes my lungs, but Jai doesn't notice or, more likely, he just doesn't care.

He wraps a piece of fabric around my eyes. A door creaks open, heavy, metallic, old. Then it locks behind me with a permanence only metal can achieve. Someone pushes me to sit on the cold, wet ground and then I wonder if I am left alone.

"Hello?" My voice echoes in the silent, cold room. My mind races without sight. Every inch of my skin crawls, and my head spins, up or down is anyone's guess. I try to focus, but the chills catch me. I'm going to be sick.

Footsteps, if they could be called footsteps, drag and scrape the concrete floor. Then someone takes off my blind-fold and the rush of light blinds me even more.

I size up the room. Two boys, bigger and dumber looking than the next, with Jai at the helm, spinning a fist blade against the filthy floor, dulling the tip with each rotation. A few cheap-looking Downlander girls draping themselves across an expensive-looking, mismatched living room outfitted with expensive rugs, chairs, lamps. Pilfered things from Central. Thieves, all of them.

My eyes land on the sun around which these people orbit: a massive, fleshy boy sitting atop a chair made from the finest materials, extinct wood, cashmere fabrics. "You must be the techie. What's your real name, techie?" His voice clicks at the end of his words, like he's sucking some old bit of food from his tooth.

I bite my tongue, then remember the name of my flatmate. "Sidharth. What's yours?"

Jai jabs me in the ribs with the butt of his blade. "If we want a two-way conversation, we'll ask for one."

"Chup, you ape," the Sun says to Jai. "Take off, eh?" He signals to the entire room and his people flee like street dogs.

"So, tell me, Sid, what do you do in Central?" He leans all the way back in his chair and it creaks under his weight.

"Data," I say. "I work for Solace Corp."

"I see." He looks pleased. "What brings you to our edge of the network? It's not every day you find an Uplander slumming it down here."

"I was just lost. I'd always heard of the Liminal Area and got lost trying to find the ruins."

When he smiles, it's clear he's replaced his two front teeth with translucent gems. "No connection must be driving you crazy."

"Actually—"

"No matter. Baitho!" He points his massive hand to a small bench across from him and I sit. "Lost, you say? No one gets lost down here because no one's dumb enough to come down here in the first place. It's dangerous, being out of your element, but you know that now."

"I am not like the other Uplanders, sahib."

"Call me Khan Zadabhai."

My heart shakes like glass. Caught by the notorious gangster. His crew runs the Liminal Area and the Narrows, and works with the Lal Hath. He is the only one profiting off of the division of the South Asian Province. And he is really profiting. Hands in everything, they say.

"Yes, Khan Zadabhai. Right, I'm a freelance coder."

"A double player. Never heard of one of those. Why would you risk everything you have in Central? Oh wait, let me guess: You like to have a little fun on the underweb. Maybe got into some gambling or drug edits or something else? Maybe

parents are pressuring you too much to be, I don't know, perfect? Getting close?"

"What are you going to do with me?" My voice feels small.

"Not kill you, if that's what you mean to ask. Everything
down here has a price, and you, techie, could probably fetch
an island-sized pile of marks on the undermarket."

"Sell me? Who'd want to buy an Uplander?"

"You'd be surprised what people want down here. Body
parts, testing. Hell, I heard of some Liminal desi who came
into a sudden inheritance and bought a whole Uplander family, just to toss 'em in the Sea. Who knows? It's not my job to
ask. These are strange times." His laugh is full of echoes and
scrap metal.

The thought of being sold and dissected like a science
project makes me want to throw up. "Look, I'm sure I can be of
benefit to you somehow. I mean I have connections to money.
People would pay for my release."

"Who, and what would they pay?" His gapped-tooth grin is
too cheerful.

"I don't know, maybe Solace Corp would. Or my family."

"Solace and Central have a no-negotiation policy," he says.

"But they do. They tell people they don't. But everyone
knows the last thing they want is for the body of an Uplander
to turn up dead. It would be such bad comms." I stand. Khan
motions for me to sit.

"Or maybe that's exactly what they want." His lack of
laughter invites chaos.

"That would be insane. Why fight for balance and the future only to blow the whole thing up?"

He lifts his massive body off the chair and moves too

close to my face. He isn't obese, just gigantic. I freeze. "Some of us do quite well with chaos and war."

Then I know. He holds his blade to my temple and presses right beneath my neural-synch. "You're not worth anything to me, but this, this pays on the undermarket."

"Wait! I have money saved. I've got 10KR marks. And I can code. I know Solace. I must be worth something."

Khan's expression shifts. Like he sees something in my neural-synch that gives him pause. "Interesting choice, with the dull finish on your neural-synch. You're from the high Stratas in Central, aren't you?"

"No, I . . ." I say, but he doesn't buy it. I should have made mine flashier like everyone else. He's reading my choices.

"You're ultra-rich, yaar, aren't ya? Trying to convince everyone that you're just an average Uplander. But you really hate it. You're embarrassed by your money. You hate your neural-synch, your privilege. You want to hide it. Blend in. You're trying too hard." Khan calls out, "Jai, get your sorry bum in here!"

Jai enters the room like a scared dog.

Khan turns to him and says, "This one won't pay, Jai, you ullu ka patha. You brought us an uppy, but the wrong kind. Get this one back inside Central without a scratch. I'll let his family know of the favor so they can bury his trouble-making. That's how we get paid. Chalo, Jai!"

"How do we do that?" Jai asks.

"I've got a job for Tiger. Need to get this uppy back home before the boss gets worried. White glove 'em."

Jai points a tube-like device at me and shoots.

"Hey, what the—?" The needle-sharp edges of a small round disc sink into my chest with metal clamps.

"It'll keep them off of our trail as we go. Just causes noise in your tech, is all."

I know Khan and Jai are talking, but I can only make out a few of their words. Something about Uplander and return and the Minister of Comms. They know.

A fabric hood falls quickly over my head and I am blind, again.

Being alone, after not being alone for so long, feels like someone removed my organs and skeleton, and stitched me back together. Empty. Like I'm not real. Like none of this could be real.

Yesterday's raid has turned the undermarket into a ghost town. The few people remaining are starving, and if they can't sell their wares, they'll have nothing to eat. Faced with the two choices of death by starvation or death by guardian, some make the choice to stay in the undermarket in case the violence lets up. Guardians are patrolling and their battle in the Narrows continues—the flying transports buzz, their soldiers smash. The mechas crunch earth. The air is bitter with smoke. Usually, the tunnels that connect the Narrows and the Liminal Area is packed with people trading goods, food, spices, electronic parts, even medicine. All things we can't get easily like the Uplanders. But now, after the raid, it's sickly quiet and dark. Dark and safe. Those who remain are scared. I can feel it. It's like it already happened here too. How am I supposed to find people who don't want to be found?

The wall catches my body. The world is spinning so fast; my face feels hot. Heat suffocates me. But something catches my foot, and I fall to my hands and knees into a puddle. Hot, foul water splashes my face.

The first thing I see are her eyes.

They're open. Lifeless.

"Taru?!" I gasp. Her face. My heart.

But no, not Taru. I wipe my eyes of the filth. A woman. A dead woman. I back away from her body and sit a minute. Was it the Fever? I don't see a blue rash. She doesn't seem sick. It's as though she went to sleep and didn't wake up. I look for wounds, but no, it was the heat. Her skin is blistered, burned. It kills just as easily as a sonic cannon, as starvation.

Her family is probably dead already. No one to care for her even after death takes her. I lift her body in my arms and carry her to the side. Cover her face with her dupatta, a sign the corpse-bearers will understand when they do their daily rounds. They will take her to the Dakhma, the high tower away from the Narrows, where they burn the bodies. Once used for exposing their dead to the carrion birds, the Dakhma is now empty of the birds that have long fled. So, everyone has accepted fire as the final change. We have no earth to bury our dead. The water would just carry them back to us. Cremation eliminates the risk of disease. It's all we have. Die from the heat, leave in the flames.

I think of my sister as I wash my hands in the market stall. I hope I haven't made her weak with my lies when all I wanted was for her to be safe, to protect her. I changed her health records to make it seem like she had a form of juvenile osteoporosis. I forced Masiji to sign off on it. I was planning on telling her she grew out of the disorder when she was older. But I only wanted her to be safe. Alive.

What have I done?

No one here will turn me in. But they won't die for me either. They've suffered enough. Thousands of Downlanders could have escaped here too. They must be hiding.

A well-worn voice calls to anyone passing, "Divination,

here. Astrology, raashifal, here!" He sings like the world isn't burning all around us.

The voice speaks in many dialects. When he speaks in Masiji's language, I pause in front of his stall. It's a lesser known language, an old-speak. Suddenly, I'm just fighting to find a way to survive this. I'm right back to feeling her ripped from my hands by the guardian. The voice belongs to a man who's probably only forty, but looks older because of the particulates and toxins that penetrate the Narrows and every cell of those who live within it.

Keep going. My boots slam hard against the wet concrete. Just what everyone needs, to waste what little they have on false hope. Maybe it's not so bad, maybe I actually believe in the horoscope and divination readers too. But . . . not today. Today I have to find the originators of the Red Hand.

A man the size of a child stands in my way. His dhoti is carefully wrapped around his thin waist over military-grade cargo pants. He wears a well-worn vest as a shirt. "You, girl, you're showing some bright colors today." It's the astrologer.

"Save it for someone who has a few marks to spare, Uncle."

His hand rests on my shoulder, not something I usually allow. But he is an elder. "Girl, this is free, a gift. Why would I want your marks when I know you don't have any?"

He reaches out to touch the necklace around my neck, my gift from Taru, and I push him away.

"Old man, I'm obviously from the Narrows, so that isn't really prophetic," I say. But there's something alluring about him, like he has a secret. Gifts, in my life, are few and far between. More like nonexistent.

"Eh, maybe I read you wrong." His smile is rich, full of

buried secrets. "It happens once in a while."

"Okay, quickly though, chalo," I say, glancing over my shoulder.

"Beti, sit, please." The old man holds onto his hip, supporting himself like a tree bending in an invisible wind. He signals to the smallest stall I've ever seen: two pillows, a small table, a bowl and a curtain that conceals the stall.

I hesitate. Sitting isn't on my list today. But during our brief exchange, I realized how tired I am. I've been going without sleep or rest for at least a day. I press my hands together and sit on the small, tattered pillow. Though I am exposed, my body gives into gravity.

"What now, Uncle?" I ask as he feeds a fire in a metal bowl with a few small, oiled twigs. They catch and a rich gray smoke works into the air of his stall, acidic and sweet.

He draws the curtain closed, dimming the stall, and sits beside me. His spectacles turn his eyes into ancient satellite dishes.

"So . . . ?" A 3D mini screen casts the solar system around us. Certain constellations are brighter than others. The stars. I know they are out there somewhere, past the smog and haze, and glare. I've never seen the whole night sky before. But this isn't the time for luxuries.

"Patience."

Enough of these dreams. I rise. "Patience? You do know that the Narrows were cleared for the Fever, right? That most are probably heading to containment? To die, or worse?" I shake my head. "My little sister . . ." I can't even finish the sentence.

"Hush, beti. I am aware." His small hand touches my replacement arm without hesitation. "Trust me, you want to see this."

He lifts a shawl and exposes a control panel. A few clicks and it lights up.

"How do you have connection here?"

"Not everyone uses the same network. They look only to the future, but it's the devices of the past that are most secure and untraceable. This is from a long, long time ago. So long ago that Central forgot."

"Interesting," I take in the strange, thick pieces of metal. "What are these? Keys? What's that?" I touch the surface of the clunky metal bits and he swats my hand.

"Eh, yes. Well, The Mechanic warned me that your veins buzz with electricity, Tiger."

"How do you know …"

"Ashiva, you're here to find the elders of the Lal Hath?"

"How do you—"

"Hang on to something."

With that, the old man turns a crank in the floor, and we begin to move lower and lower, down below the market. His thin arms tremble as he shuts a hatch above us and we continue into total darkness.

"An old elevator shaft? Where are you taking me?"

"Down, obviously. Be patient," his voice says in the dark.

It was still light out; I remember because of the auburn haze that cut through the view across Central from our flat. It surrounded the city like an apocalyptic sunset, otherworldly, and reminded me of the surface of Mars. When I was younger, I wondered if Earth was becoming like Mars. At twelve, I was still fascinated by astronomy. The new game Kanwar Uncle brought me was slow going, beyond my ability. Worst of all, Endless Planet was a single-player game that took forever and I had to solve equations in order to acquire tools. But I played it anyway, in the living room, set up my character, and launched an initial campaign into the galaxy to discover new inhabitable planets. He and Father were in the study at the end of their workday, talking, while Mother worked late. I remember everything like it was a film, and I have relived it over and over again, a million times, with forensic accuracy, in case I missed something. I've scoured the memory, like a permanent blood stain. Their voices were low, but I could hear everything, even through my headphones, because I turned the volume way down.

"Kanwar, you're being ridiculous." My father's dismissive tone was my least favorite.

"Anik, I know what I saw. Don't ask me to forget it." Uncle's sigh was volatile.

"It's easy. I do it all day long. You can pretend to forget. It was an accident. You weren't meant to see the results, the plans. Move on. Deny. Deny. Deny." Father slapped his hands together.

Lie? I remember that clearest of all. To my father, the truth was the only god.

Ice in glasses clinked. "Deny? You've known, haven't you. All this time. You've lied to me. You've lied to everyone. How can you wake up every day and do what you do? It's unimaginable."

"I do it for today, for Riza. Just because the data is abysmal doesn't mean that one of the Provinces will not find a solution. It's still possible. Have faith, brother."

Endless Planet celebrated with cheers and an explosion of glitter on the screen as my character leapt across Mars' moon, Phobos. Then their voices quieted.

"I need to make the drop, Anik. I already made the contact." Uncle's voice was tired.

"You're like a brother to me. You've put us all at risk. Promise me, Kanu. Promise me." I'd never heard my father so desperate. But what he was asking Kanwar Uncle to promise, I don't know. "They will not look upon this favorably. It's a serious offence. You have to stop sending them info."

"Okay, okay."

Kanwar Uncle was changed, though.

At the time, I had no idea what they were talking about. The Red Hand wasn't a topic we discussed. But now, reflecting back, this feels like everything. Now, it's starting to make sense. My uncle must have known something; he was agitated about it. He needed help. They talked about work over whiskey nearly every time they could. But I'd never heard this worried tone in my father's voice. It was starting to make sense now, after finding the note in Uncle's plans. Was my father was pleading with Uncle to stop sending the Red Hand

intel? Stop connecting with them, maybe? Or maybe someone else? Father asked Uncle to promise him to do something,
but what?

My father was called back to the laboratory for an emergency situation that night, something about the reactor, but
Kanwar Uncle stayed. He turned off the kitchen bots and all
the house helper bots, and we cooked dinner together.

"People are better company than machines, don't you
think, Riza?" he said with a smile.

I nodded. He made me feel so special.

"What would you like for dinner, puttar? Let me guess . . .
onion omelet?"

I laughed. It was the only thing he could make. "Yes,
please!" I put on music for our cooking time. I cracked the
eggs, he sliced the onions. The house smelled of home. We ate
together quietly.

"Slow down. You're going to choke!" he said, but I wanted
to get to the good stuff.

We washed the dishes and put them away; a job the bots
would have easily done, but he wanted me to remember how
to do it.

"Come on, I've brought you something very interesting today," he said, sitting on the couch, holding a small box.

"What is it?" Presents from him were special, not like the
things Mother and Father gave me, which were basically what
their assistants bought for me. Uncle knew me.

"First, you must swear a promise to me. That you'll never
show this to anyone, okay? It's our secret. Promise?" He
showed me his pinky finger. It was the ultimate unbreakable
promise.

"Yes!" I said, and spun my little finger around his and squeezed. "What is it?"

"Open it." He handed me a thin box. I lifted the lid and inside were small rolls of blue synth paper with code. At least twenty, each the thickness of a pen. I took one and unrolled it. The next one was the same. It was too advanced for me. Some had images of robotic plans, some had diagrams, others were just more unreadable code.

"Keep it safe for me. Okay? Can you do that?"

I nodded. "But what are they?"

"When you're old enough, you'll be able to read them yourself." He tousled my hair. "The secret is in the agribots, puttar."

"Is that all?" I was not impressed. Now, thinking back, there's a pain in my chest because I know he was saying goodbye. That he wanted me to have something of his to remember him by. He must have known he was going to die.

He feigned shock. "I thought you'd be so happy with a box." He laughed such a hearty laugh, his whole body shook. "You see right through me. Here is my real present." He handed me a small blue robot the size of a cricket ball. It had arms and legs, and big black eyes that blinked at me.

"Wow! What is it?" The mini-bot chirped and stretched out its arms as though it wanted to be hugged.

"He's a playmate. I've programmed him to play chess, to read books, to sing. But he's not very good at singing. Anyway, you can program him to do whatever you want." Uncle twisted his moustache with his fingertips.

"But I have you to play chess with."

"Of course you do. Let's play?" We played two games. He

won both, but taught me why, and I went to sleep. It was like most other nights.

I remember Uncle was sitting on the edge of my bed, the shadows falling across his face like a shroud, and my eyes heavy with sleep.

That was the last time I saw him.

His funeral was three days later.

After—when we moved—my mother made me leave his robot in the old house because it was childish.

I need to get the plans from my apartment. Now, I'm stuck in the sewers with a pagal, crazy dude, far, far away from Central. I stumble in the tunnel as we walk and laugh at myself. If only Uncle could see me now. He'd be so proud that I'd left the comfort of my home. That I'm challenging the world around me. Jai lifts my hood and the world around me overwhelms me.

"Why are you so cheerful, yaar? We're selling you to a syndicate that just might flay you and leave you out for all of Central to see," Jai says.

"Uh huh," I say.

"It would be on every comms across the Province. Did I mention the likely pain and agony you'd endure? Did you hear what I said?"

"Sure, Jai," I say. "Flayed. Central. Comms. I get it." I count seventeen steps to the next tunnel entrance.

He puts his arm out to stop me from walking. "You're an odd one. Most usually take a piss or beg the whole way."

My hands shake as I try to push my long hair into a bun. I can't control them. "But I'm no use to anyone dead, even them. Trust me."

"Hang on, what's going on with your mitts? They look a little jumbly."

Jai's a strange boy, to say the least. He's free, can do anything he wants, say anything he wants, and it doesn't matter. No one watching him, monitoring him, telling him what to do. Well, except for Khan Zadabhai. He has only one master. I have many.

A sickness steals across my body. I never let it get this far before using the auto-injector, and crashing from THink is making it worse. The gen-cybernetic doctors say my body is rejecting the neural-synch because I'm not compliant, not because I'm lacking intelligence. But my mother makes it clear that non-conformity is a fracture in her façade of perfection. That I am inconveniencing her. They agreed to give me the Injector medication for one year to see if it took. If not, they say, well, there's an experimental treatment. I don't have a say. She decides for me.

"What's wrong, mate?" Jai asks, though he doesn't sound worried, more amused.

"I'm okay. Let's go."

"No, I'm serious, yaar. You're turning yellow. Nope, wait a second, green."

And he's right. I throw up and feel better, like I can breathe again.

"Okay, that was disgusting."

I put up my hand. "Keep going. I'm fine. Just no more hood, okay?"

"For now, but I'll have to put it on before we arrive."

We meet a small boy on the corner of two tunnels, and he slips something thin and flat that looks like a data-chip into

Jai's hand. The kid takes off, and I see Jai slide the chip into a reader in his wrist. Jai is full of surprises.

"Who does the ghost tech surgery down here? That wrist reader is brilliant work. I don't see a scar at all," I say.

He ignores me, but doesn't hit me, so that's progress.

"Oh, I get it. The kid gave you directions or something. Am I right?"

Still silence. Hours pass trudging through the filthy tunnels. I count the entryways, broken signs, piles of refuse until I forget what I'm counting. Finally, we reach a shaft that goes down even further. I wonder if Central had maps of these tunnels or if Central even knew they exist. I wonder if we are below sea level because of the humidity. My legs are tired and my face is numb. The sickness is going to take me. It's just a matter of time. I want to go home now. I want the comfort of my bed, and the annoying nanny-bot Taz to make me some dinner. My life is worlds away from the living nightmare in which I'm trapped.

I count ten tunnels, and stop counting the garbage after one hundred and six pieces.

 **18 // ASHIVA**

As I follow the old man through the elevator, I consider my mission: get to the elders, find a way to free Masiji and the others. Sounds simple in my head, but the more I think about it, the more I realize this is the worst type of plan for three reasons.

1: The C.O.R.E mechas completely change the game. Humans against humans is one thing, but the scales tip in their favor with the mecha-suits. Some of us are part-machine, but none of us have an exoskeleton or the funding of the South Asian Province.

2: To find my family, I need to hack Solace, and if I hack Solace, I'll be traced as unauthorized and the SA will find me.

3: I don't trust the originators of the Red Hand. They left the Red Hand since the reorganization, and turned their backs on us.

There, I said it.

Masiji puts all her faith in them, like a religious cult, but I've never met them in person. They're phantoms that slip into conversations about the past, when she talks about life before the launch of the neural-synch. She always gets this look in her eyes when she mentions them, like they're saints, the original team that brought the Red Hand to life. I know they had a falling-out, but I never learned the specifics. But saints are dreams not worth believing in. And if someone thinks they are a saint, they are a liar or worse.

The old man leads me into a dark corridor, and I curse myself for trusting him. He could very well take me to Central authorities. Desperate people are capable of anything. Hunger motivates like no other. But still I follow. He says he knows Masiji. I have no other leads anyway. I can easily overpower him with my replacement, and I think he knows that. I hope he knows that.

"Just a little further, beti," the old man says.

If he calls me daughter, he wouldn't be setting me up for slaughter. Right?

"You know, it'll be very disappointing if I had to hurt an elder," I say.

He stops. With one swift motion, he turns to face me and presses his rough hand to my cheek. His dark eyes have shadows within shadows.

"You have every reason to hate this world, and yet you don't. Your life has been one constant challenge, a test of strength, mental and physical. I don't blame you for not trusting me. In fact, I'd think you were not the young woman described to me if you did." His chuckle is a swift breath in, followed by a coughing fit.

"You aren't selling me out for a few ration pods?" I ask as I follow him into darker and darker rooms.

"For a few thousand, maybe I'd consider it." He smiles. "No, why would that benefit me? I live in the same world as you, breathe the same toxic air, drink the same filthy water. There's no way we can prevail if we do not work together." He tosses his shawl over his shoulder. "But please, don't take my word for it." He swipes his hand in a grand gesture from left to right and my heart skips. "We are here."

"What is this place?" I take in the expansive, round room.

"This is where it all began."

The circular room is covered in dust. There are control panels on the far end, and the edges are sectioned off like it was an office of some kind a long time ago. Posters of the Rani are plastered on the metal walls, ads from a different time, a different battle entirely than the one that faces me.

"Is that original?" I touch the image of her face in black and white and red stencil. A red bloody handprint in the center on her chest. She is beautiful, stark, just a girl who got caught up in a much larger conflict.

"You know it?"

"Who doesn't? She inspired a revolution. Murdered by the guardians in their first defense of the new Central Ring. She was a schoolgirl murdered by Uplanders. Masiji told me the story many times. They named her the Rani. Queen. Her death during the Crimson Riots got Central to open the gates again, if only temporarily."

"Yes, I'm glad to see you have the story straight," he says. "I made it, you see."

"You made the Rani poster? But you're so…"

"Old, useless … I wasn't always so." His smile is almost silly. "I made more than the poster."

"What do you mean?" I scan the room and realize what a strange place this is: odds and ends of a control system, bits and pieces of ancient computer parts, monitors, all made from the same heavy metal and plastic. It's a flitting museum.

"Ghaazi made me," a woman's voice calls like fresh, cold water in the hot, dank room.

"Who said that?" But I see her before I need an answer. She's thin, tall and elegant. Her gray and white hair is pulled into a tight bun at the nape of her neck. And she wears body armor; I notice it's woven directly into her black and gray kurta and pajama. Clever. Her whole appearance says, "Don't cross me" and "Give me a hug" at the same time. Deadly combo.

"Hello, Ashiva. I'm so glad to finally meet you." She hugs me. I stiffen like a piece of wire caught in a clamp.

"Er, who are you?"

"I'm the Rani." She gently presses both her hands against my cheeks as though she wants to get inside my mind. "But my given name is Surinder. Call me Suri. Everyone does."

"Impossible! I saw the footage of your death. It was so brutal."

"Good. I'm glad even your generation remembers. Ghaazi Sahib made sure of it. How did you disseminate it to the network comms? It was genius."

The old man looks pleased. "I linked it to a comms release from Solace, so every neural-synch saw the footage. It was only a matter of time before all other networks picked it up. We super-imposed video from the Great Migration, recorded new video in a studio and edited the perspective. It's amazing what you can do."

I push away from both of them.

"Sit down, please," she says.

"I don't need to sit down." My temple pulses. "You're telling me that the Rani wasn't real? It was all a performance? I need answers. I'm looking for the Lal Hath. I need their help—we need to continue the mission." I repeat this over and over and over until the sound in my ears is gone, like the pressure in my head won't let any sound pass. I close my eyes, and see the mechas smash and light the Narrows on fire.

Ghaazi brings me water in a tall metal container. Filtered. Cold.

"Where did you get this?"

"Doesn't matter."

Suddenly, though, the crisp water is all that matters to me. It's how I imagine nectar might be. The kind they write about in the old stories. Until then, I hadn't realized how empty my system was. My hunger and thirst awake. I steady my thoughts and listen.

"Daughter, the whole thing was cooked up as a story to get our message to the world. If no one knows, no one will care. It gave us time to fight another day."

"Huh. But it backfired?" I ask.

"Not really. We gained the eyes of others and spread the mission of the Red Hand across the world before WWIII and the New Treaty forced us to separate and go underground. It didn't cause Central to tighten their grip and close the gates to their precious neocity, even as climate exiles were desperately running from the rising seas on the coasts. That was part of their plan all along. But it's easier to blame a revolutionary group for the evil decisions. Easier to say we had to keep safe from "those dangerous poor people." With their select small populations, they ramped up Solace, installed the neuralsynchs in the young and old who passed the test, and then they locked the gates. There was nothing we could do."

Hearing that an entire part of our revolutionary history is made up, an act, a performance, unhinges me. What's real? I put the water bottle down and wipe my mouth, aware now of the greedy mess I am making of myself.

"I need to contact the elders of the Red Hand. Masiji said they could help me." My eyes search the room for evidence of the great collection of revolutionaries.

The woman's voice is clear and soothing. "We are them. What's left of us at least, here in the SA."

It is like all the electricity in Central enters my body at once. "You can't be serious. You're it?"

"I'm afraid so," Ghaazi says and salutes me like a soldier. "Pilot, First Class, Third World War, Air Team."

My replacement fist clenches and the need to hurt something pulses through me, to break something, anything. "Why am I wasting my time?" I stand. "You can't help me find my family. You're only two..."

"Wait, Ashiva," Suri says.

"There's no time to wait. By now, Masiji, Taru and Zami could be..." My mouth won't let those words out, not yet. "We need new leadership, a new plan."

"But Ashiva..."

"I can't believe only two members are left. She spoke about you like you were many. What a scam. I need to find the surviving Red Hand members." I say and keep going. I'll start by hacking containment records from the Liminal Area. Surely they haven't figured out how we uplink from there. The Red Hand beyond the borders of the SA are many across the world. They have marks, but here in the Narrows we are small. And the SA stole the children, scattered us like ants.

Suri says, "I think we owe it to her, to you, to help if we can."

"How can you possibly help?" Just two people on the outer edge of life. What could they possibly do to help us?

Ghaazi lifts a tarp and dust flies into the air like ash. Underneath is a console and a monitor, ancient gear. "Let's listen to the chitchat on the underweb. Then you can go do whatever you like. Okay?"

"What network is this?"

"None Solace would recognize. The first one," he says.

"Okay, sure. But let me lead." I slide into the chair beside him and get going. The machines are even older than ours, but I figure out the basic ideas quickly. "There's something I should check on. We could use all the allies we can get." I type code to enter the massive open market cloud where the Uplander techie may have dropped the data packet. I search tags for the hacking challenge.

"What are you looking for?" Suri is looking over my shoulder like Masiji would have been if she was here.

"A hacking challenge. There it is. Kid Synch didn't disappoint."

"What is it, Ashiva? The open market is dangerous. Anyone could be watching," Ghaazi says.

I read the name of the file, "Himalaya. Let's see what you're made of."

"Wait! Don't!" Suri goes to stop my hand from clicking on the file, but it's too late. The code slips across the old screen like water overfilling a bowl.

"What the—?"

"Close the system, Ghaazi, now!" Suri says. Ghaazi scrambles and pushes me out of the way, hard resetting the system.

"It might be too late. I don't know," he says.

"What's on that file? Masiji would talk about it sometimes," I say.

Their faces are pale and stern at the same time. "You don't know then?" Ghaazi asks.

"Know what?"

"Masiji was an architect of Solace. She ran the engineering team that built Solace's code for the algorithm. This is her backup. She always named things after the mountains of her childhood," he says.

"Masiji? Solace?" My world shatters around me like so much glass. "But she hates Solace. That can't be."

Suri says, "Listen, we were the two other engineers on her team. We had philosophical differences, which led to a falling out. We weren't willing to go to the extremes that she was. She helped design the neural-synch to optimize the reduced population, so as few people as possible passed the Solace test. We couldn't stand by the neural-synch, not knowing how much control it could possibly give Central over their population. The neural-synch improved the mental capacity of the few who were allowed to thrive inside Central. Masiji thought she could decide who should live in this world. We own up to our contribution to Solace. But it was when Central wouldn't approve her next level of tests that she decided to fake her death, run away, and continue her experiments in the Narrows."

"Wait. What are you saying?"

Suri presses her hand to her mouth as though the act could erase her words. Then she lets go. "I'm sorry, Ashiva. The Children of Without is her project. She couldn't stop. Yes, on one hand she is helping the children. She teaches them, heals them. But what if she's still conducting tests? We couldn't stand by her. But we weren't strong enough to stop her. And when the Red Hand separated, no one was there to watch her closely enough."

"But that sounds like Solace, like Central. She hates Uplanders," I say.

"Exactly. She's jealous of their access to technology. She hates Solace because she knows it better than anybody. This must have been hidden in storage. How did you find the data packet anyway?"

"I didn't. A hacker who works for Solace Corp did. It was a test I set up to see if we could recruit an insider." I can't wrap my head around Masiji ever working on the program that basically ended our lives.

"I wonder, why now," Ghaazi says. "Central is always looking for a reason, an opportunity."

"For what?" I ask. "To clear the Narrows?"

Suri exhales sharply. "They've been dying to cleanse the area of their failures. The Narrows is a glaring reminder that their solution doesn't work for an entire population. The New Treaty states Provinces can't eliminate their own people outright, so they came up with reasons they can justify to the PAC. The Z Fever is one reason. Even if it wasn't really there, contagions might travel faster amongst a closer population."

"The Narrows was always hanging in the balance," Ghaazi says. "The Red Hand is always planning something. Still, there's no such thing as coincidence."

I walk to the farthest part of the round room and sink to the floor. "It has to be AllianceCon. At the last Red Hand Council meeting, Masiji talked about joining forces again. It was an in-person meeting. Even General Shankar showed his face. They were in negotiations. They were planning for an assault during the conference. What if Central found out? She said they'd been pinged and they patched the problems. But that could mean that…"

Suri stands. "There's a spy inside the Red Hand Council."

Dhat. Was Masiji right in suspecting General Shankar? Was Masiji the spy? "It doesn't matter right now." All I can see are the mechas rounding up the children like animals. Masiji was a mechanic; she needed to fix and build. But she wouldn't send her children, the ones she cared so much about, to slaughter.

Suri says, "The different cells of the Red Hand are designed to sustain massive casualties. We've done it before. This is not the first time we've had to begin again. We continue. More will follow. We are thousands around the world. Don't let Central know the truth about the losses. They'll have no way of confirming it. The council members who survived will follow the fallout protocols."

"So, pretend that we're stronger than we are?"

"Exactly."

"But who will lead until we find them?"

Suri and Ghaazi exchange looks. Together, they could easily command. They have a wealth of knowledge. Maybe they're not as in touch as they were when they were younger, but that's no matter. They could inspire people, conjure some underground propaganda campaign. They've done it before, they can do it again.

Ghaazi moves toward me. "Ashiva, you've trained your entire life under Masiji. You've protected the Children of Without. They know you. You've even stood guard at Red Hand Council meetings and probably heard more than you should."

"Yes, I have. So?"

Suri looks puzzled by me. "You should step up, Tiger. It's only natural."

"What? Me? No. I'm not ready. I'm not even a lieutenant yet. No. You both are suited for this. It's obvious."

"We need to be on the outside to find the remaining members, to guide them," Ghaazi says. "We have the External Hand connections across the globe, which are vital to reconnecting the Hand. We need to focus on that. We need you inside, to offer internal support. To run the missions. The young people will listen to you, the recruits will come to your side. We've been out so long that your network won't recognize us. We will lead the External Hand now. And you will lead the rest until we recover from these losses. People see you and will follow you. You are a lieutenant now, Tiger. Don't worry, we'll assist with everything we can."

"But I don't even know what's true. Masiji worked on Solace..." I say to no one in particular. How can I do anything if I don't even know what's real? My world breaks. The arm she gave me feels fake, heavy, unwilling. I wipe my dry eyes and swallow the guilt like bile.

"Your heart is true," Ghaazi says. "Your love for your sister is true. Your need to save the Narrows and the people is true. And honestly, there's nothing better in a leader than that basic truth. It gets so muddled when politics are involved."

I've never felt like more of an imposter in my life. I can't lead. I follow orders.

We are unloaded on a dock and sorted again. Masiji is forced to leave me and line up behind the elderly people. She doesn't say a word—something is changed in her. But I see it in her limp. She's badly injured and needs a mediport right away. I wonder what happened to her. My guesses, I pray, are worse than the truth.

They keep us in the dark at first. The warm skin of people sitting beside me makes me sweat. I don't want them to touch me, so I inch away as far as I can to be sure they won't. I jump with each jostle and loud noise outside. Like the sound is enough to crash down upon us and smash our bodies to bits. There's only enough light to see the outlines of faces. Some are crying. Others are moaning.

I think about Ashiva, and how she'd bust down a wall and break this place until most of the people are free or dead, or at least have a chance. But I'm not Ashiva. I see a nightmare with my open eyes. I don't know what's real. I have no idea who I am, so I hold onto the simple truths. "My name is Taru," I say. "It's going to be okay."

A raspy male voice rips through me. "Quiet, girl. They'll just kill us faster."

"Don't be so harsh, bhai," a girl's voice says.

"Chup," he says, "I know how this goes. I heard they burned villages in the Eastern District when they suspected disease. Not just the structures: the village, people, everything. The disease moves fast. My uncle told me about it. He watched the whole thing in the Americas. It's disgusting. People suffocate as they become paralyzed."

Children cry out.

"We have to stay calm, please," the girl says. "My name is Jasmine, Taru," she whispers.

"Thank you," I say. "Jasmine." What a beautiful name. A beautiful girl.

"Are you injured?" she asks.

"No, I just have a limp. My bones, they're brittle."

She nods. She shows me her forearm replacement. "We are all the same, sister."

I don't know how much time passes, but finally the doors open and guardians lead us into the containment shelter. Jasmine is taller than me, maybe older. We stay close, but they won't let us look at each other as we march in the dark on a long pathway made of dirt. Water is splashing nearby.

When we enter a structure, at first, I see figures that look like animals in massive room-like cages with transparent, plastic walls. But as we get closer, it's clear: The rooms are filled with neighbors, friends, children, all in different positions and states of health. Most look starved, thin, almost like the life has been sucked out of them. Some look as though they've been here for a long time, while others I know just arrived. Others are much worse, covered in bandages, sitting on the hard, metal ground, with wires embedded in their arms and heads, connecting them to a monitoring system.

They only took those of us with replacements. I recognize many faces.

"Where are we?" Jasmine asks.

We are in a dreaded place, and we aren't alone. Hundreds

or maybe more are kept here. Though I can't tell yet, there has to be a reason for the arrangement of the cubes.

"I don't know," I say. I've heard of these places from Masiji's stories. I feel badly for lying, but it's best that no one knows what I know: they can do anything they please with us. This isn't the ordinary containment in Central—the flight would have been shorter. This is something else entirely, a dark off-site. The medi-staff wanders this way and that. Their tablets, monitors and computer are in front. They look to be studying us. But for what, I don't know. Not yet. I wonder if the world knows what's happening or if it's been hidden under lies from Central.

It smells like sweat. Though they run the climate system, it isn't enough to actually cool us. And with so many bodies, it's only a matter of time before people collapse from the heat.

"Inside," is all a guardian says, and they push us in a unit already filled with a few children.

"This is it," says the boy with the raspy voice. "I wonder how long we have until—"

"Oh, cool off, bhai," Jasmine says.

There are several medi-staff roaming the facility, taking data, giving rations. Doctors, their assistants and younger people, who are probably runners. A group comes to our unit and the assistant speaks very little to us. Instead, the assistant plays a message on his device of President Ravindra that projects in a 3D holo-screen. Her fuchsia sari is beautifully clean.

"YOU ARE HERE BECAUSE YOU'VE BEEN INFECTED BY THE Z FEVER. YOU WILL BECOME VERY ILL AND MOST LIKELY WILL DIE. BUT THERE'S ONE THING YOU CAN DO TO HELP: ALLOW US TO TEST THE INOCULATION. BY BEING A PART OF THIS PROJECT, YOU CAN SAVE THE LIVES OF MILLIONS AND, POSSIBLY, YOURSELVES. IT'S THE ONLY WAY. WE THANK YOU FOR YOUR SERVICE AND BRAVERY FOR THE SA PROVINCE."

"Line up," the assistant in gray says. He doesn't look us in the eye, but the young boy wearing a black runner tunic at his side does. I recognize him from my childhood. My dear friend. Comrade.

"Rao," I whisper. My old friend. Thank god.

He looks at me and shakes his head so subtly that I have to be the only one who notices. His mouth curves and shapes silent words, "Wait."

They must've cleared the undermarket first.

They line us up by size and gender. Then they clip a sub-cutaneous port, like an IV, on the backs of our necks, which provides easy access to our nervous systems. It feels like a scorpion sting, but soon the pain recedes. They place a line in each of us and connect us to a computer that runs our stats: weight, height, temperature, etc.

"I don't feel sick," Jasmine says as they put the sensors around her head.

"The symptoms take weeks to appear," the assistant wearing a gray tunic says. "There are many types: acute, chronic, and some are asymptomatic. This outbreak has become a pandemic. That's why it's so dangerous." The assistant's neural-synch glimmers gold in the fluorescent light.

I hold the girl's hand as they run the tests and lie to her about being sick. When we are all marked and charted, Jasmine's face is damp from weeping, and the face of the boy with the raspy voice hardens to stone.

Finally, the doctor arrives at our unit. Instantly, I know him.

He scans us, and one by one his eyes stop at each of us. "We will conduct tests daily. It's easier if you comply with the orders you're given." When his eyes fall on me, his brow crinkles. "It's easier for all of us."

Dr. Qasim. He brought so many of us to safety, not that anyone knows that. Only our family. He can't be working for Central like this by choice. His weary eyes, slouching posture, all tell the story of a broken man, physically tortured. No, Central forced him.

When they are done, and the children are allowed to sit down, I stand at the edge of our unit and watch, wait. The lights dim and most of us sleep, but still I stand, waiting, pacing.

Finally, hours later, the shape of a boy walks the rows and, as he passes our unit, he tosses me some rations, whispering, "Only the dead escape. It's the only way."

I want to scream, to beg him to let us out. But I push that down, deep below my belly. When I am sure no one is looking, I inspect the ration pods. That's it? That's all he's going to do to help me?

I sit on the floor and let it sink in. Nothing makes sense. No one shows signs of the Fever in the Narrows. Masiji would have told us. Why would Central put us in containment? They hate us, but usually ignore us. There is something bigger going on . . . and I have to figure it out.

If Rao can't see a way out, I have to find one on my own.

"Here," I whisper and slip a pod into the hands of the raspy-voiced boy. "Eat." If he freaks out, it'll help no one. I'm going to need a team to work together to figure out this nightmare.

He sits up and looks at me with surprise. "Why? Why didn't you eat it yourself?"

"Not hungry," I lie.

He takes the pod and splits it into half, handing me a piece. "Share."

I swallow the dark blue pill fragment that tastes of the sea. I give him another one to save for later.

Tomorrow, I'll find a way out of this hell.

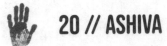

Suddenly, there's a metallic bam, bam on the door. And then, "Tiger?"

That voice. Jai. What the hell does he want? Just when things get to the worst place ever, Jai shows up to increase the annoyance level multiplied by a thousand. He opens the door and enters the room, pushing a hooded person in front of him.

"It doesn't sound like you are doing anything but wasting my time," I say and keep working.

Jai takes a few steps closer to me and sits the person wearing a hood down on the ground. They grunt when they hit the floor.

"He's a techie for Solace Corp, Tiger. He's worth something to you. You could electrocute him in Central. You could toss him flat into the sea. Whatever you want. It could be a good ol' show of defiance. A big F-U to Ravindra and Liu."

"How did you find us anyway?" I look to Ghaazi and Suri, who are busy sorting data on their ancient machines. Jai must be tracking me somehow.

"You have to listen. This could be a great partnership." He looks up at the others in the room and ask, "Eh, who are the elders?"

I ignore him. "Not interested. I'm not in the kidnapping business. Leave."

"Oh, don't be so grand. Smuggling's okay, but a little kidnapping isn't? At least take a look at him. He's an ultra-rich kid. Probably from some big-deal family."

"You're a pagal murkh. I should call Khan Zada and tell him he's interfering with Red Hand-level shit."

"Okay, look. Just simmer down. He just thought you of all people in the SA would be creative enough to use someone like a techie to your benefit. Maybe trade him for a newborn or something? Maybe he was wrong. Anyway, his words to me were: 'Jai, take this techie to the Tiger. She needs to smuggle him back into Central to keep him out of trouble.' In lieu of tithe, he wants you to be a babysitter. Then we're even. He's pretty important, so we can't risk you just dumping him at the gates and leaving him there. He needs an escort to get all the way home. You are going to be his bodyguard, get him tucked in and all, without triggering any suspicions about where he's been. Not even his people are to be trusted. Make it like he's never been missing in the first place."

"Why can't we just get him through the Liminal Area and then he could walk through Central on his own?"

"This one's special. He got picked up by the daaku already. He's smart in Central, but stupid out here. He needs to get through the Liminal, through the gates before they start searching for him. And you owe us. Otherwise, you'll have to pay with your arm."

"You're serious? That just feels like overkill, yaar." I read Jai like an Info-Run. He's telling the truth. I know Khan would try it too. Take my arm and all. Leave me without it. I'd fight, but one tiger against a sea of piranhas is as good as minced meat.

I push up against him to make sure he can feel my words. "The Narrows is gone. The Narrows is under assault by Central. The Red Hand is in ruins. You and the Lords of Shadow are done. Get out of my space!"

Jai lifts the boy by his collar and shakes his head.

"Let's hear him out," Suri says over her keys. "He could be useful to us right now. He might know how to get inside Solace."

I roll my eyes at Jai.

"Could be the break we need to find them," Ghaazi says.

I know they're right. We've got nothing. "Fine," I say.

"Don't mess up," Jai warns. "Khan's got a temper for you. Get the kid back into Central. No problems. Or else. Okay? I'd hate for something terrible to happen to you."

He sends me an air kiss.

Which is basically asking for it. I punch Jai in the chest with my cyborg arm and he flies into the wall. But my arm sighs and spins and spurts, and finally lays flat against my body, dead weight. Great idea, using my last bit of power on this jerk.

Breathe in and out.

Whatever.

My mind rushes, but all I want is for him to leave.

"Tiger," Ghaazi's voice is soft, "this could be just what we need. The boy could have access to data we don't. He could lead us to Masiji and your family. Think about it. We could connect to our network again—show the world the truth through the External Hand, across the planet."

Jai brushes off his shirt, and ego, and waits, coughing, for my reply. "Look, if it were up to me, we'd work together more. I've almost paid my debt to Khan. Maybe I can be Red Hand after all." He sighs and I've never seen him so vulnerable before, almost childlike. "I'm just the messenger, Tiger. You and I are more alike than we think."

Even though I don't trust them yet, Suri and Ghaazi are right. Everything has value.

If anything, we could use the techie to get what we want and just leave him to fend for himself.

"Right," I say.

"So, you'll do it then?" Jai's voice is hoarse. "You can do whatever necessary to find where they're keeping the Narrows kids."

"The way I figure, Khan Zada can't do it himself because the kid's wanted or connected. And you need someone who's actually good at smuggling," I say.

"Yeah and I should mention one thing, though. If anything goes south, you're supposed to disappear him." Jai whispers the last part.

"Wait, what? First you want him delivered with kid gloves, but if it goes wrong, you want us to kill him? I'm no murderer," I say loudly.

Jai shrugs. "Complicated times, love. Only if things don't go as planned." He looks down.

I lift my weak arm and Jai puts his fists in the air, weary. "I won't hit you again," I say.

"You really have a short fuse. It's a wonder you have any friends at all," he says. He shakes my hand, then he leans down toward the boy and makes like he's going to rip the disruptor device right from the boy's chest.

"Hey, no deal unless you leave that right where it is, Jai."

"Can't. Property of Khan Zada. He likes to keep track of all his devices."

"No deal unless he comes with the noise device." I cross my arms and the replacement lays heavily across my flesh.

"It'll give us cover."

"Fine, Tiger."

The boy moans like he's sick and mumbles something I can't make out.

"What's the matter with him?" I say.

"He's your problem now," Jai says as he goes to leave. "And, uh, Tiger? You know, I'd rather work for you if you'd just stop beating on me. The way I see it is that if I'm going to do dirty work, I might as well do it for the benefit of my people. I would, really. Khan's been on my back. Anyway, think about it. Maybe we can make a deal one day." He kisses the tips of his fingers and then ducks into the tunnels again.

With one quick motion, I pull off the hood covering the boy's head.

"Thanks," the boy says and squints his eyes.

He is just a boy, same height and probably the same age as me. Not an evil agent of Solace Corp. Not a wicked techie about to set up the Narrows for assault. Just a boy. An Uplander boy with perfect skin and eyes as clear as day. He looks a little ill, but ill or not, he's near perfect, in a scientific way.

"Do me a favor, eh? If you flay me in Central, just send a holo-vid to my parents? They'd hate to see that," he says.

And a dumb boy at that.

"You think it's a game?" I ask.

"Isn't it?" His hands shake. I back up and he crumbles to the ground.

"Suri, what's happening? Is it the Fever?"

"I don't think so. The disease begins with a blue rash and then slowly leaves one paralyzed, not shaking. He's probably just in shock from the whole thing. I bet Jai roughed him up. I think it's safe to touch him. Let's put him over there." She points to the storage bins, and Ghaazi makes a bed for him out of papers and scraps. Suri gives him filtered water and covers him with a shawl. Soon the boy looks to be in some kind of tortured, delirious sleep.

"Poor fellow. He's had one day down here with the rest of humanity and he's in shock." I want to smash something. "I think he's done for now. We should still use code names, just in case."

"We should contact a mediport. We'll need to block his neural-synch if he's going to be near us," Suri says.

"I say we leave him in the Liminal Area with a note that says property of Khan Zadabhai and walk away."

"Tiger..." Suri says.

"We don't have time for this. He has everything in the world and ends up down here." I go over to the boy and tie his wrists with some wires I find.

The boy says, "I'm sorry." Then passes out.

"He's an odd one," I say. "Okay, we have a pawn. Now what?" I look to Suri.

Ghaazi says, "Yes, we need to find out what he knows."

I shake my head. "We have to review the file. It's our only leverage. Open the data packet, Ghaazi. Now."

"If you say so. But there's no telling who will track us once it's downloaded."

"That's okay. We're going to have to leave this place anyway," I say.

I'm not prepared for what I see. Masiji managed to back up the entire base code for Solace. Version 1.0 pours down the screen and it's pretty crude, no finesse.

"What's that? Over there?" Ghaazi points to a portion of text in Masiji's notes. "Looks like a separate link to a basic note file."

"It's from her, from The Mechanic. It's a message," Suri says.

Ghaazi opens the file. It's a basic notation file with a ton of text inside. I don't understand the details, only the headers, and a few phrases and words stand out, like "override." But I'm no computer scientist. The language is formal and I can't make out the implications. This is not my language. But even so, I know it's all there in her detailed notes, the plans: how the Solace program will function, what types of outreach it can do, limitations to the data, how to sort genetic data points, everything. And I'm eager to know the details.

Ghaazi stands. "No, this is more like a warning."

"If you can translate her shorthand, please." I gesture to him, desperate to know the details of what they are reading.

"Something about failsafe systems in place. Who manages them. It's not very clear, but she writes about the extent to which the Solace system can override."

"Override what?"

"The human mind. Hmm . . . she was really good at covering her notes. They must've been on to her."

"There's a problem with the override? What kind of problem?" I think of my plexus, and though it's wiped and not connected to Solace, it's still a piece of embedded neural tech.

"It doesn't say. I'm reading it to you fully, promise," Ghaazi says.

"When did she leave Solace?"

"As soon as—" Ghaazi begins.

Suri cuts him off. "Maybe we should let her tell you, dear. It's not our place."

"But she could . . ." The knot in my throat twists. ". . . she could die in containment before she gets a chance to tell me."

They exchange knowing looks.

I continue. "It's not your place to decide what I learn about her either. How can I lead without information? Just give me the best information available. If you know something, you'd better tell me or I'll leave right now. And I'll leave the boy with you to figure out his fate. I'm sure Khan will send a goonda to check on his departure."

Suri says, "We only know what she told us, and she was very vague about the whole thing. We all have complicated pasts, so we never pushed her."

I flex my arm and think about how it isn't mine. It never was. I'm just a girl who's been mended by a brilliant engineer. I need to get it fixed before it stops working altogether.

"Go on."

"When she met you, you were a very small child, maybe one or two years old. You were undergoing tests for a program they were building. The Uplanders were given a chance to bring their children into Solace Corp to see if they could match the genetics required for the neural-synch. What the parents didn't know was that they were storing information on the children and testing many other things on them.

Suri continued. "Those that Solace passed were free to live in Central. Their lifespans were going to be great. Their genes were flawless, nearly disease-free. But there were so many who didn't make it, and Masiji couldn't live with the idea that she couldn't fix them too. She developed tests and studies to try to adapt a person to pass the Solace tests. She couldn't change Solace's algorithm, but she could change the person. At least she thought she could.

"For some, it worked. Gene editing. But for others, parents were desperate enough to try anything. So, she did. Transfusions, replacements, everything. It was a bloody chop shop. And the children were taken from their families." She paused and looked at me. "You didn't fare well. You almost died."

"My parents were Uplanders?"

"Listen, Tiger. I can't imagine how strange this all sounds."

"No, it makes sense." I'd always wondered. "If my mother didn't have the Fever…"

"The testing went badly, beti. It was not clean," Suri says. "Masiji lost faith in the work and was ordered to send you away with the rest. She kidnapped you and left. And they're still running her tests."

"Did they hunt for her?"

"She faked her death," Suri says.

"It was all—" Ghaazi starts to say.

I put up my hand. "That's enough. I've heard enough."

They look relieved. My questions are just beginning to form, but there is only one woman who can actually answer them. And she's locked away in containment. If Central found out she's a fugitive, she could already be dead.

"Let's go then," I say and help the tech boy up. He's not fully conscious. I copy the data packet and slip it onto my new liquid disc reader in my wrist. "There's too much evidence of the past here. We need to burn the posters, the fliers, the notes. Wipe the computers, but don't harm them. They're too valuable if we need to use them again."

Once we gather all the posters into a metal bin. Ghaazi splashes some precious oil. I strike a wire against its counter and the spark ignites the fire that consumes the old Red Hand materials.

All the faces of the Rani go up in white hot flames.

I lift the boy as we all hurry along the tunnels.

The Red Hand will be reborn.

It's like I'm already dead.

She won't tell me her name or even look at me. I've read about this technique in a military studies course at school. I know what she's doing. The less she cares, the more she ignores my humanity, the easier it will be to do whatever bad thing she's going to do: attach a bomb to my back and send me into Central. Or like Jai said, flay me.

I'm lying on the hard ground of a broken building, all twisted metal and broken glass. It's night. The small bonfire lights her face like the moon and I see her scars, her worry. She's a soldier of some kind. Focusing on whatever she's doing. There are two elders. Their code names tell me nothing. Though she is young, she seems like their leader. Or at least, she's the bossiest. Curious.

Or maybe I'm not even here. It's hard to get a lock on reality. My mind is a flurry of my past life in Central and with Solace, and in this present one. And sometimes it's difficult to tell which one is which. The one thing I see through the haze and echoes of voices and thoughts, and sickness is Kanwar Uncle sitting on the edge of my bed the last time I saw him, as my heavy eyes fight sleep. I want to leap up from my bed to tell him to not go to work the next day. To force him to stay in our house. Maybe if I was sick or something that would convince him to avoid his own death. Anything. Everything. But I watch as he leaves my room to die in a lab explosion the next day.

I don't want to be powerless anymore.

The next moment I wake, the sun is about to rise and they are taking me along the streets to what looks like a dark market: Thin people have strange items for sale set out on unsanitary plastic tarps for purchase. Baskets of old tech piled high. I count one, two, three sets of ladders, five food vendors and then I stop counting. Who wants that obsolete junk, I don't know. When they see us, most cover their things, turn their backs. A few give nods and hand the girl something. I don't know what scares them, me or my kidnappers. Or maybe it's both. It might be that my wrists are tied.

"Please," I say over and over to their silence.

"Shut up and be thankful you're breathing. We could cover your head, you know," the girl says.

We go through a dizzying maze of alleyways. I almost think they are trying to confuse me. But they keep on.

The elderly woman says, "It's up there." She reads info on her wrist reader. "Two lefts and a right."

"Finally," the girl says.

I think we are in the Liminal Area on the edge of Central. Where I got snatched by the goonda crew of street kids. I want to scratch at my neural-synch; it feels like it's growing in my head, spreading out its tentacles. It buzzes. I hum uncontrollably.

The girl comes closer. "What's with you?"

Her eyes are a reddish brown, a kind I've never seen before.

"Huh?" My eyes blink and blink, and I try to say a word, but nothing comes. It feels like I'm short-circuiting.

"I think he's fried. Maybe the neural-synch has a trigger

that injures the host if they move too far outside of Central."

"Maybe." The elderly woman is kind, but she has the look of someone who has already taken a life. "What's going on in there, boy?"

My eyes are flitting back and forth endlessly. And my thoughts race faster and faster. I moan. All I can do is moan, not make words. It's like my motor functions are crossed.

"Let's get him inside," says the elderly man.

The girl pushes open the metal door to a broken down mediport, and we all pile into the small room. Defunct. Shut down. This thing hasn't been functional for years. No one has set foot inside in a long time. I've never seen a mediport like this before. We go to Solace Corp labs for physicals and surgery updates. Nothing like this. I wouldn't even bring my bot here for a tune-up.

"Sit," the girl says, after she's already pushed me down into an exam chair and untied my wrists.

In my mind I yell, scream, beg her to tell me what she is going to do to me. But all I can say is, "H—elp."

"Yeah, yaar, we're going to. Just be chill. We aren't going to hurt you. I'm supposed to get you home safe and sound, re-member?" She goes through the contents of the cabinets and drawers. The other two reboot the machines and, miracu-lously, they restart.

The old man says, "Ha, I still have it." He holds wires in his hand. "Nothing like a bit of old school hot-wiring."

"Nicely done," the older woman says.

A mediport voice says, "Welcome to Mediport 49. We are out of service, but there's another Mediport four kilometers away. Would you like directions?"

"No. System override," the girl types commands into the 3D projected system. Commands I've never seen before. She's amazing. "We're inside."

"Inshallah," the old man says.

The tall woman sits by my side and slips her hand into mine. I don't know why she does that. But it feels nice. My heart rate goes down and my jaw relaxes, allowing words.

"Thank you," I say.

"It's going to be okay," the woman says.

The girl at the command says, "No need to get friendly with our captive."

"Ach. He's just a boy. Not a criminal, Tiger."

"He's Upland scum until proven otherwise," the girl says.

The woman leans towards me and whispers. "It's going to be okay."

I don't care if she's lying, if this is another tactic. It's all I want to hear.

"Now, try to relax," the girl presses her hand to my forehead and positions a halo system atop my scalp. Then she clips a jaw brace and my head locks into place against the chair.

"System scan launched," the girl says.

It feels like a feather running through my body, from system to system. Nervous, vascular, skeletal, everywhere it goes, my body twitches. It is painless, but terrifying.

"Done. The system says his body is rejecting the ... wait, I didn't think that was possible."

"What?" the man asks.

The girl says, "Look," and points to the visual. "His neural-synch. His body thinks it's a pathogen. His immune system is trying to override it. His body is fighting itself. And his tox levels report a high dose of THink nano drugs. That stuff's dangerous."

"He's going to need an immunosuppressant," the man says. "Ashiva, do we have the materials to build one here?" When he says her name, he stops himself.

I see the girl glare at the man and know he gave her name away by mistake. Ashiva. Remember her name. Don't forget it. I repeat it several times. Ashiva. Ashiva. Ashiva. They also call her Tiger. Don't forget.

"Yes, we can use the 3D replicator. Rani? Can you do this? But it's shocking they didn't use gene therapy bots to correct his immune-response to the neural-synch. I wonder if he's worse off than he looks."

The tall woman sits and works. "It's not a permanent solution. This is just a patch."

My eyes close against my will, but I can still hear them.

I think the man injects me with something. It stings and when it reaches my bloodstream, everything tastes sweet, metallic.

I want to live.

I try to remember that thought as I drift away into a thick blanket of nothingness.

Ashiva. Ashiva. Ashiva.

The neural-synch is more than an invention. It's a leap of faith. Overnight, the South Asian Province changed from a chaotic, beautiful place to an organized, somewhat soulless society.

Sure, there are still riots, and the Unsanctioned Territory outside of Central is still considered a threat to the stability of the Province, but something in the air changed when the neural-synch was rolled out. Masiji said it was the number of infrared rays moving through Central that altered the air, literally changing the ions. Masiji, I wish I knew what you were up to.

I know now that what we really felt was the soul of the city dying.

The boy isn't older than me. Or taller. Or smarter. Or stronger. That's clear. But he's surely cleaner. His skin is dewy and medium brown, without a single blemish. It's like he recently hatched, perfect, in this full-grown size and shape. Maybe in Central they make people in 3D cloners now. That wouldn't surprise me. But he's one of the chosen. I always thought they'd be like a different species of human.

I don't want to be perfect. My scars make me, me. I own them and earned them. And his perfect skin makes me uneasy. Hasn't he tripped over something before? Stubbed a toe? Been on the wrong end of a sliver of glass or metal? If we hadn't taken him to the mediport and completed a scan, I'd have thought he's a robot in a skin-suit.

"Stop poking the poor boy with that wire, Ashiva," Ghaazi says. "Didn't Masiji teach you manners?"

We are camping in a small abandoned building in the Liminal area. After the mediport visit, the boy went into a deep sleep. The system says it will be two hours before he's conscious. And if everything works, he'll be as right as acid rain. Immune system at bay. He's stable. But he needs to lay off the drugs and close the neural-synch permanently, and soon. At least we bought him some time. This boy's turning out to be a very large pain in my ass. I should have just paid Khan Zada my tithe. But then I'd have nothing left.

"It's not sharp," I say. "And anyway, it's not like he's our guest or something. He's our captive."

"If you treat him like an animal, we are no better than his people. And we are not equal. Never forget that. He's altered. To what extent, we'll never really know. But an altered mind and body and soul, not just replaced. He can't be trusted. We don't know how much of his humanity has been compromised," Ghaazi says.

"Ghaaziji, you really have strong feelings about this." Suri laughs. "You should go be a sadhu, preach about humanity."

He stuffs a bit of roti in his mouth and says, "Achcha, well, you're right. I'll keep it to myself. None of us needs a preacher right now."

"No, what we need is to rework the plan," I say.

"It's already perfect," Suri says.

"Since I'm the one going, I need to make sure we can get inside Solace Corp without being traced. I'd hate to just donate my body to Central without putting up a fight."

"Okay. Ghaazi and I will assist from the outside, clearing

the way for you. We can disable the UAVs and cameras temporarily."

"You can?"

"I've done it before. I'm rusty, but I can probably buy you a
few minutes here and there. We have the code ready to go.
One of the benefits of being a founding engineer on the project. We will be with you in spirit."

I toss the wire into a pile against the wall. The boy stirs
and sits upright, with all these strange creases on his face
from the blanket we gave him. Right on time.

Midnight. I hand him a can of water and a small bit of
bread.

He takes them greedily.

"Relish it, boy, that's a maharaja's meal down here."

He drinks all the water and stuffs the bread in his mouth.

"Take it easy. Don't want to lose it in your hurry."

"Thank you," is all he says.

Thank you, like he's accustomed to saying that to others
who give him things willingly. He really is some kind of pampered, ullu-brained kid whose parents pave his path with gold
bricks, cemented with the blood of my people.

"Well, time to go home," I lift the boy to his feet and he
looks at me like I'm going to eat him whole. "Don't be so
scared, boy. It's not becoming on your pretty face."

"They'll lock onto our location as soon as we step foot inside Central. You'll get caught and tossed," he says. He's cute,
trying to be all intimidating.

"Yeah, we're going to fix that."

"Really?"

"Do I look like an entertainer?"

"Yes, I mean, no. I hear an echo. Is it just me?"

"Feedback syndrome. From the neural-synch. Sounds like a bad side effect. We gave you an immunosuppressant, I think. I don't know actually. Never made one before, but the medi-port had a previous code for one, so that's all I could do. It's a fix, not a cure."

"You just gave me old code?"

"A thank-you would be nice. And, yes, we saved your ass, yaar. Why'd you let them put the neural-synch in when you obviously didn't pass the tests? Your body doesn't like the implant. It's trying to kill you."

He takes a sip of water. "My mother. She forced me."

"Your mother."

He just nods.

"Nice lady."

"You don't know the half of it."

Suri says, "Not that I need to say it, but be careful. Take no unnecessary risks." She smiles.

"And you'll meet us at the coordinates when we send them." I say, nodding.

"Promise." Suri, Ghaazi and I hold each other's gazes, and in it we say our goodbyes and wishes and hopes.

I don't look back at them as I lead the boy out of the second-story building and down into the Liminal Area streets. We have two more stops before our mission, and I've wasted too much time as it is. Taru and Masiji and Zami could be anywhere, in any condition.

"Are you going to tell me where we're going?"

He's so ignorant, I almost feel sorry for him. But his people did this to our world. They separated, killed, sorted and left us to die. Why? Because we're not as good as them? We're not compliant? Our genes aren't as perfect?

"No, I'm not. Trust is something that's earned, not handed out to one's enemy without reason. I've survived this long on my wits. Not by being nice." I laugh at him.

"Riz-Ali." His voice is gentle.

"What?"

"My name. There, you have it."

I stop walking. "Alright, Riz-Ali, what's your surname?"

He shakes his head. "One thing at a time, Ashiva."

I bristle. He knows my name. I wonder how much he learned, if he was faking his eternal sleep. If he knows we're Red Hand. I can always hide him in some dead-end tunnel and go forward with the plan on my own. Not that I want to be on the wrong side of Khan Zada. I have to keep my arm, even if Jai is pagal. I'll have to repay Khan Zada and get rid of him when I get what I need.

"You know, if you weren't so angry…"

My cyborg hand holds his face as gently as it can and strokes his chin, machine humming against flesh. "The last time I had to smuggle a boy who was a chatter box, he was delivered without his teeth."

Silence is so precious.

I hit the reinforced door three times with my metal hand. The sound echoes in the space behind the door.

"What is this place?" Riz asks and inspects the symbols that decorate the wall: hexagonal forms, chemical bonds.

I lean close to the door. "Oye, it's me. Wake up, ullus!"

Five seconds later, the process of unlocking the laboratory begins. Latches turn, levers lift, deadbolts spin, then finally a deactivation of the electrical field silences the buzz.

Then an R-77 laser cannon drops from the ceiling and we sit eye-to-eye with our own personal end of days.

"Nice touch," I say.

Riz is pissing his pants.

From behind the door I hear, "Prove your identity."

"Let's see . . . I bet, right now you're eating a snack and biting your fingernails, what's left of them."

"Okay, okay. Who did you bring here?"

"He's harmless. I need your help. It's for a special project. The one you've been dying to try."

Riz turns to me with eyes like searchlights. "Special project? Testing on me?"

The door rolls open just enough for Saachi's lovely face to show. "Good to see you, Ashiva. You understand why I have to be careful. These are evil times." She hugs me tight.

I push into the room with Riz behind me. "I know."

"Oh god, I'm really glad to see you." I wrap my human arm around Saachi's shoulders and gently squeeze.

She says, "I thought you were dead. We all did. They took everyone. I was lucky to be here when it went down. It was like watching the end of the world. Not a peep outta Central about it."

"I'm still here," a familiar voice speaks in the dark, massive laboratory.

"Brother!" I run to Zami, and the tears fall so fast I'm not sure I'll be able to turn them off.

"I know, sister. It's good to see you too."

"I thought you were gone."

"Tiger . . . I watched a guardian in a mecha-suit take families out of their homes and toss them into transports. I saw them kill a few men who tried to run. They, they … they set fire to the temple."

I pull him close and whisper, "Zami, what about Taru? Was she with you?"

He presses his lips together hard.

"Tell me."

"She was in the nursery when it all happened. I didn't have time to get to her. I …"

I hold him and lie, "I'm sure she's fine. Mistress was there. They could have made it to the catacombs."

I know she was taken.

My soul aches.

The boy I hear Ashiva call Zami examines me. "Who's the desi Uplander? Dating across divides?"

"A gift from the Lords of Shadow's own Khan Zada," Ashiva says. "I have to take a job for him. Long story."

"I've got time."

"I met with the originators of our group. Jai brought this boy, Riz-Ali, and Khan is making me smuggle this svachchh back into Central undetected so that he doesn't get in trouble. As tithe."

"Not what I was expecting. How?"

"Masiji told me I had to go back to the beginning. That the originators would help. There are two left of the old hand." She goes into a crazy story, leaving out names and locations, but the gist is about some group, and something about how now she's a sort of leader. I wonder if she's talking about the Red Hand. It's a long shot; there are so many gangs in the Narrows. But if so, she could know the Commander. I'm not sure what to do. On the one hand they can get me back into Central, past the daaku in the Liminal Area, but on the other hand, they'll definitely want something from me in return. Regardless, they have all the power now.

"Going to use him to get inside, get the info on the dark off-site? Because that's what I would do," the one called Zami says.

The one they call Saachi turns to me. "Come with me, please." Her warm hand touches my shoulder and she leads me to a comfortable chair. She uses extreme care as she ties my hands together, gently, but firmly. I wonder why she's so kind and begin to think that maybe not everyone down here is rough like Khan. "Just in case you feel like touching something in my lab, don't, okay?"

It's a mad person's laboratory. Stations with tech in various stages of disarray and chaos, tables with replacement body parts, and magnification lights make this a place of invention and destruction. And I am going to be their special project. My restraints are tight. Too tight to break on my own. I'll need to find something that can cut wire if I want to go anywhere.

The three whisper just out of earshot for nearly thirty minutes and finally they seem to agree on something. Saachi is put out, but Zami and the girl are happy, almost excited.

Saachi says to me, "Because we're not evil, I'll tell you what we're going to do. It might help your body accept the changes as well."

"Changes?" They lead me to a large, well-lit table in the rear of the laboratory and remove my wrist ties.

"Lay down, please. And I know this might not be possible, but try to relax?"

My body tenses, my arms, neck and legs suddenly fight against the new restraints on the table. I don't understand what's happening. I don't want to fight, but my body does anyway. I can't control myself.

"He's not compliant. I think it's the neural-synch, preprogrammed not to self-injure or accept injury without approval, probably a fail-safe. Zami, hand me that box over there."

"Shit, this goes deep." Ashiva says.

Inside the silver box is a syringe and a bottle of liquid.

Saachi says, "Just a simple sedative. Riz. Something that will allow your brain activity to continue, but calm your limbs."

"I ... can't ... stop," I manage through gritted teeth.

I battle the seizure, but Ashiva holds me down and her strength is that of ten men. Once the sedative is in my bloodstream, I am thankful the spasm ends.

"Okay, Riz, all I can say is that it won't hurt," Saachi tries to soothe. "It's just an update."

I see the blade in her hand and the bright light backlighting her. Words stick in my throat. I am floating elsewhere from the drugs and I don't care what they do to me. Something is injected. I let go and close my eyes, happily adrift.

When I land back on the planet, there is a bandage over my thick head. There's a metallic taste in my mouth, coating my throat.

I groan. Soon, Ashiva appears with a bottle of treated water and lets me have a few sips.

"Thanks."

Then she holds out two, small, round pills to me. "Take them. They'll help with the adjustment."

The pills seem so archaic. All adjustments are done through the system's regulation of my own adrenal and neurological systems, or through a syringe. But a pill? Won't it get stuck in my throat? Won't it take forever to work because of my stomach bile?

"You've never taken a pill before, have you?"

I shake my head slowly.

"You just put it on your tongue and take a big mouthful of

water, and swallow it down. Don't worry, you won't choke."

She helps me sit up straight and puts the pills in my hand. I do my best, but I choke the first time. The second time, they go down.

"It'll take ten minutes for them to kick in. We gave you an inject during the procedure to keep your body cool until you heal. How are you feeling?"

"What did you do to me?" My words are razors on my dry throat.

She sits down beside me. "Saachi installed a network blocker in your neural-synch. You're officially offline even when we move into Central. Solace can't see or hear you." Her expression is matter-of-fact.

"That's what you were doing?"

I'm free. "Can you take this thing out now?" The clip on my chest feels tender and all I want is to remove whatever device Jai stuck to me.

"Yeah, I hate those bugs. So annoying. Useful, but annoying to remove. Ready? One, two—" and a tiny fire hits my chest when she pulls it straight out, microneedles and all. "Done."

"Ouch." Blood pools on the bit of flesh the metal device took with it and Ashiva looks at the wound closely, almost like she wasn't expecting it.

"We have questions for you. We're not going to hurt you. We actually saved your life, I think."

"Thank you?" I listen for it, but the buzzing is gone from my brain. All of it. I smile and look around. They're kids like me. While I was out, they'd felt like gods hovering above me. Helping me. I am in their debt. Especially to the oldest one. This is their lab.

"Okay…"

"No, I mean it. Thanks."

"Well, you can show your thanks by answering some questions before we drop you back in Central. You work for Solace Corp, correct?"

"Who are you?" I look around and see a small handprint on the wall in red paint. It makes sense. The pieces fit together. The Red Hand works with gangs like the Lords of Shadow. They're supposed to be trained in all aspects of warfare, medicine, computers. They have an army of child soldiers. "I will help, of course. But tell me and don't lie. Are you the Lal Hath?"

The room quiets. No one answers.

"It's okay. I … I'm obviously not in any position of power."

"Obviously," Ashiva says.

"I know. But it matters to me, if you are Red Hand. They're the reason I got snagged by the daaku, traded to Khan and am now sitting here—not dead—with you all." The three look at each other. They look somber and confused. So, I keep going. "Just say yes, and I'll tell you whatever I can."

The boy and older girl look to Ashiva. She nods quietly. "Yeah, but what do you mean, we're the reason?"

"I left Central because I had to upload the data packet for the hacking challenge from the Liminal Area, so that I would be undetected by Solace. So much for sneaking around. I think the packet arrived. I'm not sure. I hope it did."

She laughs. For the first time I see how lovely she looks with her joyful expression.

"Hey, I'm a fair hacker, I can hold my own."

"No, it's not that. You're excellent. You're Kid Synch? The one and only?"

"What?"

She turns and says to the boy, "Oye, Zami. Let me intro-
duce you to Kid Synch."

Zami says, "What, Kid Stink in the flesh?"

"I'm serious." Then she turns to me. "That's your code
name, right?"

I nod.

"Welcome to the Red Hand, yaar. I never thought I'd meet
you. Definitely not like this. Sorry about everything before. I
thought you were just some dumb uppy."

She holds out her hand to me and waits for me to shake it.
I take it and she shows me her strength in her grip. Her hand's
covered in a glove, but I know it's a replacement. Her eyes
watch me like everything depends on my compliance. Message received.

"Um, nice to meet you," I say. I'm dizzy. Perhaps the update
is making me sleepy. Perhaps it's because the entire world as I
know it changed in under eight hours.

"Whatever," she says. "Get some sleep. We have lots to do
tomorrow."

24 // ASHIVA

I can't help but think about the moments that brought us here, to this place in time. To living in a world where children are thrown away for their imperfections, and an algorithm decides who stays and who will be left out of history. Was it when the Red Hand went underground after Central rolled out their new anti-terrorist gray-collars and UAVs? Or was it earlier, with the New Treaty and end of WWIII when the world's leaders collapsed under the guilt that they nearly destroyed the world with their war mechas and nuclear missiles? Or was it after, when the Narrows was established as the slum for those deemed unfit by Solace, and children like me were raised to be soldiers? Or President Ravindra's approval of Solace's roll-out of the neural-synch? Or is it inevitable that power will corrupt so perfectly?

A million of her little cuts ended up bleeding us out.

But how to stop the bloodshed? That is our task. And I can't do this by myself. If we can't reconnect with the global Red Hand, there's no way it will happen. To me, the big problems feel like staring at the sun, wondering how to make it night. All I know is I need to see Taru again, to see Masiji again. And I'll do anything to get us closer to finding a future in which we belong. Before the rising sea threatens the Narrows, and the Uplanders let us all wash away like another disappeared island in some natural disaster that could have been prevented, broken promises, nightmares they did their best to ignore.

I look for the moon through the one small transom window above the ventilation system in Saachi's laboratory. I can only see the soft glow of its round, silver surface through the midnight haze. I want to see it completely for once, not covered by the rings of the Alliance Space Colony spinning in its orbit. I heard it was beautiful, inspiring. Masiji told me when we searched for stars at night that starlight came to us from already-dead stars. Most glimmers of light are long gone, consumed by a supernova or a black hole. A natural death for the brightest celestial bodies. But their influence continues millions of years beyond. Then another cloud parts and an unnaturally white torus ring cuts through the moon's light. The thing about humans is, we're in such a hurry to advance that we just keep inventing things until we think we've buried our mistakes. But they're still there, festering.

That's when it occurs to me: We're going to have to end this madness somehow, and I doubt I'm the one who will be able to lead them. General Shankar is a firebrand. Masiji is the all-mighty. Me? I'm just a smuggler with a sharp tongue, and there's no way I can do this. But there's a fire building inside me. I can't stand waiting. I need to get to Taru. If she's dead, or sick or hurt, or sad or alone. It's my fault, and only I can free her. The nightmare builds around me with each moment filled with stillness.

From my seat on the counter, I watch the boy sleep on the operating table. There's only a small bandage at his temple, but his flesh isn't injured. We don't know what to expect when he comes to. Zami and Saachi are asleep on thick blankets on the ground.

He looks peaceful. My mind recalls how only hours before

his face contorted during his seizure. I remember how Saachi opened his neural-synch to fish around for the port where they could install the signal disruptor. I was relieved to see a single drop of his blood. Humanity was still inside him, even if technology had replaced his neural activity. Maybe all isn't lost after all.

I take off my jacket and roll up my sleeves. I'd injured my replacement arm somehow and ruined the silicone flesh on my wrist that Masiji had wrapped over the metal. I tug at it like a scab, and the skin lifts too easily, like a strange glove, exposing the well-worn metal. I open my hand and close it again, listening to the hum of the gears and joints as they move. Masiji figured out how to deactivate black-market tech, clean them, and use them to build a plexus that synchs our brains to the replacement parts. It works. Now I know how she knew so much about the technology, and what Solace could and couldn't connect to: She designed it.

In bits and pieces, my memories revise themselves. The history she told me about the Narrows, her ability to fix us, how she was able to know so much about our world and theirs —it's beginning to make sense now. And yet, I don't know what to believe.

"Am I still alive?" The boy's rough voice breaks the silence.

"Yeah, you're alive. Sorry about all that. We couldn't have Central and Solace tracking you, or us. It was necessary. Jai's device would have only worked for a short while."

He tries to sit up and I help him. I feel his strong body under his T-shirt. The most unusual thing about him is that even after running the tunnels and being captive for days, he smells clean, like he just showered. I wonder if there's a genetic edit for that.

"You know, I would have come along willingly, I think. But I guess my body wouldn't have cooperated anyway."

Saachi joins us and asks him, "How do you feel?"

He turns his head from left to right, stretching. "Okay, I think."

"Your eyes, can you focus?"

"Focus, squint, the whole thing. But how will we know if it's blocked?"

Saachi bites her fingernails and says, "I've calculated the precise location of the blocker and how it will impact the signal."

"You don't know, do you?" I ask.

"It's impossible to know. His neural-synch went organic. It's embedded in his brain tissue and nervous system. I didn't realize the extent of the implant. I've done what I can to stop the transmission and pick-up, but we won't know until we get him inside Central and Solace Corp."

"Hang on. You want me to go back to Solace for you? If they catch me this time, they'll put me in containment for treason and theft. And as an enemy of the state, they could kill me."

"Maybe, but maybe not. Look, you're not a typical Uplander. My job is to get you back inside without harm. I bet your family is important, right? I bet they made a deal with Solace Corp already."

The boy hesitates and now I'm sure of it. He has connections. Otherwise why would he have a neural-synch? He shouldn't have it. It's incompatible. They cost hundreds of thousands of marks. He comes from money and power. We can use him to find my family.

"I have a job to do and on our way, you're going to help me out. This will be easy for a hacker like you."

"I, I don't know."

I push. "Where are you going to go? You going to live down in the Liminal Area? Or in the Narrows? Wait, it's destroyed. You have no choice, yaar. And be thankful. People have died to be in your place."

"You're right. All I want is information you might have. I thought if I did the challenge, you and your group of revolutionary fighters could help me find it. I definitely didn't do the hacking challenge for the digi-pet. It's cute though."

A revolutionary fighter? Is that what he thinks of us? "I'm not a fighter. I'm a smuggler. I'm just trying to get my family out of containment. You know about the new Solace campaign, right? Did you hear how they used mechas to clear the Narrows? They killed people, young and old. Trampled them like trash. Took the rest to an off-site location."

"Mechas? Not war mechas. What do you mean? They were decommissioned. The New Treaty clearly bans WMDs."

"Ravindra made new mecha-suits. She got around the New Treaty somehow; they're not WMDs. She calls them C.O.R.E mecha-suits. She said they had to clear the Narrows because of the Fever."

He paces the room. "Mechas, can't be. They said it was just civil unrest and the Fever..."

"And I'll do anything to get my family out before they make another announcement that to eradicate Z Fever, they were forced to eliminate the infected. I need to find where they're holding them. Now. Get the urgency?"

He nods. Something in him changes. He is distracted. "I

get it. Help me and I'll help your cause."

"You say that word 'cause' like it's an ad campaign, a choice. It's not. Our lives aren't something to worry about for a second and then to forget." I flex my fingers and try to calm myself. I need him to tell us everything he can, and I can't piss him off. I think of Taru and pray she is still alive, still fighting like I taught her.

Zami says, "Take a seat, Kid. Tell us about this information you're looking for. If we can help, we will. You have to promise to help us, though. That's the trade."

The boy seems to give into gravity and just lets his body fall into the seat. Time is a luxury we don't have now. We have to move fast.

"I swear. Look, my uncle was a lead robotics engineer for the SA. He built the most beautiful agribots that would have solved so many problems with food production and distribution. He didn't support Solace; he was an outlier. I was young, but I remember that he was charged with treason for working on war mechas after the New Treaty. There's no way he did what they said. There was an incident in his laboratory when guardians tried to take him for questioning. He died in an explosion. I just want to know the truth about what happened to him."

"How could we possibly help?" I ask. "Seems like you have access to better intel inside Solace."

"In the records he left with me, he said I needed to reach out to the Red Hand Commander. That they'll tell me what I need to know."

"Masiji? But why?" He looks earnest enough. But he could be making this whole thing up. On the other hand, he did just go and prove his loyalty to the Red Hand by running a danger-ous hack. "What was his name?"

"Kanwar Bhasin."

I look at Saachi. "Can you check him out? See if there are any notes on the internal system about him?"

She nods and logs onto her computer station.

"Thank you."

He seems genuine. So strange what people value when they have the space to not just worry about their survival.

"That's odd." Saachi says. "This list is secure, but I have ac-cess because we sometimes use the same pool of external members to run small missions." She keeps typing. "It looks like your uncle is listed as an operative of the External cell of Red Hand."

"What?" The boy gasps.

"There's one more thing. It could be bad record-keeping, but usually the list is current, in case of emergencies or a mis-sion." Saachi looks at me puzzled and points to a green dot be-side his profile. "That little green dot means he's active."

When I open my eyes, the world around me comes into focus and the nightmare returns. I fell asleep on Jasmine's shoulder and I jerk upright to move away from her body. She looks like she hasn't slept at all. Her eyes are red-rimmed and watery. Ashiva's looked like that after she has nightmares. I'm pretty sure we all have nightmares. Lucky for me, I don't remember my dreams, even the bad ones.

It's quiet except for coughing and moaning. Then suddenly a scream cuts through the entire facility.

A blue light flashes a few units down from us.

Jasmine says, "What's happening?"

"Blue always means death," I say without thinking. The blue lights on the C.O.R.E, the blue lights on the guardian's uniforms, the blue lights on Masiji's surgery table that connects to our heart rate only flashes when someone is at risk, the blue rash of the Fever.

"Someone died?"

I look to see what they are doing as a medical team rushes to the unit. They pull a body from the unit and place it on a cot with wheels. We all watch as they wheel it past us.

A boy, maybe eleven or twelve. He's banged and bruised. My eyes freeze on his face as he goes by: rash, blue marks, every sign we've been warned about, about the Fever. It's here. If we weren't sick before, we'll be sick soon. All of us. They wheel the body through the exit and vanish.

And then it hits me: one way in and out.

I have to get through that door.

But I can't just walk through.

I'll have to die first.

"Jasmine, I need your help," I say.

"Anything."

"You sure?" I lean in close and whisper, "I want you to give me some bruises on my face."

"What? No."

"Look, I have a plan and you have to trust me. No one gets out of here alive. I don't even think we have the Fever. I think they're giving it to us."

Her eyes are fire. "And we can't just wait to die."

"Exactly. If I can get out, I can get help. I'm Red Hand . . . and I know people who can help. If I get out, then I can come back and help everyone." I think for a second. I want so badly to reach out to her, to touch her, so I do. I hold her shoulders in my hands and press gently just for a moment.

She reads me. Takes in the surroundings. "Didn't many die in the Narrows when they came for us? The mechas . . . I saw one of them use heat rays." She shudders.

"Red Hand goes way beyond the Narrows. We are everywhere."

I see the realization rise in her face. That there's is no other way. I have to go.

I think of Ashiva and how many times she's had to explain the impossible to me, to all of us, and how I'd done my best to fight her. And of how many more times she's given up trying to explain. Her life is beginning to make more sense, the way she keeps things from me. It makes it easier. She was already in the Red Hand when she found me. She had no choice, but to stay. I've always wondered what would have happened if she hadn't found me. Would I have died? Would I have been found by my family?

Before we can finish talking, a medical group comes to our unit and lines us up. Jasmine and I hold hands, and make a silent promise to each other. I'm at the front of the line. The doctor is different, not Dr. Qasim. A woman in a white coat stares daggers at me.

"You're the lucky one. Come on." She pulls me out of the unit.

"Where are you taking her?" Jasmine yells.

"It's okay," I say. "I'll be okay."

The unit door slides shut, and I look back at Jasmine and my group as I march up the walkway toward the examination rooms.

The bed I sit on is cold, ice cold. The room is like most mediports, but with more computers and screens. The doctor sits on a chair and has her assistant connect me to the main system.

"Try to relax," the doctor says. She hasn't looked at me since she signaled me from the unit.

"What are you going to do to me?" I ask. Rao isn't around either. I'm alone and begin to shiver. I realize that being brave is an act. I can't hide my fear.

"We are running a few tests. That's all you need to know," the doctor says.

The assistant says, "We should begin with basic genetic sequencing and the polygenic scoring for a baseline."

"Begin," the doctor says.

The assistant moves close to me and tries to help me lay

flat, but I jerk out of reach. "Don't touch me."

"Are you cold?" he asks.

"Yes."

He puts a thick blanket over my body. So strange, making me comfortable now when I am a caged animal. But the comfort is welcome.

"Interesting replacement foot." The doctor inspects my limb like it's the newest designer mod. "So much talent wasted..."

"What do you mean?" I ask.

"Run the sedative. This one doesn't like being touched." The doctor ignores my question.

I fight the sedation. I want to know every single thing that happens in these rooms. My eyes feel heavier and heavier, like steel doors I can't hold open.

When I wake, my vision is blurry and a voice is reading a report, "Healthy, twelve-year-old girl, no genetic diseases, strong bones, excellent cognitive function. Excellent host for the inoculation testing."

"Huh, I wonder why she's not in Central," says a second voice.

"Solace isn't perfect because it's run by humans. Human error will always ruin everything." They laugh.

"What do you mean, no genetic diseases?" My throat is hoarse.

"Why? Do you want one?" The doctor chuckles, like any joke in this place is humanly possible.

"I just thought—"

"You're as healthy as they come. Good for you. Maybe you'll survive this after all."

I grow dizzy and my eyes close against my will.

When I wake, I'm back in my unit. My head feels swollen with pain, my throat hurts and my arms are covered in bruises. Jasmine is holding my head in her lap. The phrase "no genetic diseases" and their laughter echoes in my head. But how is it possible? I'm the glass girl. Could my tests have been wrong in the Narrows? My broken bones aren't a lie. I felt every one of them. Maybe I don't have a disease that appears on their tests. Maybe I was truly injured, but not sick. But some new hope fills me even in this dark place. It's knife-sharp and fierce, like courage. And somehow, I knew it was inside me all along.

The boy with the raspy voice is pacing back and forth like an animal.

"I need all of your help now. We need to work together," I say to the unit.

They crowd around me, the body the doctors had violated with their tests.

Even the raspy-voiced boy is interested. "What did they do?"

"Doesn't matter. What matters now is that you help me."

He nods. "Yes, anything."

"Do you still have the ration? Spit on it and rub it on my face."

"Are you insane? Did they loosen a few bolts in there?"

"Trust me. Make me look like that boy who was taken. The boy who died."

"It's okay? To touch you?"

I nod. "You won't . . . hurt me. We need to get out of here."

They all finally understand.

One stands guard, the others block me from view. They paint me with the ration pill, a sickly blue, which goes along well with the new bruises I received in the exam room.

When they are done, they lay me down on the ground.

I signal to Jasmine.

Her scream is terror itself.

As still as stone is my mantra and, in a matter of minutes, the medical janitors arrive, wearing clean suits, and pile me on top of a wheeled cot. They don't even bother to check my vitals.

I hold my breath.

"Just another dead kid," says one janitor to the other.

"Yeah, would be easier if we could just send them all out to sea at once."

"Then we'd be out of a job."

"True."

They push the cot over the doorway with a bump and into the world outside containment.

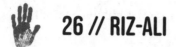

I wonder how long I can keep my identity a secret. Maybe they could run a trace, but Uplander security is pretty tight. What if they don't care? Maybe it's not about knowing what a computer thinks or thinks it knows, but about seeing what's in front of you and trusting the human. If they know who I really am, that my mother is the monster communicating their narrative, lives and deaths, that she has President Ravindra's ear, they'll kill me.

Ashiva repeats herself. This time it seems she's trying to smile and soften her hate of me and my kind. "Tell us what you know about Solace Corp's plan for the Narrows."

"I don't know much. It honestly sounds like you know more than I do," I say.

Ashiva leans back in her chair. "Yaar, don't test my charity. We admire your work and we've had such a good beginning. If you go and tell lies now, it'll ruin the whole thing. I won't trust you. And I will just have wasted a day that I should have spent looking for an off-site containment and my sister, instead of fixing the health problems of an Uplander boy who had every-thing, but gave it up for a little rebellion."

I watch the vein in her temple jump and her cyborg fin-gers flex around the arm of her chair, leaving the metal arm-rest bent and twisted. The arm whizzes and moans from the flex. Something isn't right with it.

"The last thing I want is to piss you off. Trust me. You're fierce." I mean it as a compliment, but she's got a short fuse, apparently.

Her arm moans louder as she rips the chair's arm off and throws it against the wall.

"Shiv, you should let me take a look at that," Saachi says.

"Don't touch me," she replies, but eventually gives in.

Zami approaches her, brave soul. "Why don't you take a break? You haven't slept. You haven't eaten. I know what you're going through. I'm worried about Taru and Masiji too." He holds her shoulders and leans his forehead against hers. A remarkable moment, a deep connection. I don't think I've ever felt what they do right now, that closeness, that trust. Aside from a ghost in my past that I'm chasing.

She nods. "I am hungry. And, Saachi? Let's fix my replacement, okay?"

Thank god. She leaves the room.

The boy, Zami, says, "We will get you home safe. Saachi will try to unearth whatever records or locations we can trace on your uncle's last missions. If he was in the Red Hand, we'll find the information on your uncle. But help us with one more hack. You work for Solace Corp, so you know how to locate proprietary information. All we want are the coordinates of the off-site facility where they're keeping our family. How would you go about getting it?"

I think and think; the buzzing in my brain is gone, and it's like all of a sudden realizing that there was a sound all the time. Thinking was never so complicated, and yet, I wonder if it is difficult now because I haven't done it in a while—at least on my own.

"You'd have to be an insider to get proprietary information," I say.

Zami leans in. "But you could, you know, get it."

"Maybe. I assume info like that needs the highest clear-ance. It's not like some dusty old data packet in storage. I'd have to be inside the firewall. And even then, I'm sure I'd set off a ton of alerts when I go poking around the wrong place."

"You're clever, though, aren't you? You managed to nab some dark data packet for us already. You could set some dis-tractions for Solace while you took a quick look at the coordi-nates, yeah?"

"Yeah, probably. It's risky."

"Man, it's all risky. So where would you have to be to pull this off?"

"Inside Solace. I'd have to walk into Solace Corp. after missing the last day of my internship, like nothing happened."

Zami smiles. "Like nothing happened. Exactly." He snaps his fingers.

"You don't understand. I'm not some grunt. They will have noticed my absence."

"Sure, and you'll make it right, tell a few lies, and get back into your office. Ashiva will come along as support. And since it's the AllianceCon, everyone will be distracted by the noise and fireworks, so that's cover."

"And you'll find whatever my uncle's last mission was for the Red Hand?" He reaches his hand out to shake.

"I swear."

They have no idea about my family. How connected they are. How my absence definitely is not overlooked. How Mother is probably looking for me already and monitoring Central.

I nod. Maybe I can get a connection with Solace and snag the info before the system reads my presence. They surely can't do it. They need me. I see that now. Without my connection, they won't stand a chance.

"Maybe. But Ashiva can't come. She'll blow the whole thing up."

"I heard that!" She says from the other room.

Zami says. "Eh, she'll be fine. We won't let you go alone. You'll return to your life back in happy land, with money and air and food, and life. I'm sure you can lie your way out of stumbling on a bit of old data. No big deal. Isn't that what you want?"

Return? I must've smiled because he gets excited. "I . . . I don't know . . ." I say. What will I do after all this? None of this was planned. But there's no way but through.

"Yes, that's what we are trying to do. Get you back home without a hair out of place. We fulfill our debt to Khan. Along the way, you do something legendary you can brag about on the underweb. Unless, of course, you want to make this difficult for yourself. Work with us and help us. We'll help you."

"Okay, then. Let's get ready," Riz says. "Maybe I can go back..."

Saachi runs a flesh editing pen across the scar on Ashiva's face while her replacement runs updates. Ashiva seems angry at having to undergo the genetic edit, but she looks different now, less volatile, more focused. She'll blend in better in Central. But the fire in her eyes will be harder to disguise. There's a wildness to her I've never seen in anyone in Central. So beautiful.

I know not to trust the surface of things. I've seen what she can do with her replacement arm and need no other proof of her strength. I admire her clear thinking, lack of doubt. It's like the whole world is visible to her, and she knows exactly what her purpose is. And I am a mess. My body was hacked by my mother, and now by these Downlanders. I've been monitored since birth. My body rejected technology almost like it was allergic to it. Who am I in all of this?

Alive. Still alive. So, better than the alternative. And I'm one step closer to finding the truth about my uncle. I agree to go with her just to find the location of the dark off-site, but only if she gets info on my uncle. Ashiva promises, but I know she'd leave me to die if it came to choosing between her family or me. Who wouldn't? Well, maybe I wouldn't, but my circumstances aren't normal. None of this is normal.

Saachi opens a large metal box and pulls out Uplander clothes: silks, tunics, long gloves, embroidered suits. I pull on a simple tunic and pants. I know Ashiva wouldn't want the sari, so I push it aside in favor of simple and sharp black pants, and a long black tunic: slim, silk, simple and indescribable, forgettable, but nicer than she's apparently used to. She, of course, scrunches her nose at me like she smells something rotten.

"How do you put it on?"

"The closure is here, in the back."

She tests the fabric for elasticity and I stop her. "It's silk. You'll tear it."

"Useless."

But she puts it on anyway.

Her hair is another matter entirely. Long, knotted in small braids here and there, and shaved around her ears, it looks like chaos. I hand her a brush and she looks at me with daggers in her eyes. No matter. She is fire incarnate. I will not tempt fate. She twists all of her hair together instead.

"It's great. You look great," I say.

"I feel like I'm going to suffocate." She pulls at the high collar of the tunic. She walks like she's in costume and would give herself away any second.

"Relax, or you'll come off as out of place," I say.

She grunts and readjusts her fitted jacket, walks across the room again. "I can't believe you wear clothes like this all the time. How can you stand it? I go undercover all the time and have never been uncomfortable."

"So how exactly do you fit in with the Central elite?"

She stumbles. "Not the elite, but the first few Stratas are mine, easy."

I laugh. "Can you try to be less . . ."

Ashiva snaps, "Less what?"

"Less like you are expecting to be attacked any second."

She pauses, a hand on her hip, and says, "But I am. Expecting that."

Zami steps in. "Pretend then. Or else you'll look like you just don't belong. I got you a new identity. You're now a privileged Uplander transfer from the Eastern District who specializes in combat training. You're considering joining Solace Corp as a combat tech."

"Yeah, all right. So, how do we know each other?"

I swallow hard. "Friends. Old friends? But where have I been the past few days?"

Zami smiles. "You went to pick her up and travel back with her. These are dangerous times and you wanted your friend, Avni, to arrive safely."

Ashiva says, "Avni. I've always liked that name."

"Avni. There. Now you have a story. Stick to it and get inside."

"Oh, one more thing. Here." Saachi hands us both small cases filled with lenses. "They'll block most cameras from scanning your retinas. Since there aren't body scanners, all we have to worry about are your eyes."

"Okay," Ashiva says, then turns to me. "But if you mess up, I'll—"

"Yeah, I know, slaughter me, toss me into the sea, I get it. Don't mess up. Trust me, I don't want you for an enemy."

Still, she looks prettiest when she is herself. Alive, angry, fighting. I admire her fire. Because she is one hundred percent original, herself, even with the surface edits and an arm that squeaks and squeals. I know there is no one like her in this world.

It's been two days since the raid and what do I have to show for my efforts? The worst part about it is he looks like he's having fun. Yes, he says his uncle is dead, and that his mother is terrible. But he has to be the golden son of someone wealthy. Spoiled, lacking nothing, floating through life protected from any sort of danger. It amazes me that in this world, there are still people who have food in their bellies, cool air to breathe, a future. He still doesn't know what our lives are like. His visit in the Unsanctioned Territory with us is only a temporary vacation. He can go home, even if he gets rebooted. He has a home. And a mother.

"What's your deal, Riz?" We walk along the narrow streets of the Liminal Area. He's skittish; this must've been where he was picked up.

"Deal? What deal?"

"You know. What do you want in life? Or don't Uplanders have dreams?" I scan the area and see five sets of eyes on us, all daaku waiting for easy prey. I signal to them to stand back and flash my replacement in their direction. If they're stupid enough to come at me, at us, it'll be their mistake.

He stares blankly at me, unaware of the dangers around us. Maybe they don't have dreams. It just occurs to me the neural-synch may have taken even those away.

"Of course we have dreams." His face is a ghost, though. "I've always wanted to visit the Alliance Space Colony."

I stop and laugh.

"What?" he asks. "Don't you wonder what's up there?"

"Yeah, but I'm more worried about how to feed my family or if I'm infected with the Fever rather than planning an inter-galactic vacation."

"You're right. I don't know what life is like for you. How could I? It's not my fault, though."

"Stop. Right there. You can't honestly believe that just because you were born into it, that you were given the luxury of health and life, that what happens to us in the Narrows is not your fault?" I pull my long gloves higher, tighter.

"What? I didn't make the Narrows, the Ring, Central. I'm against the neocity plans. Look, more neocities wouldn't help the rest of the population in the SA. It would only continue to develop deeper levels of exclusion. I've never agreed with it."

"Disagreeing with something and fighting against it are two different things. It's easy to disagree, safe, low risk. To stand against those who are sending families and children to their deaths outside the neocities? It's sick that we are in a world where this shows courage. It should be the very level on which humans are judged."

He's about to speak, but the words hang on his bottom lip before slipping off into nothingness. Yeah, that's what I thought.

The air around us grows thick, like my lungs can't process the pollution. And the tunic collar cinches tighter around my throat. I'm sure to lose my temper, so I do what Zami taught me to do, and I take a deep breath and count. If this is going to work, I have to stay even.

"Come on," I say. "There's going to be a line to reenter Central since it's AllianceCon."

AllianceCon will give us some cover. Central will be live-
lier than usual. The big crowds will be easy to hide in, but will
also bring an increased presence of guardians. We join the
line under a massive holo-screen projecting playbacks of the
end of WWIII, the same clips I've grown up seeing, but this
time they look different to me.

I mouth the taglines they spew about the world in which
we were born: "Born on the back of annihilation. Like the first
dawn after an endless night." Twenty-five years after the
floods and nuclear winter, after the reorganization of the
world, we should thank the PAC for their charity in how they
brought the world together. The PAC loves using the phrase
"impossible decisions" to allow Provinces the leeway to
choose how they will manage their populace.

I pause and take in the playback on the holo-screen, and
watch the North American war mecha battle the Asian mecha.
I listen to the sounds of metal crunching as the two colossal
robots collide mid-air over the Atlantic Ocean in their final
skirmish, before their nuclear missiles were launched. The
clip ends with the PAC's logo, fists destroying war mechas.

Even though I hadn't been born yet, I feel like I was there,
as I watch the great mushroom clouds rise above the disinte-
grated cities on the east coast of the North American
Province, Central Asia, and the Middle East. I can hear the
screams in my mind, as the bright flash of light consumes the
sky, and the fires inside the explosion radius burn people
where they stand, leaving statues of ash. Then the shockwave
of the blast ripples out beyond ground zero, collapsing buildings and throwing people off their feet. The worst came later,
with the fallout debris creating airborne radioactive isotopes

polluting the air, spreading radiation sickness miles away. But then the smoke from the three explosions blocked the sun and the world's food crops froze. Millions more people died around the world from fallout on the PACs' watch than from the bombs themselves. None of this is in the PAC's playback. They're the heroes who came in and gave order to our dying world.

I jump when people around us cheer at the sight of President Liu at the end of the playback, standing with the world leaders. Are they pleased at the destruction or the millions dead, or the new world order? Or are they just bloodthirsty, rich people, drunk on their wealth, so far distanced from the suffering that still continues in the world? It takes every inch of my patience to still the fire inside me. I'd love to strap on a bomb to the wall and just let it fly. I wince. No, no I wouldn't. No more bloodshed. Even here. Even with these soulless people.

People cheer at each other, saying things like "Happy Alliance Day!" and "Welcome to AllianceCon!" Beautiful people are dancing in the streets and music is pouring out of UAV speakers.

The line is long; people from the outer districts of the SA and the world are allowed inside, just on this special day. AllianceCon is a planetary event, but this is the first time the SA has hosted the event. The SA made a plea to present Solace and host the conference because they need to convince the PAC to increase the SA's funding. But most visitors are wealthy people from other regions, the European Province, the Asian Province, Americas, and even those who live on massive city barges floating on the seas. All are curious about Central. This is the first neocity, the first Ring in the world, the first algorithm like Solace. It could be the first of many.

How can they celebrate when tragedy just took place? The Info-Runs never announced what happened in the Narrows. We need to connect to the all-comms somehow, to get our message out. How can so many people come together with such a celebration while so many innocent people have been lost in the Narrows?

When we come up to the guardian's booth, I look up. Central's sub-strata is a stunning feat of engineering. The glass sparkles like a million diamonds and rises like a tsunami: up, up and up. Spectacular. I've been inside the lower Stratas, but today, I'll get my first look at how the wealthiest live.

I should've packed an explosive.

It's like he hears my thoughts because Riz says, "It's pretty, isn't it? It's so fragile."

I nod, and stuff my anarchy below my edited façade.

"Books," the guardian says and holds out her hand.

I roll down the glove on my left hand to expose my wrist reader. She scans us and it feels like eternity. But I don't sweat. I don't even breathe. I just smile wide and pout like the other wealthy girls in line beside us. One girl looks bored. Put out. Fancy. I emulate her the best I can.

"Go ahead." The guardian waves us through to the Z Fever testing. A few uppers from other Provinces are throwing fits at being detained. One didn't pass the tests and they put her inside a cube-shaped room with clear plastic walls, barred from entry and contained. She's beautiful, with long, blonde hair. Like a film star or something. But I see it. She doesn't look well. But her companion is angry. So angry, they contain him too.

We are in.

The decompression chamber cleans us of all bugs—electronic and insects. The air is extracted from the chamber, then comes rushing back in with a fresh scent. The scent Riz has on his body. It's just clean. We exit the chamber and enter Strata One's chaos.

The press of bodies is intense, and Riz reaches for my human hand. I glare at him, but when I nod and he slides his hand into mine, I feel it. Our connection. It's unexpected and comfortable. Our hands fit together perfectly. He smiles at me, a boyish grin, and I smile back. A sensation like falling takes me and for one second, I wish we were on a rooftop alone, not here, running a mission. For a blip, amidst all this horror, I adore this temporary lie we find ourselves in. But then I'm back, desperate to find my sister.

"We need to get a transport to Strata 95. Okay?"

We scan the surroundings for a transport dock. But their lines are packed, so he takes me inside a glass elevator that rises above the din, up, up and up to Strata 20. My stomach goes into my throat. It feels like floating. When I realize I am holding on tight to his hand—and judging by the grimace on his face, probably hurting him—I let go.

"Heights aren't my thing."

"And here I thought you were all perfect, invulnerable, smart, and beautiful." He smiles sweetly.

"No one's ever said that."

"What? That you're perfect?"

"Yeah."

He laughs. He's a peculiar boy. Maybe not all Uplander rich boys are soulless, wastes of space after all.

I back up, but the vertigo rushes back and I stagger. He puts out his arm to steady me and his hand accidentally touches my waist.

"Apologies, I didn't mean to..." he says.

"It's okay. Let's just get there," I say, trying to steady myself.

"We have to stop by my flat first."

"Why?" I ask.

"I want to change my clothes, eat something. It'll be quick."

He's lying. I know it. "Okay, but then—"

He stops me with a raised hand that points to his eyes and ears. "Then we visit my office for the tour." His smile is terrified.

"Got it."

Then I know. The surveillance is real, even if he is offline. We are risking our lives just being here.

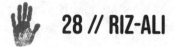

Central spreads out before us like a pulsing organism. The crush of moving bodies below for AllianceCon are reaching a critical mass. I count the floors as we rise up to the penthouse and suddenly I realize what we are doing. Going home. Anyone can be inside. Sidharth. Taz. Mother. Guardians. Father? Anyone.

"I'll be quick." I place my hand on the door lock and it pulses with heat, reading every line on my hand.

The light flashes blue. I try again.

Green. It opens.

"You live alone?" she asks.

I shake my head. "Not usually. But it looks empty now. My flatmate is probably at the festival."

Through the wall of windows, the city below glows with colorful lanterns and lights.

"Nice place," she says.

"Yeah, isn't it?"

"Funny. To have so much and just—" She shrugs her shoulders with emphasis.

"It's just where I sleep. Anyway. It's not my home." She follows me into the kitchen. "Hungry? Help yourself to whatever you'd like."

She's as still as metal staring at the central console.

"Do you need . . . ?"

"I don't need help."

"I wasn't suggesting . . ."

"I don't. I've just never seen . . ." she says, her hands pausing above the console, unsure.

I fight the urge to make a joke because it would be a huge blow to her pride, and I know what it must take for her to even acknowledge she needs help. So I open the console and program the first meal that comes to mind. In thirty seconds, the panel opens and there are ten small, white dishes domed with tiny, perfect, glass lids, containing a meal for two.

She squeals. I didn't know her voice could go that high. "That's insane!" she cries.

"Yes, it is." I'm embarrassed. She's shared her food with me, every scrap and sip. Now, knowing what I've been accustomed to, it all feels so pathetic under her gaze. Even though the meal I made is simple—daal, roti, curry, fruit—it's something I take for granted. But she's stunned.

"My mum had this put in. She thought I was looking thin. You want to meet a real master of surveillance, you should meet her."

"We could use her help. What's she do?"

"Never mind, she's in politics. Anyway, sit, eat. I'll just get some things and we can get on with it."

"Um . . . what is this?" She picks up a piece of fruit in her fingers and inspects it like it's the crown jewels, putting it close to her eyes and then up against the bright light, highlighting the star-shaped black pits inside the drab, peach-colored flesh.

"Oh, that? It's a chikoo. Delicious. Like somewhere between a pear and brown sugar. Try it."

Her eyes widen, and I realize she's probably never had a pear or brown sugar. "I'm sorry, I . . ."

She changes the subject quickly. "Are you sure they don't put strange things in your food?" She takes a bite, then slips a couple of chikoos into her pocket.

"What? No." I say, but then I think, why wouldn't they?

"I mean, it looks too perfect. Everything does."

"And that scares you? Look, eat now and forget it. What we're about to do is dangerous and it might be our last meal for a while, mind-controlling vitamins and all."

She looks at the plates, like she's deciding what to eat first. She waits until I leave before opening the glass lids on the plates. I hear the glass connect with the marble table. I think she'll eat more if I leave her alone. That my eyes will only make her self-conscious.

But when I enter my room, I get a shock. My room is packed up for storage. Sealed shipping containers line the walls. My bed is stripped. There's nothing left.

I pull the panel out of my wall and it's there. My box. The tiny synth paper tubes. Uncle's agribot plans. I stuff them into my pockets. Thank the gods. I search my drawer for my auto-inject, but it's gone. Cruel. Desperate, I search for my system. Nothing. All of it. Memory, monitors, everything gone. Nothing's left. The containers have my clothes, uniforms, a few odds and ends, but nothing important.

It's all gone. I was wiped. They can have everything ... At least I got the plans.

Then I see him.

"Taz," I say. He's offline, but his head is open and his tablet is ripped out of his chest. Obviously not a job by a techie. They would have taken more care. Even though he was trouble, he was my companion, in a weird way. I put him back together the best I can and wipe my eyes.

"What's with the empty room?" Ashiva asks through a mouthful of food.

"We have to go now," I say. "Sorry, it's not safe. We shouldn't have come."

"What happened in here? Did you just move in?"

"No, I was erased."

"Oh." Her eyes flash around the room and before she can say anything, I take her by the hand and pick up a few things, just before I hear the footsteps in the hallway outside my front door. Two sets of feet. Two people searching for me.

"We have to hide," I whisper and push her into a small storage closet in the living room. It's a tight fit, but we close it. It's hard to see from the outside; the panel slips seamlessly against the wall.

The front door slides open with a hush. Small, tinny sounds of a high-heeled person ring through the marble flat. Thick, heavy lugs of boots slink after.

A woman's voice says, "Check the bedroom."

Oh my god. I know that voice. So familiar. Mother's assistant, Geena?

A man's voice responds, "Looks like someone was here recently."

"We need to make this fast," Geena says.

I can't see her, but Ashiva's shallow breaths tell me volumes. She's getting ready.

"Madam? You should see this," the man's voice says, and I hear her light footsteps echo across the living room as they walk past our closet into my bedroom.

It's quiet.

Ashiva's voice is deep, "We have to go. Now."

I hesitate, but she slides the cabinet door open, pulls me out the front door, down the hall and into an elevator.

I press my hand to the sensor and say, "Down."

Only when the elevator moves do I breathe.

"Who were they?" she demands.

"The woman works for my mother."

"So, someone's looking for you now. This changes things."

"She probably just wants to send me to Ahimsa."

"That fancy health club?

"It's worse than that."

"Whatever. I bet they've sent an alert with your info all over Central."

"We don't know that yet. They'll want to keep this quiet. I'm not ... I'm not a model son."

"I guess we'll have to be better than them. We have to put Saachi's device to the ultimate test. If you're truly are offline, we have a chance."

When the doors open, we run out of the building and hide amongst the chaos of AllianceCon.

It feels good to be alive.

To be honest, I always wanted to see AllianceCon. Just not like this, not without Taru and Zami and Masiji. Not when hundreds of my people are locked up. Not at the expense of our freedom. There's no space in my head for the celebration around me. Any other day and I would be charged to be here. But I do my best to go with it. For their sakes.

But it's beautiful. The energy. The life. I've never seen so much money in one place. Bigger than my imagination, and louder too. The high-pitched laughter: That's what gets me first. They are all carefree, happy, chosen members of their societies around the planet, bestowed with the ability to survive and, of course, thrive.

I'm taking in the signs, banners, decorations. Sheer gold, red and purple silks hang from thirty stories above us, with little bells chiming in the breeze. Air scented with rose and sandalwood, and flowers I can't place. People from places I've only read about pass by: from the American Province with their funny accents; European Province, with their genetically edited, ridiculous facial features that make them look frozen in time. The SA elite with their tunics, saris, perfect skin and postures that make them seem almost made of plastic. Everyone is here who is anyone. Anyone who belongs to the future of the world, that is.

The rest of us will be left behind.

Central is anxious to show off their Ring and Solace Corp's reorganization. It's the first of its kind on the planet. And what better time than AllianceCon to display the newest tech, art, and ideas? They need this to work. They need this to be perfect. They need to empty the Narrows to show how at peace we are, clean up what embarrassing oversights they made, and show how the Downlanders will accept their fate and move on, or just stay quiet about it. They need to show that the difficult decisions the SA have made are for the greater good. That's why they cleared the Narrows. If this isn't perfect, the SA will not get the financial support to complete their construction on the remaining neocities, and the PAC will distribute their money to other, more deserving Provinces.

I smile at the timing. They are vulnerable now more than ever.

Entering Solace Corp on a day like today is so insane, it might work. Can we just walk in and take something? Riz seems confident, but I wonder if he's just feeling the exhilaration of illegal behavior. What does he have to lose? It looks like having his bedroom all packed away was as bad as it could get for an Uplander—so he's already hit the bottom.

The entrance is grand. Towering glass walls cut the sky. It's an engineering marvel. I freeze. This is it. This is the place that decided I wasn't worthy of continuing, that my genes weren't strong enough to add to the genetic population. This one place, this one system, this one algorithm . . . deciding thousands are unfit.

Riz pulls me close. His warm body presses against mine and he whispers in my ear, "We don't have to do this. I can go inside and meet you later. I promise to return. I won't run. It's more dangerous if you come in with me."

He still smells fresh. His breath is warm on my ear. For a second, I want to stay there, ignore the life I have, and just disappear. I imagine a moment where we meet in a different world on a different timeline. Would we . . . like each other? Would we love each other? That moment is fleeting. Images of my sister and Masiji sear into my mind. The fire will never go out.

"There's no other way," I whisper. I can't let him slip up.

"No, I guess there isn't." He slips his hand into my replacement hand and squeezes gently.

"Then I'm ready."

"Okay, Avni."

We walk up the stairs together, and the wall of glass opens for us and closes at once behind us, when we are three paces inside. Solace's motto is an insult to everyone I love: "Without Sacrifice, There Will Be No Tomorrow." We are the sacrificed.

It's quiet. There are people working today, even though the biggest AllianceCon of our lives is right outside. Unbelievable.

"It looks like an optional workday. Lucky us." Riz shakes his head. Then we both see it and freeze: A body-scanner sits at the entry. He presses my hand. "It's new. I didn't know. I swear."

We have no choice but to continue, so we do. We'd only look suspicious if we turned around now.

He leads me to the entry station and says, "Employee no. 75469. Here to give my cousin a tour of Solace Corp." His confidence amazes me. He owns this place. This is his domain.

The guard takes in Riz, then me and then turns to their screen. "Synch, please."

Riz places his forehead against a sensor. It doesn't read.

"Try again, sir," the guard says.

"Must be interference from AllianceCon," Riz says.

I just try to act as naturally as I can, which, I imagine produces less of a smile and more of a terrifying grimace, given the guard's reaction.

Riz leans against the sensor again. His mom or whoever is tracking him must have put a trace that's interrupting the sensor.

Green.

"Welcome, sir. That's odd. It's not reading your info, but it's approved your entry."

Riz responds, "Probably another update in the systems. I've been working day and night to get those to perform at night. But there are so many layers to the code, you know? I'll have my team take a look at it. It takes forever." He laughs the Uplander laugh. Not a care in the world. Nice show, yaar.

The guard just nods and smiles. "Yes, sir."

"I could easily get you an upgrade to your tech." He points to the guard's neural-synch. "We have the top of the line just sitting around upstairs."

"Really? I'd really appreciate it, sir. Your guest needs a pass. Stand here, miss." The guard points to the body-scanner and I freeze.

"Are you sure that's necessary?" Riz asks. "I'll only be a minute; she wants to get a feel for the place before applying for a position."

The guard doesn't flinch, his hand still pointing to the full-body scanner.

"Right." I step in between the panels and place my feet on the footprint-like images.

The guard initiates the scan, sending panels up and down and round and round my body. And that's when Riz gets chatty.

"So, have you been outside? It's amazing."

"No, sir. I'm on duty today."

"There are amazing Uplanders from everywhere. I saw this one woman who was so beautiful, I swear she was from Greenland."

The guard says in awe, "They do have the most beautiful girls."

The panels stop moving and I peer at the screen. The image of my body highlights my arm, flashes a silent warning, and then a really shadowy picture of me appears on the screen: "Wanted: Terrorist." My fake identification should have populated instead. They must have changed or updated their systems. That or, worse, Riz is setting me up. Sweat beads pop on my face, but I don't wipe them away. It is hot here. Maybe the guard won't notice my nerves.

Riz continues to engage the guard without batting an eye, "It's a shame you're stuck inside here. Maybe you could take a break. Just step outside for a moment. No one would notice. She was wearing sheer silk and diamonds."

The guard turns to look outside. Without moving his head, Riz reaches over to the guard's board and types something rapidly. Right when the guard looks back, Riz delivers a big grin. The warning has vanished.

"You're good to go, miss."

"Make sure to enjoy the view," Riz says.

The guard just laughs.

The gate opens and we are inside.

"Some view."

"It worked, didn't it?"

"I'll give you that. You'd be a good smuggler."

"I'll take that as a compliment."

He takes my hand and leads me up, up and up a series of walkways that spiral through the top of the round, glass-domed structure.

I keep wondering how many billion marks it took to build their infrastructure. Each mark they used from the PAC here was a mark less for us in the Narrows. This building was built on our dead bodies. For a split-second I doubt Riz. I wonder if he'll just turn me in, right here in the lion's den. He could. Even if he is wanted, erased or whatever, he could make up a pretty story about how I abducted him against his will, made him do things for me. It won't be far off. He has no real reason to help me. Yes, he knows I can do him in. And he's waiting for the info on his uncle. But he's smart. I look at him. Really look at him. And he smiles. He's the only way to my family. Without him, I'll never know where they are.

Trust him and, if he betrays you, you know what to do. Please don't betray me.

"You okay?" he asks.

I'm a good smuggler, but terrible at hiding my anger.

"I just want this done."

"In here." He leads me through a series of hallways, and then to a massive room lined with glass boxes.

"This is where you work?" I ask.

"It's strange, isn't it."

"Glass is so fragile."

"It's also transparent. They like to keep an eye on their

tech interns. But you'd probably work your own space. They have different offices in the outreach branch, if you're thinking of applying to the program." His eyebrows silently lift toward the corner of the room. I know the camera is watching us. Watching me.

"I see. Can you show me your system?"

As he sits in the chair and links with Solace, plugs her directly into his neural-synch, it occurs to me that Masiji was here, right here. She made all of this possible. Her fingerprints are on the code he's using right now, even if it's evolved since it was launched. Even with the minor block we placed, when he's linked to a hardwire, he'll have cloaked access. I hope. It looks invasive, but that's what it's about. Challenging the boundaries of humanity and machine, right?

"There's nothing to it," he says and leads me through the process. I see he's really deep-diving, hacking like the best of them.

Breathe, breathe, breathe. I fidget with my sleeve.

"I wonder if we could take a trip across the sea sometime. I've heard the views are spectacular," he speaks, like he is trying to tell me something. "There's a spa there that they say can heal even the worst ailments."

"I've always wanted to visit," I go along. He must be referring to the location. It must be near the sea.

Riz looks at me and squeezes my hand. "There's nothing to it. Let's get back to AllianceCon. I really am hungry."

"Good idea."

When we walk down the hall, he slips his hand in mine and I don't shake it off. He squeezes my replacement. My touch sensors in my metal fingers can feel vibrations and changes in pressure. I know what that means. He got the coordinates.

As we walk through the central foyer, I feel Riz's pace stiffen. Then I hear a voice.

"Where have you been?" It's a girl. She's pretty and perfect, and dainty. She is unoriginally cute. I've seen faces like hers a thousand times before, on those adverts with glowing models with clear, bright skin, threaded brows, airbrushed cheeks, be-jeweled neural-synchs. Though, hers isn't covered in real gems; they're just crystals. Rubies that size would require 24/7 armed guards.

I can take her.

"Oh, hello, Sumi. I've been on vacation," Riz says. I make to let go of his hand, but he holds my hand tighter. Like he's afraid to let go, or he wants to show this girl that we are, well, something. Whatever we are.

She looks me up and down, like she's looking through a scope on an electro-pulse rifle. "You didn't tell me you were go-ing somewhere. They were looking for you."

"Who?"

"Everyone." She glares at me with suspicion.

"Must've missed my notice. This is my friend. She's visit-ing for AllianceCon. I thought I'd give her a tour. She's study-ing tech at Eastern University."

"Is she now? I'm Sumi."

I let her hand hang in the air, an unwanted connection. In-stead I nod, look as bored as I can and say, "Riz, we really need to get back. I'm famished."

"See you, Sumi," he says as we slide past her.

When we are out of range, I say, "Looks like your girlfriend is jealous."

"She's not my girlfriend."

"Imaginary girlfriend. Whatever."

He laughs. But just as we are about to move through the guard station, I sense something is wrong. Two guards are behind us, walking in unison.

"How fast are you?" I whisper.

"Lightning."

"Let's hope so. Just run."

I run. He follows right behind me and we jump over the guard station's counter. I slam my shoulder against the sliding door mechanism, and we pour out onto the streets into the chaos.

Never look back.

A UAV careens across the sky above us and dives. It's hovering too close to the buildings and nearly hits a few onlookers as it tries to catch up with us as we run. It nearly overtakes us, but gets distracted by all of the extraordinary newcomers in AllianceCon that look and seem different than the average Centralite. The most extraordinary thing I see as we run is a collective of clones from the Americas: There are eight beautiful, androgynous people who look the same, sound the same, laugh the same. It's uncanny what Provinces choose to do with their PAC funds. Some regions invest in reforestation. Others, on building a better human. Many Provinces simply spent their funds rebuilding the cities they razed during WWIII—out of guilt, remorse, or in hopes of garnering more funding.

I slow to stare at the clones, but Ashiva pulls me and we keep running.

I've never felt so alive.

So much so that I wonder if, finally, I've been awakened and the life I'd previously lived was a dream or some kind of stasis. Ashiva awoke in me something I don't yet understand, but I want to fall completely and utterly headfirst into.

She's faster than me, but I run hard to keep up through the crowds. The rickshaw transports are cut off from the main roads to allow more pedestrian space. The festival is in full swing, with performers and tech installations, and the wealthy all fully immersed in the newest platforms. I want to scream, to laugh. But we need to keep a low profile. She pulls me into an alleyway where we wait as the guards pass through the parade. We press our bodies against the structure in the shadows. When they are gone, she turns to me.

Her voice is husky from our sprint. "So, where are they? Where's my sister?"

I cough and let my breath catch up, then release the numbers I memorized. "12.2502° N, 64.3372° E."

"What?" she looks to be calculating, using her I-Scan. "In the middle of the Arabian Sea? But there's nothing out there. They just dropped them into the deep end of the sea?" Her eyes grow wide with terror.

"No, wait, we don't know that."

"Then what? I mean, what could possibly be out there? The Bridge Project was never completed. The sea level rose too high to keep up." She paces like a predator, then lets her fist go full force into the side of the wall, splintering metal, tearing her silk glove. No blood. Only a small glimmer of her chrome knuckles shows through. I hold her hand in mine and press it.

"I don't know, but they wouldn't just waste lives like that."

"Don't be stupid. Yes, they would."

"Yes. No." My heart sinks. "I mean, if they wanted to eliminate everyone, they would have done it in the Narrows. Called it an uprising. They wouldn't bother to relocate. That's expensive." My words embarrass me, but it's true. Central's focus is monetary.

"Yeah, you're right." Something shifts in her. Her gaze sharpens, eyes widen. Ashiva turns to me and says, "The Void."

"What?"

She shakes her head at me and paces. "It is real," she says.

"You're talking about the old prison camp story?"

She doesn't stop to respond. "Or, maybe they built something like it. It could have been on the sea the whole time. They've never found it—"

"Because it keeps moving. It's the Void. Of course. It's real," I say.

"That's just enough crazy to be true," she says, and I'm thankful hope returns her face to a focused calm. "I'm sending the coordinates to Ghaazi and Suri now."

Out of the corner of my vision, I see a guardian pacing at the entrance of the alley from where we came.

"Come on, let's take in the sights until we can find a clear way out without being tracked. We can take cover in the crowd. We'll get out of here, I promise."

She nods and takes my hand, and we walk directly into the middle of the largest crowd I can find. No way the UAVs and the optic tech could keep up, reading all these faces. Along the way, we pass a vendor selling thin, color masks, and I buy two for us. Ashiva's face changes to a light green and mine goes to orange. Now we fit in. We're surrounded by hundreds of new tech exhibits from around the world. The first we pass is from the African Province, showing their new cloud machines. Another from the Australian Province is launching their new blood cleaners and regenerative science. I wonder which one will get funding from PAC to continue. We see the SA's massive AllianceCon exhibit inside a tent and decide to avoid it. But there's one that's packed more than others, so we enter that one. It showcases the latest tech from around the world, things that aren't even available to the elite to purchase—only drool over. The newest optic mods that allow you to nearly see to the microscopic level. The nano-bots that can sculpt your face and body while you sleep. I watch Ashiva as she stands, mouth agape, taking it all in. I can't read her. I pull her deeper into the tent.

Right at that moment, I want her to have everything. I want to give her everything. I want to take her away from this nightmare I am beginning to realize I'm a part of. I've never had a relationship, not really. Only crushes, flings. My family doesn't allow it. But I can't imagine being without her after all this is over. I want to have a normal day with her, without running, danger, and possible imprisonment lurking behind every doorway. I'm not sure what—if anything—she feels about me. The only thing I'm certain of is that she loves her family, and I, well, I think I love her. And I know now I have to do anything I can to help her.

"Oh, my gods, this is amazing."

But then I see it and feel so careless in bringing her here. In a case that's captured her gaze is a chrome extremity overlay. She rushes towards it and slips out of my hand.

The description reads: "Replacement Exo-Mod: Turn your body into a weapon, just for a day."

She smiles, and a sinking feeling takes me down. "This is all a game to you. To Central. You think our replacements are fun."

"This was a bad idea. Let's go." I motion to escort her out and she shifts out of my space, away from me, and watches an Uplander try on a model of a temporary replacement arm, laughing joyfully.

"What's that? Let's go see." Ashiva walks toward a crowd of Uplanders gasping and sighing at something.

"Bad idea. Stupid idea." I rush after her, but I'm too late. What was I thinking?

Behind the flurry of expensive genetic scents and planetary garb of sparkling wealth is a girl sitting on a chair. Just a girl. On a clear, lucite chair.

"It's nothing, let's go," I say.

Ashiva's ice. The girl sits in a large glass box the size of a closet. Eyes staring through space, through everything. Suddenly, her black irises turn purple and illuminate, and her head turns toward Ashiva, locking eyes with her. Her voice is slow and soft, and child-like.

"My name is A.R.I., Assimilated Reconnaissance Instrument. I am the first Neo-Soldier."

Ashiva takes two steps back into me. "She looks so real. Like Taru. Like me."

"Can we go now?"

She nods. Back on the street outside, I feel like an idiot. "I shouldn't have taken you in there."

"No, I needed to see, see how far Central has come. We'll never get ahead if we don't even know their tech advances."

She moves her replacement arm and then I know. I can almost hear her thoughts. She's probably thinking Uplanders think they're better than her. Because they can now make humans, or something better than human.

"What now?" I ask.

Her eyes focus like a laser on some invisible distant horizon I can't see. "Now, I get my family back."

"But how? I mean, if they are where we think, it'll be tricky."

I let my eyes linger too long on her, waiting for a reply.

When her eyes reach mine, she blushes. "I have a few ideas," she says.

"Do they include very bad things? I have a feeling you are thinking of committing a few more infractions, a felony perhaps?" I laugh.

"You're catching on, Synch."

"Thanks."

"For what?"

"For including me. Using my chosen name."

"No problem. You could have sent me to containment by just whispering to a guardian at any point that I was holding you against your will. But you didn't."

"I thought about it. But I don't think they'd listen to me. You've a way with people."

And she laughs.

"I would never do that," I say. "Not now, knowing what I do."

Silence stretches between us like a massive black hole. Nothing to say, nothing to do, we just take in the surroundings and, for a moment, relax. She isn't good at relaxing. I don't think her body ever has, running on adrenaline since birth. But she seems to slouch a bit, so that's encouraging.

As we sit, I feel a sudden buzz and another Info-Run cascades over the right corner of my vision. From the way Ashiva cocks her head, I know she's reading it too.

INFO-RUN
URGENT ALL
THE MINISTER OF COMMUNICATIONS IS MOURNING THE LOSS OF HER SON TO THE EX-
TREMIST GROUP THE RED HAND. HIS KIDNAPPING TOOK PLACE EARLY YESTERDAY
MORNING. DUE TO THE SA LAW, NO NEGOTIATION WILL TAKE PLACE, NO RETRIEVAL OF
THE KIDNAPPED UPLANDER. IF THEY ARE SEEN, THEY SHOULD BE REPORTED TO AU-
THORITIES RIGHT AWAY. ASHIVA, AKA, CHROME TIGER, HAS BEEN SPOTTED IN CEN-

TRAL. SHE IS ARMED AND EXTREMELY DANGEROUS. IF ANYONE SEES THEM TOGETHER, OR APART, NOTIFY CENTRAL IMMEDIATELY.

Under the Info-Run is a picture my identification card and a blurry image of Ashiva entering the AllianceCon tent that Solace took just moments ago. They are watching us. I feel the world closing in.

Ashiva takes my hand and lifts me to standing. "Let's go."

"What's happening?"

She pulls me into a crowd and down a dark street. "That's your mum, then? The flitting Minister of Comms? Ravindra's right hand?"

I can't tell if she's pissed, scared or both. Probably both.

"I didn't want to tell you. I've been trying to get away from her my whole life..."

"It doesn't matter right now who is chasing us. We need to get out of here right now, before we're seen."

A buzzing surrounds us from above and some UAVs lock onto our location as we run. But we don't stop. "Halt!" They call after us in their flat, computer-tone voice. Ashiva moves straight into a crowd and we lose a few UAVs that busy themselves with trying to identify visitors. But there's one that sticks to us, like a predatory bird coming in for the kill. It dives down and nearly touches us. "Halt!"

I know it's sending our location to Central as it flies, transmitting everything through its camera. Suddenly, Ashiva stops running and pushes me aside. She stands like she's steadying herself, and pulls her arms to her side, right fist higher, closer to her body than the left, ready for a fight.

"C'mon machchar, you piece of dung. Let's go."

It comes to her level and she crouches, then pounces upwards, just high enough to rip the drone from the sky and tears its rotors off like she's peeling wings off an insect. Then she tosses it to the ground and with one smash, she crushes the bastard to bits. That's about a gazillion infractions.

"Yes!" I yell, cheering for her.

"C'mon." She smiles and we run as fast as we can to the edge of Central, down in the elevator and into the darkness of Strata One. As the levels of Central pass us, I realize something.

"I've nowhere to go."

"Neither do I. Now we understand each other," she says. "We need to get out of Central. Then we can regroup with the others."

"Right." But a sick feeling creeps across my body. An endless weight of heartbreak. The idea that I'll never see my flat again. The idea that I'll never eat real food. The idea that my mother put out an Info-Run that declares my lack of worth. That her words may have sealed my fate as a criminal of the state. By the time we descend forty Stratas, I'm coming to grips with my future.

The doors of the elevator open when we reach Strata One.

"I just want you to know," I say, "that I want to help. I can help. I'm sorry."

Ashiva nods, nervously.

In front of us stand three figures: two armed thugs and a woman. Geena, my mother's assistant.

"Hello, Riza," she says.

This will not end well.

Run and fight. These are the two things that keep me alive. It's important to use them in that order. Running works best as the first line of defense from goondas, guardians, and general trouble. Fighting is effective only if I can't outrun them. Hiding, though, is my last resort. Most recently I hid from a C.O.R.E soldier and in Synch's closet. Nothing good comes from hiding. I should have fought on both accounts.

"I'm sorry," he says, but I'm not sure what he's apologizing for.

The three people pull us from the elevator and toss us against the wall. The woman looks like an Uplander, probably upper management, not fancy enough to be super-rich, but employed by them, nonetheless. The other two are just guards, hounds, good as dead as I calculate their height and weight, and lack of martial abilities. When they put the restraints on my wrists, they tighten them until my skin bruises. I can't show all my cards yet. If I fight now, Synch could get hurt.

Synch says, "Geena, just let her go. She didn't do this. I came of my own volition."

The woman strokes his cheek. "Why, Riza? Why'd you do it? Your mother gave you everything. Most would've killed for your place. Why'd you go and steal from Solace and trade with trash?"

One man holds him. They don't know about my replacement. Even though I tore the gloves punching a wall, the chrome is still nicely covered by the shadows.

"She's not trash."

"Do you even know what's on the data packet you gave her?" Geena asks.

"I'm getting tired of your talk. Just get on with it," I say with a smile. The guard makes a move to grab me, but I dodge him and laugh.

"Kill the Downlander scum and leave her body somewhere visible, somewhere the cameras will see. You, bring him. We're going on a ride to Ahimsa."

"No," Synch says.

The woman hisses, "We've been looking for you, Riza. What a pain you're turning out to be. But no, you have to be alive, and hanging out with a Downlander kachara. Your mummy can't be without you, so we've got to take you to Ahimsa and clear you of all this nonsense. So much extra work. Would have been so much easier if we could have pulled your body from the sea."

"She's not garbage, you fake, mindless woman. When was the last time you had a thought on your own? The funny thing is, you don't even know," he spits his words at her as she pushes me forward through the crowd.

The woman signals to the others and puts a hood over Synch's head. They're going to get rid of both of us. Quickly, they load him into a transport and leave me with the other guard in the shadows. I catch the code on the transport and memorize it. 48594. 48594. I repeat to myself over and over again.

Where'd they come from, so fast? They must be following him, following us. He said his mother would be looking. He's right. I'm so careless. Distracted. Was this what Khan was afraid of? Did he set me up for failure here? They aren't heading toward Central and Solace. The transport is moving towards the Narrows.

Nothing good will come of this.

But before that, I can't let Synch throw his life away. Not for them.

"I can make this quick, girl," the idiot guard says, turning me around to face him. "Or I can make this painful."

I shatter the restraints with a tug, relishing the shock in his eyes when he realizes I am not some meek little girl. "I vote for painful."

He takes a step back.

I move into first offensive position, one leg in front of the other, fists ahead, balanced and ready. "You first." I wink.

The goonda looks confused, but takes the shot. His top-heavy, body-builder's form tosses fists over hips and before he sees what's happening, I kneel and bring my elbow out, arm bent, and let my hook fly at his leg with all my power. He collapses like fractured glass.

"My leg! You broke it!" he screams.

So weak. What a killer. Muscles without skills. I almost feel sorry for him. But then he takes out a handgun, an M50, an illegal weapon for sure, and aims it right at my face.

One punch to his chest, and he's gone. I've got no choice. Maybe he'll survive, maybe not. He's not my concern. The gun goes flying into the water. Dhat. Would have been handy.

I run fast, my lungs cut with the wind. Jumping over curbs, around transport rickshaws, and through people. I push, shove, and run. I nab a small transport as the driver helps his fare to the curb. I've lost their position, but follow their direction.

Speeding down the road, I'm already about a quarter kilometer behind the transport, but I know the way better than they do. I swerve around and take one, two, three alleyways, and spot their vehicle about twenty yards ahead.

Something inside me is wild. Even though I have the coordinates, and I can get away back to my team and regroup for our next mission to the island containment and get Taru, I'm frozen. Something consumes me that I've never felt before.

I have to get him back, no matter the cost.

What I feel is strange. Obligation?

I made a promise to him to keep him alive. And I keep my promises.

The hood over my head is heavy and made from some sort of polymer fabric—I can breathe, but seeing is impossible. I count the bumps on the road and realize we are driving fast through Central.

I say, "You know my mother. You've known me since I was a kid."

Geena's voice is venom. "Shut up, Riza."

"At least take off my hood. Don't treat me like an animal."

When someone lifts it, I can breathe again. Three people: my mother's assistant, and two bulked up men. One is driving and the other is giving me a good once-over with an evil eye.

"Take me to my mother."

"Not in ten thousand lifetimes," Geena says. "The farther away you are from her, the better."

"We should gag him. Shut him up right," the evil-eye man says.

"It'll be over soon," she says. "Once we do the full reset and get you far away from here."

"You can't do this!" I shout as she signals to the evil-eye man, who pulls a gag between my teeth.

The transport races over the last street past the Liminal Area and down a filthy, wet path toward the Narrows. It zooms through the unmanned gates and into the two centimeters of water that covers the ground everywhere. All I can think is that this is where Ashiva is from. This is her home. I can't let them take me to Ahimsa. I know what they'll do there. I won't

be the same. They will do a complete reset. I'll never even remember that Ashiva existed. All of my memories of the past
few days will be gone. And all that will be left is a useless,
empty, compliant Uplander loser.

We reach the edge of the Narrows. A C.O.R.E soldier is
posted at the main entry in front of a twisted and broken
metal fence, like a temple icon. As it moves aside, the robotic
suit screeches and moans. I watch the curve of its helmet, the
lift in its boots, the hydraulic pumps that run outside the back
of every joint.

It looks like my mecha, the one I built in the Mecha Wars
game. The one I made that was inspired by Kanwar Uncle's
plans. I look at the machine and see my mecha come to life before me. The care in the layers of armor, the heat-resistance
paneling, all made for his agribots to withstand the heat and
extreme weather.

Mother stole the plans from my secure network?

I did this.

"Geena, did you know too? Did you know she stole my
plans?"

She flushes. "It doesn't matter, Riza. Anything you make is
proprietary and owned by Solace Corp. Employees are all subject to the same laws, even the useless interns. Didn't you read
the fine print?"

My heart races. It can't be. "But she built war machines.
She's using the mechas to quiet the people in the Narrows before AllianceCon."

"Solace ran the numbers and decided it was likely there
would be an uprising. Statistically, it was only a matter of
months before the Downlanders would decide to overthrow

the balance, to demand more. We needed to clean up the area. We couldn't take the chance because of AllianceCon."

"Do you hear yourself?" I say. "You just said that Solace decided. Solace can't decide. It's not self-aware. It's an algorithm. And even if it were, you are still a human with free will."

She glares at me and out the window, like my words don't make sense, like I'm speaking an old tongue. Like she isn't able to compute.

Stage 4 disaster. Structures are shattered, empty, and the roads are covered with sand, dirt and broken bricks of asphalt. Sandbags line the area, piled six high in places, probably to keep the Narrows above water since the sea wall was destroyed in Central's effort to get inside the area. There are workers busy moving materials from one section of the Narrows to the next. If they're Downlanders or from the Liminal Area, I can't tell. But either way, they're not here by choice. Lights are staged and lifted high above everything so they can work non-stop. They are living and working under surveillance, like they are prisoners, terrorists, or both.

What the hell are they doing here?

We move through and past them. Up and down. And yet, I don't care. Not anymore. Whatever I am supposed to feel, I don't. I can't. If the feelings that are supposed to happen came to me, I think it could kill me. Numb is the only other way to go.

I am a fugitive.

I think I'm in love.

Mother wants me alive, but rebooted.

None of these thoughts goes with the other, but they leave me dizzy.

"Stop there!" Geena yells to the driver. The transport pulls over on an empty, cemented path overlooking the Sea. "If you could have just come home without entering Solace Corp, our orders were to get you to an extraction point to meet your mother. To leave all this mess behind. But since you went ahead and got tangled up with the terrorist group, we have no choice but to keep you here and do a total reset. There's no spa, son. It's all lies."

"Ahimsa is a lie? Wait, then what are you going to do with me?" I ask.

"I connect you to Solace and she runs a system factory reset. It's a new program courtesy of the SA. They've been worried about an uprising inside Central, and we can't have that. Too much is at stake. Don't worry, it's painless and you'll be right back to where you were when you got the neural-synch implant."

"You do realize that what you are doing is illegal, right? That you're tampering with the memories of the son of a minister? Your neural-synch will record everything. What if she's setting you up to take the fall? She'd do that, you know. She doesn't care a shit about you or anyone else. If she's willing to reset her own son, what do you think she'll do to a lowly assistant?" My voice is a growl and I don't care.

"Get everything ready," she says to the driver and the evil-eye man. She turns on a tablet and uncoils wires to connect to my neural-synch.

"I'm doing what I'm told because without this, without her, I'm nothing. It's not personal, Riza. I'm just following orders."

I laugh. "What's not personal about this? Your Downlander roots are showing. Don't be so gullible."

"I'm sorry. I really am. She has my son, Sunil." She looks out at the two men. They lay down a tarp on the concrete, beside tools and a tablet. She moves close to me and whispers. "I'll distract them. They just want to get paid. Stay away from them, and I'll do what I can."

Suddenly, a screech of tires tears through the air, and the van flips. We both fall to the floor and flip with the van, over and over and over. When I land upside down, I fight to focus. Geena is unconscious and pinned under the seat that fell on top of her. I crawl to the broken window and pull myself outside. My face aches and my shoulder is in agony.

A hand appears out of nowhere: It's all chrome. "Ashiva."

She pulls me to stand and says, "Next time, listen to me, okay?"

I try to nod, but my everything hurts. "Let's go."

"I need the money. No kid, no money," the voice of one of the guards is gravel. The guard picks up a piece of metal and takes a swing at Ashiva. She blocks his attack, but slips and the guard's arm moves toward me instead.

"Wait, I can . . ." I begin, but as the words leave my mouth, I feel a bolt of lightning burn through my chest and see a scrap of metal pierce my shirt. All breath leaves me. I gasp and fall to my knees.

"No, I'm sorry. No!" The last thing I see is Ashiva moving toward me and the evil-eye man with a shocked expression.

Then all goes black and red.

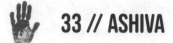

"NO!"

I'm too late. A thin man stabs Synch with a sharp piece of metal, some old scrap of rebar. And he goes down hard.

I can't tell where Synch is hurt. His blood's everywhere: through his clothes, out his mouth, over me as I lift him. Must've hit an artery; the spray is ridiculous, terrifying.

"It's okay, it's going to be okay," I lie.

I lay Synch down gently. Then I take off my jacket and press it to where his hands clutch his chest.

"Hang on, Synch. Push down here. Don't let go."

His eyes are desperate. Shit. He's gagging on blood, so I turn him on his side.

I dodge a fat man's swipe at me with a pipe, and he overextends himself and flops to the ground like a bloated barracuda. Though I am smaller than him, I'm fast. He probably underestimates me because I am a girl. Mistake of his life. I punch fat-man in the center of his back with my replacement. My chrome hits him like a ton of bricks.

"Stay down!" I yell. Fat-man groans and gets acquainted with the concrete.

Then the thin man comes at me like a fighter in his first battle, sloppy, all arms, weak legs. Idiot.

I shake my head. They have no idea what I can do. But, I guess, neither do I. Not really.

He stabbed Synch and won't be walking away from this.

The thin man takes a swing at me with his fists, like it's going to be easy to knock me down. I plant my feet and pull my replacement arm way back, releasing its full power straight at his gut. The sound is sickening. The attacker flies back, and back and back in the air, over the edge and into the water. Done.

The fat man sizes me up and takes a few steps back.

"What are you?" he stammers.

"Human," I say and chase him down. If he gets free, then everyone will think Synch is still alive. This way, Synch can become a memory, and his mother might stop the hunt.

I restrain myself and smash the fat man in the face at half power. I still break his nose and jaw. He begs and I stop because I am not a monster. And while I want him dead, he needs to deliver a message.

"Please..." He spits blood.

"On one condition. You go back to your employer. Tell her there was an accident. That everyone else died, including Synch. Everyone fell into the sea. They will not be found."

He nods as fast as he can. The blood trickles down his chin and through the new gap in his smile, courtesy of the missing teeth and my fist.

"Okay then." I slip a chip into his neural-synch and pull it out once it's done reading his info.

"I've got your code. I'll be watching you. If I find out you even hinted that any of this happened, I'll destroy you. Understand?" I hold his head and he gets it. His eyes don't lie, and now I can track him anytime I want with the info I pulled onto my hacked device. Even if he's lying to me, I can still keep track of him and use that to our benefit.

I let the goon fall back and tend to Synch's wounds.

Synch...

Oh my god.

I gather him in my arms and his eyes are fluttering closed. I know I should hold it together, but I cry anyway. I can't control it. If he dies, it means that... I broke my promise. My chest feels like it's a supernova. He can't die. Not like this. Not when I could have helped him. Not when I promised he'd be fine. Not when I made him hack Solace for me. This is my fault.

My mind races. I need to get him to Saachi now. I call her on the open comms, knowing it will be dangerous. That anyone can monitor the call.

My comms screen appears in the corner of my vision, white flashing numbers and letters. "Saach, I need a transport quick! Read my coordinates. Sending them now."

I turn to him. His eyes are closed now. But he is still breathing, shallow, shallow breaths.

"Come on, come on, don't give up." I lift him the best I can and take him near the transport that's tipped on its side. Crews in the Narrows will arrive soon to check on the commotion.

We hide in the van's shadow from view. I hear a cough and look inside the transport. The woman is pinned. She's in bad shape too.

I can't help her. This is all her fault.

When Saachi arrives minutes later in a stolen produce transport, I don't think Synch or the woman are alive. He hasn't opened his eyes, and she's stopped groaning. I've been alone with my desperate thoughts for too long.

Zami and Saachi lift Synch into the transport. I take a look at the woman. Her eyes open when I lift the metal seat off of her mid-section.

"Help me, please," is all she says. Then her eyes close again.

I want to yell at her. Tell her that all of this is her fault in the first place, that she's an evil bitch who worked for the big, bad empire. But I carry her to the transport and the heavy metal door slides shut behind me. She may prove useful in all of this. Saachi drives like a demon while Zami tends to us.

"Where are you hurt?" Zami asks.

"I'm not. The blood is his." I'm covered in gallons of the stuff by the looks of it.

"Glad to see things went as planned," Zami says.

I shake my head and press my jacket to Synch's chest. "We got the coordinates, but they were on to us. Her team came to pick him up to reset him. But it went sideways."

"His own mother? Damn, I knew Uplanders were cold, but soulless?" Zami says.

"He'll need blood. Lots of blood."

They lift me from the cot on wheels and put me down on something cold. When I hear a door shut, and their voices are gone, I open my eyes.

Bodies.

I'm on a shelf that's ten levels high in a room full of such shelves. Each shelf has a body. I am one of the bodies. Heat builds up in my gut and I try to fight it, but lose, vomiting up the last ration bit. Such a disappointment. But the smell, the smell comes in waves. Right when I think I adjust, it returns again.

Death. Death and disease.

What now? I scan the room for the living, but they're all dead. I slide off the shelf and my bare feet curl when they hit the icy ground. I look at my feet, my legs, that have been the weakest part of my body my whole life and I wonder. Was it all in my mind? Where did the lies originate? No, it was real. My pain was real. But could my diagnosis be wrong? Do I even trust the technology here? I shove these questions down under my tasks at hand. I have to be fast and silent.

There are old clothes in a bin, and I pull on the first thing I can find. A thick gray tunic and pants. I don't find shoes, but I see thick socks that will cover my replacement foot.

When I pass a mirrored glass wall, I flinch, thinking it's someone else. My friends did a number on me; no wonder the janitors didn't question my death. Dark bruises look like the Fever all over my face. In a water closet, probably used for cleaning the bodies, I scrub my face with a sponge. When I'm done, I look better. But I still feel rough.

I push my hair back into a ponytail and tie it with a string. Back in front of the mirror, I look less dead. I don't really look like an Uplander medical assistant, but the gray tunic helps.

The door opens easily. I don't know why I'm surprised, but then I remember the dead aren't supposed to move, much less walk and open doors—so why would they lock the room? The hall is empty, so I inch along. Suddenly, voices echo and I pick up the first thing I see—an offline tablet—and pretend to busy myself with it.

"Assistant." The doctor's voice is empty.

"Yes?" I say.

"They need help in Exam Room Twelve."

"Yes, doctor."

"What happened to your shoes?" he asks.

"Contamination from the last Downlander I pulled from containment. Filthy. Had to lose them," I say, though my tongue is getting thick with the lies already.

"Head to the main office for a new pair, then go to Twelve right away."

"Yes, sir." I say and start walking away.

"The other way, kid. And, what's your name?"

"Er, Jasmine," I answer.

"Hurry along."

I go. My life depends on it. I can't believe how quickly I answered his questions. Maybe I am strong, maybe I can do this. All the doors look the same in the hallway. Metal, cold, gray, steel. But there's a lot of movement near the one at the end. Must be the main office.

One push and I'm inside. Doctors, assistants, and guardians move about the room with ease; their footsteps all have a sense of urgency and purpose. Screens line the room with Info-Runs and reports. In the center of the room is a large desk with a petite and thin woman standing behind it.

I'd recognize her as soon as I would my own reflection. The Minister of Communications.

My breath evaporates. I turn my head away, but too late. I feel her eyes on me. "And you are?" she asks.

Someone pulls me. "She's with me, Minister."

Thank the gods, Dr. Qasim.

I say, "I'm here for shoes. The last ones were contaminated."

She is perfect. Perfect skin. Perfect makeup. Perfect clothes. Ageless, untouched by our sickening air. Almost otherworldly. Tidy as they come.

"Go." She waves her hand and goes back to monitoring whatever she is doing.

Dr. Qasim doesn't let go of my arm, but firmly leads me into a subset of rooms and halls, and finally into a prep room of sorts, with lockers and disinfection showers. Only then does he let me go.

"What are you doing here?" he asks. "How did you get inside?"

"It doesn't matter. I need access to an uplink. I need to get a message out. Can you help me?"

He shakes his head. "Not possible. Everything is monitored." His voice wavers.

"We can't let this happen. Whatever they're doing, the world needs to know. The Planetary Courts, the GHO and Planet Watch would not allow—"

"They've received approval for this operation. The world's fear of the Z Fever is greater than their desire for morality."

"That can't be . . ."

"President Liu sees Z Fever can undo all of their plans." How can anyone shrug off torture?

"No, President Liu is a moderate, focused on keeping us all alive. Wait. What have they done to you, Dr. Qasim?" Then it hits me.

He turns from me. "Look, you need to make a choice: Either make your escape or go back to the unit. I can't help you. I have a job to do and when it ends, I can see my family. My children."

"If you help slaughter thousands, they give you your family back?" My head spins.

"It doesn't matter, they're going to do it anyway. I . . . the Fever is real, Taru. It might infect everyone in Central eventually. That's why they're increasing the testing. It's already arrived in the Americas. They think the civilians in the Narrows are somehow immune."

"How do they know?"

"*Influenza zephyrus* breached the SA Province's water supply. It was an accident. And not a single case of Z in the Narrows has been detected. Only in Central."

"That's why they took us? For testing?" But something doesn't sit right. "Why the replacements? They only took those of us with cybernetic enhancements."

"It's something Solace missed. The Downlanders who have survived the radiation and poor living conditions are the most resilient. The ones who've survived replacement surgery are the strongest of the strong. They have fierce immune systems. Their bodies went through near death to survive the replacement surgery. The anti-rejection medication courses that we all endured, that led to a new resilience. Yes, Downlanders can still die from heat death, starvation and a lack of basic resources, but they've adapted an immunity to certain viral and bacterial strains. This is not something Central can fix with a quick nano-bot update. Central wants strong hosts for their vaccine."

He is caught in the trap. Either submit or die. He chose himself. I don't blame him.

I say, "Solace made mistakes because it conceived a world and population without taking into consideration the resilience of the human spirit and our ability to adapt with replacements. If she made that error, I'm sure she made millions more."

He nods.

Like she could have wrongly slotted me as unfit. "Just let me hook up the tablet to the main line. For five seconds. That's all I need," I say.

Dr. Qasim pauses, holding the tablet in his hand.

"Just five seconds and you can forget you ever saw me," I say.

He slips the uplink into the tablet. I go to the main comms and type as fast as I can. And just as I am about to hit send, the door opens and startles me, so I accidently let the tablet fall to the hard floor, and it cracks and turns off. Another assistant enters, covered in blood. Rao.

"Exam Room Twelve is terrible," Rao says through tears. When he sees me, his eyes widen, but he's more concerned with his state than mine. He strips and heads into a disinfection shower.

"I'm sorry," I say. But I'm saying it to myself, really.

Dr. Qasim shakes his head and picks up the broken tablet. "Do you know where Masiji is? Is she okay?"

His face is gray in the fluorescent light. "She's in critical. Her injuries are too grave. I don't think she'll make it. I am sorry. For all of this. I really am. It's better that—"

I slap his hand away from mine. "This is all your fault."

"I'll do what I can. Please get out of here. Stay safe." As he walks away, I pray he doesn't snitch on me. But he wouldn't, not now. It'd be too dangerous for him to show our connection. He tosses the broken tablet in an incinerator that destroys it instantly.

When I'm alone, the silence builds around me like a tomb.

Rao returns from the showers and gets dressed.

He hugs me. "I thought you were dead. I saw you being wheeled up on the death train."

"How'd you end up here? Working for them?" I ask.

"I'm not. I mean I am, but someone had to. I worked my way through the ranks. All the way up to clean up."

Rao chuckles.

What a foreign sound. I can't help but smile. "What do you mean, someone had to?"

"To find a way out, steal food. There are a few of us spies in the regime. Sorry about the vague message. I couldn't risk being heard. Playing dead was a brilliant plan, but where are you going from here?" Rao asks.

"I don't know. I had to do something."

"Exactly."

"There are a few others. We need to go somewhere without eyes and ears." He signals to the back of the room.

Rao opens a closet door and I follow. Kneeling, he lifts a ventilation grate and slides inside. The hole is so small, but I make it and follow him through a series of metal tunnels only the size and shape of my body. I'm weak, but only fall behind once. We reach a vent and he lifts the opening in the floor. It's dark below.

"Come on. You won't fall," he says.

I lower my legs into the darkness, take a breath, then let go. I fall, and feel a fluttering of fingers and hands catching me, and helping me to stand.

"Rao?" I whisper in the darkness.

A hand takes me and sits me down on the ground. Someone turns on a lantern and then I see: three children surround me, all in different states of health, from well and wearing assistant uniforms, to sick and bandaged.

"What is this place?"

"This is the abandoned part of the facility. It was left when a contamination alert was broadcast. Or I should say, when I broadcast the contamination. No Uplanders would dare come here. We keep it dark just in case."

"Clever. How long…"

"They took me like they took so many others from the undermarket before the raid," he says. I realize he's one of the missing, from the posters we see all over the Narrows. Have they been taking our children in secret and now they just needed more bodies? "We help whomever we can when possible. There's something you need to see."

He reaches his hand out to me and leads me toward a computer. "We've done a lot of work. Just yesterday, I think we figured out what they are doing here. Beyond the Fever."

"Don't they just want to clear the Narrows?"

"Yes and no. They're frantic. Increasing testing. Gathering anybody that's been replaced. It's their resilience they're after. Those who are able to survive the replacement surgery are stronger. Their bodies can survive terrible scenarios. We don't know why, though."

"They need an inoculation."

"Maybe."

"Have you figured out a way out of here?"

"Containment is outside Central—way outside. We think it's on an island."

"Island? There aren't any islands left."

"We think they made one."

Makes sense. Isolation. My heart sinks. "No way out."

"Only by air-transport." He pulls a light closer and shows me the plans. "It lands here, at the entrance, once a day. It leaves two hours later. Quick in and out. Four guardians or more. They bring people and supplies."

"We'll need help. Lots of help. We'll need to smuggle all the children we can into this area. They are small, easier to miss. Build a team."

"Good idea."

I think about the hundreds below still suffering those devastating tests. We have to find a way out or die trying.

"I have an idea. But it's going to take everyone in a coordinated effort. Do you have a secure line?" I ask.

"Yes, but it's only linked to the underweb. Why?"

"I have to send a message to my family. Hope they can hear me."

"You should try to rest, Shiv. He's not going anywhere." Zami's voice is calm, sleepy. He's worked all night as Saachi's assistant. They won't let me help. Said I'm too emotional. Too close to . . . whatever. I stay at the edge of the laboratory and pace for hours. Why didn't I leave him? I could be halfway to Taru by now. What's wrong with me?

"I'm fine," I say.

"We'll find another way," Zami tries to comfort me, but I'm not taking it.

I watched as they opened up his chest, replaced his lung with a balloon-like machine that will help him breathe, then replaced his shoulder and rib cage with metal bones. But the most noticeable replacement is his cheek bone and jaw. It was broken beyond repair, so Saachi installed a titanium replacement and removed the bone fragments, bit by bit, using a large magnifying glass and tweezers in her steady hand. All the while, Zami held lights, offered tools and wiped her forehead. Saachi was meticulous.

When the pair had finished stitching him up, he was reborn: cyborg.

Like me.

His perfect face is no more.

I don't know what to feel. Terrible that he almost died. Happy that he is alive. Scared that he'll hate me for turning him into this human machine. Glad he is like me. Mad at him for being so stupid and selfish. A typhoon spins round and round in my chest. I pace.

Zami gives me a five-hour sleeping tablet and I take it, knowing that rest is valuable and there's no way I'll be able to close my eyes on my own.

Saachi is starting on the woman I rescued from the transport.

"Wake me if—"

"Yeah, behanji. I'll wake you if anything happens. Now get some beauty sleep," Zami's smile is life. "You need it."

After our chores were done for the day in the Narrows, I would take Taru and Zami to the edge of the Arabian Sea to watch the fisherfolk come in with their daily catch. The fisherfolk didn't mind our watching, and fishing was the last remnant of times past in the Narrows. The fish all disappeared the following year, after the bloom of algae thickened their waters, and the ocean heated up past their ability to adapt. Most of the fisherfolk left shortly after that, to the open, rising seas, on massive floating raft-cities. Without fish, we were left with manufactured foods, and bulk lentils and grains that made their way to us through the undermarket, with which we could make flatbreads from, like roti, paratha, and naan. Not like the exotic foods in Central, meats, fruits, sweets.

No matter how much time passes, I still dream of being near the coast, watching the fisherfolk pull fish from the dark waters. There's something so comforting about the whole scene. So natural. Not like now.

I'm thankful for the rest. My heart feels settled by the gauze of happiness that dreaming gives, but as soon as my eyes open, the rush lifts my chest.

Where, when, how, what—all kinds of questions hiss in my

head like a viper and into the surrounding darkness. Zami is asleep on the floor beside me, in the same position we slept in our whole lives. Saachi is crashed in a chair nearby. It's too quiet.

"Synch..."

I find him on the surgery table, asleep. Probably forced into unconsciousness by Saachi's meds. I look at the bags he's hooked up to: serum to fill his veins, genetic meds that will speed his natural tissue's healing, anti-rejection and immuno-suppressant meds to force his system to accept the change. It's probably all that Saachi has in her arsenal. I owe her big. Now, if only I can give him a drug to force him to accept the change, that would be excellent.

He looks peaceful enough. The curve of his nose reminds me of the face of a mountain Masiji showed me in a book. It's far away in the Northern District, still, perfect, never summer and always covered in snow. I reach out to touch Synch's cheek, to see if he's comfortable, warm.

His hand takes mine, his unfocused eyes looking into space.

We don't say anything. Just sit there for thirty seconds or more, his replacement hand holding mine. All that keeps running through my head is that he can't see what I can. He doesn't know what's happened to his body. He'll blame me for everything. I want to hide. But I also just want to get this over with.

"Am I alive?" His voice is scratchy.

"Yeah, you're alive. You probably shouldn't move." I point to all the wires and tubes he's connected to. "Saachi fixed you."

"What happened?"

The big question. Can I find better words, words that won't hurt so much? All sorts of things stick in my throat like warm concrete and I shake my head, wiping tears from my cheeks.

"Ashiva?"

"What do you remember?" I say, not wanting to repeat any of the massive tragedy that I don't have to.

"First, water," he says.

I bring him a sip of water and wait.

"I left you. Then a transport picked me up. Geena took me somewhere. After that, I can't remember . . . I'm sorry I left you. I shouldn't have," he says and winces when he moves.

"Don't be sorry, Synch. We've said enough sorries to last ten million lifetimes."

His eyes search my face, then the room. "It's bad, isn't it?" He coughs.

"Take it easy. Your lung had to be replaced."

His eyes widen. "Just tell me, will I walk again?" His voice is a whisper.

"Your legs are in good shape." I take a deep breath. "It was an accident, a crash. Then you were stabbed in the chest. That ruptured your lung. And the transport accident ruined your shoulder and broke your face. But it's all fixed, I think." I clear my throat; the words burn a path through my heart.

His eyes are moons. "That's all?" His crooked smile puts me at ease. The facial muscle nerves will probably take time to catch up to the jawbone replacement.

I hold his hand and think about what I should say, and what I'd want to hear if I was on the table instead, and they are in total and complete conflict. I wouldn't believe anyone if they told me I'd be fine. But authorities always want to put people at ease. I gamble on truth.

"It's not going to be easy. There's a huge learning curve. And the Upland will never accept you like this. But you will get through. I will help you adjust. You are alive."

I see a single tear fall from his eye down to the top of the chrome replacement that now colonizes his face.

"I need to see."

I know he has to, but I wish he'd just forget. There's a hand mirror on a shelf in the surgery room. It's cold in my hands, unframed, endless. I wish I could slip inside and fall down into the forever it presents. I have no words left, nothing to negotiate, so I hand the mirror to him.

It's quiet as he looks and looks and looks.

I don't like the silence. "It took Zami a while to get used to it, but I think he's handsome with the chrome on his face."

He keeps looking, turning the mirror. I can't tell if he's going to laugh, cry, scream or all three.

"If the metal bothers you," I continue, "we could try silicone skin on the surface, but Saachi says that not for six months at least, to make sure all is adjusted and fitting properly."

"But why would I want to do that?" He isn't laughing, but he isn't crying either, so I guess we are in the positive.

"Huh? Oh, some like to give a human look to their replacements. I tore mine off. The skin isn't very strong, and I tend to bang it up. Too expensive to keep up. But Saachi's biohacker team has been studying this for years, so it should be pretty close to Masiji's work. But you're the first."

"No, I mean, why would anyone cover up their replacement at all, ever? It's amazing." He sits up from the table and hands me the mirror. "I've always been amazed by technology's ability to fix human problems. This is undermarket hacker shit. Saachi's a master."

"Oh, thank god. I thought you were going to cry or yell, or something. That would be acceptable too. Masiji said I was a tiger when I woke from my first surgery. Not pleasant."

"Nah. It's insane, yes, but I can get used to it. With time." He reaches his hand to take mine. To take my replacement. "My buddies on the underweb are going to be jealous."

I notice his eyes are watering a bit, and I hand him a cloth. Even when we accept our fate, change like this is impossible.

36 // KID SYNCH

There's a fine line between engineering a solution and creating a new problem. Scientists and technologists can be addicted to their research processes. Sometimes we get so deep into it that we fail to see the impacts of our work on the world around us. We don't even look outside our windows. It's not totally our fault; genius comes at a price. Our challenge has been impossible: find a way to survive this world with limited resources. My uncle wasn't evil. He was a curious engineer who fought to design machines to help us survive. But still, his work impacts the world, and the wrong people will make the wrong choices, as always. People like my mother. When I was eleven, Mother found my early plans for a unique, wearable cyborg arm piece. She shook her head and called me a child.

"Do you want to end up like your uncle, huh?" she'd say.

But now, she steals my plans. Profits from them. Turns my projects into monsters. Uses me and then wants to set me straight in a reeducation program. All of her steps have led me to where I am right now. Something she'd consider monstrous, with an exposed facial replacement. How could a mother do this to her son? Perhaps I'm not her son after all. Just an experiment. Like everything in her life.

Broken.

Rebuilt.

She thinks I'm dead, and all her secrets are buried. But I'm more alive than I've ever been. There's nothing more lethal than a clear mind with goals.

Here, in Saachi's lab, for the first time ever, I feel like I'm on the right side. That I'm asking the right questions, beyond my comfortable life.

Saachi, Zami, Ashiva, and I sit around a small table for a meal. I don't know the time, day or anything, but I don't care. "What's in this thing?" I ask. The beverage they hand me is fluorescent green and thick.

Saachi says, "It's a protein-building drink. It'll give you energy and focus. Your jaw is still healing so liquid food is best for now."

I take a sip and the cold, smooth mixture slides down my throat magically, sweet and sour. Perfect. The others share two portions of rations and mix the bread with some watery daal. It's the smallest meal I've ever seen, and it's the best.

I watch Zami eat. He's handsome for a kid. All arms and legs, but his thick hair and chrome bits on his face make him seem older. Or maybe his appearance is the product of living in the Narrows as an orphan.

"Eh, don't worry about it, Synch. You'll get used to it. There are benefits, you know. I can crush rocks with my molars," Zami says.

"And when exactly would that come in handy?" Ashiva asks.

"Maybe when a rock monster attacks you," Zami says with his arms waving.

"Or, maybe you'd really fancy eating a wall," I say.

"I'll tell you what, though, having a replacement arm is really where it's at," Zami says. "I've long dreamt of having one of those."

"Oh, come on, Zami," Ashiva says, taking a bite of food.

"Yeah, I've watched you, behanji, cracking open a ration can or fixing a fence or whatever with a flick of your finger. I know you keep it on the low, but I've seen it."

Ashiva shifts in her seat and puts her replacement arm under the lip of the table. "It's okay, I guess. Better than the alternative. It's not doing so well now, though."

"So much better. You're like a superhero." Zami laughs and then turns to me. "You'll figure it out. Saachi here is a perfectionist."

They agree. I find Saachi strange, and her knowledge comforting.

"I'm just happy to be alive." As I lift my stainless cup into the air towards them all and say, "Thank you." The cup flies out of my hand and travels halfway across the room. "Guess I have to work on that grip."

We laugh. Half my face lifts and the other doesn't. This will take some getting used to.

"Well, I was going to leave you, but then I thought the Red Hand could use someone like you," Ashiva says.

"I'm honored."

Saachi looks full of thought, uncomfortable. "Spit it out," I say, desperate to ease her fidgeting.

"While you were, well, in Central, I did a deep dive into External Hand's records for your uncle."

I sit up straight. "And?"

"I think you just need to see it for yourself." She turns on a screen and flips through a series of images. "It was easy to uncover the basic comms about the event that killed your uncle. But, like, it was strange that the events were recorded, in detail, in Red Hand's internal network records. Why would they have records of the whereabouts and death of a civilian engineer?"

I read the headlines: "Zealot Scientist Killed in Lab Explosion." "Solace Employee & Workplace Rage."

"I've seen it before." After his death, the SA framed his life as a crazy scientist to make an example of him.

"I figured," she says, "but something's off. The day of his death, he met with the SA government to discuss their progress on his projects. He wasn't just in his lab."

"His agribots," I say proudly.

She nods. "Do you remember anything specific about his project?"

"He'd been working on agribots that could withstand the electrical storms and acid rain of the Barrens. Here, this is all I have left of him." I pull the rolled-up plans from my pocket and hand them to Saachi.

"Amazing. This is for a battery power system of some kind. I've never seen anything like it." She inspects the plans.

"I think it might be a perpetual rare earths magnet, but I'm not sure."

"Oh." Saachi's face goes white.

"Well, speak up, sister," Ashiva says.

"I've been tracking the construction on the Alliance Space Colony through the underweb. There's been some chatter about their sudden increased funding to build a battery that will be able to power the Colony, well, forever. But they've stalled because they don't have the proper materials to build it. This is similar to the type of system they're building."

"They stole his plans?"

She shook her head. "Worse. It looks like your uncle

reached out to the Red Hand months before his death. He was made an asset for the External Hand. Also, around the time of your uncle's death, there was a payment from the PAC to an independent transport company, the same one we employ to smuggle members to the Liberation Hand. It's safer to use locals for transports. They know whom to bribe, whom to stay away from."

"What does that mean?" I ask.

"The PAC disappeared him. They probably still have him. Brains like his are too valuable."

Ashiva says, "Maybe they found out he was a Red Hand operative? Maybe he wanted out of his contract with the SA because they don't tend to let important employees go."

I sit down. "He could be alive. Thank you, Saachi. You really are the best of everyone." My mind buzzes with possibilities and plans to follow up with a trip to Greenland and the PAC, to see what else I can dig up.

Suddenly, an alert rings in my brain. The right corner of my vision flashes with white text over the world I see around me and, by the looks of it, all of us are having an identical experience. Info-Run.

URGENT I.R.
MINISTRY OF COMMUNICATIONS
IN 24 HOURS, WE WILL LAUNCH THE NEXT PHASE OF SOLACE CORP'S SHAANTI. IT WILL BE AN EVENT NOT TO MISS. ALL IN CENTRAL ARE INVITED.

Brief, clear, and concise. That means trouble. We know they will wipe the Narrows off the face of the planet, and all its inhabitants as well, one way or another. This might be the moment.

Ashiva says, "This has to be stage two of her master plan. You sure you don't know anything about it?"

"She'd rather tell her assistant than me."

Geena is in recovery from surgery. Just some banged up ribs and a few broken bones. She's lucky to be alive. Lucky I didn't kill her. Saachi sedated her and tied her to a chair. She was kind to set Geena's bones and wrap her leg in a silicone cast.

"And you all were mad that I dragged her out of the wreckage," Ashiva speaks up. "Sometimes my plans do work out, you know."

"Sure, Shivs. Whatever you need to tell yourself." Zami stands and rings his hands. "So, how do we do this?"

I put my empty glass down and speak. "We don't. I do."

Before Saachi doses Geena with a mixture of energy meds, I ready myself. I clean up, lean a few sheets of metal like a partition to block the laboratory and the Lal Hath, place a cup of water within her reach, and sit right in front of her to hold her focus.

"Go ahead," I say. And Saachi unties her hands and gives Geena the cocktail in her neck.

She comes to, and I'm not prepared for the hate that enters my being from breath to bone. She is everything that pains me, everything that causes suffering in the world. She is my mother's hand.

Steady. Steady now. Put it away.

I hold the cup of water out to her. "You must be thirsty."

Her eyes are terrified and disoriented, and she gulps the water greedily.

"Geena, how are you feeling? My friends set your broken leg and made sure you weren't going to bleed internally. You're going to be okay."

She looks at me like she's seen a ghost. "What happened to—"

"Oh, I didn't fare so well. But I'll be great. Put back together and all."

She inches away from me on her chair, just a touch. That movement tells me everything. I lean in and narrow the space between us.

"You are a cyborg now? Am I … ?"

"No, you're still one hundred percent Uplander gold on the outside. Just a little tarnished. Your insides are pretty much kachara, though. We both know that. Oh, and my mother thinks you're dead. Did I mention that? She thinks we all died in a tragic accident. I bet she's relieved. One of your guards was alive and he delivered the message to her. I'm sure he's dead now too. When did my mother become so bloodthirsty?"

"It runs in the family, Riza." She leers, but doesn't know how to hurt me.

"The funniest thing about all this? Is that you've always been so jealous of me. The whole time you've worked for my mother, you've been just on the outside. You'll never be fully accepted. You'll always be a reject of both sides. That's what happens when you sell out your people to be a servant of the Upland. No loyalty. You have nowhere to go now."

Her voice quakes, "What are you going to do with me?"

"Information. You sent the comms; you know my mother better than anyone in the world. What's the next campaign? Truth time."

She inspects her silicone cast and presses her hands to her midsection. I imagine the bruises were black on her stomach. "I am just an assistant."

"Don't lie. Not to me, Geena. I know you too well. Even from here I can do much worse to you and your family than my mother can. Sunil, right? We're already tracking him. He's at school now. Our best is already on the job." I point to Saachi, who's running a trace. I'd never hurt a child, but I'm betting she thinks the Red Hand is as bad as Central.

"Okay, please don't hurt him. What do you want?" she asks.

"You tell me everything you know, and we're done."

"I can go?"

"No, I'd like to keep you here to heal and for insurance. But after that, you're free to go."

Her eyes flash around the dark room. "You won't hurt me?

"Why would I have them fix you just to hurt you?"

"Where will I go?"

"That is up to you. I wouldn't head into Central, though. Mum's got a temper and all."

"Have it your way, but Sunil stays safe. Promise me that and I'll tell you everything."

The history I grew up reciting and the story Geena tells Synch are both suspicious. Lies, big enough to build nations on the broken backs of its people. Complete with great heroes, villains and disease, wars, economies, and hope and hopelessness. Winners and losers. They say we were on the brink of extinction. The nuclear bombs that went off around the world in Central Asia, the Middle East, and America killed millions. That if we continued to fight, the world would face annihilation. That's when the Provinces established the PAC, gave them control of the World Bank and control over all the Provinces' money. That's why they agreed to the New Treaty. The PAC has all the marks in the world. The decisions our leaders make determine our fates. And they know it. They are all power-hungry bastards, with dreams of writing their own stories in which they are the heroes.

But the thing is, you can't just make yourself a hero. You also can't help being one if you are unlucky enough to have that dumb courage inside you.

And I'm not saying Central's Ring and Solace, and the big plan to save at least a few didn't begin with grand ideas. They very well could have. They had to make tough decisions about who could live in the new world. But power contaminates the weak-minded and power-hungry; like a bit of metal left out in the sea air, rust consumes them until, one day, they're devoured and fall to dust.

I watch the interrogation on a screen from the other room,

with Zami and Saachi. Synch is careful to keep his back to the camera, not that anyone would recognize him now. We'll run a vocal distortion on him when we edit.

Geena says, "President Ravindra was demanding. She was going to get rid of the entire comms team. She was upset about the SA Province's position in the global marketplace. The East Asian Province is completely decimating us. Not to mention the European Province."

Synch shifts in his seat. "So, we launched the neural-synch. It makes one human brain work at nearly on par with AI. Faster, better, blah, blah, blah. Everyone knows how it goes. Tell me something new."

"The SA hasn't been awarded funds from the PAC for years, and without it, the SA will have to let go of their neocity plans. The rest of the cities are on hold. They will have essentially failed. If Central can't sustain itself, we'll all perish." Geena asks for more water. When she is through stalling, she begins, "The neural-synch made us competitive, yes. The best of us were optimized. But the PAC is set to cut funding to the SA. AllianceCon is our last shot. Then Z Fever came through. The Narrows provided an opportunity to test our C.O.R.E mecha-suits before AllianceCon and clean up so that we look good. Two in one."

"I can imagine this is hard for you." Synch gestures with his hands.

"Hard? What do you know of hard? I was a Downlander. I grew up in the Narrows, but worked in Central as a maid for one of your mother's friends. She wanted someone she could trust on her team. She thought she was hiring a student in me. Someone she could mold, teach, a loyal student. But she gave me work. And I never had to go back to the Narrows, to beg for food, to wonder if I would get caught by a gang and throttled to death."

"That's an easy choice."

"But every day, I saw what was happening. What they were doing. By the time I put the pieces together, it was too late…"

"Too late for what?"

"I can't…"

Synch takes her water cup and throws it against the wall. "Did I mention you're already dead in Central? It would be so easy to just—"

"Central destroyed all of the sea walls. The Narrows will be under water within thirty-six hours."

"What about the people?"

"They removed many, but their fate will not be better. Central needed bodies to host the vaccine. For the Z Fever. It came from geese, from the Arctic. They unearthed an old bacterium from the melted permafrost. The birds carried it here when we accidentally brought them here as entertainment for Central's ponds. They're spreading it everywhere. No one in Central is immune because of the genetics used to refine the population of Central. Some oversight in Solace. But…"

"The Downlanders are immune." Synch's voice rises at the end of his sentence. "So, cull the population under the guise of disease, then cover their homes in a natural disaster?"

"Solace sees the Narrows as a drain on progress. They couldn't just go in there and kill off the population. Natural disasters are expected now, since the Great Floods."

I can't hold myself back any longer and storm the room. I

rush past Synch and pick Geena up by her shirt, holding her close to my face. "And you just stood by and watched the extermination of thousands? Your hands are covered in their blood. You think you're better than us? Than us? You disgust me."

My body shakes with fire and I want to throw her against the wall, and lose myself in the anger forever.

But I can't let them win.

So I let her go.

She falls into the chair like a rag doll.

"But why is the Fever only killing Uplanders?"

"We don't know. They think Solace targeted people with certain T-cells. T-cells that are actually necessary for fighting off this disease. The theory is that Solace removed so called defects from the human DNA that were actually helpful aspects of our immune system."

"You're no better than his mother," I say. "And I hope she finds you and kills you."

Geena's face is fear and desperation, and looks like some cornered rodent about to be taken out by an exterminator-bot. She is fear itself.

"I know I'm not. But once I was inside, I had no choice. She tracked every millimeter of my movement through the neural-synch. Riza, you must know what I'm saying. She took Sunil from me."

I look to Saachi. She shakes her head, signaling she's deactivated Geena's neural-synch with a blocker.

Hers is a familiar predicament. Most who continue to work in Central after the divide had hopes of being welcomed into Central permanently. Most hold positions that robots

couldn't or were still too expensive for, like masseuses, caregivers, and assistants. But there are some bots that can do
their work too. It's only a matter of time before all the jobs are
lost to machines. Machines don't eat and they don't have feelings.

"It's strange." Geena's voice cracks. "I didn't realize how
loud my mind was with the neural-synch. It's deactivated now,
right? I can hear my own thoughts."

"What do you mean?" I ask and sit down.

"It was like a fly was in my brain, and when I'd daydream
or get off task, it would buzz and redirect me. Day and night."
She exhales heavily.

"It was doing more than keeping track of your physical
whereabouts. It was keeping track of your thoughts, you believe?"

"I don't know what to believe anymore. But, maybe."

"Was the neural-synch controlling you?"

She replies with a nod, "Yes, I think so."

I smile.

I turn to the camera in the corner of the room. "You got all
that, Zami?"

His voice calls from the other room, "Yes, recorded and
optimized for delivery across all comms."

Geena speaks up, "What? I didn't mean ..."

"You see, we've needed evidence the neural-synch is tampering with human thought. That's against the PAC's New
Treaty laws. The creators of Solace will be tried and convicted
of war crimes."

"While I sympathize with your cause, there's no way
they'll let you get that far. I envy your idealism. Don't you think

that they have people on the court too?"

She is right. We need more evidence. Concrete evidence that can't be denied. We'd have to take it beyond the SA. They could bury the government with intel and keep them tied up in the courts forever. We need to get to the GHO and other groups who are neutral.

"Huh." I swallow my pride. "What would you do?"

She looks puzzled when I cut her wrist bindings. Synch, Zami, and Saachi sit down beside me. Together, we are the Red Hand, in our strange glory.

Synch speaks first. "Geena, you have a chance to do something good for once. With your help, we could actually turn things around. We could stop the drowning of thousands and the murder of more."

Saachi clears her throat and speaks gently. "It's not a matter of sides. It's a matter of humanity. Ask yourself: Where will it end? If Solace is allowed to decide the fate of millions, how will you feel if you stand by and watch them die, knowing you could have stopped it? That you could have changed the path of our Province?"

We are still with the weight of her words. Saachi's right. It isn't about winning, not even about saving Masiji and Taru, though that is reason enough for me. This is one of those moments historians analyze after the fact. They'll question why no one did anything. Why no one saw the inevitable outcome of such reliance on technology and devaluation of human life.

"The only way to prove that Solace has illegal control over the population of Central's minds is to prove the connection, that Solace is broken. And show the world what they're doing in the dark off-site," I say. "It's the only way."

Synch says, "But how will we get inside? No one will just open the door and let us in. Not then and not now, especially with the new security. And who would go?"

"More like, how will you get there? You said it was in the middle of the Arabian Ocean? You'll need an air transport," Saachi says.

"Or we could hitch a ride," I say.

"What're you thinking?" Zami asks.

"We could do something that gets us noticed and get our own one-way ticket. We'd have to keep it contained, but big enough for a felony. Some of us will have to be outside to manage things and assist if anything goes south. With AllianceCon going on, they'll hush it up quick."

Saachi says, "You're the obvious choice. And Synch, in case you need a human shield to hide behind."

"Hey!" he says.

"Saachi's right, though," I say. "Not the shield part. But you're an insider; you know the elite Stratas better than any of us."

It has to be Synch and me.

I must be honest. "But is he ready?"

Saachi says, "Yes, he is. I've done everything I can to speed up the healing process. He's nearly at eighty-five percent, I'd say. The rest will come in time, as his body catches up."

"I'm ready," Synch says. "It's as much my fight as yours, Ashiva."

"Let's put the call-out for willing bodies on the External Hand network. We will need all the help we can get." I give in. "Saachi, can you send a coded message to the all-comms? We need all bodies, all volunteers, and everyone around the world to rise up now."

"I'm going to need to bury it in something only they'll
know, or else we might get pinged like the last comms. But
yeah, it can be done. What do you want it to say?"

My heart feels sick with this responsibility, but I shake it
off. They need a message, so let's give them a message. "The
time we've all been waiting for is now. We need to reunite or
risk certain death. We are calling on all recruits, lieutenants,
civilians, and otherwise, to take up arms, connect with your local leaders. We are coming and will not stop until we see justice."

Saachi says, "Got it. Hey, wait a second. There's something
here . . . check it.

Zami and I peer at the flashing message. A forward to the
Lal Hath from the underweb.

LOMRI: WE ARE ALIVE. IN CONTAINMENT. HELP. WAITING FOR ORDERS.

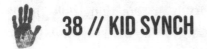

38 // KID SYNCH

For our plan to work, we'll need to cause a massive disruption in Central. And for that we'll need a C.O.R.E mecha-suit and an explosive. Do something Central can't ignore. Something that would be impossible to explain away in a comms and would disrupt AllianceCon. We'll have to commit a top-level felony in order to be sent to containment. We will take the opportunity to mess with Solace. If we're lucky, we could take out the cooling system for Solace's storage and cause some embarrassment during AllianceCon. Without the cooling, it'll only be a matter of time before the storage will collapse under the weight of the heat that's killing most of the population and cause an embarrassing media blackout during the height of AllianceCon, not to mention ruin the SA's chances of winning PAC funding. Ashiva's underweb plea succeeded in connecting with a couple of people eager to get to work.

Ashiva and I hide behind a broken wall just outside the Narrows and scope out the area below.

"We've got ten minutes, then we roll."

I nod. "Good thing I know the suits," I say to her and a nervous laugh escapes my mouth.

She raises her eyebrows. "Right. And good thing I have an explosive." She had to retrieve a device from just outside the Narrows, hidden in a lower level of some old, empty building. She said her sister Taru made it. Said it would do the trick.

"I know, I know. It's partially my design. At least if I hadn't continued Uncle's work..."

I feel her hand on my arm. "It's not your fault. People should be allowed to make things without having their creations turned into weapons. Don't forget that."

"Thanks."

"You'll find the truth. After all this. I'll help you."

I can't contain myself. I reach my hand out to touch hers and say, "Really, I don't deserve all the help you've given me. You could have just left me for dead, twice."

"You were angry. I know what that's like."

"But you always know what to do. The right thing to do," I say. "I'm lucky I picked up the challenge that day. My friends tried to talk me out of it."

"Really? You feel lucky? After all that's happened?"

I think about all that we've been through. "Yeah, I do."

She leans in close to me and presses her lips against mine, gently. I've never felt something like this before. It's perfect. Her face is centimeters from mine when she asks, "Was that . . . all right?"

I just nod, like an idiot. "Oh, yeah. Totally." I feel my face get hot and red.

She giggles. It's a strange sound. So light and cheerful, and gorgeous, amongst the din of the broken city's rubble we are surrounded by.

"Wait, you have friends?" Her gaze is too serious not to laugh.

"Yeah, I know. Surprising," I say.

There's one C.O.R.E soldier at the entrance station on the edge of the Narrows and Liminal Area. The guardians can only wear the suit for a short time, a couple of hours or so, before they have to charge up again. I know that because I built

them to be light in combat, on the underweb in a reality simu-
lation—light means no bulky battery pack to weigh them
down.

I use Ashiva's infrared binoculars to view the dock. "Charging stations." I point past the guard. "Crap."

"What? Let me see." Ashiva takes the binoculars from me.

"They have at least twenty of them. They could control
every few blocks of the city with a guard at each crossing
point."

"They're preparing for war," she says.

"After the sea takes the Narrows, people who get out will
be homeless, and move into the undermarket and Liminal
Area, or try to make it to the Northern District. Maybe they
will work together and against Central. Maybe not. Either way,
it'll be a bloody mess."

A terrible feeling of pride comes over me when I see how
much Mother has followed my design plans. But then it's
crushed by the obvious knowledge that they will be used to kill
innocent people. The one good thing I manage to do in my life,
my mother takes from me and uses against me? I don't know.

Suddenly, I feel a strange sensation in my mind, a sort of
buzzing. I've been blocked from Solace, but still have basic
network capabilities through the neural-synch. The call is
from a secure private line.

"Father?" I ask. Ashiva looks at me startled and I put up my
finger to wait.

"There you are, puttar." His voice is static. "I've missed
you, my boy."

"Do you know what's happened? Did you know mother
tried to erase me?"

"I'm sorry, Riza. I wish I was there to help you in person. I'm on the Space Colony. I don't have much time. I needed to know you were okay."

"I am, so far. It's been . . . a lot going on."

Ashiva looks at me like I'm an alien.

"Son, I need to see you more often. I'm sorry for being out of touch. Now you have the coordinates to be able to contact me directly on the Colony. It's secure. They aren't fond of us calling out. So, please just contact me directly, okay?"

He sends me the coordinates on the satellite.

"I'll talk to you soon, when it's . . . when I have more time. I love you."

"I love you too, Papa." The call disconnects.

"We gonna do this?" Ashiva shakes me back to present. "No doubts, there's no turning back from here."

"I can't go back. You know that. I wouldn't, even if I could."

She switches on her comms and says, "Bhai? You there? We're in position."

I hear a deep voice, "Tiger, we're online and ready for your signal. And don't forget our deal, if this dumb plan works, eh?"

Jai. What a jerk. What deal did she make with him now?

Ashiva speaks quietly on the comms, "You alone or with friends?"

"I've got a pal. He's from the North and ready to do what's necessary. A skilled driver."

"Okay then. Wait for our signal." She switches it off.

It's break time down on the docks. I count and all twenty C.O.R.E mecha-suits are charging. Guardians are probably doing what they do best, harassing people in the Narrows and bottom Stratas.

"There are two guardians, one at each entrance." I see them pacing.

Ashiva speaks into her comm, "It's time."

We watch as Jai limps up to a guardian. "What's he up to?" I ask.

Jai looks to be questioning him. What the . . . ? Is he crying? Clever dog. The guardian becomes more and more confused, but takes him inside the hangar, and that's where I assume Jai puts him at ease.

When he waves from below, wearing the guardian's uniform, I laugh. How he manages to pull that off, I don't know. We run down to the hangar. Once inside, Ashiva stands guard with Jai at the entrance and I make my way to the C.O.R.E. I'm in awe by their epic size. My eyes look to their batteries, searching for the one with the most juice.

Level Seven, Level Four, Level Five. Finally, Level Nine. That will be about two hours of power. I decouple the suit from the charging station and climb the ladder. When I'm on top, I glance at the entrance and they're waving for me to hurry. I slide into the mecha-suit and pull the helmet on tight.

Power up. Whoa, I'm going to like this a little too much. The suit buzzes as the control system awakens around me with a massive buzz.

I switch on my comms. "I'm in. This is crazy." I lift a weapon from the charging station and synch the electro cannon. "Ready for massive destruction."

I hear Ashiva's voice. "Don't get too excited. We've got work to do."

Stepping off the charging station is exhilarating. The C.O.R.E walks like a beast; its steps are loud and crushing as I head toward the back entrance. If we line this up right, we could take out the charging station and also make the explosion big enough to knock down one of the Ring's supports. That'll get their attention in Central.

Out back, I meet up with Ashiva, who's now also wearing guardian gear. A flatbed Central transport barrels down the road, like a demon. I jump on to the back of the vehicle and the others climb inside, and they cover me with a tarp. The driver is a tall boy with a turban.

"Halt!"

The sound stops my breath. A real guardian.

Ashiva walks up to him and says, "We have orders to take this mecha in for testing. Its battery isn't holding charge."

"I haven't received any orders for the transfer."

"Not my problem," Ashiva says. "It's above your level. Get out of the way before you make us late."

The guardian sees he's outnumbered and probably cares more about his own hide than his political views. Ashiva jumps in and, just like that, we've stolen a transport and a C.O.R.E mecha-suit and we're well on our way to starting a riot.

I really don't know if he has the guts to do the job. Synch is impressive though. Shedding your old life is tricky business. I
know well that the ties that bind us are hard to break. I'll keep
a close eye on him.

For the three of us to fit, we have to squeeze together. My
chrome arm rests against the Northerner as he drives the
transport to our destination just outside the Central Ring, under the cover of the tallest buildings around.

"I'm Ashiva," I yell above the engine noise.

"Jeet," he says and nods. "You're the new boss?"

I nod. "Just a grunt, but I've got my orders." I lie. "You ready
for it?"

"Been waiting for something like this since I was a kid."

He seems honest enough. I have no choice but to trust
him. Jai doesn't suffer fools, but he is the definition of insane.
He said he knew a guy who could take a transport, who will do
it for free. I promised Jai a chance to fight with the Red Hand,
to put his past with the Lords of Shadow behind him. Turns
out, that's all he wants. It's a four-person job. Well, six, if you
count Saachi and Zami, who are working behind the scenes to
keep the comms quiet along our route. Block by block, I pray
the cameras in Central cast images of the last ten minutes in a
loop. We speed up, up and up, into the border between the
Liminal Area and Central's Strata One.

"We have about two minutes until the whole Central District is on top of us. So just get us as close as you can and we

will do the rest. Clear out and save your own asses after I set the charge."

"Right." Jeet says.

"You don't have to tell me twice." Jai smirks.

We come up to the border and Jeet parks the transport in an abandoned building. Synch jumps down and all of us get to work: Jai secures the area with Jeet, I focus on activating the charge. We are on the outside of a wall, on the other is the storage center. I look up at the wall and smile. Inches from our destiny.

When it's ready, I place it in Synch's robot hands. "Listen, this is the switch. It'll give you only a minute to clear out, so make sure to be at least three yards away. Thik hai?"

"Got it. Okay." Crap, he's grinning.

"This isn't a game, Synch. This is as real as it comes."

His expression tells me he understands, but I can't be sure.

"Let's go!"

Jai and Jeet take to the streets, and I stay in the shadows of the building to watch it all go down.

"Comms on. Acknowledge." I say.

Jai: "I'm here, mate."

Jeet: "Achcha."

"Mech1?" I ask.

Finally, Synch says, "Copy. Going in."

I set a charge and it breaks the wall. Jai and Jeet run about two yards ahead of Synch, making sure the entrance to the Solace storage center is clear. Sparsely guarded and underfunded, the storage center isn't Central's main concern today, AllianceCon is. They focus on Solace, not her back brain. Everything happens too fast.

There are two unarmed guardians, fat from their lack of training and lazy lives without many threats to pursue. They aren't ready for what comes next.

Synch charges the entrance, with his mecha-suit fully crushing the ground. The guardians' weapons are useless against the armor, but they still shoot at him with their electro-pulse guns. Synch breaks through the wall of the data center and then disappears from sight.

I flinch. I should be the one to set the device. I know what to do, when to do it. This is my job. This is Taru's explosive. I want to control the actions, not just the orders. Being a leader is going to take some getting used to.

Too much time passes. I jog toward the entrance and go straight at the guardians, who are still aiming and discharging their weapons.

With everything I have, I slam against one of them. They fall to the hard ground. The other one hits me with a blast and I fly back a bit stunned, unable to move. But I count, and by ten I am back in control of my body. I rip her electro-pulse gun from her belt and toss it far away. The other I slam with my fist and he goes down. I feel his bones break.

Out of the corner of my eye, I see Jai and Jeet signaling for me to run. Then Synch is running straight at me. He didn't follow the timeline.

He already set the charge.

There isn't enough time.

The blast rips through the building and blows me back and back and back, until I hit something hard and everything goes dark.

40 // TARU

We all have our jobs.

The littlest: to stay alive.

The strongest: to infiltrate and gather supplies.

The wily: to gather intel.

I am the fox. Lomri. Just like my sister called me my entire life. But I'm not the broken one, the glass girl. Something in me feels different just knowing I likely will not shatter. I walk on my feet with an even pace, without a limp, instead of shifting my weight. I'm an infiltrator. I see too much, almost more than I can bear. I managed to contact the Lal Hath. Two elders are at the helm, with Zami and Saachi. They are alive. We work together to smuggle children into the abandoned wing. We've amassed a small army they think have all just died from the testing or the Fever.

But Ashiva hasn't linked up in a while. She is MIA.

Together, we build a plan. The other kids tell me about the Shaanti campaign, what it really means, that the Narrows will be underwater soon. I tell them what is happening here. At least what I know. But unless we do something massive, we will all suffer the same fate. I'm going to have to build something big. Something that will blow this facility and its leaders into the stratosphere.

These people, their experiments are horrific and nearly always lead to the death of the test host. The Uplanders are short-handed because this is a big secret project of theirs, so they take our help willingly, without questions. I guess, if we are willing to do the horrible things they ask, move bodies, clean rooms, why would they question how we come to be here? Dr. Qasim vouches for us as his assistants. They never question him.

The only thing keeping me going is that I will find a way out. That I'll see my sister again.

Until I'm called to Exam Room Five.

It's Jasmine.

She doesn't even smile when she sees me, they've taken so much from her. Or maybe she doesn't recognize me. I hope she is pretending.

"Lay her back, and administer CX29," the medical lead barks orders, like Jasmine is a machine to be tested, not a beautiful girl.

I step forward. "I'll do it."

The doctor keeps typing and analyzing numbers on their tablet screen.

When I am close to her, I realize how fully they've hurt her. I stroke her beautiful cheek. I want to cry, but I don't and I'm proud I keep it inside. I keep so much inside that I think I might burst soon.

"It'll be okay," I whisper.

She says, "I want this to end."

I pretend to insert the fluid into her IV.

"Follow me, girl," the doctor snaps. "This one will sleep soon."

Then I realize what they think I've given her. I want to take the scalpel from the table and jab it into the doctor's neck. If only I were Ashiva. But she'd just bash through the place. This is more delicate and will take patience than I have. I'll need to be able to overtake this entire place in an instant. Instead, I slip the injector into my pocket, still full of the death dose.

I lean close to her and say, "I'll get you out of here, Jasmine."

She doesn't respond. She needs food, water. I'll have to return fast to grab her before the cleaners are sent to transport her body to the cold room. I go with the doctor, pretending to do what she asks, and save a little boy from certain death. Then I return to Room Five.

Jasmine is gone.

I go to the cold room and can't find her. Rao finds her in a different room, probably taken there by mistake. I cover her with a sheet and wheel her into the dark room, then wake her and slip her into the vent. The children catch her, pull her gently into the tunnel and down below the facility into our room. They'll feed her, bring her back to life, as they have so many others.

When I am sure she's made it into the tunnel, I finally breathe. But then, I hear a voice in the hallway. A voice so familiar, all my yesterdays come flooding back.

The voice says, "There were about fifty of them, hidden in a catacomb beneath the Narrows. I know because I built it."

Someone else replies, "That's more than enough to begin."

She is alive! I want to run to the voice. I want to call out "Masiji!" but I know I have to be careful. Instead, I peer through a crack in the door and watch like a good fox.

"They're well-hidden, but alive. We could bring them here by air-transport."

The other person, a short, thin woman wearing a bloodred tunic and pants, replies, "They're all we need. Bring them here." When she turns, I know that face: the Minister of Comms. "Then we'll send them to the next location."

"Right away." Why is Masiji taking orders from her? She is alive, which makes my heart sing, but there is something different. She's different. For a second, her face turns towards mine. And though I know she can't see me through the crack, it feels like she does. Her eyes pierce my heart.

I want to scream, to shake her. To tell her what they've done to us all. But I stuff that down too. Holding in my outburst feels like trying to contain a nuclear explosion.

Masiji is working for Central. Was she all along? No. They must have done something, threatened her somehow. She wouldn't do this willingly. Not her. Not ever.

When they leave, I close the door to the room, press my face into a pile of old linens, and scream. I scream about being here. About losing my family and home. But, most of all, I scream because the one I trust the most has abandoned us to this horror. Nothing in the world makes sense to me anymore.

41 // KID SYNCH

PRESENT DAY

We wanted to get picked up. I remind myself of this and it still feels so wrong to be giving ourselves up to containment on purpose. I watch Ashiva and take comfort. She's the leader here; I'm just her student. The transport rickshaw tears through Central with its blaring siren forcing people and vehicles out of the way. There are a few others on the transport that aren't from our team; a woman in particular, who's pregnant, stands out. We planned to be picked up, but we couldn't have planned who'd already be on the transport.

"Hey, girl, where'd you get your replacement?" the turbaned Northerner yells to her. The transport engines growl as we go up and up, through Central.

"Why? You want a referral?"

He laughs. He's good at this. "Sharp tongue in your mouth must hurt."

"Not always."

The engines drown out the rest of their conversation. That, or my nervous heart throbbing in my ears. I watch as my city pours past the windows. AllianceCon below is disturbed by our explosion; several blocks are blacked out. I'm lost in my thoughts and fears when there's a sudden fight that breaks out on the transport as we careen across the bridge. The pregnant woman stands and denies the guardian her arm for testing. I want to beg her to sit. That we will try to get her out safely, but I can't make any promises. Our objective is to free the people of the Narrows. Not save a woman on a transport.

The woman stands and yells, "For the Rani, the Lal Hath."

Ashiva is too late as she lunges to stop her. The woman throws herself against the glass of the transport and falls down, down and down, into the city below. We are shaken. The woman dies on impact.

The guardians restrain us and continue through Central. Out the windows, I watch the city whip by like ghosts of my past life: the holo-adverts in Central displaying the newest Solace Corp campaign, the AllianceCon, my sky-rise apartment building that splits the sky. I remember the little fire I started there, to keep my bot at home. All the small rebellions that led me to setting off an explosion in Solace's storage system. The disruption will be unavoidable. They're going to close the Ring for maintenance, which will ruin AllianceCon. The effects could be even larger than we planned. At least we've succeeded in disrupting Solace's memory. I hope. I want to tear her apart.

Though I knew the risks, I went anyway. When your world is turned inside out, there's no way out but through. Kanwar Uncle used to say that.

It doesn't matter anymore. Uplanders think I am a criminal, just another person on a transport. I want to call out to the people commuting to Solace Corp on their rickshaw transports, passing by the windows heading to AllianceCon, and tell them to stop and go home. That this is all a façade. I see their eyes as we pass. They back away, like the contents of our transport is diseased, to be feared. The problem with Uplanders is believing the harsh reality of the rest of the world because they are so damn comfortable. Why worry about anything when the Ring keeps you cool, Solace keeps you busy? Why worry about the world outside and the millions burning alive in the heat or drowning in the rising saltwater? The comfortable only care when they themselves are in pain. Then they scream. And it's too late.

And that's when I know: Riz-Ali Singh is truly dead, and he won't be coming back.

I feel the thick, caked blood on my lips. Though I was in the suit when the explosive ignited, I was thrown hard against the ground, and the face shield exploded into shards. Engineering mistake. I put in my plans that the face shield be made from next-gen flex-polymer, not a cheap, hard plastic. Cutting corners is Central's MO.

Zami and Saachi's faces are plastered on the Info-Run signs that we pass. Which means the authorities are onto the Lal Hath. They'll go into hiding. We won't have them in our final assault on the containment. We'll have to make do. Then I see Ashiva's face too. They'll figure out her identity soon enough.

After the pregnant woman leaps to her death on the highest bridge in Central, we are devastated and reinvigorated with our revolution, all of us. I can see it in Ashiva's eyes, in Jeet's grimace. Even Jai seems to care for once.

The wind whips through the transport like an evil spirit demanding more souls. Guardians push us up against the back of the transport with their batons. Jeet fights them and for that he gets a bash in the gut. We help him stand.

"What are they going to do with us?" I ask.

"Whatever they want, now," Ashiva replies. Then she whispers, "Stick to the plan."

An air-transport comes and we are loaded onto a window-less machine. There is no escape from this one. And this is what we wanted. The guardians look pleased.

"Get in, come on, hurry up," the woman says from behind her face shield.

I can tell she would be happy to give us all a good thrashing; her expression dares us to do something stupid. They sit us all beside one another in the armored transport. Three guardians positioned across from us, unmoved by the recent suicide we all witnessed. To them, it's like it never happened. I'll never erase her death from my memory. Never.

That she called the Rani's name means there is an underground movement in the Upland that still believes in liberty and revolution. That there are civilians who believe in the mission of the Red Hand. That gives me courage.

Ten, twenty, thirty minutes pass. I calculate how far we've come and know we aren't heading for the Central authorities, but somewhere else. In flight, it's harder to know.

"Where are you taking us? It's our right to know!" I yell above the engines.

Ashiva's arm presses against mine, a subtle question. We can't let on that we know each other. She was a passerby. I was the problem in the C.O.R.E. mecha-suit. Jeet was just squatting there. Jai was just being a goonda. None of us were trying to hijack this transport.

The guardian reports, "Fl Terrorists and unpermitted vagrants found in Central are now detained in an undisclosed location during AllianceCon. Orders of the President."

"It feels like we're heading to the North. Maybe just beyond Central?"

"Chup, now." The guardian's threat is clear. *Shut up or I'll make you shut up.*

My lips press together like a steel trap.

The transport slows and the doors open. Bright lights rush in. I crane my neck and see row after row of clear, walled areas, going in every direction. And inside the cages are people, young and old. This is the new containment we've been searching for. The Void. The mythic off-site is real.

We are greeted by the hard batons of white-uniformed guardians who enter the transport. It only takes a few minutes before they subdue all of us. I am the last one. A guardian places a signal disruptor on the ground and activates it—all the cameras and devices in the room stall. Whatever happens now is off the record. I see a massive mountain moving closer, almost absorbing the light in the room, like a black hole.

The considerable man stands in front of all of us. "Look at how you've changed. Shame it'll all be for nothing."

"Khan Zada. What the—"

His eyes glimmer.

Ashiva growls, and I've never heard that before. Not from her. Not from anything. She isn't scared, she is rage itself.

Ashiva shouts, "What're you playing at?"

"It took a lot of favors to be here when they brought you in. I wasted so much currency trying to find you. You could have paid me. You could have taken the kid to the Upland and dropped him off. Clean, simple. You could have killed him. You had to blow up a memory bank and get picked up on a transport. Everything has a price, girl. I don't like being made a fool."

"Did you make a deal with the Minister?" Ashiva says.

He turns to us and shakes his head. "Nah, didn't need to. Her people aren't all so loyal." He points around the room to the guards. "But yes, we once needed each other. I kept the balance between the Narrows and Central. They let me be, and I gave them intel. We had a tight, symbiotic relationship. They were my biggest customer."

I struggle against my restraints to stand and help Ashiva up. Khan says, "Looks like you've found your courage, boy. Or you found your girl." His gapped-tooth grin expands.

"You're as charming as I remember, Khan," I say.

Ashiva speaks up, "So what? You're here to complain about business? Get back at me? I'd rather you let me free of these, so we can just work out our differences hand-to-hand, like respectable people."

Khan Zada shakes his big, sausage finger. "No claws for the Tiger."

She yells and makes a grab for him, "I don't need to use my replacement to take out your tongue." She chomps her teeth at him.

"Bas!" Khan pushes her away. "You don't understand. I get it. Look, I need you to take care of some business here for me. Then we're done." He brushes his hands like he's wiping off dust.

"What?" I say.

"The Minister crossed me. You and me? I'm used to our tiffs, Tiger. But she, she cleared the Narrows, disrupted the balance, tricked me about her son and now the PAC is going to have their eyes on me. That woman destroyed my business."

"So, you're saying...?" Ashiva asks.

He signals to a guard who goes to unbind Ashiva, but pauses. "You'll play nice," Khan tells her.

When her hands are free, Khan gives her a palm-sized device, thin as paper. "I want you to blow this place to bits. It will cost them dearly to lose this prison."

"A micro charge. This is . . ."

"Yeah, it's a pretty mark. Just rig an explosive and it'll vaporize the place."

"All that way for this ball of fire . . ." she says.

"Can't be too careful. I want them to pay. Some projects you must oversee yourself. I'm sure you know what that's like."

The guardians shove us forward into the prison facility. But this is no ordinary facility, it's high security. The place is clean. The floors, the walls, not a single nob or button anywhere. Everything is controlled by a hidden system.

"And you, Jai . . ."

Jai looks terrified. "I don't work for you anymore, Khan."

Khan smacks Jai.

"Lies come so easy to you, Jai. You can never leave me."

"Get on, then." Khan kicks Jai, and Jeet, forward too.

"This isn't my problem, yaar," Jeet says. "I'm just a driver."

"A driver, you say?" Khan makes the sound of sucking something from his teeth. "You drove my product, so you are involved."

We all stumble as guardians push us to follow the large man. The off-site, or wherever we are, is different than I thought it would be. It's organized. There's a reason for the arrangement of things. The doors in the all-metal hallways are sealed. Cameras are everywhere, watching us as we pass below. There are sensors in the air. Everything is being moni-

tored. And it has an antiseptic aroma that verges on the bitter,
like the smell you get when burning nonflammable things.

People move aside when we come through. Guardians,
men and women, who I assume are doctors or scientists because of their clean suits. When we reach the last doorway, we
are pushed inside. Five guardians wait with weaponry I've
never seen before. We are pushed to kneel on the hard
ground.

Khan waves to his guardians and then unshackles the rest
of us. "I've never been here. You've never seen me. You're on
your own. I haven't given you permission to take out this off-
site. I'm a goddamn ghost and we are even."

"Deal." Ashiva and Khan Zada hold each other's forearms.

She shakes her head. "We have work to do."

Khan picks up the signal disruptor as he backs out of the
room with Jeet and Jai.

The cameras click back on. We are left with the guardians.
There are five of them and two of us. But they have weapons,
and we don't stand a chance. Before long, we are both sub-
dued and separated. I hope she knows what she's doing.

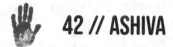

My dream begins with my voice whispering her name: Taru, Taru, Taru . . . I watch her float backwards, away from me, her silhouette against the rising sun. The dream is so real it pierces my body, shakes me to my bones. I feel her and then drown in failure. I can't put the images into words, but I don't have to. I know what it means.

Taru is gone.

I'm frozen. The pressure of a thousand warm blankets surrounds my body, making it impossible to open my eyes, move at all. I'm not sure I want to anyway. A sedative runs like thick poison in my veins. At one point, I see the world flashing past, and one person in a white coat and one in a gray tunic are leading my cot down a white tunnel.

When I open my eyes again, this time with awareness, I'm in an all-white room. White floors, white walls, white everything. I can't see a door anywhere. I'm sitting on the hard ground. My clothes are gone and I am wearing a white gown. My arm exposed, metal. I wondered if this is real.

"Hello?" I stand and feel pain shoot up my leg. Someone stitched me up. Why? Then I remember the explosion. Synch, where is he? Memories flood into my mind.

A light flashes in front of me and a holo-screen plays. President Ravindra looks so clean and confident in her bloodred sari.

YOU ARE HERE BECAUSE YOU'VE BEEN INFECTED BY THE Z FEVER. YOU WILL BECOME VERY ILL AND MOST LIKELY WILL DIE. BUT THERE'S ONE THING YOU CAN DO TO HELP: ALLOW US TO TEST THE INOCULATION. BY BEING A PART OF THIS PROJECT, YOU CAN

SAVE THE LIVES OF MILLIONS AND, POSSIBLY, YOURSELF. IT'S THE ONLY WAY. WE THANK YOU FOR YOUR SERVICE AND BRAVERY.

When it's done, it disappears like smoke. I'm inside containment. Taru, if she's alive, is here.

"Bullshit," I yell. "Liars!"

I feel like a caged animal, without anything to take my anger out on. My head shakes with every step as I pace across the white floor. White floor, white walls, outside of time and space—it feels like drowning. My thoughts quicken with every heartbeat. Buried alive. That's how I feel.

I must have hit my head pretty hard in the explosion. I try to calm, settle. We are inside containment. That was one of our goals. It didn't happen the way we wanted it to happen, but still, I'm inside. I can get Taru and Masiji, and whoever else is trapped in this nightmare, out as soon as I get out of this goddamn room.

"Hello?" I whisper because my voice is hoarser than I expected. A minute or two passes, then the white panel on the door slides open.

A team of three Uplanders move in. A woman with the confidence and ego of a doctor, someone who seems like an assistant, and a grunt who lingers behind, nearly invisible.

I hold my tongue. I'm compliant. They love that crap.

"Doctor? Where am I? Why am I being held?" I ask, as clearly as my injuries allow.

She shakes her head and motions to her assistant to pull a cart and cot toward me. They hesitate. I don't blame them. I can smash him into bits if I want. I probably look wild.

The doctor speaks, almost bored, "If you comply with our tests, it will make things easier. I find stressed subjects don't give clear results." It's the business-as-usual doctors who do testing that scare me the most. She's done this a lot. She's not even thinking about the moral ramifications anymore. When we cease to be people to them is when they frighten me the most.

"I'm being held against my will. I was supposed to go to containment, not a medical facility."

The medical assistant clamps restraints around my ankles and wrists.

"Take it up with the President. New law. Any and all prisoners of Central can be held in the medical facility for testing of the Fever."

"I intend to," I say.

"Will you comply?"

I nod and stuff my fire deep down. Wait. Just wait. Be patient.

"Don't worry. Most of it won't hurt," she says.

The small grunt who's been standing like a shadow behind the group moves into sight. She shakes her head and puts her finger to her lips.

Taru, my sister.

My dear sister.

My body fills with fire and every molecule tenses up.

I fight hard not to jump up, take her hand, and run. To not kill these devils and carry her far, far away from this place, away, away, away. They'd destroy us if we try to escape now. I must wait.

She knows what I'm feeling and again puts her fingers to her lips. Her face says, "Wait." She's different. Changed. Strong.

The team installs an IV port in my neck and plugs me into their system. The doctor takes some blood, tissue, and hair samples.

When it comes to the physical exam, the doctor spends a little too much time on my replacement.

"Such beautiful and crude work you do in the Narrows. How do you do it?"

"You wouldn't expect such genius from a low-life Down-lander, would you?" I say.

"No, not that," she replies. "But without the proper surgery, cybernetics is complicated." Her hand strokes my hacked plexus that Masiji built to connect my replacement to my neu-rological system. "This took some insider knowledge of the technology."

"You'd be surprised how simple your systems are to hack," I say. How could she go through with this work, and be so completely enamored by me, while treating me like an ani-mal? I can't understand.

Taru is in the background, handing tools to the team as they work. What's the plan here? I try to read her body lan-guage, but come up blank. She turns from me as they continue to measure my body and take notes. They feed my blood into a cart where a computer runs tests. All I can see is data. I have no idea what it means.

I watch Taru, trying not to give her away. Her face is bruised; I can see that. She is scared, but strong. Her replace-ment foot is hidden under boots that are two sizes too big. There's a distance between us I've never felt before. It's more than these circumstances. She's different.

"Lay back on the cot. This will hurt," the doctor says.

I close my eyes and feel a surge of electricity shoot up my spine, into my limbs and head. My whole body seizes. They take measurements. Analyze me. When they are gone, I'm exhausted. I watch them leave the room. As the door is about to close, I feel a warm presence and a hand on my forehead.

"Ashiva, I . . ."

Sister.

"I'm sorry I couldn't get here sooner," I whisper, my voice hoarse. "We need to get the boy who came with me, Synch, in front of a computer. I need to get to the transport. We're here to get you out of here. To save everyone."

She nods. But pauses. "We have a group of children already working on an escape. We didn't know if anyone would find us."

I'm so proud of her. "Good. That's good. Let's connect our plans and teams. Work together. First, can you get to Synch?"

She says, "Yes, I can."

"Good." We discuss how long we might have until the guards are alerted to our actions, the signals to watch for. She doesn't sugarcoat the risks. "There's no guarantee. This all could go very wrong, Taru."

"I know. But we have no choice. We're not dying here."

I hold her hand longer. I don't want to let go. If she leaves my sight, I can't be sure I'll see her again. "Here take this." I pull the micro charge from a gap in my replacement. "When the place is cleared out, use this to vaporize everything."

She says, "Shiv, you have to listen to me carefully. Masiji, don't trust her."

"What?" I recall what Ghaazi and Suri told me about her working on Solace.

Taru's face is more serious than I've ever seen—it is stone. "I think she's working for Central, for the Minister of Comms. Don't trust her."

My heart shatters. "That can't be. Surely you're mis—" But I know my deepest fears are confirmed. Maybe her work was more important to her than we were.

She shakes her head. "There's no time for doubt. I must go. Stay alive. And I'll do the same. I love you."

"I love you. We need to get Synch a moment with their computers. He needs a chance to access it from the inside, download their internal files as evidence. Can you manage that?"

She cocks her head sideways. "Yes, I think so. It won't be easy. I have to go. Wait for my signal," Taru's voice is a young lieutenant's. She slips a thin piece of metal into my wrist restraint, then puts it in my hand.

Lock picked. Good girl.

The door closes behind her.

She isn't the young, fragile girl I forced her to be. She is fierce and beautiful and strong, in spite of me and all I've done to shelter her.

Sister.

When I saw her for the first time, I wanted to scream at her. To yell and demand information about the tests that were run on me in the orphanage. Why she and Masiji determined I had juvenile osteoporosis. Ashiva must have known about this. I need to know why they told me I would break. I need to know if she knew. If it was true or a mistake. But there isn't time for that. Not yet.

By the time Ashiva and her friend arrive in containment, I'd been busy. The small network of teens who reintegrated into the workforce of containment had connected with others. Our reach is now across every unit. The only way something like this can work is if we do it together.

In our small room, we plan, plot, coordinate. The little ones are listeners and thieves. The older ones have made connections with doctors and assistants who are here against their will. The ones who have families. We make promises to smuggle notes to their families in exchange for small favors.

I found the boy Ashiva came in with and get him her message. I'm not sure if he believes me, but the boy named Synch, he seems to understand. I can tell he is one of us because he is kind to me, not frightened or superior. I'm surprised I haven't met him before, but there are so many of us living in the Narrows and Liminal Area outside the Ring.

"Today, we have only one chance to get this right," I say to the children in the contaminated room. "Deepak, did you pull the data from their charts?"

The small boy nods.

Rao says, "And everything else is set. We're just waiting to go."

"Okay," I agree. "If anything goes wrong, come here straight away. Don't look back."

They each acknowledge my words in their own way. I turn to Rao and he helps the little ones up through the ceiling vent.

He pauses before going up. "If anything goes wrong . . . with your sister, Synch. They'll probably be taken into the testing room together . . ."

"It'll work, Rao. No matter how it turns out," I say.

I hug him and he leaves without me.

I go through the steps again in my head, the ones Ashiva and I decided. Rao delivers the message to containment, that we'll take the children and hide them. Separate those who can't fight from those who are able. I'll set the charge myself. I kept that part from Ashiva; she still thinks of me as someone to protect, and I can't risk her keeping me from doing what needs to be done. I won't break. Not this time. Never again.

It's late, or at least, it feels late. I haven't slept in days, aside from micro-naps when my eyes can't stay open. But I am ready. Now that Ashiva is here, our clock has sped up and we have to move faster.

The halls are less busy, but a few medi-staff are moving about as I make my rounds. I steal the key from the first assistant I come in contact with, a bump and snag. The first thing Ashiva taught me how to do.

With the key, I slip easily into the control room. There are three of us in the room; the others are working with medi-staff, listening to instructions. Dr. Qasim is here.

I nod to him.

He nods back.

Dr. Qasim says, "Okay, I need assistance with handling the less receptive patients right now. It's crucial we get their new samples or else a large part of our study will be lost. I need everyone to come with me, now." The guardian backs up, and follows him and his group.

I am alone. But only for a moment. The guardian is in the hall and could return any minute.

I put the key into the reader. It takes forever for it to accept it, but finally: green.

When the screen turns on, I find the containment prison door system control. I look at the clock. We've coordinated our clocks to work together. In five seconds, four, three, two, one. I submit my request to unlock the system.

Before I can stand up from the station, a light flashes silently. That's how I know it works. That's how I know I just unlocked all the clear plastic walls inside Containment where they keep all of us.

All of us working together only have a few minutes before guardians descend.

With the key in my pocket, I run as fast as I can back into the hall, and go down, down, down, into my position in our ventilation system, and wait.

44 // KID SYNCH

When the boy with the unruly hair enters my room, after the medi-staff is done with me, I wonder what new devilry they'll try this time. They've already injected me with god knows what, sequenced my DNA, tested me for the Fever, and didn't bother to tell me the results. Not that I'll believe them anyway —but it's becoming clear this is a ruse. Do they think I'm an Uplander? Or maybe they know I am not who I say I am. The doctor is easy to read. He triple-checked results.

Calls me an anomaly. And I don't say a word.

The boy, however, is tiny, tough, skeptical. He has the Narrows written all over his expression.

I say, "They probably are feeding you and keeping you from the testing. But don't work for them. It's not worth it."

The boy, no more than seven years old, closes the door behind him and ignores my words. He says, "Synch, is that your name?"

His voice is small. I nod.

"I have orders from Taru to get you to the nearest uplink location in containment. Please follow my instructions quickly."

"What? How? Who?"

"Hush, brother, we only have sixty seconds before the cleaners come. See, they think they've just offed ya." The kid flashes an inject. "I'm taking you to do your job. The strong one, the Red Hand lieutenant, Ashiva," he leans in very close and whispers directly into my ear, "says you'll know what to do once you get to an uplink."

"Say no more."

The boy says, "Hurry, and be quiet. Also, I'm sorry about this."

"About what?"

He lifts a body bag up onto the bed and signals for me to get inside. Once I'm in, he closes the sides with snaps and darkness surrounds me. I want to close my eyes, but fear won't let me. I try to take measured breaths, but my heart is racing out of control.

"Just stay still as you can and try not to breathe," he whispers.

"How am I supposed to do that?"

"Shh," he rolls me out of the room.

I think we are in a hall. I can hear shuffling feet and the air is acidic and cold, maybe ammonia. A few minutes pass and I fill with doubt. We roll over a couple doorways. Then, finally, we stop moving. He unsnaps the bag and I sit up. The room is pitch black, so my eyes have no contrast to which they can adjust.

He flicks on a small flashlight and slides it into my hand.

"This is an old workstation. We just temporarily connected it to an uplink, off of Solace's radar."

"Impressive." I flash the light across the console. The old machinery is definitely hacked to work. Old wires connect and splice to new modifiers. It is dangerously overloaded. "Did you have to optimize the—"

"No, since it's the old system, we made it slow and quiet. Might take a while to connect and send. Probably something you're not used to."

I pat the kid on the back. "This is brilliant work. Thank you."

He beams. "I'm going to leave you to it. Cut the line when you're done."

"Achcha."

He turns to exit. "I almost forgot." He slips a chip into my hand. "The data. All that you'll need."

"You guys are really organized."

"Been here for a while. Taru, Ashiva's sister, is the leader we needed."

Taru. I wonder how Ashiva is doing in all of this. I hope we make it out of here, but I don't have time for silly, self-defeating thoughts. Not today.

"Oh, and bhai? Ashiva said to meet in the bay. That she'd have the transport ready."

I slide the chip into the reader and connect to the link. He is right. It takes forever. But it loads. I hear someone pass by the door and flick off the light. But soon as I am alone again, I enter the code that will run the info comms through the Space Colony. The line my Father used to contact me—I figured out how to use that as a bridge to the powerful satellites on the Space Colony and reroute it back into the global comms. Sure, some of the information will be lost, dropped packets and all, but even with that data loss, it'll be easy to patch the information together and redistribute it Earth-side once it's in the hands of the Red Hand's allies around the world.

I watch it load.

And load. I imagine how the data moves through air across wireless networks, through bursts of energy.

And load . . . I pray it makes the leap to the satellite and doesn't get blocked.

The file must be huge because the system is stuttering.

Doubts pour in. I push them out. What if I can't load this? What if Ashiva can't get a transport? What if we all die here? No. No. No. Useless thoughts. Everything in me stills suddenly: my heart, my breath, my thoughts, as I watch it load.

And.

Finally.

It does.

I want to scream. To celebrate with someone, but being completely alone, I just clench my fist, then cut the wires. The records of what's happening here in containment will be in the hands of the GHO and External Hand in seconds.

If we don't survive this, at least the world will know about the testing and Central's lies. At least, maybe, we can save others.

The hall is dark as I make my way through to the end with a tiny, flickering light. Suddenly, a voice rings through my body, soul, and mind.

The voice says, "We need to calibrate. Or else it'll all be for nothing."

I peer through the doorway into the main hall. There a woman stands. Perfectly outfitted, fashionable amongst all this death. Like the queen of all this horror in her maroon sari. Beautiful. Terrifying.

Familiar.

Or is she? Outside her natural environment of pristine Central, she wanes, a bit. Less colorful, less perfect. Smaller too. And yet, so much power in such a petite form.

Sweat covers my skin. What I wouldn't give to just beg and cry, and yell at this woman. And collapse at her feet and be held by her. The one who brought me into this world. The one who decided to erase me from it.

Mother.

My long hair braids easily, and I leave the sick wing of containment. I pocket a few injectors, just in case they come in handy. My mantra: Get the transport. Taru will get the people. Synch will get the evidence. We'll all get out.

Yeah, I'm not naïve enough to believe we can walk out of here without a snag. This is their house, not ours. So, I'll have to go hard. I'll have to fight. But I am ready.

The first doctor I run into gets an injector in the neck and goes to sleep. Doesn't see it coming. The second one I have to hit in the head with my chrome arm, but it only takes one hit. The third one is a kid, so I let her go. Tell her to stay clear of the bay until she hears the signal, but she already seems to know what I am talking about. Taru did her job and got the word out. She began emptying the cubes in the back first, the ones that aren't as closely monitored by guards. Maybe this will work. Maybe some will get out without getting caught in the inevitable fight.

Containment isn't as big as I first thought. Where they keep the people is the largest space. The mediports they built around, like a circle, were poorly constructed, half-assed, like they had to rush this whole massacre. Pretty quickly I find the route Taru told me about, the one the cleaners take, the one for the dead. And I stick to it. It's grim. The worst. Death, death and death. But also quieter than hell.

All the devils work in Central.

The last row of doors lay in front of me like a test. I almost hesitate, but shake off that feeling. If I can just get to the transport bay, Taru will bring the others, and Synch will get the evidence sent to the GHO and our allies around the world. It has to work, I remind myself.

When I push open the last doors and feel the spray of real, unfiltered saltwater air, I smile. We're on an island. Ocean waves curl and crest and roll around me like an impassable slick-backed creature. But when I look again, I know we aren't even on an island—it's a barge floating in the middle of the Arabian Sea. There, below me, sits a series of amphibious hover-transports that look as though they can traverse the seas and air. We will stuff each and every living person into the transports, leaving not a soul behind aside from the Central scum.

The wall offers a little cover, so I hide behind it and survey the surroundings. We'll have to make sure everyone gets outside and into the hover-transports pretty quickly. Moving that many people will be tough enough, but while we load them up, we'll take on some fire from guardians, surely.

Which reminds me: the guardians, where are they? There have to be a few out here protecting their most precious connection to the world...

"Stop, girl." The voice is metallic, inhuman, and echoes through the salty air. Only when I turn, I know why.

A mecha.

A goddamn C.O.R.E soldier.

I back up as its shadow stretches across and past me. It stands at least twice my height and is every inch a wonder of mechanics. I'm tough, but this? I tremble as I scan its form for an inch of vulnerability. I search desperately for any corner, any surface that might be less than structurally perfect. If I wasn't so terrified, I'd be in awe.

Synch built you.

And I'm going to take you down.

"I'll only say it once, girl." The guardian inside the suit is a woman with bright red hair that has been through too much henna. It stands out straight and spiked. Her scowl shows she means what she says.

I pause. But only long enough to understand her weapons. Suddenly, she levels her giant fist with the electro-pulse cannon at the end in my direction. I know what is coming and run as fast as I can.

BAM!

The C.O.R.E's cannon unleashes a fury of electricity at me. I get away by mere centimeters: the heat rushes against my arm and burns a hole on my skin. The mecha-suit is big, but being small has its advantages. I run against the rail that loops around the containment. The suit can't follow because the path is too narrow. I feel it watch me, waiting for me to slip into the depths of the ocean.

Around the corner, I climb the structure and wait.

"That was my last warning, Downlander," the guardian says.

"I'm counting on it." I wipe my sweat from my face with my flesh hand and focus.

Its footsteps fall, metal on metal, shaking the structure. It must weigh a ton or more. I remember what the C.O.R.E did to the Narrows and tighten my grip on the rail, and let my rage fuel me.

When it turns the corner around the other side of the structure, I fall on her shoulders and dig my replacement hand deep into the soft metal joint on her neck, tearing the only flexible part of the suit. It rips, and I hold on tight as she spins around, trying to get a grip on me.

She thrashes like a beast, but I hold on. That is until her robot hand takes my foot and pulls me off of her, and tosses me into the sea. I dive deep and swim under the edge of the platform, knowing she will come for me to make sure I am gone for good. The shadow of the mecha-suit comes close and its reflection shadows the surface. I'm like a fish; I can hold my breath forever, so I wait. Not a single bubble rises to the surface.

The shadow crouches and she's going fishing. When her hand comes into view I lift my head and shoulders out of the water and yell, "Over here!"

She faces me and I thrust my replacement arm up and into her neck, through the suit. The inject slides into the gash I opened previously, and I give her every bit of the paralytic medicine. She staggers backwards. I climb out of the water and watch.

Her expression is strangely annoyed. She doesn't have a clue what's coming.

"Go down," I say through clenched teeth as I back up out of the way.

The beast stumbles and turns, and suddenly her form careens toward me. The guardian looks dizzy now, and momentum propels her toward me. I feel her grab my replacement arm as the suit spills toward the water.

The mecha holds tight and twists.

One ton of metal tears at mine.

"No!" I scream.

As the guardian's eyes close, and she dies in the suit, my arm is still in her grip. She falls into the ocean and I brace myself against the decking, as my replacement arm is ripped from my body.

My hand slides over my empty shoulder. I cry out to the ocean. The pain is lightning, shooting through my nervous system, but I am alive. I still have a job to do. I steady myself, making sure I don't faint and count. Focus. One, two, three. Breathe.

Pick yourself up, Ashiva.

Blood meshes with wires, and bone. Most nerves in my joint had died long ago, before I even had the replacement surgery. I know what shock is and I'm not in it. I take deep breaths. Steady girl. I wrap my torn shirt around my shoulder and compress it.

The transport isn't far. The door opens with ease.

Once in, I pull up a comm, and speak to my brothers and sisters inside containment.

"Downlanders, this is Chrome Tiger of the Red Hand. It's time. We've unlocked your cages and we will not be taken. Your oppressors aren't immune. We are. It's time to fight. Your lives depend on it."

I slide down against the controls and watch the blood pool around the ground beneath me.

Then I feel a gust of wind like a hurricane and look through sweat and salt-stung eyes, and see the most glorious transport I've ever seen. It descends like a massive pelican. The four tilt rotors let it rise and fall vertically, but the upturned wings mean it can go long distances. The underbelly has water skis that hover just above the water and then it lands clumsily on the surface of the water making a huge wave. I look for a weapon and pick up a gnarled piece of metal in my flesh hand.

Then I hear the voices as clear as water cascading in my ears. "Aye, Lieutenant Tiger!"

"Ghaazi! Suri!"

My body falls to the platform with agony and relief.

46 // TARU

I hear my sister's voice on the all-comms and I know she's not well. In fact, she's very injured and needs my medical assistance. But first I need to do my job and get these people out of here, so I hurry.

"Come on!" I pull myself out of the vent and run to the blocks of containment, guiding the free survivors outside to the transport.

Guardians rush the prisoners in containment with their electro-pulse rifles drawn, ready to put us all down. I watch as my friends and neighbors tackle guardians together, beat them and rip their weapons from their belts and hands, then redistribute the weapons to each other. A little girl, no older than seven, manages to get an electro-pulse baton and uses it to shock a guardian, then runs up the walkway toward the transport dock. I watch as some win and others get shot with an electro-pulse to their little bodies, shake with agony and fall to the ground. I ignore my hot tears and don't hide my face behind my hands, even when the life leaves a boy's eyes. I scream, a ferocious growl that comes from deep inside my heart and my chest. From a room where I've locked away every single moment of frustration, anger, hunger, fear, for every single child here who deserves to live, to be free. I duck and dodge, and try to stay upright as I move into the fray and don't stop until I've stolen an electro-pulse rifle and lift it over my shoulder. When I pull the trigger, I'm surprised by the flash of fire that pours into a guardian's body just as he's about to punch Rao. The guardian's body falls to the ground. I help up my friend, and we stand back to back and attack, just as Masiji and Mrs. Zinaat and Daadaji and Poonam Auntie, and all of our teachers showed us. Don't stop, their words echo in my mind. Don't stop until you're safe, until you all are safe.

When I see how everyone rallies, I know we have a chance. But the guardian's weapons are potent. One barrage from an electro-pulse can stun a few people at a time.

Then I hear it. The smallest cry. A young child left on the containment floor. How is she still here? Why haven't I smuggled her out? She's alone. A baby. It will only be moments until they kill her too.

I'll fight with the rest of them.

"Rao, I'm going back," I yell.

"What? No! You can't."

"Take the others down to transport. Ashiva will be waiting."

He hugs me. "I'll try to cover you. Go!"

It's bloody chaos. When I reach her, I pick her up and hold her close.

"Don't worry, baby. I've got you," I whisper as I run.

All of containment is a blur. Bodies, fighting, adults taking guardians' weapons and using those against them. There's a chain of people sending survivors into the halls out to the transport.

But then, I feel a presence and the cold, white end of an electro-pulse rifle pointed right at me.

The guardian's gaze is dead anger. I see his fingers turn the weapon to lethal. No amount of pleading will help me, I know it.

In the blink of an eye, I run, but another body comes be-tween me and the rifle, and they intercept the blast of white-hot voltage.

"Dr. Qasim!"

He gasps, "Go! I'm sorry," then lets out his last breath.

We run with the others. I don't know how many die trying to leave, but fighting is all we can do. We have to try to survive.

I carry the child down the hall, all the way to the end, and outside into the sea air. I hand her to someone. "Take her on board."

"Aren't you coming?" the man asks.

"I have one more mission."

I rush back to containment. I have one more job to finish. To make sure none of the work done here will continue.

I watch her until the alarms bleat and the lights flash. I can't let her pass by. "Mother!" I scream over the din.

The tablet in her hands falls to the ground, shattering. "Riza?"

People rush past, guardians, medical staff, others. But we stand locked in a gaze that can never communicate the truth necessary to bridge the gap between us.

She stumbles toward me. "My dear son, what happened to you? You should be at home, safely reset by now. Not here."

I take her hand from my face, from the replacements, and throw it down. "You did this to me. You sent them to kill me."

"I don't know what you're . . . Son?"

The alarms pulse, lights flash and we're stuck in the middle of a moment of total and utter confusion.

The guardians run past us, and we are in a countdown. All who can get to the transport will, and it will take off as soon as it is full. We all agreed to that. And if Taru's posse is right, no one will be standing at the end.

"Come on," I pull my mother's hand and drag her behind me.

"Where are you taking me?"

"Shut up." I can't leave her. There is too much I need to know, too much I need to say. It is selfish, sure, but I also know if I leave her here, it'd be as good as leaving her for dead.

I'm not like her. Not a killer.

And, there is something off about her. Something strange, not connecting.

The battle on the dock is devastating, but someone gets ahold of a few electro-pulse batons and the strongest bodies are covering the entrance as guardians exit the containment. I see stray restraints on the ground and get an idea as I pick them up.

Where is Ashiva?

We make our way with the others through to the transport and pile in.

"Mother, you try anything and I'll not have any control over the mob that wants to toss you overboard, you hear me?"

She presses her hands to me in offering. The restraints make a satisfying click as I slide them on her wrists.

I can't hold it in. Sometimes the need to know is stronger than life itself. "How did you get my mecha plans? I encrypted everything."

Her eyes plead with me. "But you shared them with someone, didn't you?"

"Only MechTech and Generix."

"Ever wonder who they really were? That you'd actually have real friends on the underweb? I hired them to befriend you on your silly games. Keep an eye on you. We have teams of agents online working for us. You mess up, and I'll lose my job and so much more. You have no idea."

"You?!" Heat fills my body and I want to smack the oddly calm look off of her face. "Why?"

"How else could I get the plans? You'd never share them with me. They were illicit in Central. I knew Kanwar left something with you, but we could never find it. We had to harvest information from the underweb."

"Harvest? You stole from me. Your own son." I push her

forward and question keeping her on the transport. I look outside and it is a long way down. For a split moment, I consider
it. But, no. Her fate won't be so easy. "What happened to Uncle? You know." I stop and search her face, ready to test my
theory. "He's alive, isn't he?"

"He might be, yes." She acknowledges my words, but
there's no time. Not for this. I need more time.

We keep moving. We need to know the full extent of her
plans, otherwise we'll just be one step behind the whole time.
Afterward, we can leave her to the highest planetary authorities for trial. We can't stoop to her level; we must be humane
now above all else.

I must find Ashiva. I have to take her with me.

The transport can hold hundreds. The space is a cargo
hold, an open bay filling with people. She'll be at the docks. I'd
need to find the cockpit in this massive transport.

My heart races as I push past the injured and sick. Where
is she? Surely, she made it. Otherwise this transport wouldn't
be open, these people wouldn't have been able to enter. Doubt
flashes in my mind along with the lights, sirens. What if we are
being sent to our certain death, trapped in a loaded transport?

"Ashiva? Where is she?" I question those I pass. No one acknowledges me, they are so caught up in their own survival.

The rails and stairs that lead to the front of the transport
shake as I climb them. There is a circle of people at the entrance
to the flight deck. I hand my mother to a guard and tell him to
keep her safe, that she's vital to our survival. It's the biggest
transport I've seen—probably meant for a mass evac. It's an air-
and water-transport that can float and fly, so I hope we can stay
high in the sky and get far away from the off-site, quickly.

"Don't let her out of your sight and let me through." The guards in front of the flight deck don't budge.

"No one gets to the Commander," one girl says.

Then a voice like a wish comes through. "Is that Synch? He's okay."

When I see her, I want to weep.

"I knew you'd get here," she says.

Her replacement arm is missing and there's a rag tied around her shoulder, heavy with blood. She's standing behind two elderly people sitting in the captain chairs, charting our course: the elders of the Lal Hath.

I can't help it. I need to hug her. Carefully. Thankfully, she doesn't resist.

"You should see the other woman. Oh wait. You can't. They're at the bottom of the ocean."

"You need medical attention," I say.

"She's going to be fine," the old man says. I suddenly remember him from the Narrows. "She's tough. It looks worse than it is."

"Ghaazi?" I ask.

He bows. "We got a lift on a fishing transport when Ashiva sent the coordinates. Here just in time, I see."

"I need to get us airborne," Suri replies.

"We've got 120 seconds until we depart. How're we looking?"

Ashiva turns to the others. "Still filling."

"Once Taru checks in, we are out. Tell 'em to get on board. Clock is ticking. Send the message to the entrance," Suri says.

"Right," Ashiva says and nods to a boy to send the message down.

"Ashiva, I have to tell you something."

"What?" she says as she plugs in coordinates onto the screen.

"I don't know how to say this..."

"Just spit it out then."

"I brought my mother on board. I think she could give us answers. After that, she will go to the Planetary Courts."

Her eyes are ghosts. I watch as anger, confusion, and then acknowledgement wash across her mind. "Bring her in."

I nod to a guard.

When she stands before Ashiva, Ghaazi, and Suri, she looks so small and useless and powerless. How could one person do so much damage? They can't. This is not all her doing.

A boy returns to the room. "Taru has arrived, Ashiva. She completed her mission."

"Thank god," Ashiva says. "She did it. She set the micro charge."

"I'm surprised you let her do that," I say.

Something in Ashiva's expression shifts and I can't tell if she is exhilarated by her surroundings or genuinely at peace. "She deserves to fight like everyone else."

"Sit," Suri says to my mother and the old man shoves her into a chair. Suri turns to her and smiles. Everything in that moment is surreal. I feel the floor beneath my feet shake as the engines roar.

Ashiva rises to her feet, the red of blood washing down her side. "You must have a lot of information in there, somewhere. If you want to earn a spot on this transport, you're going to have to offer it up."

Mother stammers and falls to pieces, trembling.

Suri says, "How do we make sure that Solace won't hunt us down? Where can we go? What can we do to hide?"

My mother is pathetic as she weeps. But it's not normal. Something's way off. "I made a fail-safe in case I needed to start over. I've seen too many people on my team disappear to not cover myself. Wipe the records."

Suri leans into my mother. "Minister, we don't have time for your emotional reckoning. Just give us something."

Mother's eyes are desperate, pleading. "The fail-safe code has a request for armed UAVs. They're airborne. Coming to cover this up. They'll be here soon and they've already locked onto this quad-transport."

Ashiva says, "Well, call it off!"

I look at my mother, begging her with my eyes to tell us something, anything. She fights for composure. "The beacon is linked to my fail-safe. We need to disengage the beacon if you want to get out of this transport alive. But if you do disengage it, it will also wipe my records. It's all connected. I had to protect myself."

"We've already sent the data packet of this hell place to the Space Colony," I say.

"Not all of it." Her eyes widen. What's she playing at?

"There's more?"

"If you don't disengage my fail-safe code now, the UAVs will be here in two minutes and they won't stop. They'll never stop."

"How?"

"My direct uplink." She points to the glittering chrome device that feathers across her temple. Of course, her neural-synch. "You need to hack it, son."

"Synch, get on it," Suri says. "Do it now. We have to hope there's enough in our comms to convict all of them. If we don't survive this, what will be the point?"

I plug into her neural-synch with a cable connecting to the control panel of the transport.

"You mess with us, lady and you'll learn what pain is." Ashiva pushes up against her.

She nods. "It'll work. If you don't do it, Central will find this transport and blow it to dust as soon as you are in range. They have explosives at the ready, armed UAVs in the sky."

"That's a pity," Ghaazi spits his words and readies the transport for take-off.

Ashiva looks at me. I know what she is thinking. Can we trust this woman? And I really don't know. I shake my head.

Down at the dock, shadows gather around the entrance to the containment. "Ashiva, we have to get airborne."

"Taru checked in?" she asks.

I nod. "Yes, she's on board."

"Well, what are we waiting for then?"

Then suddenly the entire transport shakes with such violence that most of us fall onto the hard, metal ground.

BOOM.

"There's something holding us at the dock," Ghaazi says.

"I'm going down. Push off as soon as we are able," I yell to the ones at the helm.

"No, Ashiva," Suri holds me back. "You're badly injured. Let me go."

"We need two to pilot this thing. You and Ghaazi. Without you, none of us will survive. I'll be back, but you know what to do if it goes badly. Promise me."

"Got it." I know in my soul that Suri understands.

"Synch, take care of the fail-safe. And Ghaazi, give me three minutes. If I'm not back by then, get this thing in the sky and to the Northern District. Got it?"

"Copy." Ghaazi tips his fingers to his forehead. I know I can count on him, even if it means leaving me behind.

The transport comes heavily armed with weapons I've never even dreamed of holding. Hardware lines the walls of the cockpit of the transport for easy access in an emergency. From small, handheld weapons for the crew and for hand-to-hand combat, to controls for massive cannons that line the exterior of the ship, the transport designer thought of many potential dire scenarios a Central captain might encounter. The electro-pulse pistol is compact but basic and I can manage it on my own, so I take it and run down the stairs, through the bay packed with people, and all the way back to through to the massive ramp that's still sitting open, like the mouth of a metal monster.

BOOM.

Metal creaks and aches. I know what it is. Another night-mare come to life. The mecha-suit guardian is holding the transport's massive ramp door in its fist. The door is halfway closed, like a gaping mouth. It can't close fully.

"Everyone, back to the highest level inside. Now!" I scream to the few stragglers still lingering by the entryway. "Head into the main cargo hold and take cover."

Before I get there, the C.O.R.E turns away from me and lets go of the ramp. The metal falls with a thunderous slam that shakes the entire transport.

"What the—?"

The C.O.R.E. guardian takes on fire from the distance and staggers backward before ending up on one knee. I crane my neck and see another guardian leaning against the deck, tak-ing aim with a rifle at the beast, at its own.

I have to get the ramp up, and now that it's damaged, I'll have to bring it up manually. Which means I'll have to set the crank, and that can take more time than we have.

The guardian open fires again on the C.O.R.E and when it turns, I see who is driving the machine: Masiji. Her expression is shock and apology and fight. Half of her suit has been badly damaged, already-shredded metal, scalded by the firefight.

She leans down on one knee and with the massive cannon on her fist, she aims and takes out the other guardian and half of the entrance too. The fire scorches the structure. What's she doing? Defending us or hurting us?

"Get inside the transport, Ashiva! I've got the ramp."

"Masiji!" I don't know whether we can trust her or not. That she sacrificed herself for our escape tells me volumes.

but not everything. "Don't do this!"

"I'm sorry. It wasn't meant to end like this," was all she says as she pushes the gate ramp up with her robotic arms and holds it half closed. "The children, our children, were stronger than theirs. I made sure of it. I ran experiments on them, more than just the replacements. I made them stronger. Central found out about my genetic modifications to make them resistant to the harsh world. Because of the immunologic updates, they became immune to the Fever."

"What? What do you mean?" I think about Masiji's replacement surgery being more than a cyborg addition. There was always something else we couldn't figure out. I think about all the people who died in the Narrows, every day.

"What about the people in the Narrows who died?"

"Think, Ashiva. All heat deaths, water-borne illnesses, or starvation. But not the children. I couldn't help everyone, but I had to help a few."

I watch the fire behind her grow, and I know we only have a minute or two, but there are so many questions I need to know.

"Why are you working with the Minister of Comms?"

Her head shakes. "I knew they were going to flood the Narrows to clean up the slums before AllianceCon, so I promised they could test the children to make a vaccine for Uplanders, as long as they gave the children a place inside Central afterward. They were meant to live inside the Ring. They were made to withstand everything. They're the cure. The Fever was going to decimate Central. I had to get the children out somehow. Even if I promised them as tests for the inoculation. Forgive me. Promise me, Ashiva. Live." She pushes the transport ramp closed, with me inside and her out.

The last thing I see is her face, and her smile.

"NO!"

My tears come like a monsoon, uncontrollably, all-consuming. I feel the transport lift off into the sky. And a few moments later, we all hear the micro charge explosion consume the nightmare below. I watch the facility explode and vaporize, pieces of it flying into the air, with the heavy parts sinking into the sea. I watch until we are carried high into the clouds and into a world I've never seen.

49 // ASHIVA

"The transport won't make it. We need to land—now!" Ghaazi yells above the roar of the engines.

"Can't we go a little further, just over the Pass at least?" I can feel the aircraft dropping several feet at a time, rebalance, then drop again.

"I'll try." Ghaazi says.

The scenarios I run through in my mind all lead to our death. If we don't land near a village, in this weather, we will all die of frostbite, hypothermia, or both, trying to find one on foot. The flight from containment over the sea and now over the Himalayas has been nauseating. The vibrations of the air-transport, the cries from the children, the stress of what's to come echoes in my mind until my fears give me focus.

"We need to drift down to a lower altitude. We're losing oxygen, Ashiva. Now!" Ghaazi yells.

I get on the comms and say, "Brace yourselves."

Ghaazi takes the air-transport lower and we hover. I think it's over. That we'll recover and keep going. But the cloud coverage and storm make visibility only a few meters, and that's not enough. Turbulence shakes the transport like a ragdoll, and we spiral.

"Air's too thin for the rotors. I'm going to try to land it." Ghaazi says, through gritted teeth.

"Everyone hang onto something!" Suri yells.

The air-transport careens like a wounded bird and I fight

to stay focused. Ghaazi's flight prowess is clear. A former pilot in the wars, he never sweats, only calculates; he's been here before. His face is an unflinching grimace. "There, there we'll land." I can't see what he does, and I hope it's enough of a runway.

He counts, "Brace for impact in five, four, three, two..."

When "one" comes, we all stiffen and close our eyes. It feels like being in a whirlpool caught under the waves. But then, just as suddenly, it ends with a massive jolt and we land. The aircraft is on its side and I'm dangling from my seat awkwardly. Synch is okay. Taru seems fine. Ghaazi nods at me and lets out a nervous laugh. Suri coughs, but is alive.

"Well done, Ghaazi. Well done." Then I scramble to unfasten my harness and grab the comms mic. "Please help those you can. We will need to gather our gear and send our search party out right away."

Moments later, we all stand at the aircraft's ramp as it lowers. The same one Masiji closed with the mecha-suit. I shudder, but blame the cold; I can't think about her yet, not yet. Ghaazi and I are wrapped in layers of clothes, everything warm we can find. The rest of the hundreds of children will stay inside the air-transport. Better safe here until we know how far we are from the nearest village. The stories about the North, it's hard to know what's true. Is it even here? Is what Ghaazi says true? Are they waiting for us?

"Where are we?" Taru asks as we stand shoulder to shoulder. The snowstorm spirals before us.

Ghaazi looks at his tablet. "Close. By my calculations, we are only a few kilometers from the nearest village. At least, well..."

"What is it?" Taru asks.

"Where the nearest village was, about twenty-five years ago. The landscape has changed drastically. Let's just hope they're there. At the monastery."

A gust of frozen air pushes against us. Even with all the clothing we have wrapped around us, it won't be enough. My shoulder is stabilized with bandages and numb from the injection Suri gave me on the transport. Ghaazi and I go ahead; we all agree with his navigation skills and nothing is stopping me from going. I can't risk another life today. We can't wait for the storm to pass. We need food, water, and shelter immediately, in this unpredictable area.

As we step down the ramp, I look at Ghaazi. "You sure it's only a few kilometers?" The rush of cold air steals my breath and causes me to yelp uncontrollably. I've never been so cold in my life. None of us has. It's remarkable.

He shakes his head and laughs at the ridiculous blizzard already covering our faces in snow. "I do hope so."

I turn, and look at Synch and Taru before descending into the blizzard. "I'll see you soon." I don't wait to hear what they say; leaving the conversation unfinished gives me hope that we will return.

It's white and blinding, like the sun. Sometimes it's soft. Other times the snow falls with clumps of ice that bites and stings. The land all around is more gray than white, like a bone that's been out in the sun too long. I laugh even though it's painfully clear how hard hiking through the snow will be. I've been fighting the effects of the sun and heat for so long, and now I wonder if all the heat I've built up in my body will sustain me through this place. The wind whips our faces and I follow in Ghaazi's footsteps so as to not lose him. All I hear are our footfalls crunching and my breath. Hours pass. It's timeless here. My usual markers in the sky are useless, white above, white below. I keep my flesh hand against my body, all the while wishing I still had my replacement. I feel vulnerable, deprived of my cyborg arm and weapon. We take many breaks, but it's easier to keep going.

Suddenly, a calm falls upon us like a blanket, and the sound and sight of the storm recedes. And then it becomes clear just how beautiful the world is we've been walking through.

"Wait, Ashiva." Ghaazi pulls the fabric down from around his face and I can make out his massive grin. "Look, Tiger!" He points above us. "Look!"

The snow blinds, and my eyes burn with glare. Things take shape slowly, as I try to readjust my sight. We are standing at the top of a crest, peering up at the mountains above us. Ghaazi is crying. And still I see nothing but white. So I take his binoculars. Looking through the lenses, I finally see what he does. Before us is a snow-covered mountain, with sharp, gray rocks jutting here and there, like dragon spines. The buildings built atop the mountain are so perfectly matched to their surroundings that if he didn't turn my shoulders and face me in the right direction, I'd never see them. The entryway, the monastery. Our first stop to finding the Northern Fort. If this is real, maybe the Fort is real too.

As we walk up toward the tidy, small, white square structures that are snowy, like the surrounding rocks and outcroppings, a village comes to view. It's as though it was carved out of the mountain itself. The monastery and village look like they're trickling down the rocky terrain, and in the center, above the tallest building, is a massive hole in the mountain. A cave. There I see one or two dim lanterns flickering. In the distance, on the lowland, there's a thin strip of blue and gray, sharply contrasting against the endless excess of white. The river. This all lines up with the stories I've heard about the North. I fall to my knees and weep. The scene is the most beautiful I've set my eyes on. The air is cold, cleaner than in the south. And it's quiet.

Ghaazi and I climb up to the village, and when we walk through the archway leading to the center, the first five people we see look at us like we are ghosts. We might as well be. The roads have been impassable for decades, from mudslides and avalanches and the altitude. People haven't attempted the journey for fear of radiation, and the myths of the beasts that survived the fallout. Soon, others meet us in the narrow alley between the buildings. There are families, women, men, children, monks and civilians.

"Where did you come from?" A brave child yells from the comfort of his mother's robes.

Ghaazi says, "We came a long way, child. Can you help us?"

His mother comes toward us and holds out her hand to me. "You must be very tired. Come."

She leads us into a stairwell, then through a small doorway that enters into a room with pillows on the floor and a roaring fire at the front. She asks us to sit down and wait. Her smile is clear of fear, and there is only kindness on her lips and in the way she moves. I don't know how to respond. The buildings have reddish wood doors and frames, and massive wood beams run along the low, white ceilings. I've never seen a place like this before, untouched by technology. But then I see it's wired. There's a local network running along the walls. The very sophisticated tech gives me pause. This place isn't what it seems. It must be a front for the Fort.

"Ghaazi. I, I can't believe we made it."

"I know." He is overwhelmed too. "It hasn't changed at bit. Not in twenty-five years."

"So, you have been here."

He grins. "I thought it was destroyed in the mecha wars. The nuclear bombs dropped north of here, and we heard there were avalanches and earthquakes. I really wasn't sure it was still standing."

A man and two children enter a few minutes later, with metal cups of hot tea and a bowl with a thick paste inside.

"Yak's butter," he says. "It'll warm you."

He scoops out a dab with a spoon and flips it into each cup. It floats and creates a slick oily surface atop the tea that coats my throat when I take a sip.

"There are more of us. In the valley. We escaped the Narrows, outside the Unsanctioned Territories of the Central District," I say, not wanting to say too much, but just enough.

The man takes us in without acknowledging my words. He smiles. "Wait. He'll be here soon."

I nod. Ghaazi told me about their leader. How the region considers itself a sovereign area independent of the SA, even though the SA doesn't see it that way. As long as they stay off the grid, they can do what they want.

A man who tells us he is Governor Tenzin enters the room with a plate of porridge. Ghaazi and I share it, and my hand shakes.

"Sir, we wish to claim exile status."

He nods. But his silence doesn't inspire confidence.

Ghaazi asks, "Is there another? Another leader we need to address?" His eyes glimmer with hope. I wonder…

Tenzin says, "Let us help you first; then we can talk." He leaves and sends in a woman to care for us. They take Ghaazi into a separate room for privacy. At first, being alone feels impossible. But my shirt is peeled off, stuck to my skin with blood, and the kind woman drapes a towel over my chest for modesty. As she cleans my arm, and the blood that has long since dried on my body, with a wet sponge and hot water, I give into the feeling of comfort, one that's unfamiliar to me. The water in the bowl turns red quickly, and then a brownish color, and it swirls as she dips the sponge again. You can't wash off the past so easily. Her touch is too gentle. This will take hours.

"It doesn't hurt, it's numb. I had a replacement. I lost it. In a battle. It's gone now." My words feel hollow, silly.

"Astonishing," her voice has an unfamiliar accent that cuts her words short and she smiles as she speaks. As she changes my bandages, it's clear she's interested in my metal shoulder joint. She gives me a towel to dry off with, and offers me fresh maroon robes and thick boots to change into. I am thankful to get rid of my blood-stained clothes. The new ones are warm. Maybe we can begin again, here. At least we can start anew and take the time to build a plan, regroup properly. She leads me back into the large room where we ate.

"Ghaazi will meet you later. For now, your presence is requested. Please." She points to the front of the room.

There's a figure standing so close to the fire blazing in the stone hearth that I worry he'll catch fire. His back is to me, and all I see is his tall form and his impossibly broad shoulders, leaning forward, hand against the fireplace wall, pushing with so much pressure it looks as though he's holding up the whole building. A cornerstone. The shadow he casts is epic and meets my boots as I enter the room. I stop, paralyzed by the possibilities. Is this the person who holds our fate in their hands?

"Sir, I am Ashiva, Chrome Tiger from the Red Hand Narrows outpost. We just freed the civilians from the Narrows who were illegally held in the dark off-site known as the Void. We are exiles seeking assistance to reconnect with the remaining Red Hand members." My voice echoes in the room. "Sir?"

The figure breathes in and out. Is this whom I'm supposed to be speaking to?

I continue. "Sir, we need to hurry. There are still many young children left in our air-transport a distance away. They need our help. Please."

He doesn't move, doesn't even acknowledge my presence in the room. I clear my throat, unsure what to do. Maybe he didn't hear me.

"Many died. We are being hunted now and need help. Maybe you—"

He turns and faces me. My heart stops. It's him. But how? "General Shankar?!"

Thick bandages run across his face and neck, but for the most part, he's still an icon, the one I saw for the first time in the Red Hand Council meeting days earlier. "General Shankar, sir. I thought you were dead. The fires. Oh, thank the gods."

"Don't thank the gods, Ashiva. They had nothing to do with it." I think he smiles, at least as far as he can. Maybe it's more like a grimace; the burns and ghosts in his expression only allow modest levity. "Or should I call you Commander?" He smirks and presses his right replacement hand to his chest, and I long to do the same. I use my left hand instead today.

"I'm no Commander. I'm not even a lieutenant yet."

He shrugs. "Well, maybe not. But you could be, one day."

The Red Hand lives. For the first time I feel like we actually have a chance, we have a leader. He points to the floor and we both sit cross-legged on the thick pillows before the fire. "I knew The Mechanic set a trace on me."

"I'm sorry. I didn't want to."

"I know she didn't give you a choice. I would have done the same. The Mechanic and I have trust issues. Always have." He clears his throat.

"She did it. I didn't know it then. But she brought you all in the Narrows. I bet she faked the hack on the system too."

He nods, lips thin with certainty. "I knew she was a double player, but how far it went . . . I didn't trust the summons to her meeting. I dodged your trace and tried to leave right after the first strike. Not soon enough, but at least . . ."

"You're alive. The Red Hand is alive."

"Some of us are. I'm not the only one." He turns and points to a person standing in the doorway.

"Hello, Tiger." The woman stands, and she looks even more childish and haunted than ever.

"Poonam Auntie." I rush toward her and she puts both of her arms around me. "I'm so glad you made it."

"I did. Can't kill a cockroach, right?" She laughs at herself.

"You're not a cockroach, Auntie. You're amazing."

She smiles awkwardly and says, "Yes, I made it."

"Did she, though? The Mechanic?" General Shankar asks.

"No." The memories come rushing back. Of Masiji wearing the mecha-suit, protecting me. But why? "She went down in the explosion on the dark off-site facility." If she survived the explosion, she would have drowned in the ocean afterwards. This stays with me, a nightmare.

General Shankar says, "She had her reasons. She couldn't move on from her contribution to the Solace algorithm. She loved the children, but she couldn't let go of the idea that her technology would save them. She was a fanatic. I think she knew they were going to clear the Narrows, and she tried to find a way to get the children out—even if it meant offering them up for testing for the Z Fever vaccine."

"We'll never know," Poonam Auntie says.

He nods. "We are regrouping now. The External Hand has been reconnecting with Red Hand operatives across the world. But we can't stay here forever. We can't risk bringing conflict to this peaceful village. If the SA tracked your transport..."

"Right, of course." And all my dreams of never leaving this paradise dissolve. "Maybe some of the children can stay. The ones unassociated with the Red Hand?"

He nods.

"Let's get the Children of Without."

50// ASHIVA

A week has passed and my first lesson in this new place: the stars are brightest when the sky is clear and impossibly cold. We'd never seen snow before we arrived in the Northern District, deep in the Himalayas. And now we're surrounded by sheer cliffs of stone peaked in snow, endless cold, and limitless stars at night. Stars that were sitting under the heavy, polluted air of the SA. They were there all along. I realize that cold feels like just fire if you close your eyes. Most of us are still awake at night and sleep during the day, our rhythm to avoid the Narrows' heat. On my night walks, I see galaxies spin across the sky, some older than time, some stars already dead, reminders of the infinite. Of what exists beyond this world. It makes me feel small, yet somehow miraculous.

Learning that this pristine place always existed while we fought to live, to breathe, to die with dignity, cuts deep. Our work has just begun. The Northern District welcomes us as exiles. They have an independent tribal leadership that governs the village. Central's UAVs aren't here. They aren't being watched. When I ask why, Governor Tenzin says, "They can't fly at high altitude." They've been here since before the neocity. Most people have always lived here. We are the first to come, to fight our way over the mountain. Saachi and Zami send a comms to us on the underweb, they will find a way to meet us soon. That they are safe. We'll wait for them.

At the first community meeting since our arrival, we listen to Governor Tenzin and General Shankar talk about their limited resources. Taru nods and stands. "The Children of Without are trained in all aspects of survival. Some of us are Red Hand, with experience in medicine, comms, and military training. We are not just children, we are an army. We will be useful to you, not a drain on your resources. We will work. You will benefit from our presence."

Her confidence is alarming. Governor Tenzin nods. "An army, you say?"

"Yes, sir. We can help train your people."

To this, he smiles subtly. "We will have to expand our farming and ration the yaks, but we will make it through the winter. Together. The smallest children will live with each family in the village, and contribute to the farming needs and defensive needs of the District. There are some of us who are also like the Red Hand. We can work together." He winks at Taru.

We survived. The children survived. And now we will combine our efforts.

Taru, Synch and I live in a small house with a few children from the orphanage and a local family. Synch is different since the containment, since his mother was taken into custody.

Synch's files reached the satellites and were transmitted to the GHO and Planet Watch. President Liu of the Planetary Alliance Commission and his counsel will need them to run a proper trial. That is, if they aren't corrupt. The Minister of Comms was taken into custody and is being transported to the PAC now, on the Northern District's only air-transport. General Shankar made sure of that. We wait. In hiding.

The tragedy in Central and the Narrows has already been cast across as many comms as we can, to warn to other Provinces across the world with similar nightmares: the loss of life, the testing, the Fever. Not to mention their numerous attempts to find a solution to the impossible problem: Who will survive in this world, how, and who will decide? For our protection and theirs, we give the Governor's scientist our blood and genetic sequences, so they can make their own vaccine if the Z Fever arrives here.

But there's also a backlash, anger, and confusion from the masses. I don't have space to think about it yet. It's like a looming hurricane, just around the corner. We hear snippets of Info-Runs from Central's new leadership about how the Central District is in transition. How a rebel group destroyed the Ring and Solace, and other garbage. Lies, lies, and more lies.

Transition. Rebels. Blame.

The language Central uses kills me. You can't soften the horror of exile with carefully chosen words. Homelessness is another nightmare just beginning. I avoid being alone with Taru, until one night she corners me in my small bedroom after the community dinner.

I hate the quiet. The stillness is stifling. "Masiji, she must've been in over her head, you know?" I say fidgeting with the one item in the room, a thick blanket. I try to fold it, but it's asymmetrical and flops onto the floor instead.

"Shiv," she says picking up the blanket, "that's not how it went. I saw her talking to the Minister. She was all in."

"She was lying." I grab the blanket back.

"When?" Taru asks.

"Then."

"Sister, she lied to us." Her words fall on me like lead bullets.

"No."

"She was like your mum. No way you'll really see the full truth." She folds the blanket and puts it far out of my reach. Then she takes my shoulders in her hands and forces me to stop moving, stop buzzing, but I can't focus.

"Masiji couldn't have . . ." I say, my words a whisper.

"She sent us to our death. Made a deal with the SA government to take us in for Fever testing. She built us just to save them in the end."

"Stop it!" I yell. "You don't know that! She said she wanted us to be in Central, not them. I still don't believe she was all bad."

The silence divides us further. It's snowing outside again, and the walls of the small room feel like they're shrinking on us. I want to go on a walk, so I put on my robes and the jacket they gave me.

"I know, behanji. I know what you did." Her voice is a knife.

"Sister, I've done so much. But everything I've done has been for our survival."

"You sound strangely like Masiji. Like President Ravindra. Like President Liu. Everyone seems to want to make decisions for others. But somehow they all just end up hurting more people."

"I'm not like them. Don't say that." My heart breaks hearing her words, knowing the truth.

"Ashiva, you were wrong. You made me afraid. I learned in containment that I carry no diseases. All that time I imagined that at the slightest touch, my skeleton would shatter into a million pieces. Do you know what that's like? Living with so much fear? Fear of being touched? I thought you were protecting me, but you just needed me to be broken. To feel superior, strong. I'm not broken. I am strong. Without you."

"Taru, I was so scared when they broke you when you were a child. You almost died. I didn't know what to say to keep you safe, to make everyone stay away from you, so I lied. All I ever wanted was for you to live."

She shakes her head at me. "You wanted to control something. If I lived, the world lived. I get it. But this isn't about me, it's about you. Don't do me any favors, Ashiva. I don't want your help anymore. I am my own hope."

When she leaves me, I pray it's not forever. I cry, alone, for the first time. I'm relieved at not having to hide the lies anymore, but I'm overwhelmed with how I'm going to fix everything again. Maybe I won't have to do it alone. Either way, this world will keep falling and we will always keep fighting. I'm proud, so very proud of Taru. Even through my embarrassment, guilt, and pain, I smile through the tears. She's beautiful.

When I speak with Synch alone, on a midnight walk under the stars, I wonder if he thinks about his old life in the Solace Towers.

Instead I ask, "Have you seen snow before?"

"No, not before we came here. It's amazing."

I nod and gaze hard at the outlines of mountains around us in the moonlight. We look at the Alliance Space Colony spinning in the shadow of the moon. The distant look in his expression sets me on edge, but I try to ignore it.

He smiles, acknowledging me. "I need to find him. My uncle. General Shankar told me Kanwar Uncle's plans will help the Red Hand. That they'll be useful in bargaining with the PAC."

"I'll help too."

"Ashiva?" He reaches out and holds my flesh hand. His eyes are strained.

"Yeah, Synch?" I wish I could read his mind.

"Um, I just wanted to tell you thank you. For..."

"Just shut up," I say and lean over, and kiss him on the lips.

GLOSSARY OF TERMS

THE CHILDREN OF WITHOUT

A note on language: India has over twenty-two core languages with hundreds of dialects. Many words in this book have been borrowed and evolved from Punjabi, Hindi, and Urdu. As the world of this novel is a fictional place based on a mash-up of some of the diverse cultures in South Asia, this seemed appropriate. Also, the Romanized version of Sanskrit-based words have infinite spellings. So, I compromised and used what was familiar to me personally.

Achcha – well, good, okay
Arre kya – Hey, mate?!
Bachcha – child
Bas – enough
Behan – sister, -ji big sister
Baitho – have a seat
Beti – daughter
Bhel – bhelpuri is a popular snack with puffed rice, vegetables, and savory tamarind sauce
Bhai – brother
Chalega – it'll work, it'll do, good enough
Chalo – let's go, hurry up, come on
Chota/choti – little (m/f)
Chup – quiet
Daadaji – paternal grandfather
Daal – dish made of lentils, with a soup-like consistency
Daaku – daku (singular) bandits
Desi – local; a person of Bangladeshi, Indian or Pakistani descent
Dhat – crap
Dhoti – fabric tied around the waist and covering the legs loosely
Goonda – rogue, hoodlum, gangster
Haan or haanji – yes, yes formal
Haraami – bastard
Inshallah – if God wills it
Ise rok – right now
Jalebis – jalebi (singular); donut-like dessert
Kachara – garbage
Kurta – tunic
Lal Hath – Red Hand
Ladki – girl

Langar – free vegetarian meal for everyone, usually served in a gurd-wara (Sikh temple)

Lomri – fox

Maa – mother

Machchar – mosquito

Maharaja – ruler, king; literally "great king"

Masiji – mother's sister, formal

Murkh – fool

Nahi – no

Pagal – crazy

Paratha – flat, round, stuffed bread cooked on a griddle

Puttar – son

Rajaiyan, rajai (singular) – quilt

Raashifal – horoscope

Roti – flat, round bread cooked on a griddle

Sadhu – holy man

Sahib – sir

Salam – Greetings

Seva – service

Shaanti – peace

Shukriya/Shukran – thank you

Svachchh – spotless

Thik hai – okay

Ullu – fool

Ullu ka patha – dumb; literally "son of an owl"

Veerji – older brother

Wahe guru – mantra in the Sikh faith meaning god

Walla – wala, wallah, is one who does or sells the thing denoted

Yaar – dude, friend, mate

Zara rastha dijiye – give way, or coming through

Works Cited:

Delacy, Richard. *Tuttle Pocket Hindi Dictionary: Hindi-English, English-Hindi.* Tuttle, 2017.

Hares, W. P. *An English-Punjabi Dictionary.* Asian Educational Services, 1998.

ACKNOWLEDGMENTS

Writing a book is a singular process. However, it takes a team of people to publish a book. I have many people to thank.

Maksim, when you are old enough to read this book, I hope that you will know that this is what Mommy was doing when she went "to work" all those days. I hope you know it's because I believe in you, in the future. You give me hope. You're *our* world. I love you so much.

David, thank you for bringing laughter to our discussions about the perilous worlds I build. None of this would be possible without you. Your belief in me, in us, and the fierce confidence in what I'm doing even on the days where I feel like I can't find a word, is everything.

Eric Smith, my literary agent extraordinaire, thanks for finding me during #DVpit and for taking me and this book on. You are a fearless advocate for the most precarious stories and I am thankful for your support every single day. Thanks to P.S. Literary and specifically Curtis Russell for your counsel. Thanks to Sarah Guan, astute editor at Erewhon Books for believing in this book and asking the hard questions that made it what it is today. Thanks to Martin Cahill, Erewhon publicist, and Liz Gorinsky, publisher for enthusiasm about this project. Also, thank you to the stellar team at Erewhon including Jillian Feinberg, Cassandra Farrin, Kelsy Thompson. Thanks also to Lakshna Mehta for your keen eye and for noticing my reference about the Rani of Jhansi.

Thank you to my parents, Kiki and Kanwar Jit Singh Chadha.

who have always believed in me. Whose passion for science and nature have inspired me to see a world that will be inclusive and possible. You both inspire me every day. My brother, Ranjit, and sister in-law Kavita, thanks for supporting me always. Thank you to my in-laws, Michael and Deborah, whose enthusiasm is infectious and whose kindness is unparalleled. To Dani and Steve, for your endless support. And to the future children of our families: Ava and Shane, and Layla and Harper, you are all going to do great things, of that I'm certain.

To my dear friend and colleague, Dr. Robert Buchwald at the University of Colorado, Boulder, who spent many hours discussing viruses, flora, and fauna in this world. I appreciate your friendship and generosity. To Dr. Paul Strom, I am thankful for your friendship and for many engaging conversations about the ethics of technology. To all of my colleagues at the University of Colorado, Boulder Honors Program and Honors Residential Program what a great place to work. To my students in the Honors Writing Club through the years—I'm rooting for all of you! Keep writing.

My critique partner, Christine Macdonald, thank you for carefully reading early drafts, for rushing to read late edits, and for always being my favorite person at writerly events. Rocky Mountain SCBWI, for offering an open and inclusive environment to explore studying the craft of YA and children's literature. And of course, the Big Sur in the Rockies Conference— where I received feedback on early chapters and connected with talented friends Susan Gose and Adra Benjamin.

And finally, to my debut group with too many names to list, you all are so important in my career and sanity—I adore the entire 21ders team.